Kandy Shepherd swapped a career as a magazine editor for a life writing romance. She lives on a small farm in the Blue Mountains, near Sydney, Australia, with her husband, daughter and lots of pets. She believes in love at first sight and real-life romance—they worked for her! Kandy loves to hear from her readers. Visit her at kandyshepherd.com.

Michelle Douglas has been writing for Mills & Boon since 2007, and believes she has the best job in the world. She lives in a leafy suburb of Newcastle, on Australia's east coast, with her own romantic hero, a house full of dust and books, and an eclectic collection of sixties and seventies vinyl. She loves to hear from readers and can be contacted via her website: michelle-douglas.com.

CINDERELLA AND THE TYCOON NEXT DOOR

KANDY SHEPHERD

CLAIMING HIS BILLION-DOLLAR BRIDE

MICHELLE DOUGLAS

MILLS & BOON

First published in Great Britain 2024
by Mills & Boon, an imprint of HarperCollins*Publishers* Ltd,
1 London Bridge Street, London, SE1 9GF

www.harpercollins.co.uk

HarperCollins*Publishers*, Macken House, 39/40 Mayor Street Upper, Dublin 1, D01 C9W8, Ireland

Cinderella and the Tycoon Next Door © 2024 Kandy Shepherd

Claiming His Billion-Dollar Bride © 2024 Michelle Douglas

ISBN: 978-0-263-32130-2

05/24

MIX
Paper | Supporting responsible forestry
FSC
www.fsc.org
FSC™ C007454

This book contains FSC™ certified paper and other controlled sources to ensure responsible forest management.

For more information visit www.harpercollins.co.uk/green.

Printed and Bound in the UK using 100% Renewable Electricity at CPI Group (UK) Ltd, Croydon, CR0 4YY

CINDERELLA AND THE TYCOON NEXT DOOR

KANDY SHEPHERD

MILLS & BOON

To my fellow *One Year to Wed* authors,
Michelle Douglas, Ally Blake and Rachael Stewart,
for helping to make writing this book such fun!
I loved every minute of our collaboration.

PROLOGUE

Garrison Downs,
June, first day of winter

ANASTASIA HORVATH HUNCHED her shoulders and pushed herself back as deeply as she could into the padded leather arm chair, trying to make herself invisible. She felt uncomfortably conspicuous in the grand office that had been her late father's centre of operations at his vast family property, Garrison Downs. The intensely masculine room was furnished with fine furniture and antiques as befitted his status. Holt Waverly, billionaire grazier, public figure, custodian of this one-and-a-half million-hectare cattle station—one of the largest in South Australia—and dead aged sixty-four, tragically felled by a falling tree branch.

It was unbearable that she would never again see her vibrant, larger-than-life father. But she wasn't allowed to show her grief. Her black dress was the only indication of her loss. She bit down on her lip to stop it from trembling and gripped her hands tightly together. More than twenty people had congregated in the office. She only knew one, the elderly lawyer set to read her father's will. But she recognised two others from photographs and media reports. Sitting in her line of vision were two of the three older half-sisters Ana had never met—not once in her twenty-five years.

Ana found it difficult not to stare at Matilda and Rose Waverly—the youngest and oldest of Holt's daughters with his late wife Rosamund. The middle sister, Evelyn, was nowhere to be seen. Matilda and Rose looked like the wealthy, socially well-connected people they were—utterly confident of their rightful place here. Just, in fact, like the girls who had bullied her at the private girls' high school her father had insisted she attend. As far as she knew, they had absolutely no idea she, their youngest sister, existed.

Rose, the oldest sister, tall and slender, brown hair in a ponytail, sat upright in her chair. She looked like she'd just slid off the back of a horse. Rose kept glancing out of the big bay window to the classic Outback scene of red dirt and eucalypt trees as if she'd much rather be outside. Matilda, also tall but curvier, with a mane of blonde hair, sat with her socked feet curled under her on a velvet chair, hugging an embroidered cushion to her chest.

The sisters looked nothing like Ana, with her straight dark hair and slight figure.

Except for their eyes.

Even from across the room she could see her half-sisters had the same piercing blue eyes she had. The same eyes as Holt Waverly—the father she'd only ever seen a few times a year, the father who had never publicly acknowledged her and never given her his name. She was his secret love child.

Her mother had always insisted on calling her a 'love child', when there were other less kind words aimed at children who were born out of marriage to a man's mistress. Her father had met her mother Lili when he'd sincerely believed his marriage was over. Her mother had loved him and had believed she and Holt would be married after the planned divorce. But he'd reconciled with his wife. Neither Holt nor Lili had known Lili was pregnant with Ana when he'd left her. He'd taken responsibility for Ana, but he'd had nothing to do with Lili, except on issues concerning his fourth, secret daughter.

Ana had never been able to rid herself of a sense of shame, fed by the secrecy that had defined her life—no one must ever know who her father was. She hadn't been allowed to call him 'Dad' when they were together on his infrequent visits to Melbourne, just in case she was overheard. Instead she'd called him *apa,* the Hungarian term for dad, as suggested by her mother and her Hungarian grandparents.

And she missed him terribly. For all the distance and constraints, she had adored her father, a larger-than-life figure. Yet even after his death a month ago she had not been able to acknowledge her link to him, her shock and pain at his loss. Such was his importance, he'd been given a state funeral. She and her mother had, of course, not been invited. They'd only seen glimpses of the ceremony on the news.

No one knew about their existence, except for this elderly lawyer who now sat behind Holt's outsized desk. It was he, George Harrington, who had organised the purchase of the house where they'd lived in the inner-city Melbourne suburb of St Kilda, paid Ana's school fees and administered the annual allowance paid to her mother for the secret daughter's upkeep. When Ana had turned twenty-one, she'd been surprised to be told her father had organised an allowance to be paid directly to her to replace the allowance to her mother.

Now Ana was on display in this personal study of the father who'd had such a public life but had kept her existence a secret. She cast her eyes downward to the antique Persian rug. She could almost feel the barbed thoughts aimed at her from all corners of the room.

Who are you? What are you doing here? You don't belong.

A wet doggy nose nudged her arm—a beautiful old Border Collie, its muzzle grey with age. Rather than the usual black-and-white, it was the silvery grey-and-white known as lilac. This must be River, her father's beloved dog. Apa had told her about River, a working dog who had retired to become a pet with house privileges. Now he was nuzzling her affectionately. Did River recognise her as family, if only on the outer circle? Did he sense the tight rein she was holding on her emotions and want to comfort her?

She patted him, fondling his soft ears, loving the contact. 'Thank you,' she whispered to the sweet animal. She had always wanted a dog, but her mother had said a firm no. Animals were too much work and cost too much.

Her mother had kept to a strict budget. 'Your father looks after you now, but we can't count on that. If anything happened to him, those funds could be cut right off. His family wouldn't take kindly to you. Who knows what could happen when Holt dies?'

Ana was about to find out.

George Harrington had already told her that her allowance would continue. But she was required to be at the reading of her father's will at Garrison Downs today.

Her mother had refused to accompany her. 'This is something you have to do on your own, my darling,' she had said.

Ana wished she had her best friend Connor O'Neill with her. She wouldn't feel so vulnerable if she had him there. But Connor now lived in a different state. And they'd argued. As kids they'd squabbled, often about something inconsequential, but had always made up. This time was different. He had a new girlfriend, who Ana didn't think was worthy of him, and she'd told him so. Connor hadn't agreed. He'd told her she'd gone too far and to stay out of his love life.

Ana had found that hurtful. She only wanted the best for him—and clearly that girl wasn't it. As a consequence, they hadn't spoken for weeks. He hadn't replied to her texts telling him about her summons to Garrison Downs. She missed him.

Maybe she'd lost him.

That was an unbearable thought.

Suddenly the dog's ears pricked up and he turned his head towards Matilda. Ana looked towards Matilda too and, for a startling moment, their eyes met. Ana couldn't help a shiver of terror. But to her intense relief Matilda smiled, a warm smile edged with uncertainty but no recognition. Ana smiled a tentative smile in return.

Her sister!

River padded over to Matilda and jumped up onto the sofa next to her. Her sister—only a year older than she was—couldn't be too bad if a dog could look at her with such devotion.

In his wavering old man's voice, the lawyer announced that Evelyn Waverly would be joining the meeting via video call. As he spoke, a large painting on the wall slid into the ceiling to reveal a screen. Ana had to twist herself around to see it from where she was sitting. Then her third half-sister was there. Evelyn was so different from her sisters. City-smart in a tailored suit. Blonde hair pulled back in a tight bun. But she had the same blue eyes as the others—as Ana did herself. Evelyn's expression was contained, even a little stern, and didn't give anything away.

The lawyer started to talk about properties, investments and the robust state of the Waverly family's financial standing. Ana didn't have a clue about any of the business matters, but it appeared her father had been even wealthier than she had thought. The family cattle station, Garrison Downs, had generated much of that wealth.

Mr Harrington cleared his throat, then paused for what seemed like an abnormally long time. The room hushed in anticipation of what they were all there for—the contents of the will.

Finally, he read from the document. 'To my daughters, I leave all my worldly possessions, including, but not limited to, Garrison Downs.'

Ana realised she'd been holding her breath and she let it out on sigh of disappointment. Nothing for her, as her mother had anticipated. But Ana had hoped against hope for some recognition in her father's will. She had only ever been given the crumbs of his affection. It wasn't his money she'd wanted, it was his love, and by not leaving her anything in his will he'd let her know even the crumbs had been swept away. She tried not to let the hurt show on her face.

She had to get out of here.

Mr Harrington continued. 'Let it be known that it is my wish that my eldest daughter, Rose Lavigne Waverly, take full control of the management of Garrison Downs, if that is *her* wish. If not, I bow to her choice.'

Ana looked at Rose, saw her flinch. Surely she wasn't surprised? Apa had spoken proudly of how Rose had helped him run the property for the last ten years. Had he been unaware of how every word praising his 'real' daughters had hurt like a stab to her heart? She'd seen so little of him. She doubted his secret, second-best daughter rated as anything much—certainly not worthy of being acknowledged as a Waverly.

Mr Harrington hadn't finished. 'Ah. At this point,' he said, peering over the top of his glasses, 'could we please clear the room of everyone bar family?'

Ana got up to leave the room, relieved. She wasn't sure she could keep it together. Wasn't sure she wouldn't cry out that it wasn't fair, that her life hadn't been fair, that she'd deserved more than a distant, part-time father. But Mr Harrington indicated she should stay. Perhaps there would be some small bequest for her after all. She sank back into the chair.

Along with her half-sisters, she waited in silence while the other people filed out of the room. She ignored the curious glances sent her way by her sisters and those departing. Perhaps they assumed she was the lawyer's assistant.

'Now,' Mr Harrington said. 'There is a condition placed over the bequest. One that has been attached to the property since its transfer to your family years ago.'

Did this have anything to do with her? Ana wondered. Was that why she'd been asked to stay?

Mr Harrington took off his glasses. 'As I'm sure you know, the history of Garrison Downs is complicated, what with your great-great-grandmother having won the land from the Garrison family in a poker game in 1904.'

Really? Ana wondered how such a thing could actually have happened. Garrison Downs was immense—why would someone have risked it in a poker game? How bizarre.

'Any time the land has been passed down, certain conditions had to be met.' He paused before reading directly from the will. 'Any male Waverly heir, currently living, naturally inherits the estate.'

'Naturally,' Rose murmured.

'But,' said Mr Harrington, lifting a finger, 'if the situation arose where there is no direct male heir, any and all female daughters of marrying age must be wed within a year of the reading of the will in order to inherit the property as a whole.'

Ana stifled a gasp. Although it wasn't anything to do with her, she grasped the magnitude of it—and the injustice. It was obviously the first her half-sisters had heard of it.

'What?' said Matilda.

There was an exclamation from on-screen Evelyn too.

'I don't understand,' Rose said, shaking her head.

Neither did Ana. As an accountant, she had worked with the beneficiaries of some odd wills but nothing as archaic as this.

'The land,' said Matilda slowly, 'is entailed to sons. If there is no son, the Waverly women *can* inherit, but only if all of us are married.'

'That can't possibly be legal,' Rose said, her voice hoarse with disbelief. 'Not in this day and age.'

'Too right, it can't be,' Evelyn said from the screen. Ana hadn't heard as much about Evelyn from her father as she had about Matilda and Rose, but she knew she was a high-powered PR executive.

'It is…arcane,' agreed Mr Harrington. 'But it has been a part of the lore of this land for several generations. So far as I see it, and so far as your father must have wanted, it stands.'

'How has this never come up before?' asked Rose.

'Sons. Waverlys have always been most excellent at having at least one strapping, farm-loving son,' said Matilda dryly. 'Until us.'

'And what happens if we refuse to…marry?' asked Rose.

'If the condition is not met, the land goes back to the current head of the Garrison family, Clay Garrison.'

Ana, keeping apart from all this, couldn't help but feel sorry for her half-sisters. She was puzzled that their father—*her* father—had let this happen. It seemed cruel.

Rose rolled her eyes. 'That old goat Garrison. He can't tell the back end of a bull from the front. And as for his son Lincoln… If our land, our home, the business we've built, fell into their hands… I—I can't even *think* about it.'

'Don't waste your time worrying about it, Rose,' said Evelyn from the screen, assertive and professional. 'Because that's not going to happen. Not now. Not ever.'

Mr Harrison interjected. 'As it stands, unless all four of Holt Waverly's daughters are married within twelve months of the reading of this document—'

Four daughters? Ana wasn't sure she'd heard right. She barely had time to process what might have been a slip of the lawyer's tongue when Matilda confronted Mr Harrington. 'Wait. You said four daughters. There are only three of us.'

Ana's thoughts raced.

Her father hadn't forgotten her after all.

Matilda spun to face Ana.

'Who are you?' Matilda asked, not unkindly.

'Ana Horvath,' Ana said, getting up from her chair, her voice not as steady as she would have liked it to be. She realised she was wringing her hands together, something she did when stressed.

Then Mr Harrington got up from behind the desk. 'Come forward, girl.'

Ana took a small, hesitant step towards him.

'Anastasia, this is Matilda Waverly,' he said. 'That there is Rose. And up on the screen there is Evelyn. Girls, this is Anastasia Horvath.'

'Hi,' Ana said, weakly waving her hand.

'Impossible,' said Matilda, her voice breaking.

Matilda looked at Ana more closely. Ana endured her scrutiny. As an only child, Ana had sometimes fantasised about meeting her sisters, about them all becoming great friends. Could that actually happen? She was reeling from the revelation she—her father's love child—was an equal beneficiary of his will. She could have expected hostility from her half-sisters, yet they seemed shocked and curious rather than hostile. Was there actually a chance they would welcome her?

Be careful what you wish for.

Ana had wanted to be acknowledged by her father and to get to know her sisters. And now they were all dependent on each other to gain their inheritance. An inheritance that could gift her millions. How did she handle this? How would her sisters handle *her*?

Oh, Connor, why aren't you here to advise me?

Had she pushed him away for good? They'd grown up next door to each other and he'd always been there for her, warning off the bullies at primary school, letting her cry on his shoulder when she'd been hurting. He was the only person aside from her mother and grandparents who knew the truth about her father. Two years older than she, he'd always been wiser than his years, always able to be trusted. Now, when she most needed his advice, she would have to face this on her own.

She'd had no expectations from her wealthy father other than the continuation of her monthly allowance. Yes, she could walk away from this. But, if she did, her sisters would lose their birthright.

But it was her birth right too.

The wealth involved would make an enormous difference to her life. She'd be a fool to turn her back on that.

'Rose?' Matilda said quietly.

'Hang on. Evie, did you *know*? Is this why—?' Rose began.

'I have to go,' said Eve, looking as pale as the white walls surrounding her, before the TV turned to black.

Rose, visibly disconcerted by the shock contents of the will, got up and headed towards the door. 'I can't— I don't have time for this. I have a station to run,' she threw over her shoulder. At the door she stopped, turned, pointed at Ana and barked, 'Stay!' And then she was gone.

Stay. At Garrison Downs.

Her father's property had attained mythical status in Ana's eyes. She had always wondered about it. Never thought she would see it. And now she was here—welcomed by her half-sisters.

Ana nodded. But Rose had already gone and Ana wasn't sure if she had seen her give her assent. She looked at Matilda, kind-eyed Matilda, with whom she already felt a tenuous connection. Matilda smiled and rolled her eyes a little, as if to say, 'You know what Rose is like'.

But Ana didn't know what Rose was like. Or Matilda. Or Evelyn—Evie, her sister had called her. But she wanted to get to know her sisters.

They were of her blood.

For any of them to claim their inheritance, all four of Holt Waverly's daughters had to be married within the year. They would have to work together. Ana couldn't be the one to ruin it for the others.

She had to find a husband.

CHAPTER ONE

Melbourne,
December, first day of summer

IT HAD BEEN six months since that drama-laden reading of her father's will—six months to go until the deadline for all four sisters to wed, so as to secure their inheritance. And Ana was no closer to finding a man to marry. She had tried, really tried, only to end up with a string of dead-end dates. In six months, she hadn't met one man with whom she could remotely imagine sharing her life.

But both she and her new-found sisters had so much to lose if she didn't find a husband. Matilda had dropped the bombshell that she was already secretly married—to a European prince, no less. In August, Matilda and Henri had had a grand, official royal wedding ceremony in Chaleur. In November, Eve had married George Harrington's son, Nate. Rose was still single. But Rose was so formidably efficient, Ana had no doubt she'd be married by the end of the year—although there didn't appear to be any contenders yet.

Ana, the secret sister her half-sisters had embraced so wholeheartedly, couldn't be the one to let them down by remaining uncoupled. She was losing sleep and losing weight from the pressure of the relentlessly ticking clock—

at the same time dealing with her grief at the loss of her father. Sometimes the pain slammed into her, hard and unexpected. He was gone and he would never visit her in Melbourne again.

But there was anger along with the grief. Why hadn't Apa ever given her some clue about what his will held? And, after his wife Rosamund had died, couldn't she have been allowed to meet her sisters then? She felt sad that she'd gone twenty-five years without knowing the wonderful women her sisters had turned out to be.

Not that her link to Holt Waverly was now any less secret than it had been all her life. She and her sisters had agreed that both the condition of the will and her new role in the family should be kept hush-hush until they were all safely married. Otherwise the media would certainly pounce on the story. Then their lives would be hell.

That was one reason she hadn't told any of her dates about the inheritance her marriage would trigger. The other was that she wanted marriage for the right reasons, not because she was suddenly an heiress. But the more she tried to meet the right man, the more stressed she felt. She was beginning to wonder if she was driving away potential partners rather than attracting them.

With six months to go and no husband in sight, her mother, Lili, had called a family meeting. Lili had been as stunned as Ana at the terms of Holt's will that placed her daughter as an equal to his legitimate daughters.

'He loved you, he truly did,' she'd said through her tears. Ana's grandparents had not liked or approved of Holt. However, they felt Ana's inheritance went some way towards mitigating the way Holt had seduced their only daughter, Lili, with false assurances of marriage.

None of them could understand why a twenty-first century bequest would have such an archaic requirement for marriage.

It was two hours before Saturday evening opening time at the Hungarian restaurant run by her grandparents in the beach-side suburb of St Kilda. Four of them sat around a round table—Ana, Lili and her grandparents, Dori and Zoltan. Two chefs were busy at work in the kitchen. In the early days, her grandparents did all the work themselves. Now they were easing down as they got older. If— *when*—she got her inheritance Ana vowed to help them financially. Refugees who'd fled Hungary many years ago, their early lives hadn't been easy.

The restaurant had always been her happy place. Ana loved the eclectic décor comprising wooden floors, bent-wood chairs, crystal chandeliers, art prints of old Budapest, the always present aromas of delicious Hungarian food and the warmth and welcome. As a child she'd often sat at this very table doing her homework in the gap between school ending and her mother finishing work in the city and coming to take her back to their nearby home. When she'd been in primary school, Connor had often sat here with her.

Her grandfather started off the meeting. 'Anastasia, we can't have you risk losing your rightful share of your father's billions because you are too picky with—'

Her mother glared at Nagypapa and corrected him. 'Because she's finding it difficult to connect with suitable men, you mean?' Lili paused. 'I've been thinking. Perhaps we need to widen the husband-hunt net.'

'The *hunt*? The *net*?' Ana pulled a face. 'That sounds so predatory.' She took a breath. 'Do I seem predatory? Maybe I'm scaring guys off—coming across as too keen for commitment. Too needy, perhaps.'

It was bad enough dating a stranger, but knowing she was assessing them as a possible husband made her feel even more awkward. From the number of guys not pressing for a second date, they might also have felt the same.

'Or the ones who are serious about settling down sense that you really don't want to get married,' her mother said. 'To anyone.'

'Perhaps,' Ana said, shifting uncomfortably in her seat.

She'd thought of marriage as something in her future. Now, at age twenty-five, she wanted to be independent, to live her life on her own terms, not someone else's. The wealth that could be unlocked to her by the inheritance would give her every chance to do that. She wanted to quit her boring accountant job at the insurance company and concentrate more on her fledgling online jewellery business.

Why on earth did that caveat in the will have to force her sisters and her to marry? It was ridiculous and unfair. Evelyn had tried to challenge it, but it had seemed the clause was set in stone.

Her grandmother shook her head. 'The problem isn't you, *kicsim*—you're beautiful, smart and kind. You'd make the right man a wonderful wife. It's these dating apps that you young folk rely on, they're the problem. Who knows what could be wrong with men who have to look for women online?'

Ana cleared her throat. 'Actually, Nagymama, they're people like me. I'm on those sites too, remember?' She'd tried them all, swiping left most of the time.

'You're too good for them,' her grandmother said with a dismissive sweep of her hand. 'And there is no substitute for an introduction to a suitable man whose family is known to your family.' She looked at Ana with narrowed eyes. 'Your mother is right. I need to widen my net.'

'Oh, no. No, thank you, Nagymama,' Ana said quickly. 'No more introductions, I insist. You can't imagine how embarrassing it was both for me and the "eligible" guy who was forced into meeting me because his grandparents are your friends.'

There had been one such family friend who had sparked her interest. Then he'd told her he had agreed to see her just to put off his parents, as he wasn't ready yet to come out as gay. But she'd made a new friend that day, so it hadn't been a total waste of time, like the others had been.

'What about letting me help?' said her grandfather. 'My friends at the Hungarian Club are always boasting about their grandsons. I could ask—'

Ana flung up both hands in protest. 'No. Thank you for the kind thoughts, both of you, but no more matchmaking. Please.'

'Darling, you've only got six months to get married,' said her mother. 'Surely you should be open to all possibilities?'

Ana shrugged. 'I'm not doing well on my own, I admit it. Perhaps I need help with updating my profiles on the dating apps—you know, to better promote myself.'

'I don't know that I could help with that,' said her mother.

'Or me,' said her grandmother with an expressive lift of her brows.

Ana smiled. 'I wasn't actually thinking of asking for your help. I'm going to ask Connor to help me get a more effective message across.'

'Connor? But isn't he living in Sydney?' said her grandfather.

'He's back in Melbourne.' Ana looked at her watch. 'And should be here to meet me very soon.'

Not long after the reading of the will, he'd contacted her to say she'd been right about his girlfriend and he'd ended it.

'We're catching up tonight.'

Her family's faces lit up. They all loved Connor. He'd lived next door to her mother and her in St Kilda, along with his doctor parents and younger brother. She and Connor had constantly been in and out of each other's homes. Everyone thought of him as a big brother to her. It was why she'd never really thought of herself as a lonely only child. For as long as she could remember, there had been Connor.

Her grandmother got up from her chair and prodded Zoltan into vacating his. 'We must get *gulyas* ready for him. It's his favourite.'

Ana laughed. After her grandparents headed to the kitchen, she and her mother reminisced how teenaged Connor had always angled for an invitation to go with them to the restaurant for a meal. He was energetic, sporty and always seemed to be hungry. As he'd grown up, he'd had his own friends, his own ways of spending the evening rather than with his next-door neighbour's family. But there had always been food on the table for Connor, and room for him in the Horvaths' hearts.

And in *her* heart? Connor was a friend. Just a platonic friend. He'd made that very clear to her the one and only time they had shared a kiss at her Year Ten formal. He'd said it was because they were too young to get involved that way and it would be weird. When she'd suggested they lose their virginities together, he had paled.

'You know I think of you as a sister, right?' he'd choked out, backing away.

Of course, she'd hastily backtracked to say she'd been joking. But she hadn't been. She couldn't remember when her attraction to Connor had started. Probably when they'd both reached puberty and skinny, gangly Connor had filled out and grown into his height. Or maybe she'd become aware of him in that way when girls from school had wanted introductions to her 'hot neighbour'. But he'd made it clear he didn't see her as anything other than a close friend and she'd had to settle for that.

Ultimately, it had been the right decision. Boyfriends came and went; a friend like Connor stayed in her life. She would never want to risk losing him by trying to push him to be something else.

'So your best plan is to improve your profile on the dating apps?' her mother asked.

'And to continue going to the gym, socialising with people from work at any opportunity, borrowing a dog to walk in the park where the cool guys walk their dogs, enrolling in male-orientated hobby courses...'

'Oh, dear, that sounds like hard work,' said her mother. 'The trouble is, you can't go out chasing love. Love comes to you when you don't expect it.'

'Love? Why are we talking about love?' Ana had been thinking of attraction and compatibility as criteria for the husband hunt. Not necessarily love.

'Isn't love the only reason to get married?'

Her mother had a wistful look on her face. Ana knew she had loved Holt and believed he had loved her; had thought they would marry after his divorce. Until he'd gone back to the marriage he'd sworn was over. It had taken her mother a very long time to find love again with Ben, whom Ana liked very much. Ben wasn't at the meeting.

He wisely stayed out of any discussions to do with Holt, or the repercussions of Holt's will.

'Well, yes,' she said.

'So aren't you looking for love? Isn't that why it's proving so difficult for you to find someone?'

Her mother knew her so well, Ana thought. She'd had a few nice boyfriends whose company she had really enjoyed. She'd had one not-so-nice boyfriend who'd lasted longer than the others but had proved to be controlling and domineering. She shuddered at the very thought of Rory. But had she ever really been in love? In love enough to get married, that was. Would she recognise love if she tripped over it?

She sighed. 'Okay, so I should be out looking for love.'

'Or being open to love finding you,' her mother said.

Ana was about to ask her mother what exactly she meant by that when the door from the street opened and there was Connor, framed in the doorway.

Her breath caught in her throat. Connor. The same familiar, handsome Connor—tall, long limbed but, in some shockingly subtle way, different. Different enough for her to feel, for the first time in their lifelong friendship, a little awkward. She stayed glued to her chair rather than rushing up to greet him.

In faded blue jeans and a black T-shirt, his dark-blond hair streaked gold from the sun, he seemed broader in the shoulders, more muscular, more *powerful*. Surely he couldn't be taller? Not aged twenty-seven. It must be the way he was holding himself. She hadn't actually seen him for more than six months; video calls weren't quite the same as being together in person.

Then he grinned, the big, friendly, all-encompassing

grin he'd had even as a seven-year-old. With that open look on his face that said he expected life would be good to him.

She smiled back, buoyed with sudden joy, and jumped up from her chair to step near and greet him. 'You're back. It's been so long. I've *missed* you.'

He looked deep into her eyes, as he always did. 'I missed you too.'

Then she was swept up into his arms. 'Your biggest, best-est, Connor bear-hug,' she said, her voice muffled against his shoulder. His chest was hard with muscle. He must have been working out while he'd been away. She closed her eyes in the bliss of having him close again.

Her best friend.

Her mother was next in line for a Connor hug. Then her grandparents were there, bearing steaming bowls of *gulyas* and buttered noodles. They placed the dishes on the table. Connor hugged each of them in turn.

'You must be hungry,' said her grandmother, doting on him as she'd done since he'd been a little boy.

'How did you guess?' he said with that heart-warming grin. He sniffed, loud and exaggerated. 'And, if I'm not wrong, you've made me my favourite meal.'

'Always,' said her grandfather, smiling, not hiding his delight.

Ana knew that Connor probably was genuinely hungry. He always seemed to be hungry. But even if he had just eaten a three-course meal he would still have said he was hungry because he knew it would please her grandparents. That was Connor all round. Not a people pleaser, but a person who was kind and truly considerate of others. She couldn't risk losing him again. The weeks they hadn't spoken had been hell.

'How could such a gorgeous-looking guy be so darn

nice?' her friend Kartika had said when Ana had first introduced them.

Ana had shrugged. 'Dunno. He's just like that. Always has been.'

He was super-smart too. It was no wonder his family had expected him to become a doctor. His parents were doctors. His grandfather had been a doctor. And his great-grandfather before that. But Connor had studied medicine at university for one year and decided it wasn't for him.

To the consternation of his family, he'd left, with the stated aim of becoming wealthy. Connor being Connor, he'd succeeded at that beyond everyone's expectations. He'd become a multi-millionaire by the time he'd been twenty-one. Without ever being obnoxious about it, not even for a minute.

Then he'd studied what he'd always wanted to study: veterinary science. He was now a qualified vet doing volunteer work for, as he said, 'animals and the people who love them'. Indigenous animals in danger were his main focus.

Ana knew Connor had his demons—his parents' divorce had affected him badly—but he was the kind of person who didn't want his pain to impinge on others. Sometimes over the years she'd wondered if that reticence was actually a good thing.

Her grandparents doted on him. He'd been part of their lives for so long, the grandson they'd never had. As she watched him chat with them, she realised what was different about her friend. He'd always been the boy next door. Now she couldn't call him that. He no longer lived next door, but that wasn't it. At twenty-seven, Connor was definitely a man. And every fibre of her being was aware of it.

'Come. Eat. All of you,' ordered her grandmother in her soft Hungarian accent.

Ana realised she was hungry too. The relentless pressure that came with having to find a husband had lifted. Connor was here. Of all people, he knew best her good points and her bad. He would help her present a more wife-friendly image to the online dating arena. She knew she could count on him.

Actually, now she thought of it, why not ask him if knew of any possible prospects among his friends and acquaintances?

CHAPTER TWO

AFTER DINNER, Ana walked beside Connor along the St Kilda foreshore on the palm-tree-lined pathway that ran parallel to the beach with a view over Port Phillip Bay. She was feeling ridiculously happy that he was with her. In recent years they hadn't seen as much of each other as they'd had when he'd lived next door. That was inevitable. Life got in the way. Boyfriends and girlfriends who felt threatened by their friendship got in the way.

But it had been too long a break from seeing him. Her life had been turned upside down during that time. And she had struggled to work things out without his support.

'It's good to be home,' he said.

The sigh that accompanied his words was uncharacteristic. Connor didn't do sighs. What had happened up there in Sydney? She knew he'd broken off with Brandi, the woman Ana hadn't liked. But break-ups didn't usually affect Connor. He'd always shrug and tell her the relationship had run its course. Then he'd bounce back. He might go long stretches between girlfriends—he was fussy about whom he dated—but there would be another one soon enough. Connor didn't need to chase women— they chased him.

'It's good to have you home,' she said. Mundane words,

perhaps, but they were heartfelt. Somehow, already her world seemed on a more even keel.

It was a balmy, early summer evening. Melbourne was notorious for having all four seasons in one day because of its volatile weather. Not so today. People were still on the beach—some brave souls swimming, a group of kids chasing a ball around on the sand.

Connor and her didn't hold hands. She didn't slip her hand into the crook of his elbow. He didn't put his arm around her.

They were friends.

A hug, a kiss on the cheek in greeting, was the extent of any physicality between them. It had always been that way. Except for that one, memorable kiss back in high school. That kiss had started as something light, experimental, but had quickly turned into something deep and passionate and utterly heart-stirring. It was the kiss she had never imagined a kiss could be. The first time she had felt the first thrilling stirrings of desire. She had wanted it to last for ever. If the kiss had to end, she wanted another. But to Connor that kiss had not been the right thing to do. Not with the girl next door. Not then, not ever. He'd made it very clear.

They walked towards a group of buskers playing a throbbing, inviting rhythm on African drums. Ana found herself timing her steps to the beat. Connor laughed when he realised what she was doing and joined in. Then, as they reached the drummers, he swung her into a spontaneous dance on the pavement. Laughing, Ana followed his lead as she lost herself in the compelling drum beats, the full skirt of her vintage-inspired dress swirling around her.

Connor danced with a sensuous, rhythmic grace. A lock of his blond hair fell over his forehead, his eyes gleamed green with energy and enthusiasm. He was, undoubtedly, hot. But she couldn't allow herself to want him. She had long ago trained herself not to be aware of her friend as sexually desirable. Or to think even for a moment what an asset a good sense of rhythm could be to a man. This was just Connor.

Other passers-by joined in, until there was a group of strangers dancing with them. They were uninhibited, laughing, enjoying themselves. Ana felt warmed by the good will that surrounded them. This was fun. Connor waved to the small audience that had congregated to watch the drummers and the dancers. They clapped. Entirely un-selfconscious, he bowed to them.

'Why does this kind of thing only happen when I'm with you?' Ana said, a little breathless from the pace of the dance.

'Because of the company I keep?'

He answered her question with a grin and another question that didn't answer anything. That was Connor being Connor. Not for the first time, Ana was glad she was his friend and not his girlfriend. He had broken more than a few hearts, while her heart remained intact. And she still had him in her life. Staying just friends was worth it.

The drums stopped. The dancers came to a halt and they started to disperse, the rhythmic bond that had drawn strangers together broken. As an older lady walked past, she patted Ana on the arm. 'You two make such a cute couple.'

'Oh. I… We…we're not—' Ana stuttered, taken aback.

'Thank you for saying so,' said Connor graciously. He always seemed to have the right words to hand. In this case, he didn't confirm or deny their coupledom, but Ana was saved from an awkward moment. The woman chose to take it as an affirmation and seemed pleased.

Connor pulled his wallet from his pocket and threw a generous number of dollars into the drummer's busking hat. Ana and he resumed their walk.

'Okay, Ms Heiress, bring me up to date with the search for a husband,' he said.

'There's not much to update you with, unfortunately.' She looked up at him. 'But, Connor, before we talk about what my mum calls the "husband hunt", before I update you on how things are going with my sisters, I want to talk to you about—'

'It gives you a thrill to say that, doesn't it? Your sisters.'

'It does. I still can't believe they're in my life. *I have three sisters!* I have to pinch myself to make sure it's all real.'

'They don't resent you?'

'Far from it. They're upset they had a sister all this time and no one told them.'

Connor's eyes narrowed. 'Surely your sudden appearance at age twenty-five must have been hard for your sisters to accept? Especially when you're making a claim on a substantial inheritance that's suddenly split four ways instead of three. I wish I'd been a fly on the wall at the reading of the will.'

'I wished you'd been there too—not as a fly but as you. It was quite scary.' If only she'd been able to have even a phone call with him, she would have felt better about facing the challenges Apa's will presented. 'Rose and Tilly must have been shocked but they graciously welcomed me, they really did. I expected hostility but I got hospitality instead.'

'Tilly?' he said.

'That's what Rose and Eve call Matilda. She asked me to call her Tilly too. And Evelyn is Evie, or Eve.'

'That's very nice, isn't it?' His tone laced his words with something less than positivity.

'Please don't sound so cynical. They truly are wonderful women.'

'Because they need you on side so they can claim their inheritances.'

'There's that, I suppose.' She paused. 'But I believe they're genuine in their welcome to me.'

'What about the sister in London?'

'I met Eve when she came back to Australia to visit in September. She turned out to be just as lovely as the other two. She came and had dinner at the restaurant with me and my family. We had a surprise visit from Nate, too, which was very romantic.'

'That's significant?'

'Absolutely. I was anticipating disaster. After all, when you come down to the truth of it, my mum had an affair with her dad. He had another child his family knew nothing about. Can you imagine? Eve accidentally found out about the affair when she was a teenager. As a result, she became estranged from the family and very bitter towards her father. But it seems she no longer holds a grudge against my mother, and we all got on really well. Even my grandparents fell for Eve and Nate. They're family now. Mum was nearly in tears by the end of it. Even though she genuinely believed Holt was getting divorced when she got together with him, she always felt she'd wronged the Waverly family.'

'I'm glad Eve doesn't blame you for what happened with your parents,' he said. 'The sins of the fathers and all that.'

Ana rolled her eyes. 'Literally the sins of my father.

Who knows why he let my mother believe he would marry her? Tilly was only a tiny baby at the time.'

Connor was the only friend with whom she could talk about her father in any depth. And it still felt weird to think about Holt and Lili as lovers. Who ever wanted to think about their parents in that way?

'Simple. It was a sure-fire way of getting her into bed. I can't imagine gorgeous Lili would have been an easy seduction.'

She gasped. 'Connor! That's going too far.' She shuddered. 'That's my mother you're talking about.'

'It's a guy thing.' He shrugged. 'You know what they say—a horny guy has no conscience. Love. Commitment. Marriage: He'll spin any yarn if he thinks it's what she wants to hear. Anything to get him into a girl's pants.'

'Stop! I don't want to know your seduction techniques.' She paused. 'Have you ever—? No. I really don't want to know.'

He laughed. 'You rise to the bait every time.'

'And you're such a tease,' she said, smiling in spite of herself.

'I try,' he said with that irrepressible grin.

'I prefer to believe that Holt genuinely loved my mother. But circumstances at home changed and he made the right choice for his family. Remember, they didn't know Mum was pregnant with me at the time they ended their relationship.'

'But he took responsibility for you. Tried to maintain a relationship.'

'It was never enough. I was just getting to know him again and I'd be waving him goodbye.'

'I remember how sad you'd be after he left. But he made it up to you at the end with his will.'

'Too late for me to thank him.' She fell quiet for a moment, remembering. Connor gave her time with her thoughts before he spoke again.

'But you inherited sisters,' he said. 'Tell me more about Eve.'

'She might have held the circumstances of my birth against me at first but we're all good now. She needed closure. I felt honoured to be her bridesmaid last month when she married Nate. And guess what? Eve is an expert horsewoman. The other two ride as well.'

Ana and Connor shared a love of horse-riding. They'd been sent to a horse-riding camp one school holiday when she'd been ten and it had become a passion for both of them. She rode whenever she could. A long-held ambition was to own her own horse. Becoming part-owner of Garrison Downs might help achieve that ambition.

'Did you check out the stables when you were there?'

'Only quickly. There were some magnificent horses. Stud horses for breeding, as well as working horses.'

'I understood those mega cattle-stations mustered using helicopters and motorcycles instead of horses.'

'They do, but apparently Apa was old-fashioned when it came to being on horseback. He rode for pleasure too.'

'That's where you must have got your love of horses from.'

'Is it an inherited thing?'

'Why not, if it's something you have in common with your sisters?'

'I guess so. Rose has taken over Apa's stallion, Jasper. Jasper still grieves the loss of his rider.' She fought the tremor in her voice. 'That day, Rose showed me where… where Apa is buried in the family graveyard.'

'That must have been difficult for you.'

'Yes,' she said, hit by a fresh wave of grief. 'But it was good to hear what had happened from my sisters who were there. Apparently Apa was hit by a falling branch from a gum tree—what they call a "widow maker". He got back on his horse and said he was fine. But then two days later he suddenly collapsed and was taken to hospital by air ambulance. Tilly went with him and Rose stayed for the muster, as Holt would have wanted.'

She paused. 'Rose was in the house when suddenly River, his dog, started to howl. It was eerie and sent shivers down her spine, Rose said. Then the phone rang. It was Tilly telling her their father had just died. River was howling his heartbreak at the loss of his master.' Ana fell silent. It was still unbearable that she'd never had a chance to say goodbye to Apa. She'd been told of his death through a formal communication from Mr Harrington.

'I'm sorry about everything you've had to go through. About River's behaviour—animals just seem to know. There's no explanation for it. And I'm sorry I wasn't there for you.' They walked some more in silence before Connor spoke again. 'Do you have a favourite of your new sisters?'

'That's a tricky one. They're so different. Each sister is so nice in her own way. Tilly, maybe. Though I really like Rose and Eve too. I think everyone loves Tilly. She's warm, open, kind, though she speaks her own mind. You know where you stand with her. Did I tell you she's now a princess? A genuine princess.'

'As distinct from an Outback princess?'

'All three of my sisters are Outback princesses,' Ana said. 'But Tilly is also Princess Matilda of Chaleur. It's a small Mediterranean principality. She's gone back there to be with Henri, her husband. Did I tell you Tilly asked me to make her wedding band for her official royal ceremony in August? I was so thrilled.'

'And you?' said Connor. 'Aren't you an Outback princess now too?'

Ana shook her head. 'I think you have to be born to it—the Outback, I mean. Besides, I'm from the wrong side of the blanket, as they used to say.'

'Don't put yourself down, Ana.'

She sighed. 'It's true, though. A love child, my mother always calls me, as you know. I don't think I could be an Outback princess even if I wanted to be—more an Outback outsider. Garrison Downs is…daunting. It's like a kingdom. The property in its entirety is probably larger than some small countries. With billionaire Holt as its king and his three beautiful princesses.'

'You're a princess too,' Connor said fiercely. 'Don't you forget that.'

'More Cinderella, really. It's what I feel like.'

'Not so. Your dad recognised you as an equal daughter when it came to inheritance. Step up to it, girl. You're an equal heir to the kingdom. Don't let anyone think any different, especially not you.'

'A red dust kingdom. Remind me not to wear white sneakers the next time I go there.' She paused. 'It's magnificent, Garrison Downs; you should see it.'

'I hope I will one day. I'm counting on an invitation to visit.'

'The second I feel I have the right to invite a guest, the invitation will be yours,' she said. 'I've already picked out a good-looking gelding named Zircon for you to ride. I've fallen for a sweet mare, Ruby. The horses are all named after gemstones. Some whim of my father, apparently.'

'When I heard your news, I looked up everything I

could about the property,' Connor said. 'I found pictures of your father's study where he met with visiting states-men, the ballroom where they hold charity events, endless shots of enormous herds of cattle. By the way, the station is known for its high standard of animal welfare, I'm sure you'll be pleased to know. But there wasn't much about how the family live.'

'In the utmost comfort, I can assure you. There are two fabulous houses and a tiny old settler's cottage going back to the very early days of the property. What they call the old house is the beautiful heritage house where Apa grew up with his parents.'

'And the other house?'

'A mansion. That's the kingdom's castle. Extravagant. Over the top. Like out of a designer magazine. When I stayed there after the reading of the will, Rose put me in the yellow suite. It's like something out of a very posh English coun-try house—or what I imagine one to be. Air-conditioned to the hilt, of course, and run by a housekeeper and staff. Apa had the new house built for his wife Rosamund when he went back to her.'

'To make up for his cheating?'

'Could be. That's not something I could very well ask. The new house is modern—or modern for twenty-five years ago—but timelessly elegant. Rose told me it has her mother Rosamund's stamp all over it. There's an in-door swimming pool because their mum liked to swim. And it's surrounded by beautiful gardens that were their mum's passion too.'

'A garden in the red Outback? They must have good water supplies.'

She smiled. 'Trust you to think of that—always prac-tical. Apparently, there's no shortage of water. In fact, there's a river nearby, but I didn't see that. There's so much I haven't seen.'

Connor stopped walking and turned to face her. He looked into her eyes in that searching way he had. 'It's your heritage, Ana. You need to get to know Garrison Downs. How it works. Where you want your place to be there. Let the others hear your voice. Claim it as your own, equally with your sisters.'

Ana nodded. 'And yet it seems to have been Rosamund's domain. Where does her husband's secret love-child fit in there?'

'Where she makes her place, with the help of her sisters.'

Connor made no mention of the fact there would be no place for Ana to take at Garrison Downs if she wasn't married within six months. Her sisters wouldn't be living there either. The despised descendants of the original owners would be draining the pool and trashing the gardens—or so Rose predicted.

'Wasn't the wife English?' Connor said.

'Half-English, half-French, Tilly says. Apparently it was a terrible shock for a sophisticated, cultured woman to find herself isolated in the heat and the dust of the Outback. No amount of Waverly money could make up for it.'

'It must be strange for you to be immersed in stories about Rosamund Waverly and her influence. She was the rival for your father's affections—Rosamund won, Lili lost.'

Ana shook her head. 'Mum never thought of it that way. Rosamund was his wife, the mother of his three children. If he wanted to make a go of his marriage, my mother thought it was the right—the moral—thing for him to do. Even if she was left heartbroken when he went back. She believed his marriage to be dead; turned out it wasn't. You know I loved my father, but he was far from perfect.'

'You've come to terms with that?'

'A long time ago. Right about the time when I realised I was the only girl in that awful private girls' school who never had a father turn up for school events. Not once. The divorced fathers came but never mine. He couldn't risk his family finding out about me.'

'I remember. So you told them your father was dead.'

'It seemed easier that way. And now...and now he really is dead.'

She sniffed back sudden tears. Cleared her throat. She couldn't give in to that grief now, not in public. 'You've distracted me by talking about my sisters. Before we talk any more about me, there's something I need to say to you.'

'Fire away,' he said. His wary eyes told her he'd been expecting this.

'I'm really sorry we fell out over Brandi. You were right to tell me to butt out of your love life. It wasn't my place.'

A muscle tightened at the corner of his mouth. 'Nothing to forgive. You were right. Turned out she was, shall we say, overly interested in my bank balance.'

'Not your handsome face and charming personality?'

'I think my fat wallet was more appealing. I didn't see it at first. But she got greedy.' There was an edge to Connor's voice.

After Connor had dropped out of medicine he, two other clever guys and a genius girl had formed what they called The Money Club. They'd each wanted their own wealth so they'd be able to take charge of their lives, be independent of their families. The four of them had traded crypto-currency at exactly the right time. They'd invented of-the-moment apps and sold them to the highest bidder.

They'd invested in property with perfect timing before a huge boom in prices. The more money they'd made, the more they'd invested and the more they'd made.

The club continued to this day, although the four founding members were now scattered around the world. Connor was a very wealthy guy. With the money to do anything he wanted, he'd decided to go back to uni. Now he'd graduated as a vet. He'd spent much of the past year volunteering on a project working to improve the health of an endangered colony of koalas.

'You really liked Brandi, didn't you?' Ana said.

He hesitated and she wondered if he would brave it out. Connor didn't do vulnerability. 'Yeah. I did. I liked her a lot. I even didn't shut her down when she started to hint about moving in together.'

'That was serious for you.' Connor was notoriously anti-marriage, anti-commitment. His parents' nasty divorce when he'd been a teenager had traumatised him.

'Turned out she wasn't the person she said she was. I should have listened to you and spared myself some drama.'

'When have you ever done that? You hate anyone telling you what to do. Which is why we didn't speak for weeks. We can't let that happen again.'

'Sorry about that. I really am. Even the mention of your name caused a screaming match.' He shuddered. 'But it's over now. I don't want to talk about it.' When Connor broke up with a girlfriend, that was it. A clean break. No keeping in touch. Her number deleted from his phone.

'Maybe you should talk about it,' she said gently. 'Spill the details. Cry on my shoulder. Work it through. You know I'm here for you.'

'And I appreciate that, as always. But there's no point.

Brandi is in the past. Right now, I'd rather hear about the hits and misses of your campaign to find a husband.'

'All misses, no hits, I'm afraid.'

'The guys you're meeting must be both blind and stupid.'

She smiled. 'Thank you, friend. It's been quite a hit to the ego, that's for sure.'

'Let's head for the pub. We can talk over a beer about how I can help you. There must be something you could do better. You've only got six months. That's probably not even time to organise a wedding, let alone find the husband to front up to it.'

CHAPTER THREE

CONNOR WAS USED to other guys looking at Ana when he was out with his beautiful friend. Tonight was no different. There'd been admiring, appraising glances from the moment he'd walked through the door of his favourite pub, with Ana sashaying in beside him. She had a subtle but sensual swing of her hips that was pure Ana. He knew she was still fired with the rhythm of their impromptu dance. With her lovely face, slim figure and dazzling smile, she turned heads.

You're a lucky guy. He could read that in the pub patrons' gazes. And he was lucky to have had Ana as his best friend since they'd been little kids.

She'd been five and he seven when the cute little girl next door with her hair in pigtails and a scattering of freckles across her nose had burrowed her way through a gap in the dividing hedge and fallen into his back yard. He and his brother Billy, who had been playing there at the time, hadn't known what to make of her. But little Ana had joined in every rough and tumble game with him and his brother, who was three years younger than he was. She was a whiz at cricket. Swam like a fish. Her slight, slender frame made her good at gymnastics.

His parents had expected that Ana would play more with Billy, who was closer to her age. But there'd been a bond between Connor and Ana from the word go. Almost, he thought, from the moment he'd picked leaves and sticks from the hedge out of her hair. He'd always felt protective of her and she of him—not that he'd needed protecting, especially by a girl.

When she'd been fifteen, she'd gone on holiday to Budapest with her mother and grandparents. He'd missed her. But, when she'd come back, she'd seemed different. It had taken a while for him to get used to a new, more *girly* Ana. She'd dressed differently and had found an interest in jewellery, having spent time with a great-uncle who was a jeweller of some repute. Connor's guy friends had started to take an interest in his lovely, very feminine neighbour.

Yet he had always been determined to keep their friendship just that. Ana was out of bounds as far as dating went. Never spoken of, but never forgotten, was the kiss they'd shared when he'd escorted her—as a friend—to her school formal. He'd suspected it was her first proper kiss but it had sizzled—the heat of it totally taking him by surprise. But he was two years older than she was. She'd been too young for the kind of kiss that had screamed 'going exclusive'. He wasn't ready for that, and she certainly hadn't been either—no matter what she might have thought.

He'd known stepping out of the friendship zone could be a risk, and back then he hadn't been able to bear the thought of losing he. Not at a time of immense change for him with the disintegration of his parents' marriage. Teenaged Connor had clung to Ana for support and reassurance during the time when his mother had discovered his father had cheated on her throughout their marriage. Ana's friendship had given him stability at a time when he couldn't have dealt with more change. She'd been the only person he'd been able to confide in about what was going on. Ana was accustomed to keeping secrets. Even today, he felt she was the only person he could truly be himself with.

Now he sat opposite Ana in the privacy of a corner booth. She was looking particularly lovely tonight, with her black hair tied back in a high pony-tail, her cheeks flushed pink from dancing, her astounding blue eyes defined with dark make-up. Who'd have known those eyes would bond her to her newly found half-sisters?

He'd wondered if the three Waverly girls would insist on a DNA test when Ana had appeared, seemingly from nowhere, as a claimant to the will. But it seemed her father's acknowledgement of a fourth daughter and the Waverly eyes had been enough. Still, he'd warned her to be careful about giving too much of herself until she knew for sure that the sisterly love was genuine. Not that she seemed to want to listen to that particular piece of advice. She was enchanted by her new sisters.

'Okay, spill,' he said. 'Tell me all about the husband hunt.'

Over the background chatter and clinking of glasses, he listened with increasing incredulity as Ana regaled him with tales of her desperately bad dates. The condescending creeps. The guys who had obviously lopped off twenty years from their real ages for the dating apps. The seriously weird and the just plain boring. Then there had been the guys who'd thought insults were a form of flirtation.

He heard about her grandmother's well-meaning attempts to find her a suitable husband. And her dread of reporting to her sisters how she was no closer to finding the all-important man—or woman, for that matter. It didn't state in the will that it couldn't be a same-sex marriage, but he knew Ana didn't swing that way. He hated seeing her so anxious about a clause in a will that was so archaic and constricting. Ana had always been slim, but she'd lost weight. There were bruise-like shadows under her eyes and a frailty about her that he found alarming.

Finally, he put up his hand in a halt sign. 'Stop! You're going about this in entirely the wrong way.'

Her eyes widened. She stopped mid-word. 'What do you mean?'

'Seems to me you're preparing to throw your life away for the sake of your inheritance.'

'You mean by getting married? Of course I wasn't planning to get married just yet but—'

'I mean by forcing a marriage. The condition in the will says all four of you have to be married within a year, right? Otherwise, bye-bye Garrison Downs, the source of much of the Waverly wealth.'

'And the beloved home of my sisters,' she reminded him.

'Where does it say in the will that it has to be a real marriage?' he said.

Ana paused. Only because he'd known her for so long was he able to get a clue about her feelings from reading her face. She'd had to keep so much secret for so long, she'd mastered the art of masking her emotions. Now he saw confusion. 'Um. Nowhere, to my knowledge.'

'Or does it state somewhere that it has to be a lasting marriage? Or, indeed, a love match?'

She frowned. 'Nowhere.'

'Or that it has to be a consummated marriage?'

Ana flushed, which told him she was thinking what he was thinking about consummation. Only in his thoughts he was with her, not she with some stranger she'd married. He forced thoughts of *that* from his mind—as he'd been doing for years. He had never allowed himself to think of

Ana in a non-platonic way. That hadn't always easy. But staying just friends worked best for him.

'It…it certainly doesn't say anything about…about consummating the marriage anywhere in the document,' she said.

Connor sat back in the booth. 'So why are you running around trying to find happy-ever-after love to fit some artificial deadline? You can't force it. No wonder you seem so tense and anxious when you talk about it.'

'I am not tense and anxious.'

He stared pointedly at her hands, which she was wringing together so tightly, he could hardly tell which fingers belonged to which hand.

'Okay. Maybe a bit tense and anxious. Actually, more than a bit.'

'No wonder. Even if you find a guy you think you could spend your life with, what kind of pressure would be on him? On both of you? Have you thought past the wedding to sharing a life together?'

Her mouth turned downwards. 'I haven't met anyone who I'd imagine spending a weekend with, let alone my life.'

'So why do that?' He leaned across the table, closer to her. 'Look at this marriage thing as a business proposal. Instead of trying to force happy-ever-afters, find someone who you can marry to fulfil the terms of the will. Pay him a substantial fee. Then quietly divorce after the inheritance is settled on all four sisters.'

His friend was so smart, he wondered why she hadn't thought of this, or her sisters.

She frowned. 'You mean, hire a husband?'

'I wouldn't put it quite like that, but yes.'

'Bizarre idea, but…' He could see the cogs turning. 'How would it work?'

'You'd draw up a contract for his services to be your husband, in name only, for a year, starting with a fake engagement, leading to a wedding and then a discreet divorce.'

'A fake marriage?'

'It would have to be a legal marriage before a celebrant to satisfy the terms of the will. You couldn't risk it unravelling if it was found to be fraudulent. But it wouldn't be fraudulent if the marriage didn't work out and you separated soon after.'

She nodded thoughtfully. 'I think, under Australian law, you have to be separated for a year before you can file for divorce.'

'All that would mean is you couldn't marry anyone else for at least a year.'

She shrugged. 'As I don't want to get married at all, that wouldn't be a hardship.'

He wasn't sure why she was so vehemently against marriage. It might date back to the awful guy, Rory, the longest-lasting of her boyfriends. He'd been a manipulative bully. Connor had seen that, but it had taken Ana a while to wake up to it.

He was no fan of marriage either. Especially after his experience with Brandi. He'd had a close escape. How viciously she'd turned on him when she'd realised he'd seen through her. Everything he'd thought had been spontaneous about her had been calculating. He could only imagine how much worse it would have got if he'd stayed.

'The guy you choose to sign up to the contract would have to be a good actor,' he said. 'And attractive enough for it to be believable that you would fall for him so quickly.'

'Someone I wouldn't have trouble pretending to fancy. But…it would be a marriage in name only.' She grimaced. 'No sex. There couldn't be sex.'

'Not if you didn't want it.'

'I wouldn't sleep with some guy just to—'

'Inherit millions of dollars? Of course you wouldn't. Some might. But I know you would never contemplate that.'

He couldn't help a grin. She smiled back. 'How would I go about it?' she asked.

'A water-tight contract. Confidentiality clause. And a hefty fee. The inheritance will make you a very wealthy woman. You can afford to pay top dollar to make it worth your potential candidate's while. Borrow against your house if you have to. The pay-off from your inheritance would be worth it.'

'Where would I find such a candidate?' she said.

'You're considering it?' He was surprised, as Ana was usually pretty much a go-by-the-rules person.

'It's kinda out there,' she admitted. 'But I suppose it could work. I'm open to all ideas to allow me to get that inheritance. Not just for me but for my sisters.'

'Good,' he said.

'But where would I find this…this fake husband?'

'Let me think,' Connor said. 'Your guy would have to be good-looking and a good actor. So why not an actual actor?'

'That's a thought,' she said slowly. 'Not that I know any actors.'

'Actors have agents,' he said.

Her eyes narrowed. 'But could you go through an agent with such an unconventional role? I doubt they'd let me through the door. It would also mean another person I'd have to let in on the secret.'

'Good point. The fewer people who know about the hire-a-husband contract, the better.'

'Understood,' she said.

'Were there any actors on the dating apps?' Connor asked.

'You mean the genuine kind, as opposed to the ones who were pretending to be someone they weren't?' she said. 'I thought I recognised two. I wondered at the time why they would put themselves out there on an app.'

'Genuinely looking for connection, I suggest. Finding a compatible partner isn't easy for anyone. I reckon some celebrities could have problems being appreciated for their genuine selves.' He knew now to be concerned that someone—a person like Brandi—could be with him for his wealth. It had been kick-in-the-gut hurtful to find out the truth about the woman he'd been infatuated with.

Ana's finely winged eyebrows rose in alarm. 'That might be so. But I can't have a celebrity. The fake husband couldn't be someone well-known. That would totally attract the wrong kind of attention to the wedding.'

He nodded. 'A struggling, unknown actor might be the best candidate.'

She sighed. 'It's a good idea. But I'd have to be so, so careful. How on earth could I put that kind of trust in a stranger? They could break the contract and go to press with the truth of a fake marriage. The repercussions of being exposed don't bear thinking about.'

'True. There's a lot at stake.'

'Not just for me, but for my sisters.'

He thought about it but came to a dead-end every time. 'What about someone you actually know?'

She paused. 'There is someone. Maybe. One of my grandmother's matchmaking efforts. He's gorgeous, fun and hiding the fact he's gay from his family. I liked him a lot and we've agreed to stay in touch. He's establishing his own business, so might welcome the money.'

'Could be worth considering.'

It was strange but all this talk of Ana getting married was stirring up some unfamiliar emotions—the most insistent one being jealousy. One day, each of them would most likely get married. Even him, although that seemed the remotest of remote possibilities right now. It would be lucky if they each married someone who tolerated their spouse having a straight best friend of the opposite sex. Brandi had hated him having contact with Ana. Ana had only had a few serious boyfriends. They hadn't exactly encouraged her to spend time with Connor. One of them had been outright hostile. But he couldn't be jealous of a hire-a-husband. He couldn't be jealous of anyone. Ana was just a friend. That didn't stop him from wanting to protect her, though, as he always had.

'Wait, now that I think of it, that won't work,' said Ana. 'My new friend has a partner. He wants to get married as soon as they can, once he comes clean to his family about his sexuality. They wouldn't welcome not being able to marry for more than a year because he was legally tied to me.'

'Shame. Count him out, then,' Connor said. 'But you've only just started thinking about this alternative marriage possibility. There must be other possibilities—an anonymous advertisement on the Internet could be an idea.'

Ana vehemently shook her head. 'I can tell you right now, I wouldn't do that. Way too risky.'

'You're right,' he said. 'Of course you are.'

'I'll ask Kartika if she has any thoughts,' Ana said. Kartika was Ana's best female friend and a really nice person. Ana had met her at university. Kartika was Indonesian and now lived back in Jakarta, working in her wealthy family's business. She was also Ana's partner in their online jewellery store and was as keen as Ana was to expand it.

'Is that wise?' he said. 'Bringing another person into your confidence?'

'I trust Kartika implicitly. If I went ahead with this crazy scheme, only you and she would know anything about it.'

'If you say so.' Connor drained the last of his beer. 'We've got a ticking clock against us. We really need to put our thinking caps on, as my grandmother used to say. I'll go get us more drinks and then we can get a recruitment plan into action.'

Ana sighed. 'Or we can forget all about what is a completely off-the-wall idea.'

'That too,' he said. He still felt uneasy at the thought of Ana actually marrying a stranger. What if he became abusive? Tried to scam her? Or what if she chose someone so compatible it actually became a real marriage? He wasn't at all sure that was a good idea.

There was a queue at the bar. When Connor eventually got back to the table, it was to find Ana scrolling through her phone. She looked up, eyes alight.

'What you propose is called a "marriage of convenience". It's more common than you might think, when oddly worded wills that specify marriage are in play.' She smiled. 'And apparently popular in romance novels.'

'Really? I'm more than a bit miffed to find it wasn't a brilliant original idea of mine,' he said lightly.

As he pushed Ana's glass of wine towards her, Connor was surprised to see how animated she was—excited, it seemed, about a possible marriage of convenience.

'So you think my idea is a feasible one?' he said, more

than a little chuffed that she should think so. And more than a little concerned about the possibility of her marrying a stranger.

'The more I think about it, the more I think it could be an excellent solution to an impossible problem.' She took a sip from her wine and looked across at him, head tilted to one side, very serious. 'I've even thought of the perfect man to be my pretend husband. He fits every criterion we discussed. He is absolutely the one. There could be no other choice.'

'And who might that be?' Connor asked.

Ana put down her glass and moved closer to him across the table. 'You.'

CHAPTER FOUR

ANA WATCHED IN alarm as Connor nearly choked on his beer, spluttering and gasping for air. She slid round in the booth so she could pat him vigorously on his back. Finally, he got his breath back.

'Me? Are you serious?' he choked out.

'Very serious,' she said. 'I don't know why I didn't think of it straight away. You would be perfect as my pretend husband.'

'Perfect? Me?' His green eyes glazed with disbelief. 'What makes you say that?'

Ana wasn't sure whether to be offended or amused that Connor appeared so shocked at her proposal. *Proposal.* There was a proposal in a business context, or a proposal in the context of asking someone to marry you. This was, she supposed, neither one nor the other.

'The fake marriage was your idea. You'd be able to carry it through better than anyone. When I thought about it, I realised you so perfectly fit all the criteria we discussed.'

Her friend shook his head, obviously bewildered. 'You know I'm usually not lost for words, but I... I don't know what to say.'

Ana could see he wasn't just shocked. Connor was obviously appalled and horrified. She was mortified. His reaction shot her right back to the time she'd so foolishly suggested they lose their virginities together. She'd gone too far. Taken too much for granted. Totally ruined their reunion after six months apart. She shuffled back from where she sat next to him to her place opposite in the booth. She wished she could shuffle right out of the pub.

Her cheeks burned with humiliation. She could hardly bear to look at him. Frantically, she tried to back-pedal. 'Of course it's a terrible idea. I'm sorry. Forget I mentioned it. Silly of me.' She attempted a carefree laugh, but it came out as a strangled, hysterical squeak. She looked down at her watch and faked surprise at seeing the time. 'Anyway, I think I need to go.' She went to get up. How could she ever live down this fiasco?

'No. Stay.' Connor reached over the table to put his hand on her arm to stop her. 'I was surprised, that's all. You know I'm not the marrying kind. Just a mention of the word gives me shivers of aversion. And I don't like lies or dishonesty. We talked about acting skills, but really it would be lying and deception on a grand scale that would be required.'

'I should have known better than to even suggest it.' Ana squeezed shut her eyes, wishing that when she opened them she could be anywhere but here. When she did open them, it was to see Connor, no longer horrified but concerned. Compassion and understanding warmed his eyes. He knew her so well.

'Quite rightly, you felt you could ask me,' he said. 'We're friends. We help each other out. I've always looked out for you. You need help now. It's just—'

'I know,' she said, wanting to extricate herself from the confines of the booth, feeling edgy with embarrassment.

'No, you don't know. You're jumping to conclusions.

You shocked me. Now I've got over my shock, I want to hear what you have to say. Run me through those criteria again.'

'You'll just laugh,' she said, knowing she sounded a little sulky, unable to help it.

'I won't. Well, I might laugh at the ridiculousness of me being anyone's husband, even a pretend one. But I wouldn't be laughing at you. Never would I laugh at you.'

There was an edge to his voice that made Ana put her embarrassment aside and focus on Connor. He'd just gone through a bitter break-up. She knew he feared he could never be faithful to a woman. That was why marriage—a real marriage—was something he didn't think he could succeed at. He'd grown up being told he was just like his handsome but unfaithful father in terms of looks, brains and personality. Then the image of his father had been shattered and so, in some way, had his image of himself. She hadn't realised it went quite so deep.

'You know that's not true,' she said. 'When you find the right person, you'll be a wonderful husband. You're a more honourable and loyal person than your father in every way. I really believe that.'

Connor's mouth twisted wryly. 'You know I'd like to believe you, but I'm not so sure I'll ever want to marry for real. So tell me why I'd make a good fake husband.'

'Are you sure you want to hear me out?'

'Absolutely sure. I'm not saying I'll say yes. I just want to hear your rationale for my fitness for the role.'

'I don't expect you to say yes. Well, obviously I was hoping you might say yes, or I wouldn't have suggested it. But in light of your spontaneous adverse reaction, I've completely revised that expectation. Weighing up the probability, I—'

'I love it when you talk like an accountant.'

He was smiling at her, that gorgeous Connor smile that she had never been able to resist. She couldn't resist it this time either. She smiled back. Then they were laughing together, as they had done so many times before. This was Connor. Her best friend. She had completely overreacted. The husband-hunting thing had her on edge.

'The criteria?' he prompted. 'And please don't ask me again if I'm sure.'

'Okay,' she said, relaxing back into the booth, happy they'd got over the awkwardness. She couldn't bear it when things weren't good with them. Those months when they hadn't spoken had left their mark. She had missed him every day. 'First, a marriage between us would be believable. We've known each other most of our lives. That woman earlier this evening wasn't the first one to take us for a couple.'

'There have been others, yes. And we've each helped the other out when in need of a date. We would be believable.'

'We know each other so well, we wouldn't trip ourselves up with details of our lives that would make people suspicious we weren't for real.'

'True.'

'There are other reasons you'd be ideal. You're not in a relationship, you're in no hurry to actually get married and you're so ridiculously rich you wouldn't try to blackmail me to cash in on the inheritance.'

'Correct on all counts,' he said. 'But I—'

Ana put up her hand in a halt signal. 'Can we save the objections to the end? You know how difficult this is for me. Let's face it, employing a fake husband is tantamount to admitting I can't find a real one.'

'Ana, that's not true. You're everything a guy would want in a wife—beautiful, kind, smart.'

Just what her grandma had said. What about sexy, exciting, adventurous? But Ana knew, up until now, she had trod the safe path. That was her family's influence. They were obsessed with security. She owed them so much. As a good daughter and granddaughter, she'd gone along with what they wanted for her—a degree in finance with a sure job at the end of it. A secure role in a big accountancy firm, where she felt both bored and trapped. The inheritance opened new horizons for her. The freedom to follow her creative impulses. Her own business. Security of a very different kind. And the chance to change.

'Thank you,' she said.

'I meant if a guy was ready to marry. Not like me. You know why I don't have marriage on my radar.'

Ana knew Connor feared his capacity for fidelity because of his father's multiple betrayals. It was why he got out of relationships when talk of commitment came calling. She hoped his experience with dollar-signs-in-her-eyes Brandi wouldn't embitter him.

'I don't want to get married either,' she said. 'I want to fly, Connor, without having to take into consideration someone else's needs. I don't want to be tethered any longer by other people's expectations of me. I've loved studying part-time for my jewellery-design qualifications. It's not just a hobby for me. I want it to be my career. You know that. I want to invest my time and my money in my business with Kartika. I need to be free of obligations so I can travel to where we source the materials and have the jewellery made on a more commercial scale. We need to do marketing and publicity too. The inheritance will give me all that. I can't be tied down by a marriage. Not a real one. Or a fake one with someone I don't trust.'

'Trust has to come into it on both sides,' he said slowly.

'I know I can trust you above anyone else. I know you would play the role convincingly and with sincerity. With you as my fake husband, I know there would be no leaks to the press and no blackmail attempts down the track. I can trust your integrity.'

'You can always trust me. That goes without saying. I know I can trust you. We've kept each other's secrets since we were kids. But this is really serious, Ana. I believe the fake marriage idea is a good one, considering your circumstances. But you and I have so much history, and so much to lose if it didn't work out.'

Connor leaned closer across the table and took both her hands in his. They rarely touched, so Ana could tell how seriously he took her proposal.

'You're going to say no?' she said. She swallowed hard against a lump of disappointment that threatened to choke her.

He looked directly into her face in that way he had. 'I'm going to say I want to think about this. You know I'm always on your side. But something about this "marriage of convenience" proposal scares me. And that's apart from the prospect of lying to our families and friends.'

She frowned. 'Scares you?'

'You know how much I value your friendship. What if we went through with this and it didn't work out? It would be a really big thing to go into, and an equally big thing to come out of. I don't want to risk losing you. You know what I say: girlfriends come and go, but Ana is for ever.'

Ana wondered if he would again say he thought of her as a sister. Because ever since that kiss they'd shared, she'd never thought of him as a brother.

'We'd be aware of that,' she said. 'I wouldn't want to risk losing my friendship with you either. I value it so much.'

She tightened her grip on his hands. 'Don't think I would ask this of you if I had any other choice.'

'I'm aware of that,' he said.

'We're both intelligent people; I think we could make it work. Please, Connor, help me out. This was your idea, after all. I can't even contemplate a fake marriage with a stranger. It's too risky and I fear it could backfire on me. Yet I have to marry within six months. It would be so unfair if my sisters missed out on their inheritance because I couldn't find a man. Unfair on me too, because Garrison Downs and the wealth it generates is as much my birth right as it is theirs.'

'Understood,' he said.

'I also want to claim that birth right for my mother, who brought me up pretty much as a single mum. She put her own life on hold for way too long. And for my grandparents, who spent so much time and love on me and were civil about Holt—a man they loathed—for my sake.'

'You make a compelling argument for me to consider,' he said.

Ana realised it was so compelling that, by trying to talk him into the plan, she'd talked herself into it one hundred percent. Now she believed there could be no other way to meet the requirement of the will than to go through with a fake marriage to Connor. Panic gripped her at the thought of him refusing to step up.

But there was one big problem that suddenly blazed into her consciousness. Something she couldn't share with him. If he agreed to her proposal, she would spend way more time with him than she had since they'd been children. They would be thrust into an enforced intimacy. What if she found herself unable to keep up the pretence that she wasn't attracted to him?

* * *

Connor realised his hands were still entwined with Ana's across the table. And that they had leaned so closely towards each other, their heads were nearly touching. Just as well. That way, no one could possibly have overheard what they were saying. And they really didn't want this conversation to be overheard.

He gently disengaged their hands and Ana drew back. Her cheeks were flushed pink, which served to make her eyes seem even bluer. Tendrils of her dark hair had come loose from where they'd been pulled back in her ponytail, and they wisped around her face. Her bold red lipstick had worn off, but her mouth was naturally pink.

Her mouth. It was a part of Ana that Connor never allowed himself to focus on. Her full lips were eminently kissable, but he could never acknowledge that. Back in their teenage days, when she'd suddenly turned so feminine and elegant after her trip to Budapest, the boys at school had certainly noticed. He'd been protective and had refused to facilitate introductions. He'd guarded her.

'If you don't want her, mate, don't hog her to yourself,' the boys had said.

He'd growled back that they weren't good enough for her.

He had wanted her. But she'd been too young and he hadn't been ready. A two-year age gap had loomed large in those days. And then everything had fallen apart with his family. His father had moved out and he'd stayed in the family home at St Kilda with his mother. Next door to Ana. He'd been happy for her to remain the girl next-door who offered uncomplicated friendship. He'd needed that so badly. From then on, they'd stayed firmly in the friendship zone. She'd lost her virginity to someone else—

her first serious boyfriend at uni, most likely. He hadn't asked, hadn't wanted to know, still didn't want to know.

'How long do you need to think before you can make a decision?' she asked.

Ana had offered him friendship and comfort when he'd really needed it. She'd been a loyal friend in the intervening years. Now was the time to return the favour.

She needed him.

'I've had enough time,' he said.

'Really?'

'I've made a decision.'

Her eyes widened. 'And?'

'Ana Horvath, will you marry me?' he said.

'*What?*'

'I'm stepping into the role straight away. I realise I'm a traditional kind of guy when it comes to marriage, even of the fake kind. I want to do the proposing.'

'Oh, Connor. Thank you. I… I'm so grateful. So grateful I could kiss you.' She stopped. 'Should I kiss you?'

For a long moment, their gazes met, full of unspoken questions. *Yes!* he wanted to say. But that would complicate this raw, new agreement between them.

'Not now,' he said, finding it remarkably difficult to utter those two words. Suddenly all he could think about was kissing her. He tried very hard to avert his eyes from her mouth. 'You'll have to kiss me at some stage soon if we're to make a relationship believable and authentic. We'll have to sort out how we handle the…uh…public displays of affection.'

'Yes. We will. PDAs to be choreographed.' She looked down at the table, unable to meet his gaze. Did she feel any of the same pull to him? Or was he just a convenient solution to her problem? 'But we're both private people,' she said. 'We can probably keep the PDAs to a minimum. No one we know would expect us to…to be all over each other.'

He cleared his throat. 'Perhaps not.'

Ana all over him? Now that was a thought.

She looked up again. 'We'll figure it out.'

'But, in the meantime, are you accepting my proposal or not?' he said.

'Yes, I am,' she said. Connor saw the worry lift from her face to be replaced by relief. That made it worthwhile. She laughed. 'I can't believe we're doing this!'

'Consider ourselves engaged,' he said. Never would he have imagined himself saying those words. Ironic that it was just a game.

'That seems kinda weird, doesn't it?' she said, her head tilted to one side.

'If I was a real fiancé, I'd be affronted you said that. But, as I'm a fake, I'd have to agree. Yes. Seriously weird.'

'But I'm so grateful.'

'And I'm so glad I can be of help.'

'What's next?' she said.

Connor didn't have to think hard. 'We tell the right people that we're getting married.'

'Who first?' she asked.

'Your sisters. Face to face, with a visit to Garrison Downs. Then your family. Then mine. Billy, of course. He'll be gutted. He's had a secret crush on you for years.'

Her eyebrows rose. 'Your little brother, Billy?'

'Not so little now. He's only a year younger than you are. He can be my best man.'

'Best man? Oh, my gosh, we'll have to have a wedding, won't we? A proper wedding. I hadn't thought of that.'

'We haven't had time to think about a lot of things,' he said. 'But surprise engagements are like that.'

'You're right into the play-acting already,' she said, smiling. 'I'm impressed.'

'If we don't get deep into it straight away, we might have trouble ahead of us,' he said. 'From now on, you have to seriously believe you're engaged to me. I won't be the only one acting. Do you think you're up to it?'

'Of course I am,' she said. 'If you remember, I took part in a few university revues.'

'Indeed you did, but you didn't invite me,' he said.

'I was a bit too self-conscious,' she admitted. 'But I think the experience will help me play the role of besotted bride.'

He frowned. 'Besotted?'

'Come on, Connor. Have you ever had a girlfriend who wasn't besotted with you?'

'I wouldn't say *besotted*…'

'You're very handsome, clever, a decent human being and very, very wealthy. I would definitely say besotted. If I—'

'If you what?' he said.

'Nothing,' she said, casting down her gaze again.

'You can't say *nothing*. Come on.'

She looked up. Her cheeks flushed a deeper shade of pink. 'If I were seriously dating you, and wasn't your friend who's known you since you were a grubby little boy, I… I would be besotted.' She paused. 'That's not to say I *am* besotted, you understand. I'm talking about a hypothetical situation.'

'Hypothetical. Of course.' Just the same, he couldn't help but feel pleased. Because wasn't it the truth that she'd always been special to him, even when he'd been a little boy? 'Hypothetically speaking, if I wasn't the boy who had to wipe up your bloodied knees every time you crashed my skateboard—'

'If I recall, it was one of your doctor parents who tended to my bloodied knees. And I only crashed your skate-board because you dared me to go too fast. You kept on daring me.'

'And you kept on crashing my skateboard.'

'Until the day I got my own skateboard.'

'And we went down that hill side by side.'

'Yes,' she said, smiling. 'Really fast.'

How innocent those days had been, with both his parents living together at home and available to patch up knees and elbows or put stitches in a gashed forehead. Without thinking about it, he put his hand up to his head. He still had the scar, faded now, just below his hairline. The scars caused by his parents' divorce went so much deeper.

'So…you were saying?' Ana asked. 'Hypothetically, that is?'

'Hypothetically, I'd be besotted with you.'

'Really?'

'Like most of the neighbourhood boys were. But you didn't even notice.'

'Don't be silly, of course they weren't. They were interested in tall, tanned, leggy blondes.'

'Not all of them. Some were very keen on you. Don't worry, I fought them off for you.'

'You *what*?'

'I didn't think they were worthy of you.'

'Like I didn't think Brandi was worthy of you.'

'Touché,' he said.

She laughed. 'I don't remember those boys very well. I

would, if any of them had interested me. Also, if you remember, my grandparents and mother were really strict
with me. After all, my mother had got pregnant to a married man at age twenty-five. They were going to make
darn sure that no such unplanned pregnancy happened to
me. They loved it when we took up horse-riding because
it was ninety-five percent girls at the horse camps.'

'Me being the five percent boy.'

'That's right. The girls made such a fuss of you.'

'And I stuck with my friend, Ana,' he said. 'It wasn't a
hardship. You're very lovely, you know. And you were very
cute when you were a teenager.'

Their eyes met for too long. Hers were the first to drop.
'Nice to reminisce,' she said briskly. 'But that's not pro-
gressing our marriage-of-convenience agenda, is it?'

'Spoken like you're chairing a meeting,' he said.

'Which I often do at the office,' she said. 'I can't wait
to hand in my resignation.'

'Perhaps you should do that soon. Can you afford to?'

'If I'm careful, yes. But I can't count on the inheritance
until all four of us sisters are married. I'm not sure there's
anyone on the horizon for Rose. Perhaps we should share
our idea with her.'

'Not a good idea,' he said. 'I don't think we should tell
anyone the truth. Not your sisters. Not your family. Not
Kartika. There's no need to take her into your confidence
now that I'm the fake fiancé. You and I can be the only
ones to know it's not for real.'

'Understood,' she said. 'Safer that way.' She paused. 'A
ring. We'll need an engagement ring.'

'I can buy one.'

'I can make one.'

'Make it blingy,' he said. 'I don't want to be seen as stingy.'

'Blue sapphire and diamonds, I think,' she said. 'Something modern and simple. I can wear it on the other hand after the divorce.' She sobered. 'That also sounds weird. I'll spend the rest of my life as your ex-wife.'

'And me as your ex-husband,' he said. 'But let's make sure we're the kind of exes who stay friends.'

'Absolutely.'

'Do you need me to sub you for the ring?' he said.

'No. I can pay for the gems myself—easier that way.' She paused. 'Do I need to pay you that substantial hire-a-husband fee we talked about? I'd rather not have to mortgage the house.'

The title to her family home in St Kilda had been transferred to her, under the terms of an agreement with her father, when she'd turned twenty-one. It had been a welcome surprise. She had lived there alone since her mother had moved out to live with Ben. One of the bedrooms had been converted to be her jewellery workshop.

'Of course you don't,' he said. 'I don't know why you asked.'

'I didn't think so. It's not as if you need the money. But I had to check to be sure. We have to be spot on with our communication.'

'Let's agree that, if there's something one of us is not sure of, we keep quiet until we can discuss it with the other.'

'Understood.' She sighed. 'I can't tell you how relieved I am that I can stop the husband hunt. It was awful. Thank you. Thank you, *darling*,' she said, then ruined the effect with a peal of giggles. 'Did you like that?'

He rolled his eyes. 'Darling. Sweetheart. Honey. You decide. I'd rather just be Connor.'

'I quite like *my love,*' she said.

'I'd still prefer Connor,' he replied, more abruptly than he'd intended. 'Nothing personal, I just find such terms insincere.' All the time he'd been cheating on her, his father had called his wife 'honey'. Total hypocrisy. He shifted in his seat. Time to change the subject.

'You said once you could read my mind. You failed dismally. Do you want to try again?'

Her brow furrowed. 'Okay.'

'What am I thinking right now?' he challenged her.

She narrowed her eyes almost to slits as she perused his face. Then her eyes widened. 'No, Connor. You couldn't be.'

'Couldn't be what?'

'You couldn't be hungry. Not after the *gulyas* and the strudel that followed.'

'That was a few hours ago. Of course I'm hungry.' He paused. 'How did you guess so quickly?'

She knew him so well.

'Years of observation,' she said dryly. 'You didn't exactly look deep in philosophical thought.'

He laughed. 'The burgers are good in this pub. While we're here, we might as well order one.'

'You can. I'm not in the slightest bit hungry. Besides, as you know, I don't care for fast food. You remember the way I was brought up—only home cooking will do.'

'You know the way I was brought up—your classic latchkey kid. Parents running a busy general practice. Often with out-of-hours emergencies. Never on top of their paperwork. For medical practitioners, they knew surprisingly little about nutrition when it came to feeding two hungry boys. Burgers, pizza, and fish and chips featured often on the menu.'

'Fortunately for you, and Billy too, the girl-next-door's grandparents ran a restaurant not far from our homes.'

'Very fortunately for me. But I did acquire the taste for a good burger. And I want one now. Are you sure I can't order one for you? Last chance.'

'I'll just nibble on a few of your chips,' she said.

'Spoken like a true fiancée,' he said, laughing.

'Let's have fun with this fake marriage,' she said. She leaned across and took his hand. She stroked the palm with her slender fingers. 'First PDA,' she said, with a husky, sensual voice he'd never heard from her. She looked into his eyes and pouted with her lush mouth. 'How am I doing?'

'Well,' he said. He cleared his throat. 'Uh…very well.' *Too well.*

Because he was getting aroused. By Ana. That couldn't be, even if she was his fake fiancée. *Especially* because she was his fake fiancée.

CHAPTER FIVE

TEN DAYS LATER, Ana peered out of the window of the two-seater private plane piloted by Connor, taking them to Garrison Downs for the weekend. They'd been flying over endless tracts of red dirt punctuated by hummocks of spinifex grass, coarse scrub and stunted trees. This was truly the Australian outback: harsh, unrelenting, with its own wild beauty. She noticed a small mob of kangaroos bounding along the bed of a dried-up creek.

Suddenly there were signs they were nearing their destination: more vegetation, fencing, pastures, vast herds of cattle, cattle yards and a river surrounded by rocky outcrops. Then she recognised the buildings at the heart of the kingdom surrounded by an oasis of green as Connor circled, preparing to land.

She snapped a few photos with her phone to show her family. She could, she supposed, caption the photos as 'my new home'. But could she ever shake off the feeling that this place was, in fact, home to her father's *other* family—what she still could not help thinking of as his *real* family? Who had used that phrase during her childhood? Her mother? Her grandfather? It had stuck.

She and Connor were wearing headphones and microphones so they could communicate over the sound of the twin-engine plane. Right now, he was getting landing instructions from Rose. Connor was so competent, sure of himself, and she had utter confidence in him. He'd got his recreational pilot's licence while he'd still been at university. When he'd suggested the private plane, rather than commercial flights and long drives, she'd jumped at it. They'd set off from Melbourne's Moorabbin Airport.

Was there anything Connor couldn't succeed at? He could pilot a plane, perform surgery on animals and make money on a large scale. He really was an excellent choice for a fake fiancé. She knew her sisters would be impressed. His practical skills and knowledge would be valued out here.

And that was on top of his personal charm.

Connor was the kind of person people naturally gravitated towards. Who would blame them? She'd spotted how attractive he was when she'd been five years old and had dived through that hedge. She still remembered how she'd wanted to play with that boy and nothing had been going to stop her. What would it be like to play with him now—that boy all grown up? That man, now her fake fiancé? She felt a little shiver of desire at the thought. There was too much at risk for her to allow her thoughts to stray that way. Nothing had changed between them. They were still just friends.

'That, below, is what it's all about,' Connor said. 'Your birth right. How are you feeling about it all, now we're so close?'

'To be honest? Anxious and a tad overwhelmed,' she admitted. 'It was all very well planning our fake engagement in Melbourne but, actually being out here, I realise it's such a big deal. I feel enough of an imposter as it is.'

'You are not an imposter. Your father's will says four daughters will own this place, not three. Keep that in mind.

You're doing your best to play your part in securing it for all of you.'

'So are you,' she said. 'I'll always be grateful for that.'

'Don't worry, I'll think of ways you can pay me back for years to come,' he said, smiling.

'I'm sure you will,' she replied, also smiling. She refused to let her thoughts run to exciting ways that payback could happen. Because he had made it very clear he simply didn't see her as anything other than a close friend. 'Look, more kangaroos,' she pointed out, glad for the distraction.

In spite of Connor's reassuring words, Ana realised she was twisting the engagement ring round and round on the third finger of her left hand. She hadn't created a ring for herself in her workshop back in St Kilda after all. She hadn't had time—or, truth be told, the inclination. Connor was right: they needed attention-grabbing bling to shout out her engagement to a very wealthy man, not the discreetly elegant sapphire ring she'd want if she were really getting engaged. This needed to be a megaphone of a ring.

She'd contacted a friend from her jewellery design course and purchased wholesale a gorgeous four-carat, emerald-cut diamond solitaire, with small diamonds studded all around the band. It was as big a diamond as her slender hand could take. When she'd shown it to Connor, he'd stared. 'Can you afford that? You have to let me pay for it,' he'd said.

Ana had laughed. 'Impressive, isn't it? They're laboratory-made diamonds, not mined diamonds, so it's pricey, but not horrendously so.'

'I can't tell the difference,' Connor had said.

'Not many people can,' she'd said. 'Fake diamonds for a fake engagement. Appropriate, I thought.'

'And yet the diamonds appear to be real.'

Just like their relationship would have to appear.

'If anyone asks, let's say we chose the ring together,' she had said.

In the days before they'd left Melbourne, she and Connor had spent time getting their stories right. Still, she couldn't help but feel nervous about actually acting out the engagement. It was so important they didn't let on that it was a charade. Nothing could be allowed to jeopardise the inheritance. There was too much at stake for their marriage to be revealed as a fraud.

Connor executed a perfect landing on the Garrison Downs airstrip and taxied the plane into the hangar. Rose was there to meet them in a four-by-four covered in red dust to take them to the house.

Her oldest sister was wearing jeans, riding boots, a checked shirt and an Akubra hat. She looked very much part of Garrison Downs in a hands-on, managerial manner. Apa had always told Ana how well Rose ran the show. Now Ana realised how fortunate she and her other sisters were to have her. Managing such an enormous enterprise as the cattle station was a task beyond her imaginings.

Without a moment's hesitation, Rose hugged Ana in greeting. No matter what Connor had warned, Ana truly believed in her sister's embrace of her into the family.

Ana introduced Rose to Connor. 'He and I have been friends since we were in primary school. I really wanted to show him Garrison Downs.'

'So pleased to meet you, Connor,' Rose said, with a firm handshake and a speculative glance.

When would be the right moment to tell Rose she and Connor were engaged? Ana had wanted to do it face to face, but somehow actually being with Rose made it seem more difficult. Announcing an engagement would usually happen in an organic way, because there would most likely be an existing relationship. Not by blurting out a hastily contrived plan.

The midday December sun blazed relentlessly down on them. Ana pulled her hat from her shoulder bag and jammed it on her head. It was a stylish city Panama, not a bushman's hat like Rose's. Like the other times she'd been to Garrison Downs, she felt out of place, intimidated by the vastness that surrounded her. She wore jeans, sturdy sneakers—not white; she'd had to throw her red-dust-stained white shoes out after her first visit—and a long-sleeved vintage shirt patterned with quirky representations of cacti. She couldn't pretend to be a rancher like Rose and Matilda, who had spent most of their lives here.

The night she and Connor had become 'engaged', Connor had asked her to read his mind. Now she got the feeling he was reading hers, because he took her hand and squeezed it reassuringly. It was if he sensed her feelings of inadequacy, a return to the private girls' high-school days, when she had felt intimidated by girls like her sisters, who were so sure of their place in the world. Not that Rose, Tilly or Eve had treated her with anything other than kindness and welcome.

She and Connor did not do holding hands. Now it seemed they did. For so many years she'd felt utterly at ease with him. Now she was confused. Was Connor holding her hand as an affectionate gesture because of their long-standing friendship, or as a ruse to appear authentic in their fake relationship? Whatever the reason, she liked the feeling. Although she knew she shouldn't get used to it. It would be too heart-breaking when Connor became her ex-husband and there would be no need for such false expressions of affection.

Rose focused on their clasped hands. She looked from Ana to Connor and back again. 'Ana, I forgot to ask. We've got the yellow suite ready for you. I know you were comfortable there the last two times you've visited.' She looked at Ana straight, with the same blue eyes Ana saw every time she looked in the mirror. 'Do you and Connor need two bedrooms or one?'

Ana hesitated, paralysed by indecision. She wanted to say, 'Two bedrooms, please'. The thought of sharing a bedroom with Connor suddenly became impossible. She could maybe stutter an explanation to Rose that they were waiting until their wedding night to share a bedroom, but Rose didn't know yet that they were getting married. And who would believe they'd wait? She closed her eyes firmly at a sudden, disconcerting image of Connor and her in bed, naked, sheets tangled around them.

No!

'One bedroom, please, Rose,' said Connor firmly. He still had hold of Ana's hand.

Rose looked again at the 'not just friends' way they were holding hands, then at Ana again. 'Ana, that ring— it's like a beacon. Does it mean—?'

'We're engaged,' Connor said with a big, Connor grin. 'You're the very first to know.'

'That's wonderful! Congratulations,' Rose said.

'Because me getting married is so important to Garrison Downs, we wanted to share the news with my sisters before we even told our families,' said Ana.

Ana could see her sister was genuinely pleased for her and Connor. But she sensed relief there too. Three sisters partnered now and only one to go, Rose herself. It was easy to imagine the pressure she must be feeling. Ana wanted to commiserate but, knowing how the husband hunt had worn her down, she didn't dare.

'I didn't know you were dating someone,' Rose said.

'I wasn't. I mean, we didn't date. Not in that sense, anyway. Connor isn't *someone*. He's my best friend. We hadn't seen each other for six months. And, when we did, we… er…realised our friendship had grown into something much deeper than…than friendship.'

Too much information, Ana.

'We realised we'd fallen in love,' said Connor, as if that was the simplest possible explanation. Which, of course, it was. Why hadn't she thought to say that, instead of rambling on?

Truth was, it cut too close. Ana had probably been more than a little in love with Connor for most of her life, but she could never admit it to herself. Hearing him say it was like a painful stab to her heart. Because he'd always made it so clear that he could never be in love with her. But she reassured herself that Connor's words weren't a total lie. It took a kind of love for her friend to go along with a fake marriage for her sake. Connor would get nothing at all from the arrangement. He was going along with the charade simply to help her out.

'Isn't this just the best news?' said Rose, smiling. 'Show me the ring.'

Ana splayed out her left hand. The diamonds glinted in the sunlight and looked very impressive. Quite the ring one would expect from a multi-millionaire fiancé.

'It's stunning. Did you make it?'

Ana shook her head. She had made both Tilly's and Eve's wedding rings. 'This is too complex for me—at the moment, anyway.'

'Eve and Tilly will be thrilled with your news. When are you planning to get married?'

There was a note of concern in Rose's voice that Ana, also driven to desperation by the need to find a man to marry, recognised. There were less than six months for them all to be wed.

'Well before the deadline set by the will,' she said. Then realised that, while that sounded reassuring, it didn't sound very romantic.

Connor jumped in. 'I've waited so long for her to grow up, we don't want to wait any longer to get married.'

Waited for her to grow up? What? She glared at him. She was only two years younger than he was. He could never resist teasing her. Still, his explanation sounded genuine, and that was all that counted.

'We thought a January wedding,' Ana said. 'Just a small one. Family and close friends.'

Australian law required at least a month's notice for a marriage. She had lodged the application the day after Connor had agreed to marry her. She wanted to be absolutely sure she was legally wed well before the deadline of the last day of May. After all, the will didn't state she had to spend time being engaged. It specified she had to be married. She wanted to get it done and dusted in plenty of time.

'Sounds great,' said Rose. 'Now, hop in the car and come on down to the house. Lunch is waiting for you. Clever of you to come by private plane, but it's still a long trip, and you must be hungry.'

Ana looked up at Connor. Their eyes met and they both burst into laughter. Rose looked somewhat taken aback. Ana hastened to reassure her. 'One thing you need to know about Connor is that he's always hungry.'

Rose laughed too. 'He won't go hungry here.'

This was Ana's third visit to Garrison Downs. She'd first come in June, for the reading of the will, and to say farewell to her father with a few private words at his graveside in the family cemetery. Then just last month for Eve's wedding to the super-hot Nate Harrington. She had been thrilled to be her bridesmaid, along with Rose and Tilly. The reason for the hasty November wedding had immediately become apparent: Eve was expecting a baby next June. Ana, from having known no family on her father's side, could now look forward to being an aunt, and she was delighted about it.

The newlyweds were waiting for Ana and Connor at what the family called either the new house or the homestead. Rose had already relayed the news about the engagement by phone, so they were greeted with excited congratulations. Eve hugged Ana, and Connor too, when Ana introduced him. The men shook hands.

Nate was the son of Holt's lawyer George Harrington—keeper of all Apa's dealings regarding his secret daughter in Melbourne. Nate had taken over his father's practice so, not only was he now Ana's brother-in-law, but also the Waverly family lawyer.

Eve was glowing. She was barely showing, with just the tiniest of bumps, but it wasn't just her blossoming pregnancy that seemed to have softened the brittleness Ana had sensed in her video call during the reading of the will. It was happiness too, and contentment.

When Eve had visited Ana in Melbourne, she had told her how, as a teenager, she had accidentally found out about Holt's past affair with Lili. Disillusioned and angry, she'd pretty much checked out of the Waverly family and gone to live with her mother's family in London as soon as she could. Now she was back, living at Garrison Downs for good. She and Nate were renovating the old house so they could live there—a move made after consultation with Ana.

The new house, opulent and elegant, made Ana feel again like she was stepping into the pages of a glossy design magazine. Page after page of large, high-ceilinged rooms with elaborate cornicing, cream walls and polished wooden floors. Everywhere she looked, she saw vignettes of immaculately styled antique and contemporary furniture, art and accessories. On her first visit, she'd thought it was the kind of French-inspired mansion she'd expect to see in Toorak, the wealthiest part of Melbourne, not in the middle of the South Australian desert. Yet, in a gesture towards the Australian climate, it was surrounded by wide verandas and shade-giving trees.

According to her sisters, the house was pure Rosamund. Her daughters hadn't changed the interior design since their mother had died seven years ago. Why would they? The house was a masterpiece. But it was here, in this house that had been Rosamund's haven, where Ana most felt like an interloper. She doubted that her name on the deed would change that.

Eve and Rose led her and Connor into the family dining room. Thankfully, she was seated with her back to the large portrait by a famous artist of her father, his wife and three daughters that dominated the wall. It had been painted when the girls had been pre-teens, showing a joyous, united family.

Holt's real family.

It was a beautiful piece of art, and she knew she shouldn't let it bother her. But she couldn't help but let the portrait feed her feelings of exclusion and lack of belonging.

Rose noticed. 'I'm sorry, Ana. I'd meant to have that picture moved before your visit. We can't very well paint you into it at this stage. It's now no longer relevant.'

'But that was your family as it was then. A slice of history. You don't need to move it for my sake.'

'We do,' Eve said firmly. 'This is your home too now, just as much as it is ours. I suggested we commission a new painting of all four Waverly sisters to replace it.'

'We've talked about that with Tilly,' explained Rose. 'We all think it's a good idea. A new painting for new beginnings.'

Ana felt moved at her sisters' thoughtfulness. 'I'd like that. But you don't need to move this one,' she protested. 'Really. I do have my own lovely family in Melbourne.'

But not her father.

She paused. 'And I had Connor too.'

Always, she'd had Connor. And she couldn't let this fake engagement mess up their long friendship. Because she couldn't imagine life without Connor.

'Nah, it's toast,' said Rose in her no-nonsense way, although she accompanied her words with a wink. She got up to go to the kitchen to confer with the housekeeper about lunch.

Eve turned to Connor. 'I heard all about you, Connor, when I had dinner with Ana's family at the restaurant,' she said. 'But I believed you were the best of platonic friends. Now you're engaged?' She looked to Ana, her eyebrows raised.

Eve was astute. But Ana had a story and she was sticking to it. She looked up at Connor. It wasn't difficult to make it a loving glance as he really *was* her dearest friend. She was glad and grateful to have him here supporting her.

She took a deep breath. 'As I told Rose, Connor had

been working in Sydney for six months. When we saw each other again, well, it was somehow different. We...we fell in love.' And she had to be constantly on her guard that she didn't really develop deeper feelings for him.

Just friends.

'We'd been friends for twenty years,' said Connor. 'But friendship was no longer enough. I asked her to marry me. Fortunately, she said yes.'

Connor smiled, then dipped his head to kiss Ana lightly on the mouth. It was the perfect thing for a fiancé to do. Possessive. Protective. Confident she would welcome his kiss. He hadn't kissed her since that first time when she'd been sixteen. She closed her eyes at the sheer bliss of it.

Connor was kissing her and she was loving it.

She returned the pressure of his mouth, aching for more. Then realised where she was and pulled back. She forced an easy smile to hide her bewilderment at the strong feelings that simple kiss had evoked. She must not let herself want more than friendship from him.

'Oh, my!' To Ana's surprise, Eve gave a breathy exclamation and blinked back tears. She snatched up a napkin and dabbed at her eyes. 'Ignore me, my hormones are all over the place. That kiss... You two really do look perfect together. To think, two of us are married and you are engaged, and all with six months to go...'

Eve's gaze drifted to Rose's vacated seat. 'Although I don't want to put any pressure on Rose. We've all been lucky to do it for love. The idea that she would have to...' She dabbed at her eyes again. Nate put his arm around his wife and smiled at Ana.

Ana scarcely heard Eve, too lost in a mist of sensual euphoria from Connor's kiss. Connor cleared his throat. Was he as affected by that brief touch of his lips on hers as she was? Or was he embarrassed? It was all very well in theory to talk about feigning physical affection to make their relationship appear believable. The actual practice wasn't so straightforward.

She would be sharing a bedroom with Connor.

How was she going to manage that and the intimacy it implied?

CHAPTER SIX

CONNOR LOOKED AROUND him as he strode away from the homestead. As far as he could see, and far beyond, lay the land belonging to Garrison Downs—one and a half million hectares of it. The landholding of a billionaire cattle baron. Land that encompassed lush grazing, bushland and scrubland. He imagined the wildflowers would be spectacular in spring, transforming the landscape into a riot of colour. He'd been told a river that ran through rocky outcrops, as well as underground bores, brought water to even the furthest paddocks. He took a deep breath, filling his lungs with the clean air scented with eucalypt, and another more earthy, familiar smell that let him know that stables were nearby.

Nothing Ana had told him about the place had prepared him for how it felt to actually be at Garrison Downs and take in the magnificence of the property. For Ana to be a part owner would be a privilege beyond measure. He felt suffused with the energy and determination to help her find her rightful place here. It wasn't just immense wealth the sisters would gain but also responsibility as caretakers of this land.

Ana still felt intimidated by her inheritance and all that came with it. That was understandable, considering the circumstances. He wanted to help her embrace what Garrison Downs could mean to her. Family. Connection. Freedom. And a place to ground her when life got tough in the city. All this was hers to share with her sister. With enough funds for it to run smoothly and to keep on delivering a torrent of dollars to her bank account. It made him happy that Ana had finally been acknowledged by her father. But how much longer would she have had to wait if he had not died prematurely?

Connor had met Holt Waverly on a few occasions, as the best friend next door who was in on the secret of Ana's birth. Her elusive father had been a towering, robust man. Handsome in a rugged way. A deep, booming voice that resonated authority. A man of the land who strode the city streets with confidence. Sure of himself to the point of arrogance. Connor had liked the man, although he was not sure he admired him. He had not liked how sad his daughter always was after her father went off home to his world of Garrison Downs. A world that Ana could never share. Until now. Thankfully her father had left his secret daughter a legacy of recognition, part-ownership of this magnificent place, and—arguably most important—sisters.

Eve and Rose appeared to be everything Ana believed them to be. Connor liked them a lot—Nate too. He hadn't expected that. He had counselled Ana to be wary. To watch out for ways the sisters might try to minimise her share of the inheritance. To expect they might ditch her after the inheritance was disbursed. Now Connor was willing to admit he could have been wrong. The sisterly love seemed genuine. He could see Ana's confidence flourishing. Not just because of the hand of sisterhood the three women had extended but also because, through his will, her father had formally acknowledged her importance to him and her right to be a Waverly and be part of Garrison Downs.

Connor would do what he did best—look out for Ana. It was what he had always done. And what he would continue to do for as long as she needed him.

As a friend.

He had agreed to the marriage of convenience scheme to help her. Privately, he'd had his lawyers look at the will, only for them to agree with the lawyers the sisters had engaged. There was no way out of that archaic clause requiring marriage for the four sisters.

But there was danger in the benign agreement between he and Ana that he hadn't anticipated. Kissing Ana had been like lighting a fuse which had set off a series of explosions that had rocked him. Lust. Desire. An urge to possess her.

He wanted her.

He'd wanted her for a long time. But above that, on an entirely different plane, he cared for her. He had seen the wonderful person she was even as a child. That admiration for her, that looking out for her, that *friendship* had endured. He didn't want to lose their friendship, which wasn't tainted by the unrealistic expectations and disappointments of a romantic relationship. He never wanted to hurt her the way he knew he had hurt the girlfriends he could not commit to.

Although he always tried to be honest with them. There was something about a man who said he didn't want commitment that was like a flag to a certain kind of woman—like Brandi.

He and his business partners in The Money Club thought of themselves as low-key nerds who had never courted publicity. Somehow, Brandi had heard of them and tracked him down. What had seemed to be a spontaneous meeting in a bar in Melbourne had actually been a calculated hunt. Ana had sensed something not right about Brandi from the get-go. He should have listened to her. She knew him better than anyone. He'd thought she might be jealous. Instead it had turned out she'd been right.

He knew Ana was attracted to him. She had been aware of him as a man long before he'd been aware of her as a woman. He could not take advantage of her vulnerability. Ana was not the woman for a fling. Especially not a fling with him, a man who cared about her. A man who wanted to keep her in his life. A man who didn't want to risk losing her for the sake of a sexual interlude because they were forced into proximity in a fake relationship. He did not want Ana to be another woman's phone number deleted from his phone and his life.

'Connor, wait up. We're nearly there,' Ana called.

Lost in his thoughts, he hadn't realised he'd got so far ahead of Ana and Rose on their way to the stables, which were some distance from the house. They were keeping pace with the beautiful old border collie, River, who was accompanying them. River was very old, with a stiff-legged gait that spoke of arthritis. When Connor had petted him, he'd given him a surreptitious examination for any of the suspicious lumps and bumps that could be found on a dog this age. All clear. His eyes were good for a dog so old, and his teeth too. Connor was relieved. Ana had already become very fond of Holt's canine friend. River was a remaining link with her father. There should be some good years still left in the old boy.

'Ana tells me she's picked out horses for us both,' he said to Rose.

Ana had told him how their mutual love of horses had helped her bond with Tilly, Eve and Rose. That they'd realised they had more in common than their blue eyes.

'She did indeed,' said Rose. 'You'll be riding Zircon and we've put Ana on Ruby. Can you ride with a stock saddle?'

'Yep. So can Ana. We learned to ride Western as well as English.'

'She told me you learned together when you were kids.'

'Kept us out of trouble,' he said. Their shared love of horses had also helped keep their friendship flourishing.

'Did Ana tell you that we went on a junior jackaroo and jillaroo school holiday camp when she was fourteen and I was sixteen? We were both very keen to go and pestered our parents until they agreed.'

'My mother worked in an office full-time and Connor's parents were busy doctors,' Ana said to Rose. 'They were always looking for holiday care for us. We didn't have to pester them too hard to get us off their hands.'

'My whole life here was like a jackaroo camp,' Rose said with a laugh. 'I reckon I was in training to be a stock-man from the time I could walk.'

'And you loved it, didn't you, Rose?' Ana said.

'I resented every minute I was away from here,' Rose said. 'Garrison Downs is my life, and I will do anything to keep it in our hands.'

The three of them fell silent. Connor could tell Ana was aching to tell Rose about their marriage-of-convenience idea. But they'd agreed that they couldn't take any risk of their marriage being declared fraudulent. It was best to keep quiet about it.

'Although Ana might appear the perfect city slicker, she is very at home on horseback,' he said. 'Years of pony club on the outskirts of Melbourne and holiday horse camps.'

'Nothing was as good as the jillaroo camp,' Ana said. 'It was held at a working cattle station in the west of Victoria. Nothing on this scale, of course. We slept in bunk beds in an old barn. I thought I'd gone to heaven.'

'Me too,' Connor said. 'We didn't just ride and look after horses, we also learned how to muster sheep and cattle.'

'So I can put you to work here, Connor?' Rose said with a grin.

'My skills are a little rusty,' he said with an answering grin.

'I bet you haven't forgotten how to lasso a steer or crack a stock whip,' said Ana.

'You were pretty good at cracking a stock whip, if I recall,' he said. She was so petite but she'd been determined to make that whip crack, and she had.

'My grandmother went hysterical when she heard I'd been cracking whips,' said Ana. 'She thought it was dangerous and told my mother off for letting me go to the camp.'

'She didn't know the half of it,' Connor said. 'We were fearless. We wanted to try everything. We didn't care if it was dangerous.'

'We were always supervised,' Ana said primly.

He laughed. 'Yeah. Right. Remember when you and that other girl decided you wanted to ride a pig and sneaked off on your own? Luckily it was a sweet, tame pig or it could have ended differently.'

'You tried to ride a pig?' said Rose. 'Bareback?'

'Of course bareback. They didn't have pig saddles.'

'She slid off into the mud,' said Connor. 'I remember it so well.'

'He doesn't let me forget it,' Ana said.

'And I never will,' he said.

'The owners weren't happy and threatened to send us

home,' Ana said. 'They made us clean out the chicken shed, which wasn't as much fun as riding a pig.'

'But just as smelly,' said Connor.

Ana flushed and laughed. She looked as cute as she had covered in mud when she'd been thirteen. Those were times when he'd still thought of Ana as a sister. He hadn't thought that way after that first kiss at her school formal. But he'd refused to acknowledge the change in his feelings. Platonic friendship was the way to keep her in his life.

'Sounds like fun,' said Rose.

'I'm grateful for those experiences because, although it was kid stuff, it means I'm not completely ignorant about how a farm works,' Ana said. 'Although nothing could prepare me for the scale of Garrison Downs.'

She turned to Connor. 'Remember how excited you were when you were allowed to give a vaccine injection to a horse? Under supervision, of course.' She turned back to Rose. 'I think Connor first got the idea he wanted to be a vet then, although he's never said that. At that stage he was still set on becoming a doctor, the family profession.'

'Did you go back to the jackaroo camp?' asked Rose.

'The next year my grandparents took me to visit Budapest.' Ana pronounced it 'Buda*pesht*'. 'My grandmother wanted me to have other influences. She didn't think whip-cracking was a safe or ladylike thing to do. Good thing I never told her about the pig.'

'Budapest? Is that where your grandparents were from? What was visiting there like?'

'Awesome. Budapest is the most beautiful city you can imagine. So sophisticated to my fifteen-year-old eyes. It was like stepping into a different world for me. I loved it.'

'Did you have family there?'

'Yes. My great-uncle owns a jewellery store. It was a

revelation. That's where I really got interested in jewellery. His daughter has a gorgeous fashion boutique near the opera house. She took me in hand and helped me to choose clothes that suited me and how to wear them. I had such fun.'

'Ana came back quite the girly girl,' Connor said.

He remembered how shocked he'd been. She'd had her hair styled differently, and for a moment he hadn't recognised her, only to acknowledge how lovely she was. His buddy had grown up.

As they got closer to the stables, Ana tried to recall the last time she'd gone horse-riding with Connor. It was well before he'd headed off to Sydney. It wasn't that their interest in horses had waned, more that different, more accesible activities had intruded as they'd grown up. Particularly at weekends.

She'd moved high school for the final two years, away from the bitchiness of the girls' school, with its popular girl cult which had totally excluded her, to another private school. Apa had insisted she attend private schools and, as he'd paid the school fees, her mother hadn't argued. The new, co-educational school had been closer to home, more laid back and inclusive. She'd been so much happier, although she'd continued the fiction that her father was dead. She'd made other friends and got involved with school sport, playing competitive tennis at the weekend to cement new friendships.

There'd been an increase in study load, particularly for Connor, striving to get into medicine. The university course required an incredibly high mark for entry. When her time had come for final year studies, she'd buckled down too. Horse riding had become a special treat rather than a regular routine.

Now she was excited at the prospect of riding with him again, and on Waverly land. She and Connor had changed into their riding boots back at the house. They carried their helmets with them. It looked much cooler to be on horseback wearing just an Akubra hat. But neither of them rode without a protective helmet, especially on an unfamiliar horse. Connor's parents had insisted. They'd seen too many head injuries to allow otherwise.

The Garrison Downs stables was a substantial complex. As well as the working horses for the stockmen, there were the family horses, and the valuable stud horses. As they neared the stable, Sally, the stable manager, rushed out to greet them.

'Rose, glad you're here!' Sally said. 'I'm worried about Jasper. He's gone lame—front right hoof. He's obviously in pain.'

Connor looked at Ana. She nodded. 'You know Connor is a vet?' she said to Rose.

'I'd be happy to look at Jasper,' Connor said.

Jasper had been Holt's horse and Ana knew he was particularly precious to Rose. 'I couldn't bear it if anything happened to him, Ana,' she said. Rose untied and tied her ponytail, something Ana noticed she did when she was troubled.

Ana put a hand on Rose's arm. 'I know. But Jasper is in good hands with Connor.'

Jasper was a black stallion of more than seventeen hands. He was very obviously lame. 'He's the sweetest boy,' said Rose, stroking the horse's face. 'He'll behave for you. He likes men. Dad raised him from a foal.'

Connor rolled up his shirtsleeves to reveal his strong,

tanned forearms. He washed his hands then donned surgical gloves from the large, well-stocked equine first-aid cupboard. Jasper nickered a greeting when Connor approached him. Ana watched as Connor spoke to the big horse in a low, soothing voice. 'Let me have a look at that hoof that's causing you so much trouble.'

Jasper let Connor examine his hoof. 'I'm looking for evidence of a puncture, a stone bruise, laminitis, cracks, white line disease.' After a long moment, he looked up to Rose. 'I've found the problem. An abscess, which is a build-up of pus and infection within the hoof.'

'I've treated abscesses before,' said Sally, the stable manager. 'I know what to do.'

'Sally is a trained veterinary nurse,' Rose said.

'Good,' said Connor. 'Do you know how to get his shoe off?'

'I can do that,' said Sally.

'Then we need to get his hoof into a bucket of warm water with Epsom salts and iodine. The solution will encourage the abscess to burst so it can drain.'

'I can do better than a bucket,' said Sally. 'Holt bought a special boot for the horses that we can pull up over his hoof and fill with the solution.'

'Excellent,' said Connor. 'Then we apply a poultice, using a drawing cream to help or—'

'We have drawing treatment, bandages and tape for the poultice,' said Rose. 'We've got antibiotics too, anti-inflammatories and pain medication if you think Jasper might need them. We're a long way from the nearest vet, and have to be prepared for emergencies.'

Ana watched with growing respect as Connor worked. He was so competent. So reassuring. And kind. He knew how upset Rose and Sally were at seeing this beloved animal in pain. He reassured them, as well as murmuring a litany of soothing words to the horse. Her heart swelled with affection for him. She was proud of him. There was a new assurance to her friend, an air of authority that he knew exactly what he was doing and that he was doing it well. He was…extraordinary in every way. It made him even more desirable. If she allowed herself to think of him in that way.

Once the poultice was on, Connor turned to Rose. 'I'll check on Jasper again this evening. Then again in the morning and before we leave after lunch. After that, it will be your call if you need to contact your vet.'

Rose hugged him. 'You're going to be an asset to Garrison Downs, Connor. I don't suppose you'd consider moving here after you're married, as our resident vet?' She was joking, Ana knew, but there was a note of seriousness there too. Connor certainly looked the country boy in his moleskin trousers and checked shirt. But then he looked perfect in the city too. Darn it, Connor looked the part wherever he was. She dreaded the moment she would have to tell her sisters she and Connor were getting divorced.

'That would be entirely up to Ana,' he said. 'Garrison Downs would be an awesome place to live.'

Ana clenched her hand around the strap of her helmet. Was he serious? Or was he playing along with the premise that they would be married in a month and that him living here could be a possibility? The further they got into this charade, the more difficult it would be for both of them not to blur the boundaries.

Did she want to live at Garrison Downs? It was too early to tell. Besides, she wasn't yet married, and neither was Rose. There was no guarantee owning Garrison Downs would actually happen. What was that old saying? 'Don't count your chickens until they're hatched.'

One of the stable hands had Ruby, a sweet-natured chestnut mare, saddled ready for Ana to ride. A handsome bay gelding, Zircon, was ready for Connor. The stable hand had warmed the horses up for them on the sand arena.

Once Ana and Connor were mounted, Rose gave them directions for a ride to the river. She gave Ruby a friendly pat on the rump and told Ana she'd see them back at the homestead when they were ready.

The ride took them past the well-tended private grave-yard known as Prospect Hill where her father was buried under the shade of a flame tree. Both she and Connor dismounted to pay their respects. The last time she'd been here with Rose, she'd been too overwhelmed with grief over her loss to notice anything about the other graves. This time she saw that Rosamund was also buried there. Holt's parents were too, Katherine and Cecil Waverly.

'Your middle name is Katherine,' Connor said as he examined the headstone with her.

'Apa insisted I have a middle name from his family. I always liked having that connection. Now I'm told by my sisters Katherine could be cantankerous and domineering and gave their mother, her daughter-in-law, hell.' She laughed.

Connor laughed too. 'You're not cantankerous and domineering, so that's all that counts. Well, I guess you can be cantankerous when you want to be.'

'Careful, or I'll show you cantankerous,' she said, punching him lightly on his arm, laughter still lingering. 'It's interesting, though, to find out about this side of my family. I've never known anything about them. If you remember, Garrison Downs was won in a poker game by my great-great-grandmother. Imagine that. She must have been one feisty woman. Tilly is a historian—she's Dr Waverly, you know. Her speciality is old letters. Wouldn't it be great if she could find out more about the Waverly ancestors?'

'What would be really great is if she found evidence enough to ditch that punitive clause in the will.'

Ana laughed. 'Trust you to describe marriage as *punitive*.'

He smiled. 'Point taken. But I don't deny it. You know my views on marriage. Don't tell me that requirement hasn't caused you a lot of stress.'

'Thanks to you, some of that stress has been lifted. Now I worry for Rose.'

'You've become attached to your sisters, haven't you?'

She nodded. 'Very much so. But I'm still not sure that I belong. I'm trying to adjust to the massive change Apa's will has brought to my life. My sisters have such a deep sense of birth right and attachment to this place. I'm not sure they could ever understand where I come from. What it was like to have our father drop in and out of my life. How I coped by telling people my father was dead. How I was his dirty little secret.'

'Don't call yourself that,' Connor said, frowning.

'It's true, though.' She looked towards Rosamund's headstone. 'Their mother had to be protected at all costs from knowing about me, as if I was something to be ashamed of. She would never have let me set foot on the property.'

'From what you know from your mother, Rosamund had pushed Holt away. Didn't want him near her. They were on the brink of divorce. That's why he fell for Lili.'

'Not quite as simple as that, according to my sisters.

It's only since Apa died that Tilly discovered her mother's diaries.'

'Hidden diaries? The plot thickens.'

Ana nodded. 'So much fell into place for them. They had never been told about Lili and certainly not about me. Eve found out about Lili accidentally when she was fifteen, but she didn't tell anyone. She hated the hypocrisy of them presenting as the perfect marriage, when in fact the marriage had been far from perfect. When she finished school, she went to live in London and it caused a family rift.

'The diaries showed that Rosamund suffered undiagnosed severe post-natal depression after Tilly's birth. Both she and Holt were deeply unhappy, their marriage on the rocks. That's when Holt found comfort and love with Mum. But, when Rosamund was finally diagnosed and treated, Holt ended his affair with my mother and gave their marriage a second chance. Apparently they were then very happy.'

Connor went quiet and Ana realised this talk of infidelity must be hitting a raw nerve for him. 'I'm sorry. I hope hearing about people being unfaithful doesn't bring back memories.'

'Yeah. It does. It reinforces my reasons for not wanting to get married—lack of trust being the biggie. How could Holt's wife ever trust him again? How could your mother trust another man?'

'We don't know about Rosamund. But, although my mum didn't date much at all until after I left school, she did meet Ben, and they're very happy.'

'This case is different from my parents' story,' Connor said. 'Holt and his wife worked together to repair their marriage. My father was a serial cheater, going right back to the early days of their marriage. There were multiple liaisons.'

'And you were the one to—'

'Catch him out with one of his support staff. And I didn't have the guts to tell my mother.' He kicked against a stray weed with his riding boot. That was at the core of the damage inflicted on him by his parents' divorce. And Ana was the only person with whom he'd shared the trauma that he'd known what his father was up to. But he hadn't been able to bring himself to tell his mother.

'You were sixteen years old. It wasn't your place. Besides, you did tell her, in a way, by warning your father if he didn't come clean with your mother you would let her know what you'd discovered. It was brave of you.'

'After it all exploded, I was left with the suspicion that Mum had known all along about the other women but didn't want to confront it. I don't think she's ever forgiven me for disturbing the status quo.'

'Again, not your fault.'

'Maybe it was. Maybe it wasn't. But I'm like him, Ana. You know that. I look like him. People mistake our voices on the phone. What if I am as incapable of fidelity as he is? Unable to be trusted? If I ever married and had kids, I wouldn't want them to go through what Billy and I did.'

His face was contorted with anguish. It tore at Ana's heart. Even now, he tormented himself over what he saw as his role in the break-up of his family. And that history might repeat itself if he married. If only he could see how wrong he was. He did look like his father but that was as far as it went. His father was superficially charming. She'd liked him and he'd been kind to her as a child. But Connor was the real deal, genuine in a way his father wasn't. The father was the one with the problem, not the son.

Why had his mother let Connor blame himself the way he had? So many times Ana had tried to comfort him and reason with him that he was tormenting himself for no purpose.

'As I've said before, you are not your father. Not anything like him in everything but looks. Listen to me, who has known you for most of your life—I've never had any cause to distrust you.' She paused. 'Have you ever cheated on your girlfriends?'

'Never,' he said. 'But I can't give them what they want.'

'Because it's not what you want. You haven't met the right person yet. When you do—'

'People start off marriage thinking they've met the right person. Where's the guarantee in that?' he said.

'There can't be guarantees. My grandmother says you can never see inside someone else's marriage to know what's really happening.'

'Your grandparents are an example of a good marriage,' Connor said.

'Yes, they are. They fell in love when they were eighteen. They went through hardships we can't even imagine, but their love kept them going And I know lots of people in what appear to be happy marriages.'

'And just as many that suddenly explode when the cheating is revealed.'

His mouth had a cynical twist she didn't like to see on his handsome face. She needed to kill this conversation. 'What would I know?' she said. 'I'm twenty-five and don't have the slightest interest in getting married. Not yet. You're twenty-seven and haven't found the right person yet. Fortunately for me, you're free to help me out in this weird situation, where I have to get married whether I like it or not.'

'What are friends for?' he said flatly.

'Indeed.' She choked out the word through a suddenly constricted throat.

Friends. He could never see her as anything more than a platonic pal.

He was silent for a long moment. She knew him so well, she could see he was forcing himself out of his dark moment. Connor being Connor, he had to hug all that pain to himself.

'Seeing all this makes me very glad I'm helping you—in my own hire-a-hubby way—and your sisters to claim what is rightfully yours.' He waved his arm to encompass their surroundings. 'Garrison Downs is worth it. It's a prize beyond value.'

'And I'm very grateful.'

The more Ana thought about what she'd asked of Connor, the more she realised what a big deal it was. She had pretty well asked him to put his private life on hold for more than a year. Though, once they were married, he could discreetly date…

No! She clenched her fists by her sides. She couldn't bear the thought of him being with another woman. Nausea rose in her throat. She had to fight that thought with all she had.

For how long had she been kidding herself? *She wanted him—and not just as a friend.* But it couldn't happen. Not when all the feelings were only on her side.

Rose had showed her where a cleared track of red dirt wound up a rise to the lookout over the river. 'Right now, I want to take advantage of us having these beautiful horses to ride. What do you say?'

'I say race you up that track to the lookout.'

They quickly mounted their horses again.

'Starting from now,' Connor said.

Rose laughed. 'Game on! C'mon, Ruby.'

Rose had always wanted her own horse. She'd found her in Ruby. The mare was beautifully trained, responsive, strong and good-natured. Ruby was a dream come true. Another reason to make sure her marriage of convenience helped to ensure the inheritance.

She reached the lookout just behind Connor. He looked so good on horseback, relaxed, in control, as one with his mount. There was something very appealing—okay, say it—something *sexy*, about a handsome, well-built man who could control a strong, powerful animal with skill and kindness. He would never use spurs or a whip. Neither would she, of course. She wondered if somehow her lack of success with men was because they could never live up to Connor.

They slowed their horses to a walk when the incline became steeper. The view that opened up to them from their vantage point on a rocky outcrop of red sandstone made her catch her breath. The shadows of the opposing stony ridges were starting to lengthen. Down below them, the slow-moving river, its waters blue in the afternoon sun, snaked through banks of large pebbles, eucalypts and scrub. A ghost gum, which had most likely been hit and killed by lightning, stood proud, its bare white branches stark against the greenery. A flock of pink Major Mitchell cockatoos took flight, swooping by, the sun glinting on their wings, their raucous cries breaking the silence of the landscape.

'Wow!' Ana breathed. 'What else can I say?'

'Anything you and your sisters have to do to retain ownership of this place will be worth it,' Connor said, sounding almost reverential.

She turned Ruby to face him. 'You've fallen for Garrison Downs, haven't you?'

'Who wouldn't?' he said.

Maybe me, she thought. The property was truly magnificent. The income would bring her wealth beyond her wildest dreams. But would she want to actually live here, like Rose and Eve? It was so isolated for a person whose home ground was Melbourne.

'I see a trail going down to the water,' she said. 'Shall we take the horses down? I reckon some of that water is shallow enough to ride them through. They'll love splashing through it.'

'So will we. Can you imagine how much we would have loved this place when we were kids? You wouldn't have been able to keep us away.'

Kids. Children at Garrison Downs. Eve was expecting a baby next June. Tilly would soon, no doubt, be expected to bear an heir to the throne of Chaleur. And her? Kids weren't anywhere on her radar. Not now. So why when she imagined her future children here, happy on horseback, did she see a little green-eyed boy who looked just like Connor?

CHAPTER SEVEN

ANA HAD NEVER felt more awkward with Connor than she did standing with him in the air-conditioned splendour of the yellow suite. *Their* room.

They'd just got back from their ride on Ruby and Zircon, which had ended in an exhilarating gallop back to the stables. Connor had checked on Jasper before they'd headed back to the house. Such luxury to leave the horses with the stable hands to take off their saddles and bridles, wash them down and groom them. Although, on the walk back to the house, she and Connor had agreed that they actually liked that time with their horses after a ride. Next visit, she'd allow enough time to look after Ruby herself.

She and Connor had pulled off their riding boots in the mudroom on the way in. Now she stood with him in the bedroom in their socked feet on the pale, floral patterned rug. It was the first time she'd shared a bedroom with him since she'd been, maybe, seven years old and bunked down with both O'Neill brothers when his parents had been babysitting her.

The suite comprised a large, elegant bedroom with a king-sized bed, a study area with a chaise longue style sofa, over-stuffed arm chairs and a full-sized en suite bathroom. Her gaze kept being drawn to that bed.

She couldn't share a bed with Connor.

No bed could be big enough. Not, she realised, to save herself from Connor. But to save Connor from her. She was on guard while she was awake. But she couldn't guarantee that she could continue to dam her feelings of attraction to him if they had to sleep together in the same bed. And that could lead to disaster for their fake marriage plans.

The suite had obviously been designed with excellent taste and a big budget. The crisp, high-thread-count linen was in tasteful shades of lemon and white with piles of coordinating cushions. Framed botanical prints of wildflowers adorned the walls. It was like a suite in a luxury hotel, with everything provided for a guest's comfort. Ana admired its beauty, though she preferred a less fussy style.

That bed!

It dominated the room. She had to force herself to look away from it. Was Connor feeling as edgy as she was?

Connor being Connor, he didn't show it. 'Man, this is such a girly room,' he said, looking around him. 'In fact, this entire house is not exactly guy-friendly.'

He had a point. 'Maybe,' she said. She didn't want to criticise anything about the interior of the house. Because that could be seen as criticising Rosamund, and she couldn't be drawn into anything like that.

'I can't imagine your father coming into the house and kicking off his boots after a day mustering cattle. Especially in that room with the white carpet.'

'I guess that's what the mudroom is for. To kick off the boots, I mean, like we did. But Apa's study is very much a guy room.'

'It's very much *his* room. How many portraits of the man can there be? It seems a bit—'

'Self-important?' She hardly dared voice the words. She had adored her father. But she hadn't known the public side of him. There were some high-powered people in those photos with Holt on the walls of his study. Her father had been so respected, he'd been given a state funeral.

'You said it,' Connor said.

'I really like his study,' she said. 'I feel close to him there. It's likely my sisters feel the same. To be fair, I don't know if that overtly masculine décor was him or Rosamund. Or whether it was him or her who wanted to hang that multitude of portraits and photos. The house was her domain. From what I knew of Apa, he would have let her do what she wanted. The outdoors was his domain.'

'It was good of Rose to have that family portrait moved,' Connor said. 'That showed sensitivity and thoughtfulness. I like her.'

'I thought you would. I was touched by how considerate she is. And what a great idea to get a portrait painted of all four of us, though when we'll all be together I don't know. Tilly was only here a few weeks ago for Eve's wedding. It's not like she can drop her royal duties and fly all the way down here for a girls' lunch.'

'True,' he said.

'Rose seems to be very much the outdoors type, like Apa. I don't think she pays too much attention to the finer points of interior design.' She looked up at him. 'However, she might want to make changes to the house. Why don't you ask her about it over dinner?'

'No thanks. I'll avoid contentious topics. I'll be too busy making sure I say the right thing about our engagement. It would be only too easy to slip up.'

'Connor, you're doing great. You actually fit in here better than I do. I thought Sally was going to swoon when she was watching you tend to Jasper. Seriously, you're a big hit with everyone.'

'That's only because they care about you. As it should be. They want you to be happy.'

'I guess. But I worry that after we—'

'After we get divorced it might be messy?'

'No. I—'

'I know you, Ana. That is precisely what you were thinking. What comes after doesn't matter. It's now that counts. Establishing our credentials as a genuine couple. Moving towards the wedding next month. Afterwards, I can be the villain.'

'You could never be cast as a villain, Connor. You will always be the hero. To…to me anyway.' She paused and looked up at him to meet his green eyes. His hair was all tousled from where he'd run his fingers through it after he'd taken off his helmet. He'd never looked more handsome. 'I wish…' She stopped herself. For a scary moment there, an uncalled-for thought had clamoured to be voiced.

I wish we were a couple for real.

He met her gaze intently. 'You wish—?' There was an edge to his question she didn't recognise.

Flustered, she stepped back. Her words spilled out. 'I…I…wish we had two bathrooms here, because I'd like a shower.'

'That's it?' he said, frowning. 'That's your wish?'

She took a step back from him. 'Er. Yes. It was hot out there. I feel sticky and probably smell of horse.'

He laughed. 'If you do, I do too.' He paused. 'Do you want me to ask Rose can I use a different bathroom?'

'No. Please.' Ana put her hand on his arm. 'That would be giving the game away. Do you mind if I shower first? I'm sure I'll take longer to get ready for dinner than you will.'

'Go for it,' he said. 'And I won't say take as long as you want to, because I know you will anyway.'

'You'll never forgive me for using all the hot water at horse camp, will you?'

'That was so long ago. Do I hold grudges? There's nothing I love more than a freezing cold shower in an open barn in the middle of winter.'

Connor paced the room. What kind of torture was it to share a bedroom with Ana? Wherever he turned, that big bed was in sight. But the worst torture imaginable was hearing the shower going and knowing Ana was naked in there behind those glass doors.

He didn't have to work hard to imagine her soaping her body, twisting and turning under the water. He had to dial back on the fantasy of opening that bathroom door and offering to wash her back for her. Perhaps joining her under the water… He shook his head to clear it of such untoward thoughts.

He had never seen Ana naked. Why would he have? They were *friends*. Friends kept their clothes on. When they were children, he and Billy had cheerfully run around without a stitch on but Ana had always been modest.

He paced some more. She was taking for ever in there— he would have been in and out of the shower in five minutes—but that was what girly girls did. He wouldn't have her any other way.

He couldn't remember when he'd last enjoyed a day so much. He could be completely relaxed in Ana's company—even when she confronted him about his attitude to marriage. Even then, he knew she understood him and cared for him. That criticism came from a warm place in her heart. Fact was, he had never felt so at ease with any other woman. Perhaps because there was no romantic relationship between them, there were no unrealistic expectations on either side. No demands. No manoeuvring for change. Whatever her magic was, he felt happy when he was with Ana. It was a good feeling.

Ana had always been there for him. And he would drop everything to be there for her. Realistically, he knew that could not go on for ever. Not when possible future partners might come between them. It was irrational of him to want it to. But he found it difficult to imagine life without his long-time friend. Those weeks when he'd cut her off for criticising Brandi hadn't been fun. In fact, he'd been miserable. It wasn't until he'd walked into the restaurant that night to see Ana there that his spirits had finally lifted.

He heard the glass bathroom door open. He turned his back to it and stepped away, as a gentleman should when a lady who was not his lover emerged from the bathroom. There was a possibility she might be wearing only a towel that didn't do a good job of covering her. Or a skimpy little robe that fell open as she moved, revealing tantalising glimpses of slender thighs and high, firm breasts.

No glimpses for him.

Not even the tiniest peek.

This was Ana.

He focused resolutely on a painting of a pretty, purple wildflower. He had no clue as to what it was. He could identify indigenous animals but flowers weren't his thing. Ana liked them, though. He'd been away for her last birthday so had sent her flowers. She'd been inordinately thrilled with them.

Her voice came from behind him. Towel or robe? 'You seem very interested in that flower,' she said.

'Not really. I was just turning my back to give you a chance to get out of the bathroom. In case you, uh—'

'Didn't have any clothes on?'

'Uh…yes.' She was pretty good at reading his mind. But he wouldn't want her to be party to the fantasies he'd been having about her.

'I took my clothes in with me so I could get dressed there. I'm decent. You can turn around.'

She stood there, face flushed, eyes so blue they hardly seemed real, hair tumbling to her shoulders. She was wearing a short black dress with thin straps that skimmed her curves.

'You look lovely,' he said, suddenly short of breath.

'You know what they say, Melbourne girls only wear black. Can't disappoint people.'

'You would never disappoint anyone.'

'Th…thank you,' she said, looking up at him.

Their gazes held for a long time. He took a step closer without breaking eye contact. 'Would now be a good time to practise kissing?'

She stood very still. 'There's no one to witness it. So… what would be the point?'

'We don't want to look like we're new to kissing each other.'

'I think we…we fooled them at lunchtime.'

'Practice makes perfect,' he said. His heart pounded. *All he could think about was how much he wanted to kiss her. Ana.*

He could see in her eyes she wanted to kiss him too.

His gaze dropped to her mouth, her lovely pink mouth with the generous lips that made him ache to taste them. He dipped his head. She rose up on her toes to meet him, putting her hands on his shoulders to balance. His mouth touched her lips for just a fleeting moment. He couldn't really call it a kiss. It was just the merest brushing of her lips to his before she broke the contact and pushed him away.

She stepped back. Crossed her arms over her chest. Her cheeks were flushed and her eyes glittered. 'We…we don't need to do this. This…this kind of kissing is dangerous. We don't need to practise. We've each kissed other people and know what to do.'

But they hadn't been Ana.

'I want to kiss you.'

'You do now. It's just proximity, Connor. If someone like Brandi were nearby, you wouldn't be wanting to kiss me. Not for real, that is.'

'That's not true.'

'I think you'll find it is. I'm not your type.'

He frowned. 'I don't have a type.'

'Please. Don't you? Think back to your girlfriends. All tall. Curvy. Blonde mainly. A couple of redheads.'

It was true. Yet why did he think petite with black hair and blue eyes was more his type? If he had to have a type, that is. Because he'd never let himself acknowledge it.

Because he didn't want to risk losing her. He'd put barriers up against being anything more than friends when they were teenagers because he hadn't been ready. Now they'd plunged headfirst into a fake marriage to complicate this…this stirring of attraction.

He went to get his clothes, still reeling at how Ana had pushed him away.

'Connor?' she called after him. She looked at him with a teasing smile. 'I promise not to peek.'

Ana was pleased that the conversation over dinner with Rose, Eve and Nate started by them admiring the bracelet she was wearing. It was a gold chain bracelet hung with a sliced piece of amethyst in a gold bezel setting.

'Is this from your online store?' Eve asked.

'It might be. Or I might keep it exclusive.'

'Did you make it yourself?' asked Rose.

'I didn't actually make the bracelet myself. I had it made by one of our external workshops. Then I added the amethyst, which is one of my favourite semi-precious gemstones.'

'I believe your store is very successful,' said Nate.

'It started small but, fingers crossed, it's growing,' she said. 'I'm an accountant by trade.' Not for much longer, she hoped. 'But I've always been interested in creative stuff.'

'Creative accounting can be a thing,' Connor said, and they all laughed.

'My great uncle Istvan in Budapest is a jeweller. When I visited as a teenager, he let me spend time in his workshop with him. I was hooked. Under his tutelage, I grew to see jewellery as wearable art. To please my family, I studied accountancy. But my heart has never been in it. I studied part-time to qualify in jewellery design and gemology.'

'When did you start the store?' said Rose.

'I met my business partner and dear friend, Kartika, at uni. We're so like-minded. She's Indonesian. On holiday with her in Bali one time, we met up with a community of artisan jewellery makers she knew. We started to sell some of their designs online. Then we commissioned that group to hand-make jewellery to our designs as well. We specialised in original but affordable designs that are just that bit different. It grew from there. We got a real boost when a Hollywood celebrity posted our earrings on social media. We now have our designs made in Jaipur, too. We're looking to source certain items worldwide—to sell worldwide, too, of course. A percentage of our profits goes to women's health projects in the countries where we source from.'

'How exciting,' said Eve. 'I'm very proud of you.'

'Thank you.' It meant so much to hear those words from these sisters who had been kept from her for so long.

"I really love your bracelet," said Eve.

'Me too. You're so talented,' said Rose.

Ana looked at Connor with a questioning raise of her eyebrows. He answered with a nod.

'I'm so glad you said that,' she said. 'Because I've made a bracelet for each of you and for Tilly.'

'You haven't!' said Eve.

'I was planning to give them to you for Christmas. I've got them with me. You can either wait to unwrap them on Christmas Day or—'

'We can unwrap them now,' said Rose.

'Yes, please,' said Eve.

Ana rose from her seat. 'They're in my room. I'll go get them.'

'You stay,' said Connor. 'I know where they are.'

As soon as Connor left the room, Eve leaned over the table. 'Connor is gorgeous. We approve.'

'He is rather wonderful,' said Ana. No need for creative fibs there.

'And fantastic with the horses,' said Rose. 'What an asset to Garrison Downs. Thank you for bringing him into the family.'

'Does he have his own veterinary practice?' asked Nate.

Ana shook her head. 'That's not what he wants. He's independently wealthy and wants to use his vet skills where he's needed as a volunteer.'

'That's so admirable,' said Rose.

Ana smiled. 'He's admirable all round.' Again, no need to lie.

'Not to mention hot,' said Eve. 'Was there ever anything more between you when you were younger?'

Ana could feel the blush warming her cheeks as she remembered that one, passionate kiss. 'No,' she said. 'We were just friends.'

'And yet, you've fallen for him now. What's changed, do you think?' said Eve.

Ana shrugged. She and Connor had anticipated this question. 'We spent six months apart. I think we both changed in that time. We...well...how can I explain falling in love? There's no reason to it.'

Eve exchanged a lingering glance with Nate. Ana saw the real love in their eyes. She was happy for her sister. Would she ever find love herself? Her mother was right. She'd never before come close to it.

'Are you two getting married so soon because of the will?' asked Rose.

'The short answer is yes,' said Ana. 'We might have waited longer for the actual wedding otherwise. But we both felt there was no point in waiting when so much is riding on us all getting married.'

An uncomfortable silence fell over the table. Ana didn't dare look at Rose. There was so much pressure on her older sister now.

Rose broke the silence. 'We're not going to lose the station,' she said. 'I promise.'

Just then, Connor arrived with three small parcels, exquisitely wrapped. 'Shall I be Santa and hand them out?' he said.

'Why not?' said Ana. Had she ever seen a Santa as good-looking as Connor? Even in a baggy red suit with a pillow down his front and a fake white beard, she'd want to climb onto his lap.

She waited until he put two of the parcels in front of Eve and Rose. 'I call these "the sister bracelets". That's the name I'll give them if we launch them in the store.' The gold in the four bracelets was of a much higher carat than used in most of their jewellery in the store. To keep prices reasonable, some pieces were gold-plated. Sterling-silver pieces were their best sellers.

'Can I go first?' asked Eve, eyeing her package with delight. 'Pretty please?'

'Before you open it, may I explain my choice of gemstones?' Ana said. 'All gemstones have a meaning, intrinsic to their qualities. Some people believe they can heal.' She held up her wrist. 'Purple amethyst is supposed to calm the emotions and encourage clarity of thought. But I just love the colour.'

Eve ripped open the paper to unwrap her gift. The bracelet was identical to Ana's, with its round gold links, but with a pure, pale semi-precious green stone. 'It's beautiful, Ana. I love it. Thank you!' Nate helped her fasten it on her wrist. She held her hand out for the others to see.

'The gem is amazonite,' said Ana. 'It's known as the gambler's stone, and is believed to bring good luck and success to those who wear it.'

Eve laughed. 'I wonder if our ancestor Louisa May, who won Garrison Downs in that poker game, was wearing amazonite at the time.' She blew a kiss across the table to Ana. 'I shall cherish my sister bracelet. Thank you.' She turned to her other sister. 'What's your stone, Rose?'

Rose unwrapped her parcel methodically. She stilled when she saw what was in it, swallowed and fastened her bracelet on her wrist. She held it up for the others to admire. Her gemstone was burnished golden with dark stripes.

'It's called tiger's eye,' said Ana. 'The gem promotes confidence and courage and helps keep balance and strength. I think you have those in spades, Rose.'

'So thoughtful of you,' Rose said. 'Thank you, Ana. This means a lot.'

'I love it too,' said Eve.

'The third parcel is for Matilda, right, Ana?' said Connor.

'Yes. I was going to post it to her and hope it got there in time for Christmas Day.'

'No need,' said Rose. 'Leave it with us to send over with our gifts. We get to use a diplomatic courier organised by Tilly.'

'Thank you.' Ana slid the parcel over to Rose.

'What gem did you choose for Tilly?' asked Eve.

'I debated over it but chose lapis lazuli. It's a beautiful blue. Fitting for a princess.'

'What are its qualities?' asked Eve.

'Lapis is said to promote wisdom and awareness, as well as to bring harmony to relationships,' Ana said. 'She might need that to be co-ruler of Chaleur.'

'A wise choice, Ana,' said Eve.

'Matilda chose such a different path to her sisters,' said Connor.

'I think love chose that path for her,' said Ana.

'Too right,' said Rose. 'And if anyone can make a success as a princess of an ancient principality, it's our Tilly alongside Henri.'

They decided to make a toast to Tilly. 'To absent princesses,' said Eve, holding up her glass.

'To Outback princesses present in this room,' said Connor, to Ana's surprise. He really did fit in here. He made the toast in mineral water. No wine for him, as he was piloting a plane the next day.

'Except I don't think I really qualify as an Outback princess,' Ana said in a small voice. 'City Cinderella, more like.'

Rose turned to her. 'You absolutely are one of us and don't ever think anything different. You have a blood connection here. One day you'll feel a heart connection to the land too.'

After the toast, Ana asked Connor to take some photos of the three sisters with their hands overlapping and their bracelets on show. There were lots of laughs before they got it right.

'Would you mind if I put this photo on the website if we launch this product? No identifying details, of course.'

'Absolutely,' said Rose.

'Shall we share these photos with Tilly?' Ana asked. 'If we do, it would ruin the surprise of her gift from me, as we'd have to tell her about ours.'

'Let's keep it a surprise,' said Eve. 'Rose and I will be here for Christmas, you'll be in Melbourne with your family and she'll be in a foreign country.'

'It's not foreign to her now,' said Nate. 'Chaleur is her home. She has responsibilities that will keep her there.'

'Nevertheless, these bracelets will be a way to unite us, wherever we may be,' said Eve. 'I'll always think of my sisters when I wear mine.'

'Me too,' Ana said at the same time as Rose.

Ana was so tired by the time she and Connor got back to the yellow suite, she wouldn't let him argue about who was getting the bed. It was all she could do to summon the energy to get into her pyjamas. 'This is my house— or it will be—and I say I'm taking the sofa. You'll need all your wits about you to pilot that plane tomorrow. Just toss me the extra pillows and I'll make myself snug with this throw, okay?'

She didn't make herself snug. The *chaise longue* was hard and uncomfortable. Ana suspected it was designed for looks rather than comfortable sitting, let alone sleeping. She didn't know what time it was when she finally admitted defeat and sneaked into the big, divinely comfortable bed. Trying not to disturb a slumbering Connor, she tucked herself in on the edge of the bed as far as she could be away from him. But he stirred, opened his eyes, smiled a sleepy smile—though she wasn't sure if he was actually awake—and reached out a hand to her across the expanse of crisp, white sheet. She reached out her own hand and let him fold it into his. She couldn't help an answering smile before she went to sleep, holding Connor's hand, feeling blissfully happy and secure.

When she awoke to the morning sun streaming through the shutters, the bed was empty, the sheets rumpled on Connor's side of the bed. She could hear him in the shower. Had she really been holding hands with Connor all night?

She dismissed it as a dream.

CHAPTER EIGHT

ANA KNEW HER mother and grandparents would be happy about her engagement to Connor. But she hadn't anticipated just how happy. She hadn't expected her grandmother to burst into tears of joy when she and Connor announced their news on their return from Garrison Downs. Or her grandfather to be quite so proud and excited at the prospect of his granddaughter's wedding. Everybody loved Connor. And they loved the idea of Ana and Connor as a couple.

Her grandmother had immediately demanded to know if the hastily planned wedding was because Ana was pregnant. But Nagymama didn't care if she was. Because Connor was the father, and they loved Connor and knew he would do the right thing by marrying her. In fact, Nagymama seemed disappointed when Ana told her she wasn't pregnant. 'I hope you won't wait too long before giving us a great-grandchild,' she'd said. What a difference a wedding ring made.

Only her mother had pulled her aside to gently ask if she was sure, that this had happened very quickly.

'I've known Connor for most of my life, Mum,' she'd said. 'You can hardly say we don't know each other.'

'You know each other as friends, not as lovers,' her mother had said.

'I know the difference, Mum.'

If only she did!

Since the trip to Garrison Downs there had only been affectionate kisses on the cheek, some hand-holding and the odd arm around her shoulders. All in the interests of appearing to be a happily engaged couple in front of other people. Nothing like the heat of that almost-kiss moment in the privacy of their shared bedroom in the yellow suite.

The fact that soon into the new year Connor had been called away to an animal rescue on the other side of the country was fortuitous. Her wanting him for real was becoming like an obsession—one she had to hide from him. Yet other people expected her to be obsessed with Connor. After all, they were getting married.

'Yes, I miss him. Of course I miss him. Yes, I can't wait for him to be back.' She'd said all that, acting the lonely fiancée, and meaning it. She did miss him. Every day, in fact. But, in a way, she was relieved. The more time she spent with him, the more she found it difficult to fight that growing attraction.

It was as if she was looking at him differently from how she had ever done. And liking that new Connor way too much. Because although Connor had wanted to kiss her—seriously kiss her—it had not been in the context of anything deeper. Friends with benefits. Was that the way he saw it happening between them while they were forced into proximity? Or was it just because they were both available? What had he said about how a guy would say anything he thought a girl wanted to hear to get her into bed?

'If you're sure this is the right thing for you both, I'm very happy for you and Connor,' her mother had said. 'I couldn't ask for a better son-in-law. And, of course, you getting married will help fulfil that archaic requirement of your father's will. Your sisters must be very pleased. Only Rose to go now, isn't it?'

There wasn't a moment when Ana didn't feel bad about deceiving her family. But it had to be done. They couldn't risk there being any legal implication for the inheritance if their marriage was seen to be fake.

In the plane heading back to Melbourne after their visit to Garrison Downs, she had told Connor she would plan a simple, quiet wedding for the middle of January. Maybe in the registry office—they only needed two witnesses.

She should have realised that was never going to happen.

'Your grandparents would feel cheated, darling,' her mum had said. 'After all, I didn't ever have a wedding. Would I feel cheated too? Yes, I would. I want to see my daughter a bride. If you're getting married, let's do it properly.'

Ana had agreed to a 'proper' wedding. But what she wouldn't agree to was a religious ceremony. That would be just too hypocritical.

Before she knew it, the rest of December, Christmas and New Year had been pretty much taken up by wedding plans. She soon discovered that planning a wedding at a month's notice wasn't that simple. Wedding venues booked out sometimes years ahead. So did celebrants, florists, caterers and cake-makers. And custom-made wedding dresses needed to be ordered up to six months in advance.

But the community Ana's family had lived in since her grandparents came to Australia pulled together to help Dori and Zoltan's granddaughter get married in style. It soon became apparent there could be no other choice of venue—her grandparents' restaurant, where she and Connor had spent such happy times over the years and was like a second home. The restaurant was closed on Mondays and Tuesdays. That made a Tuesday the ideal day for Nagypapa and Nagymama to host the wedding. A week day also made sense, as wedding suppliers were booked out for weekends in January.

Everything started to fall into place. A friend of a regular customer had a friend who had a friend who had just qualified as a marriage celebrant. One of Nagymama's friends owned a wonderful St Kilda cake shop and wanted to gift them a wedding cake. Lili's florist friend insisted she do the flowers.

Ana found the perfect dress in a sample sale at one of Melbourne's best wedding designers. It was nineteen-fifties-inspired in ivory silk, full-skirted, tea-length, off the shoulders and laced down the back. And she loved it. She couldn't resist a short veil, retro and perfect. After all, would she ever dress as a bride again? Kartika, her bridesmaid, was bringing a beautiful soft blue dress in a similar style with her from Jakarta.

If it was a real wedding, of course Ana would want her sisters to be bridesmaids too. That would be a dream come true. But it wasn't possible anyway, because the sisters were still keeping their relationship secret. Rose and Eve would, however, be at the wedding as guests. Tilly had been in tears when she'd explained why she couldn't be there. There were royal occasions in Chaleur at which she simply had to be present. To be away in Australia would be a breach of royal protocol the newly minted Princess Matilda simply couldn't make.

Ana had made the wedding bands herself, thinking all the time she could melt them down after the marriage was dissolved. She could perhaps make earrings with the salvaged gold and platinum. But would she ever have the heart to wear them?

All Connor had to do was get suits for him and his brother Billy, who was his best man. It turned out Connor had a suit he'd never worn, a wheat-coloured linen three-piece he'd had tailor-made in Hoi An on a vacation to Vietnam. Perfect.

Her best friend would be the best dressed, most handsome hire-a-husband Melbourne had ever seen.

In the lead up to the wedding, Connor found himself strangely edgy. On more than one occasion, Ana had given him the chance to back down from their arrangement. There was no way he would do that. There was way too much at stake. And had the marriage of convenience—which he'd started to call the mock—not been his idea in the first place?

Fortunately—or unfortunately, as he found himself missing her every day he was away—he'd been called to an emergency rescue of sea birds caught in an oil spill in Western Australia. The number of pelicans with their feathers covered in oil and choking on it was tragic. He was grateful for the veterinary skills that enabled him to help save them.

That had taken him away from Melbourne from just after the new year to just a few days before the wedding. It was a relief in a way, because their sudden engagement after twenty years of just being friends had put the two of them under the microscope. And under a microscope was an uncomfortable place to be—especially when he and Ana had to be so careful not to tangle themselves up in the web of lies they were weaving around the wedding.

How many times had he fielded the question, 'Why get

married in such a hurry? Is Ana pregnant?' As if it was anyone's business but their own if she was.

Not that there was any chance of Ana getting pregnant. There hadn't even been a kiss between them since they'd got back from Garrison Downs. But he'd thought about kissing her. A lot.

Now today was their wedding day. Their mock-wedding day, that is. Although the ceremony was totally legal, it was never going to be a real marriage. It seemed surreal that today he and Ana would officially become husband and wife in the eyes of the world. But, when he thought about the magnificence of Garrison Downs, he knew it was worth it. When he thought about Ana's anticipation at taking her jewellery business to the next level and beyond, he knew it was worth it. When he thought of how much she cherished her relationship with her sisters and the future they had planned as a family, he knew it was worth it.

Fortunately, he knew the major players in this wedding well. Not one person had expressed anything but happiness that he and Ana, best friends for so long, were getting married. Her mother. Her grandparents. Kartika, who had flown down from Indonesia two days ago. His parents— his mother here with her second husband, his father with his latest girlfriend—were as delighted as Ana's family. As his mother had said, 'Finally, you've recognised what has been under your nose for so long. Ana is the one for you.'

It wouldn't be easy to face them when he and Ana engineered a divorce. Their 'break-up' would hurt and disappoint the people closest to them. That wasn't something he'd thought about when he'd come up with the idea for the mock marriage.

It was late afternoon and the clock was ticking for Ana to come downstairs from where she was getting ready with Kartika in her grandparents' flat above the restaurant. The restaurant had been transformed with swathes of airy white fabric, fairy lights and masses of beautiful flowers in pastel shades. Girly? Yes, but that was Ana, and it seemed just right both for the room and the occasion.

It was...romantic. Even he couldn't fail to recognise that. An area towards the back of the restaurant had been chosen for the ceremony to take place. He and Ana would make their vows under an arch that had been completely covered in fresh, pale-pink roses.

A guitarist strummed quietly as the guests gathered. There were more than thirty guests in the restaurant waiting, with him, for their first sight of the bride. The guests were a mix of family and close friends. Only one of his Money Club partners had been able to make the wedding at such short notice—Adrian Chong and his delightful wife Chloe had flown down from their home in Singapore.

Two out of three of Ana's sisters were there. It was Matilda's first winter as a princess of Chaleur and she had no way of getting out of her traditional role of presiding over the winter festival—a very big deal in that small principality. She had sent an extravagant gift, plus an elegantly hand-scripted note of loving good wishes on embossed paper headed with her royal coat of arms.

Connor chatted with Eve, Nate and Rose. He noted the sisters were wearing their sister bracelets, and he knew Ana planned to wear hers. None of the other guests knew Ana's sisters. They were part of that web of secrecy regarding her father that still enmeshed Ana. He let the other guests assume the sisters were university friends.

The door to upstairs opened. Ana's grandfather asked people to take their places and to clear the makeshift aisle between the tables as the bride would soon be arriving. He and Billy, in a deep-blue linen suit, took their places at the side of the rose arch. Connor was nervous, cracking the knuckles of his left hand, until Billy hissed at him to stop. Kartika came through the door first, lovely in a powder-blue dress, smiling at him. Something in her smile made him wonder if Ana had confided in her the truth about the wedding.

Then he saw Ana. Ana looking ethereally beautiful in a white dress he was seeing for the first time, as tradition dictated. And he had eyes for no one else. Ana, like he'd never seen her before.

His bride.

She was a bride A full-on, traditional bride. Ana marvelled at how she'd got here. She'd tried so hard to keep it simple, because the wedding wasn't for real. But no one else but she and Connor, and now Kartika, knew that. So she'd succumbed to the pressure from her family and got swept up in the glamour and fun of it. So here she was in her dream dress, the skirt held out with layers of stiff, retro petticoats, her face covered by the cute, chin-length veil and wearing high-heeled, peep-toe white pumps. 'You look like Audrey Hepburn,' Kartika had said after she'd finished her bridesmaid's work of helping the bride get dressed in her finery.

Now Ana stepped her way down the short aisle towards her husband-to-be.

As she got closer, she could tell Connor was as nervous as she was. They were in this fraud together. Each only too aware of what could be at stake if they were exposed. She glanced around her to see the smiling faces of people who cared about her. She knew they wished her a lifetime of happiness with Connor. She felt a distinct twinge of guilt at the deception. Then she caught Rose's eye and remembered exactly why they were doing this.

Rose and Ana subtly raised their hands to show they were wearing their sister bracelets. Ana was clutching her hand-tied bouquet of roses and eucalypt leaves, so couldn't risk a wave back in return in case she dropped it. But she could tell her sisters saw she was wearing her bracelet over the long white gloves her wedding dress had called for. Her other jewellery comprised a two-strand choker of baroque white pearls, and the pearl earrings her mother had given her for her twenty-first birthday. And, of course, that elaborate engagement ring.

Connor looked exceedingly handsome. She was so proud of him. Of everything he'd achieved. Of what a good person he was. If the look in his eyes was anything to go by, he admired the way she looked too. And that look made her feel beautiful. He had always made her feel good about herself, way back to those days in primary school when he'd protected her from bullies. Or when he'd assured her that the braces she'd had to wear on her teeth for a year when she'd been twelve looked cute. She felt a rush of affection and gratitude towards him that swelled her heart.

This really was a wonderful occasion, surrounded by well-wishers, a superb meal to come and music for dancing. A celebratory party. That's how she should think about it to wash away the guilt of their deception. To think it could ever be anything else could only lead to heartbreak. She knew she was in danger of falling in love with her old friend, and she simply couldn't allow it to happen. Not if she wanted to keep him in her life when it was all over.

She neared the rose arch where Connor waited for her. He was either as overwhelmed as she was by the waves of goodwill in the room, or a darn good actor, because his affection for her shone from his gaze. That look made her heart feel quite fluttery, as if it were accelerating a beat or two—not a feeling that proximity to Connor usually evoked. Not until recently, anyway.

Ana handed her bouquet to Kartika and let her bridesmaid help her slide off the long white gloves. Kartika then took her place next to Billy. Ana took the few steps that would take her very close to Connor. Then she lifted the wisp of a veil back from her face. Offering herself in marriage to her man. According to wedding etiquette, her father should have done that after he'd walked her up the aisle. She felt a surge of sadness that Holt was not with her. Not that he could have been acknowledged as the father of the bride. But she banished that sadness in the warmth and admiration of Connor's smile.

To the delight of their guests, she walked into his arms. She stood on tip toe to nuzzle into his neck, her lips on his warm, smooth skin, and murmured so no one else could hear. 'I know this must seem ridiculous. You probably want to laugh. The way I'm dealing with it is to pretend that this gathering is a celebration of our friendship. Twenty years of friendship and caring—it really is something to celebrate. Let's relax and enjoy it without worrying about what might come next.'

She felt Connor relax, and he smiled that familiar Connor smile. 'Great idea,' he whispered. 'You always know what to do.'

'Let's get you two married,' said the celebrant, a charming, articulate young woman.

Ana felt like a spell had been cast over her as she repeated her wedding vows to Connor, framed by the rose arch. He seemed to be under the same spell as he confidently spoke the vows in his clear deep voice, sounding sincere and convincing. No one would believe this wasn't for real. She had to make sure *she* realised it wasn't for real. Because when Connor looked into her eyes and said, 'Anastasia Katherine Horvath, I take you to be my lawful, wedded wife,' she found herself thrilling to the illicit idea of what it would be like to be in a real relationship with Connor. She noticed his hands weren't quite steady as he slid the wedding band onto the third finger of her left hand, above the elaborate engagement ring that was as fake as the vows they'd just exchanged.

What would it be like if they were for real?

It seemed only moments before the celebrant intoned, 'I now pronounce you man and wife. Mr and Mrs Connor O'Neill.' Their guests started to clap and applaud.

But Ana startled at those words. Through all the time spent preparing for the wedding, she hadn't even thought that people might call her Mrs O'Neill. Surely she wouldn't be expected to change her name? That would bring all sorts of complications.

It brought to front of mind the reasons why she didn't want to get married—married for real, that was. For so long, she had fulfilled the expectations of her family when it came to her career. She had undergone this fake marriage to gain her inheritance. That inheritance would give her the means to soar free to follow her own interests. To grow her business. To travel. To answer to no one but herself. Certainly not to a husband. A man who might expect her to take his name. And who might clip her wings.

The celebrant continued. 'Connor, you may kiss your bride.'

Ana looked up at Connor, smile set in place, expecting a sweet kiss on the cheek.

Instead, Connor took her by surprise by wrapping his

arms around her, pulling her in close and bending her back into the classic bride swoop. Then he kissed her, firmly on the mouth. To all intents and purposes, he was claiming his woman. *Well played, Connor.*

There were cheers and more clapping from their guests. But Ana was oblivious to the rejoicing, too intoxicated by Connor's closeness. By Connor's mouth on hers, his arms tight around her, his warmth, his strength, the familiar scent of him. She kissed him back, wanting more, wanting *him*. He swooped her back upright without breaking the kiss. She wound her arms around his neck, pulling him closer, deepening the kiss, caressing the seam of his mouth with the tip of her tongue, feeling his in return, not wanting it to end. She could tell herself that, conscious of an audience, she was only kissing him in such an exaggerated manner to emphasise the genuine nature of the marriage. But she knew she was kidding herself.

Her only thought was to be closer to him.

She was kissing Connor for real.

'Woo-hoo!' called several guests.

'Get a room, you two. You're married now!' called another.

Ana broke away from the kiss, flushed and laughing. But she didn't take her eyes from Connor's. Because for one long, exhilarating moment she saw in his green gaze the same mix of surprise, awareness and desire that she was sure he could see in hers.

That look gave her hope that perhaps something more might come of this. Maybe even a negotiated friends with benefits scenario. She wanted more than kisses from Connor. But she wasn't sure how to get there. Not when they'd tied themselves up in so many conditions relating to the mock marriage. Not with that long history of hands-off, platonic friendship—a friendship she didn't want to risk losing.

Within seconds, she and Connor were swept up in congratulations and hugs. The tearful embrace of them both by her mother. 'My new son!' she said, through happy tears. 'I couldn't be more pleased.'

There were more, 'Congratulations, Mrs O'Neill!' than Ana could keep count of.

Then there was the sit-down meal, featuring their Hungarian favourites. A few mercifully brief speeches. The cutting of the magnificent two-tier cake adorned with roses. Dancing. And then the evening was over.

They'd done it. She and Connor had pulled it off.

They were married.

There was one more traditional touch to the celebrations. The tossing of the bride's bouque. Whoever caught it would be the next to be married. Ana stood with her back to the group of single ladies then tossed her bouquet backwards over her shoulder. When she turned round, it was to find it had been caught by Rose, who stood holding it awkwardly in front of her. Ana could see the startled surprise in Rose's blue Waverly eyes. And something else passed between her, Rose and Eve. Hope.

Three sisters wed and one to go.

Ana had resisted the idea of a honeymoon. But Connor had pointed out that he needed a holiday, so did she, and that it would seem odd if they each returned to their separate homes the day after the wedding. Her grandfather had apparently taken Connor aside after they'd announced their engagement and suggested they honeymoon in Budapest—and had offered to pay for it. Connor told her he had thanked him but insisted on paying for everything. With no contribution from Ana either. He could well afford it and would brook no arguments, he'd said, over her protests. Budapest. There was nowhere else she'd rather go. Then Connor had thrown in the extra surprise of a visit to Matilda and Henri in Chaleur on the way home.

They left the reception in an elegant, chauffeured vintage car, organised by Connor as a surprise, and headed to an airport hotel where they could crash for the remaining hours of the night before taking a very early flight to Hungary.

Two weeks alone with Connor. Who knew what might happen? She had pushed him away in that yellow suite at Garrison Downs. Maybe next time they shared a room she might have to let him know how much she wanted him. How much she was prepared to risk taking their relationship to the next step.

She might have to convince him to seduce her.

Connor sat in the back of the vintage 1964 Rolls-Royce Silver Cloud, headed to the airport hotel. The guests had cheered when the very stylish vehicle had pulled up in front of the restaurant. Ana had laughed in delight. She'd been expecting the standard limo, but he'd wanted to surprise her. He'd known the car would appeal to her love of vintage. It was his contribution to a wedding where she'd done most of the work. He kept casting glances at her, sitting beside him on the luxurious leather seat. She was still in her wedding dress, although the sassy little veil and the sexy gloves had come off for dancing.

Ana, his childhood friend, was now his wife. He had mixed feelings about it. Foremost, he was glad he was able to help her attain her inheritance. But the shared vows of the ceremony had triggered a shift in his feelings about marriage that was percolating through his thoughts.

She yawned. 'Didn't it go off well? Such a good party. And we played our roles brilliantly, didn't we?'

'We did,' he said.

Was it still just a role for her? The thought was disconcerting. Because during the ceremony he'd found himself so involved in his role of pretend husband, he'd started to believe in the possibility of a marriage with Ana. When he'd slipped that platinum ring on her finger, he'd felt he was securing her as his wife. It had seemed so real and somehow so *right*. And as for that kiss... He'd started it as something playful, but very quickly it had become something altogether more passionate. The more he thought about that kiss, about those heartfelt vows, the more possible it seemed. Ana. Him. Married. For real.

Obviously exhausted, Ana yawned again and put her hand over her mouth. For weeks, she'd worked so hard to get the make-believe wedding organised. It had gone off flawlessly. 'Sorry,' she said. 'So tired. I didn't get much sleep the past few nights.'

Without a word, he pulled her to him. With a sigh, she nestled her head against his shoulder, her soft hair brushing across his neck. Within seconds her breathing changed and he knew she was asleep. Connor inhaled her sweet, warm, familiar scent.

He felt an immense wave of tenderness for her. Fate hadn't dealt his friend the easiest of hands with the way she'd had to exist under the cloud of secrets and lies surrounding her birth. Never able to tell anyone that she had a living father, let alone who he was.

Yet she'd never complained. Even though he knew how heartbroken she'd been every time her father had left after one of his fleeting visits. He knew she would have thought about Holt today, although not a mention had been made of the father of the bride. Yet in the wording of his will Holt had shown how much he had cared for her—and bequeathed Ana her three sisters. The acknowledgment by her Waverly family had made a difference to her.

To ensure she got what her father had wanted for all his daughters, Connor had stepped up. He hadn't regretted it for a second. Never had Connor felt more protective of her. Not just protective. Possessive. With his right arm around her, his other hand lay on his knee. In the darkness of the opulent car interior, the brand-new gold wedding band on the third finger of his left hand gleamed. In the eyes of the world, he was married. It didn't feel as weird as he'd thought it would.

As Ana snuggled in against him, Connor thought about his long friendship with her. How important she was to him. How much he'd missed her when he'd been working away with the pelicans before the wedding. How he felt more at ease with her than with any other woman—in fact, with any other person. Ana Horvath was, when he really thought about it, his favourite person. Smart, kind, funny, unstintingly loyal. What a huge, horrible hole would be left be in his life without her.

There was also the not insignificant fact that he desired her. Was becoming obsessed with wanting to bed her. Rather than thoughts of stepping back from crossing the friendship line, his mind was flooded with thoughts of galloping across it.

She had never looked more beautiful than today. He wanted her so badly, it had showed in the hunger in his eyes as he'd watched her chat with their guests. Or so both his brother and Adrian had informed him. Then relentlessly teased him about it. But that was okay. He and Ana were married. People expected him to be passionate about his bride at their wedding. Expected that kind of teasing about their wedding night. Ana would no doubt put his reaction down to his good acting. But he hadn't been acting.

He thought about what his mother had said at the announcement of their engagement. 'Finally you've recognised what has been under your nose for so long. Ana is the one for you.'

Was there any truth in his mother's words? Could it be that the other women he'd dated had fallen short when compared to Ana? Was that why they'd never lasted? He feared marriage. But his anti-marriage stance rested mainly on a platform of distrust. Ana had never given him cause not to trust her. She hated the deception she'd grown up having to tolerate. Would he trust himself to be faithful to her? For the first time ever, he thought he needed to consider the fact that marriage to Ana fell in a completely different basket than marriage to anybody else.

Their luggage for the honeymoon had been sent ahead to the hotel. All they had to do was check in when they arrived. He gently awakened Ana from where she was sleeping on his shoulder. Startled and still half asleep, she looked up at him, then smiled a slow, warm smile of recognition that sent tingles down his spine. She had never before looked at him like that.

'You,' she said sleepily, a wealth of emotion shining from her eyes. 'It's you.' Then she blinked, shook her head and pulled back from him. 'Sorry. I… I was dreaming. But I can't remember…'

Dreaming of him? If yes, he hoped it had not just been a happy dream but possibly an erotic one. He stilled. What if she'd been dreaming about another man? He felt shocked by the jealousy that knifed through him.

Extra solicitously, he helped her out of the car, to be

greeted by the steamy January night air. 'Hard to believe we'll be in winter tomorrow,' he said. A mundane comment to disguise the tumult of his thoughts. Not at all what he'd really like to say to her.

'I can't wait,' she said. 'I love Budapest. I'm sure you will too.'

Ana had booked the airport hotel room. Connor wasn't surprised to see there were twin beds. He remembered the fuss she'd made about a bed at Garrison Downs. She should be very pleased with the Budapest hotel he had booked.

Ana staggered into the room ahead of him, exaggerating each step. 'I only had two flutes of champagne,' she said. 'I'm walking like this because my shoes are killing me. They're new and I didn't have time to wear them in.'

He smiled. Still the same Ana. She'd developed a taste for shoes that looked so uncomfortable he didn't know how anyone could wear them. But she always looked fantastic in them.

She threw herself back onto one of the beds and kicked off her shoes. 'We only have a few hours here before we need to be at the airport. It's hardly worth getting undressed.'

'So you'd get on the plane in your wedding dress? Could be uncomfortable.'

'You're right,' she said with a sigh, sitting up on the bed. 'But, Connor, I can't get out of this dress by myself.' She got up from the bed and turned her back to him. Looked over her shoulder with imploring blue eyes. 'See? It's tightly laced all the way down the back. The lady in the bridal shop said a zipper was simply not romantic for a wedding gown.'

Connor had noticed. He had noticed the way the silk

laces crisscrossed her body, cinching in her already narrow waist. She was all wrapped up in that dress, like a beautiful gift just crying out to be unwrapped. Romantic, perhaps. Sexy as hell, yes.

During the reception, the thought had crossed his mind about how it might be to undo those laces. To watch that dress slide off her shoulders down her body to pool in a froth of white on the floor. In his fantasies, she had stepped out of the dress wearing only those sexy, high-heeled shoes. She might even had smiled a sensual, come-and-get-me smile. More than once, that fantasy had played across his mind.

'Kartika had to tightly lace me into the dress,' Ana said.

Connor had to clear his throat. 'Now you're asking me to unlace you out of it?' he said hoarsely.

'Yes. Please. If you don't mind.'

He gritted his teeth. This prosaic request was hardly what he had been fantasising about all evening. 'I suppose I must,' he said, more grumpily than he had intended. How would he be able to hold back from distinctly un-friend-like behaviour when she was inviting him to undress her? If this were anyone but Ana, he might think she was teasing him.

He forced himself to stand behind her and calmly loosen the laces that crisscrossed her back, then pull them open. Her skin was smooth and warm under his hands. Did her breath quicken at his touch? Or was that wishful thinking? The dress started to slide down her shoulders and off her body, revealing the creamy skin of her back. The front of the dress loosened too. Ana clutched the fabric to her chest. She wasn't wearing a bra and the curves of her breasts were tantalisingly revealed. Were her nipples peaking at his gaze? Connor valiantly fought the temptation to slide his hands over her shoulders and down the sides of her breasts. To push the dress over her hips. Was she wearing panties?

She turned to face him. Her face was flushed, her eyes dilated. 'Thank you. I... I can manage now.'

'Are you sure you don't need any further help?' he said through gritted teeth.

'Quite sure,' she said. Her tone wasn't as certain as her words suggested.

He couldn't stay here, with her in that alluring state of semi-undress, for a moment longer. He stepped back. 'I'll go shower while you change.'

'Good idea,' she said, still clutching the dress to herself to preserve her modesty. The action pushed her breasts upward in a most enticing way but she seemed oblivious to it. He, who knew her so well, couldn't detect even a touch of regret in those beautiful Waverly blue eyes. Let alone any hint of desire. Certainly not the kind of high-level lust he was feeling. He'd obviously read more into her response to his swooping kiss at the wedding than had actually been there.

After his shower, he stepped back into the room to find Ana fast asleep on the bed, wrapped in the white towelling robe provided by the hotel. She slept with her cheek resting on her hand. Her make-up was smudged dark around her eyes. She looked vulnerable and alone. He pulled the cover up over her, as the air conditioning was quite chilly.

So much for any ideas about a real wedding night.

He slipped into the other bed. But he couldn't sleep. Two weeks alone with Ana in Budapest. What had he let himself in for?

CHAPTER NINE

SEDUCING CONNOR INTO seducing her was top of Ana's wish list for their Budapest 'honeymoon'. She'd wimped out back in the Melbourne airport hotel, too exhausted to do anything about her desire to lure him into bed. Just as well, really, as they'd only had a few hours before their flight left Melbourne. It could have been excruciatingly awkward.

However, once in Budapest, her secret hopes that he might have the same agenda for the honeymoon were dashed on their arrival in the glorious city of her ancestors. Her generous husband-in-name-only had booked them into a fabulous five-star hotel in a grand, historic building overlooking the River Danube. In a luxury suite with two separate bedrooms and two bells-and-whistles marble bathrooms.

'No need for either of us to have to sleep on the sofa,' Connor explained.

'Or squabble over bathroom time,' she agreed, trying to sound cheerful.

There went the 'only one bed' scenario for seduction. Darn Connor for being so thoughtful. But he was working on out-of-date information concerning her attitude about sharing a bed with him.

'I thought you'd be pleased,' he said, sounding rather pleased with himself in his own gruff way.

Not, she thought. 'Of course,' she said through gritted teeth.

Now was her chance to say she would have been more than happy to sleep in the bed with him. However, perhaps it wasn't quite the right moment. Not when she'd made such a fuss of sleeping on the back-breaking sofa back at Garrison Downs. But that had been before the wedding. Before that exhilarating kiss when she'd thought, for the first time, he might want her too. Before the exciting touch of his hands on her bare skin as he'd unlaced her wedding dress.

Had that affected him at all? And did he remember holding her hand as she'd fallen asleep, in that big bed in the yellow suite at Garrison Downs before Christmas? Perhaps she had dreamed it, but it had seemed so real at the time. She couldn't forget how blissfully happy the contact had made her. She'd been hoping, somehow, to recreate it. And more.

Anyway, what was the big fuss about making love in a bed? There was the sofa, the carpet, up against the wall; even the bath tub, for heaven's sake. If she got the chance to get physical with Connor, she wouldn't care about the comfort factor of a hotel bed.

They'd just arrived after the very long, but exceedingly comfortable, first-class flight from Melbourne via Dubai. She hadn't flown first class before and it had been a revelation. Gourmet meals, an on-board spa, even a bar serving drinks in a first-class lounge. Utterly exhausted after the wedding, she'd slept for a lot of the trip, in the first-class pyjamas, on the flat bed made up with crisp sheets. *Thank you, Connor, for your generosity.* She'd nearly fainted when she'd seen how much the fares had cost.

Now she did a twirl in the ballroom-sized living area.

'This suite is amazing,' she said. 'Clever you for getting it for us. Thank you.'

'I thought you'd like it,' he said.

The room must have cost him another small fortune.

She walked over to the window and pulled the curtains further back so she could see the view in its entirety. She caught her breath. Snowflakes slowly drifted past, enhancing the already beautiful view of the famous Chain Bridge. The elegant, nineteenth-century bridge spanned the River Danube to connect the Pest side of the city, where their hotel was, to the Buda side. Across the river, a dusting of snow covered the Fisherman's Bastion and the Matthias Church with the elaborate spires and turrets. Places she wanted to visit.

'Budapest is even more beautiful than I remember,' she said. 'The buildings all frosted with snow make it look like something out of a fairy tale. I'm aching to get out there and show you what an awesome city it is.'

Connor joined her at the window. 'It's magnificent: the river; the old buildings; the snow. This is a world away from Garrison Downs Yet each place is spectacularly beautiful in its own way.'

Ana was very aware of him standing by her shoulder, his height and strength. He was wearing black jeans and boots and a lightweight black cashmere sweater. It wasn't his usual look and she found it incredibly attractive. Although they'd freshened up in the first-class lounge during a short layover in Dubai, he was sporting a sexy stubble. She liked that too. How would it feel against her cheek if she kissed him?

Again, she was struck by the realisation that, in some ways, Connor was different. Had he changed so much in the six months he'd been away in Sydney? Or had she not

noticed cumulative, ongoing changes in her childhood
friend usually masked by everyday familiarity? Then,
wham, she'd been hit by that change when she'd met him
at the restaurant after a half-year absence. When she'd
realised he was no longer the boy next door. Not a boy at
all. A man.

A man she wanted.

If she'd wanted him as much then as she wanted him
now, she didn't know how she could have maintained a
platonic friendship through recent years. Now the fake
intimacy they'd needed to cultivate for the sake of the
wedding was accelerating those disturbing new feelings.

They were married.

It was almost as if that fact gave permission for something different to happen. Besides, didn't the marriage
have to be consummated to be legal?

'What do you know about Budapest?' she asked as they
both looked out at the view.

'Not a lot. I've chatted with your grandparents about
the events that drove them to Australia. And I've heard
from you about your visits here when you were younger.
But there's much to learn.'

'For me, too,' she said.

He turned to look down into her face. His expression
was serious.

Did he get more handsome by the minute?

'This is your heritage as much as Garrison Downs. The
culture. The architecture. The music. They all speak to
your Hungarian side. After all you've gone through with
the shock of your father's death and the drama of the will,
I wanted to bring you here. To restore some balance to
your view of yourself.'

'Really?' She felt flooded with gratitude for his understanding. 'Thank you, Connor. That seems very profound and…and very perceptive. You know me so well. As if you haven't done enough for me by acting as my husband.'

She was going to add, 'What would I do without you?' But she didn't think it wise. Because those weeks when they hadn't communicated, because of her dislike of Brandi, had let her know exactly what it was like not to have Connor in her life. It had been awful, like a great, gaping hole in her heart. Yet, at the same time, might it be worth taking a risk to see if there could be more than friendship between them? Though, that hadn't worked out too well on their wedding night.

'You know I wanted to help with the mock. Now there's a signed marriage certificate in hand,' he said.

The 'mock' was what he called the marriage of convenience.

Distancing himself, perhaps, with humour from their deception of so many people who cared for them. 'Your grandfather told me how much you wanted to come back here. He felt you needed it. We cooked this trip up together.'

Did she need it? Maybe she did, to have some distance. To overcome that nagging sense that she didn't really belong at Garrison Downs. That the place was all about Rosamund and her daughters, with the secret daughter banging at the back door to be let in. What had happened in the last seven months had been overwhelming at times. Apa's death and the terrible grief she'd felt at his loss. The complications of the will. The unproductive and demoralising hunt for a husband. The way her attraction to Connor had burst out of the boundaries she had put around it for so long.

'It's true what Nagypapa said. I've been saving for a trip

for ages. My grandparents knew that. They've always encouraged me to feel connected to the family we have left
here. This will be the third time I've visited but the first
time I've been here by myself.'

'By yourself?' he said. 'I'm here, aren't I? Or are you
planning to ditch me?'

She expected him to nudge her on the arm in his jocu-
lar, we-are-good-mates style, the way he had always done.
But he didn't. He sounded light-hearted but the shadows in
his green eyes said something else. Had she hurt his feelings? She couldn't bear it if she had. Who knew with all
the play acting that had been going on between them in
the interests of the mock marriage? Did she really know
how Connor felt?

'Oh, Connor, I'm so sorry. That's not what I meant at
all. I meant the first time I've travelled independently. I'm
so grateful you're here with me. I wouldn't even be here
if it wasn't for you.'

Now. She took a deep breath. Now she should say some-
thing about a change in direction for their friendship. *Now.*
But she couldn't bring herself to say the words. 'I meant,
the first time I was with my grandparents. The second time
I was on the budget bus tour with my university friends.'
And wishing he'd been there too, to share in the fun.

'In your second year. July holidays. I remember.'

'Yep. Eastern Europe in two weeks. We were only in
Budapest for one night. Not nearly enough to sample all
that there was to do here. But the trip was a lot of fun. We
all loved the ruin bars.'

'A ruin bar? A bar where you get ruined? Isn't that what
students do anyway?'

She laughed. 'That, too.' Not her, though. She never allowed herself to get drunk. Not when she was sitting on

that big secret of her birth. Wariness with strangers who wanted to get to know her had become second nature.

'Budapest ruin bars are cool bars that sprung up in dilapidated buildings, abandoned warehouses, ruins—even underground. They're mainly in the downtown Pest area. You know this side of the river is Pest, the other side is Buda?'

'I didn't know that. I do now. I'm up for visiting ruin bars,' he said. 'You'll have to be my guide.'

'I have some cousins our age here. I'm sure they could show us where the locals go.'

'And how to avoid tourist traps,' he said.

'That too. My first trips were in summer and autumn. But Budapest in winter is different altogether, and so beautiful.'

'Especially to Australian eyes, having come straight from summer.'

Leaving steamy, summer Melbourne to land here in the cold and snow was a shock to the senses. A shock of a very good kind. She loved it.

'I believe there's a big outdoor ice rink in the City Park,' she said. 'You've never ice-skated, have you?'

'No.'

'Didn't think so,' she said. 'Neither have I. Do you want to try it?'

'I'm always game to try something new.'

What about making love with me, with a choice of two beds?

She paused to get her breath back at the very thought.

'Me too,' he said.

'Before I go any further, we need to talk.' She looked up at him. It hurt to say this, as there was nothing she wanted more than to spend all the time with him. But she had to play the game. 'How do you see this trip going? I mean, do you want to do things together? Do you have an agenda? Or do we go our separate ways during the day? Maybe we meet up for dinner some nights?'

She had to be sure, one way or another, to make this work with Connor. They had the marriage certificate as proof they were legally married. But they needed to stay married—or at least appear to be married—until after that thirty-first of May deadline. Then, after an appropriate interval, Connor would become her ex-husband. Would their friendship be the same after spending so much time together?

Connor frowned. 'Why would we go our separate ways? I'd assumed we'd spend the time together. You'll want to meet with your family, I'm sure, and I'll need to spend some time online for Money Club business. But apart from that—'

'The family will want to meet you too. Remember, they think we're married. They'll want to meet my new husband. We'll have to play the role for them or it might get reported back to my grandparents.'

'I'd like to meet your cousins and any other members of your family. Your Australian family have been so good to me. It will be interesting to see what they're like here. Those who stayed.'

'I wasn't sure if you'd want to…to get that personal,' she said.

Connor put his hands on her shoulders and looked down into her face. 'Mock marriage aside, we're still friends, aren't we?'

'Of…of course we are.' She forced her voice to be steady. Cheerful, even.

Friends.

There it was again, that definitive word. It was as if he wanted to reiterate that friends was all they could ever be. In spite of those mixed messages he'd sent her at the wedding.

That kiss!

Or had she simply misread him? Was she deluding herself to think they could ever move outside the friend zone into something deeper. Even if it was simply friends with benefits?

'I can't imagine anyone who I'd rather see Budapest with than my best friend,' he said. 'Especially when I know how much this place means to you.'

'Me too,' she said. 'Be with you, I mean.' It was true. Should she really risk attempting to make it more than that?

They were married. That meant absolutely nothing—it was a means to an end. Connor had performed wonderfully in his role as bridegroom. She needed to forget anything other than he really was the best friend a person could ever have. And she couldn't risk losing that friendship.

Maybe her seduction plan wasn't such a great idea. She'd never seen a friends-with-benefits arrangement that had worked out. One partner always seemed to want more commitment and ended up getting hurt. Maybe it was the nature of intimacy that people got attached to people they had sex with. Not all the 'it doesn't mean anything' words in the world could change that. Did she want to risk that kind of pain? For her. Or, indeed, for Connor?

If Connor had invited her to Budapest on holiday a year ago, she would have jumped at the chance. She would treat the time here as if she and Connor were still just buddies. Separate-rooms-type buddies. That was all they'd been and all they were likely ever to be. She would enjoy this break in this beautiful city that had such significance to her family. But two weeks alone with Connor might be too much for her to hold off trying to seduce him, even staying in separate rooms. She wanted him so much. She might have to work out a way to go back to Australia earlier before she made a fool of herself.

'Budapest and my Hungarian heritage mean a lot to me,' she said.

'As they should.'

'I might have had an absent father, but I had grandparents who were determined to make up for Holt's absence. They're truly like second parents, as you well know. I grew up knowing I was Hungarian by descent. Our family here can be traced back a long time, through Hungary's turbulent history. Whereas I knew nothing much about my Waverly side—although my sisters have given me a crash course. I want to learn about what it means to be a Waverly of Garrison Downs without losing sight of how important my mother's family is to me too.'

'Of course you do,' he said. 'Remember when I said you must have inherited your love of horses from your father? I think your creative side comes from your Horvath family. That's such a part of you. You need to fully embrace it.'

Connor's kindness and understanding made her feel quite weepy. No one got her like he did. She sniffed. 'Sorry. Jet lag.'

'Come here.'

He pulled her into one of his special Connor bear hugs. She relaxed into it, resting her cheek against his shoulder as she had done so many times, feeling his strength surround her. She realised then that the nocturnal hand-holding had been the same kind of friendly comfort Connor's hugs had always been. There hadn't been any other meaning to it or anything sensual. She'd read too much into it.

'It's been quite the roller coaster for us over the last month or so,' he said. 'I wondered if we would get it all done on time. The trip to Garrison Downs. The engagement announcements. Then the wedding itself, with all that entailed. Mainly thanks to you, we pulled it off. You were brilliant. And worked so hard.'

'As the wedding was all about me, and what I would gain from it, me going all out to organise everything was to be expected. Fortunately, I'd resigned from my job to give me the time to act as wedding planner. It turned out to be a good party, though, didn't it?'

'The best of parties,' he said. 'I really enjoyed myself. In the end, I wasn't aware I was pretending. Like an actor who must get so deep into their role they say their lines without thinking.'

'Me too. I got so caught up in it. Accepting everyone's congratulations. Telling them how happy we were. Thanking them for the gifts they brought even though we stated no gifts. They'll have to be returned, of course.'

'And no one was any the wiser it wasn't real.'

'My mother had her doubts. But did you see how close she was to tears when she welcomed you as her son? Tears of joy, I mean. She ended up believing in us.'

Ana felt bad about that. Really bad. But she knew her mother would understand when she found out the truth. She wouldn't want her daughter's inheritance to be at risk because her daughter hadn't been able to find a real husband.

'Did anyone ask you if you were pregnant?' Connor said.

She laughed. 'My grandmother outright. Others skirted

around it, but it was very obvious they thought it likely. A few of the older people actually stared at my stomach. Did anyone say anything to you?'

'Yes.'

She laughed. 'Some people simply don't have boundaries.'

'Did you tell Kartika the truth about the wedding?'

'I was nearly bursting with the need to talk to someone about what we were doing. Besides, she had to know. I asked her to be my bridesmaid at a fake wedding.'

'So, yes, then?'

'She can be trusted one hundred percent. She approved of our plan. I swear she would never tell anyone else. By the way, she said to say thank you, from one of my best friends to the other, for stepping up to help me.'

He paused. 'You were the most beautiful bride. I… I couldn't take my eyes off you.' His voice was husky and his arms tightened around her.

'Why thank you, dear friend,' she said, forcing her voice to sound light-hearted, glad her face was hidden from him. 'That means a lot, coming from you.'

'Seriously. You looked exquisite. Radiant. A dream bride to any man who—'

'Hadn't sworn off marriage?'

'Yes. Seeing you like that made me see you in a different way. As if a filter had overlaid a pre-existing image of my childhood friend. If…if things were different I—'

'You what, Connor?' she said, her heart racing.

'I would—'

The buzzer to their room sounded, shattering the moment.

Darn.

Most likely a bell boy, delivering their luggage. She decided to ignore it. But it buzzed again. It was too urgent to ignore. Regretfully, wishing she had just another minute—even a few seconds—to follow through on the conversation, she pulled away from Connor. Did she imagine he'd let her go with some reluctance? 'I'll get it,' she said. She opened the door.

'Your luggage, Mrs O'Neill,' the bell boy said.

Ana stilled. For a moment she was about to tell him he'd got the wrong room. No Mrs O'Neill here. But then she realised he meant *her*. She turned back to Connor. He was trying not to laugh at her disconcerted expression. 'That's you,' he said, his green eyes dancing.

'I... I guess it is,' she said.

For the time being, that is.

The bell boy wheeled the cart with their luggage to the larger of the two bedrooms. As anyone would, for a newlywed couple on their honeymoon. She thanked him, speaking in Hungarian, and tipped him with some Hungarian *forints*.

She turned back to Connor. The moment was lost. Would she ever know what he'd been about to say?

'Okay, Mr O'Neill, I guess we now have to toss for who gets the larger bedroom.'

'You, of course,' he said. 'I wouldn't be much of a gentleman if I nabbed it for myself.'

That was the trouble. She was hoping that, alone in this palatial suite, Connor might act less like a gentleman and more like a man who appreciated her as a desirable woman.

CHAPTER TEN

WHO WAS THIS WOMAN? Connor wondered. This different Ana. Elegant, assured, *hot,* speaking in rapid, confident Hungarian? She wasn't usually a person to draw attention to herself. A hangover, he supposed, from having to keep the truth about her father a secret. Yet here she was in a short, tight black skirt, black tights, cute little high-heeled boots he found incredibly sexy and an attention-getting red sweater that hugged her curves. Perhaps it was because no one in Budapest knew or cared about Holt Waverly or his family. Ana could be just Ana.

And Connor liked it.

It was both exciting and perturbing to be in such close quarters with this different version of his long-time friend. He'd found it difficult to keep that hug—what Ana always made a thing of calling 'the Connor hug'—platonic and comforting. When what he'd wanted to do was pull her into his arms and kiss her. To take up from where they'd started at the wedding. And not stop kissing her. Until kissing was no longer enough. What they should have continued at the airport hotel—if she hadn't fallen asleep.

He'd been saved by the buzzer from confessing that his feelings for her had changed. That since the wedding the idea of a bride—not just any bride, but an Ana bride—had seemed seductive rather than scary. He wanted her. And it was getting more difficult to hide it. He didn't want to push her into something she might not be ready for. It was difficult to tell if her feelings towards him had also evolved.

She was such a good actress. He didn't know any longer what was genuine and what was play-acting in aid of the mock marriage. That kiss at the wedding had seemed so real, so passionate, the kiss of a bride looking forward to her wedding night. But had it been part of the fake wedding game? A performance for the enjoyment of their guests? To have everyone there believing the marriage was the real deal? Had she not realised what she was doing by asking him to unlace her on their wedding night? Surely she couldn't be that naïve?

Back at Garrison Downs, before Christmas, she'd made such a fuss about the bed. He'd doubted she'd got any sleep on that poor excuse for a sofa, yet just now she'd seemed miffed that he'd booked her a room of her own. He didn't know any more exactly where he stood with her.

'I didn't know you could speak Hungarian,' he said.

'You mean after twenty years of friendship I can still surprise you?'

'Indeed you can,' he said. And he wasn't just referring to her language skills. 'I've heard you speak the odd words with your grandparents but you sounded so fluent talking to the bell boy.' The bell boy who had been discreetly ogling her. She looked so cute in that short, tight skirt. It taken him all he had to stop himself from telling the guy to keep his eyes off his wife.

'I told you I've been saving for a trip to Budapest. I decided that by the next visit I wanted to be able to speak the language. During the six months you were away in Sydney, I had some intensive lessons with Nagypapa. When he thought I was ready, he took me along to the Hungarian Club for conversation with his friends there. I'm pretty fluent now. The test will come when I get into conversations with people who won't make allowances for me.'

'You picked it up quickly,' he said admiringly. 'Well done.'

'Yes and no. I've always been surrounded by the language. Apparently, I had a lot of words when I was little. I learned Hungarian alongside English. Then I got to the stage I didn't want to stand out as different and refused to speak it any more.'

'But the language must have stayed in your subconscious.'

'I believe so. That's what my grandmother says. Anyway, it should make it easier for us to get around if I can speak the language. That said, English is widely spoken here. For example, the announcements on the metro are in both Hungarian and English. My cousins learned English at school.'

'I'm raring to get out there and see the city. To just walk around and get our bearings before we do any actual sightseeing.'

'Me too. We'll have to be careful what shoes we wear. A lot of where we'll be walking has cobblestones that might be slippery with the snow.'

'Understood,' he said.

'There's something else you need to know about Budapest.'

'And that is?'

'The food is amazing.'

He laughed. 'Like at your grandparents' restaurant? Then I'll love it.'

'There's traditional food to die for, but also contemporary food that borrows from other cuisines. While I was on the plane, I looked up some restaurants we might want to try. And I put together a list of sights we should see.'

'Won't you have seen it all before?'

'Not really. Remember, I was fifteen when I was first here and hanging out with family. Next time I was with a bunch of students just for one night. Now I'm with you.'

'And we're both so grown up and sophisticated.'

'Of course we are,' she said, striking a pose and pouting her mouth. Her lush, seductive mouth he'd kissed so thoroughly at the wedding. *Their* wedding.

When had she got so sexy?

The image of her with her wedding dress sliding off her shoulders as he unlaced her returned to taunt him.

'Shall we have quick showers and get going?' she said. She glanced down at her wrist. 'My watch has adjusted to Budapest time—that means lunch soon.'

'Lunch sounds good,' he said.

Surprisingly, he wasn't that hungry. He'd eaten so much on the plane. Then there was the fact his gut was twisted in knots about what he wanted to say to Ana. Would she welcome a change to the status quo? Did she want him the way he wanted her?

'We have his and her bathrooms,' she said. 'You go to yours and I'll go to mine.'

'Done,' he said, immediately revisiting the fantasy of being in the shower with her and helping her to soap her lovely, naked body.

'Oh, and, Connor?'

'Yes?'

'Don't shave.'

He put his hand to his bristly chin.

'I like that stubble,' she said, with a narrow-eyed, speculative look that made him wish he could tell what she was thinking. Because it seemed like it might be X-rated.

'Stubble stays,' he said, feeling bemused. And more than a touch aroused.

He was in and out of the shower as quickly as he usually was. But, surprisingly, he didn't have to wait overly long for Ana. He was in the short passageway between their rooms, still wrapped in the luxurious deep navy hotel robe, when she emerged from her bathroom wearing her robe. Disappointingly, it wrapped very tightly around her, giving no glimpse of curves.

Her face was set in a very determined expression, her cheeks flushed. 'You're here—good,' she said.

'What's up?' he asked. 'Something wrong with the shower? We can call housekeeping if there is.'

'There's absolutely nothing wrong with my shower. It's an excellent shower. No, it's me that's the problem.'

'You? Are you ill? You look okay but—'

She waved her hand dismissively. 'Nothing like that.'

'Then what?' he said, alarmed. He had never seen her like this.

'I have something to say to you and I'm not going to bottle it up any longer. I've been thinking about it in the shower.'

'Right,' he said. He wasn't sure what else he could say.

'I notice you didn't shave.'

'You asked me not to and I didn't.'

'Good,' she said. '*Argh!* There I go again. Prevaricating. Not saying what I really want to say. Although I really do like that stubble on you.'

'And what's that you want to say, Ana? Is it something I've done? Or not done? Let it rip.'

'It is and it isn't.' She started to wring her hands—not

a good sign. He gently picked them up and disengaged her fingers. She scarcely seemed to notice.

'It's about me. Always feeling I need to think of others. Putting my own needs last. I think it dates back to the fact that my birth ruined my mother's life. And once I became aware of that I tried to make it up to her.'

'What? Your birth did no such thing. Your mother adores you.'

'I ruined her life,' she stated again. 'I wasn't really aware of it until I got older. Recently, I've thought about it a lot.'

'You really think that? I'll bet she doesn't. I know she thinks you're the best thing in life that ever happened to her. She actually told me that, just after we got engaged.'

'She was twenty-five with a promising career ahead of her. Then she was suddenly a single mother. Her chances of meeting someone else were immediately diminished. But she didn't want to date anyway. Not with a little girl to bring up. Then there was the complication of Holt. Always a presence in her life because of me. She would have preferred to put him firmly in her past.'

Connor noticed how Ana referred to her father by his given name, instead of Apa, when she was trying to look dispassionately at him.

'Mum was always concerned Holt would dump me as a daughter, the way he had dumped her. She constantly worried about money because she didn't trust him not to stop the allowance he paid her for my upkeep.'

He frowned. 'Do you think he would have stopped the allowance? That doesn't seem like something Holt would do.'

'How would we know? You talk a lot about trust. I don't think Mum ever trusted him again. By the time she actually fell for another man, it was too late for her to have a baby. I know she wanted more than one child. I had to make it up to her by...by being the best possible daughter.'

'You would have been that anyway. It's in your nature. I don't know why you can't see that.'

The same way he had difficulty coming to terms with his role in his parents' divorce? He hadn't known this was a scar from her past she bore. He'd been aware of some of it, but not the depth of what she was feeling now. Perhaps Ana being the same age as Lili had been when she'd met Holt had brought it front of her mind. He wanted to take her in his arms and hug her, tell her how wonderful she was. But it didn't seem the right moment.

'So I studied for a degree I didn't want to study,' she said. 'Got a job I don't like for the sake of security. To please not only my mother but also my grandparents. Now I'm doing it again.'

He frowned. 'What do you mean you're doing it again?'

'This holiday. This...this *honeymoon*. I asked you what you wanted to get out of it. Here. Budapest. But we didn't talk about what I wanted out of it. Maybe because you've paid for it and I don't want to be indebted to you.'

That stung. 'You could never be indebted to me.'

'I can pay you back once I inherit.' The flush on her cheeks was deepening.

He put his hands on her shoulders. The robe slipped to the side, baring her throat and the enticing curve of one breast.

'You will not pay me back. We don't work like that. We never have. Now, tell me what this is really about.' He spoke again before she had a chance to reply. 'I think I see where it's going. We didn't talk about what you expected from this holiday. That's me being male and selfish.'

Her eyes widened. 'No! No one could ever accuse you of being selfish. You're too perfect for that.'

His mouth twisted. 'Why does "perfect" said that way sound like an insult?'

'Argh! I'm getting it wrong again.' She looked up into his eyes, hers wide and sincere. 'I would never want to insult you. Ever. Or hurt you. You are, quite possibly, the most wonderful man alive.'

'I like that,' he said, taken aback.

'Good. You're meant to like it. And I mean every word.'

He felt he was still no closer to understanding what was bothering her. 'Ana, just tell me what you want out of this holiday. If it's different from what I want, we can compromise.' He liked to get straight to the point. But he'd learned over the years that Ana had her way of getting there. Usually in a circuitous manner that he had learned to navigate.

'Shower time is good for thinking,' she said. 'Negative ions from falling water inspire creativity.'

'I didn't know that,' he said, puzzled by her train of thought. Sometimes he really wondered if there was something in that 'men are from Mars and women from Venus' theory.

'I've always found it so. In fact, I came up with the idea for our best-selling earrings in the shower.'

'Okay…' he said.

'While I was in the shower just now, I decided I wasn't being honest with you about what I wanted. Because that's a difficult thing for me to do.'

He nodded, hoping it would encourage her to get to the point. He was distracted by the way her robe was falling off her shoulder. He doubted she wore anything at all underneath it.

'Okay,' she said. 'If I don't say this now, I probably won't ever say it.'

She took a deep breath. The robe slipped a little further. Much more, and a nipple might come into sight.

'Understood,' he said.

'First, I am not Mrs O'Neill, so please don't call me that. Even if I was married for real, I would not be Mrs O'Neill. I don't mean that as an insult to you and your nice name. I wasn't deemed worthy of the Waverly name. Horvath will stay my name. It honours the people who wanted me and cared for me.'

'Okay,' he said. Curse Holt Waverly for leaving her with this legacy of insecurity. Despite everything Connor had said to her about claiming her rightful place in the Waverly family, that second-best feeling seemed to be lingering.

'Let's get another thing clear. I'm so over you thinking of me in a sisterly way.'

Funny, he'd had the same thought. He'd be glad to give up the role of protective older brother he'd played for so long. Now he had a different role in mind.

'Call me the girl next door, your horse-riding buddy, your friend…but *not* your sister.'

He felt deeply entrenched barriers falling away. Realised that he'd hidden behind the fiction that she was like a sister to him to stop himself from wanting her when circumstances hadn't been right for anything beyond friendship. Now there was nothing to stop him letting her know how he felt about her. The fake marriage had served to focus his thoughts on what a marriage might be between two people who had known each other most of their lives and who could truly trust each other.

She had more to say. 'I can assure you, I do not think of you that way. In fact, I fancy you like hell. I've been attracted to you since we were teenagers. I think you know that. And you've always let me down lightly when my attraction bubbles over and I throw myself at you. But if there is a reason for you to push me away—a real reason—then let me know. Just don't tell me it's because you think of me as a sister. There are better ways of telling me you're not attracted to me.'

He looked at her for a long, intense moment before he spoke. 'What makes you think I'm not attracted to you?'

Ana stared at Connor. He had never looked more handsome with his hair still damp from the shower, that sexy stubble, the dark robe loosely tied and open at his bare chest. He smelled deliciously of the designer toiletries from the bathroom that enhanced his natural, familiar Connor scent.

Her mouth suddenly went dry. 'Wh-what did you say?'

'Are you about to throw yourself at me again?'

'I'm… I'm considering it.' That was the whole point of her spiel.

'Then know this. I think you're beautiful, desirable and very, very sexy. I've spent years denying how attracted I am to you. Because you were too young. Because I needed things with you to stay the same when other parts of my life were spiralling out of control. Because I feared losing you if a relationship didn't work out. Because you had a boyfriend or I had a girlfriend, and the time wasn't right for us. No more denial. I've never wanted you more than I do at this moment.'

A delicious thrill tingled through her body at his words. The look in his green eyes told her even more.

'Are you serious?' she said.

'Very serious.'

'You're not teasing me? It would be cruel if you were teasing me, Connor.'

'I'm not teasing you, Ana. Are you teasing me about threatening to throw yourself at me?'

'Of course not. I mean, I'm not teasing you. Or threatening you. I want you too.' Her voice broke. 'So much.' This was Connor offering everything she wanted from him.

His eyes narrowed in a very sensuous way she had never seen before in their twenty years of friendship. It sent shivers of awareness coursing through her. She felt his gaze on where her robe was slipping off her bare shoulder.

'How do you plan to go about throwing yourself at me?' he said, his voice deep and throaty.

'Um…' She was so surprised and pleased at his response, she hadn't actually planned the logistics of a seduction. The staged unlacing of her wedding gown hadn't done the trick.

'Do you plan to take a run at me and fling yourself against my chest?'

She laughed at the image that conjured up. 'No. Don't be silly.'

'How, then? Would you care to demonstrate?'

She smiled, a slow smile of appreciation of this gorgeous, gorgeous man she wanted so much. Had wanted for so long. And who she knew so well. But as a friend, not a lover. She stepped closer and looked up at him, her gaze intent on his face. Her heart started to race at the awareness in his eyes, the sensual set of his mouth.

This was Connor, but not a Connor she had seen before. A private Connor for her eyes only. She wanted to know him as a lover. She wound her arms around his neck, drew his head down to hers and kissed him.

It wasn't a show kiss for the benefit of anyone watching.

Or a practice kiss. It was a kiss that came from her heart, singing a message to him that she was his to take. Kissing Connor. Wanting Connor. His tongue slid between her lips to meet hers, and the kiss quickly moved from tentative to exciting, to passionate and demanding. All those years had passed since their last proper kiss. It was just as exhilarating, just as arousing, just plain wonderful. She wanted so much more than kisses. But she would enjoy these kisses in the meantime.

She broke away to steady herself, to catch her breath, to make sure this was real.

'Why haven't we done this before?' she said, her heart beating in triple time, her breath ragged.

'Because we weren't ready,' he said simply.

Through her haze of excitement and mounting desire, she realised he was right. This was the right time for them. Whatever came of this, she would have no regrets. They had time, opportunity, privacy and a choice of two beds.

'Is this what you want?' he said. 'Because if you'd rather wait—'

'Wait for what, Connor?' she said, teasing.

'For us to make love,' he said, his voice husky.

She was ready. Oh, yes, she was. She was very aware he was naked under his robe. And it was obvious he was ready to take this sensual adventure further.

'I'm ready when you are,' she said. Then laughed. A bit too nervously. A bit too giggly. 'That's something I would have said to you when we were teenagers. Sorry.'

'No need to apologise. I think it's cute. And I take that for consent.'

'It's consent, all right,' she said. A rush of desire for him made her feel suddenly light-headed, her nipples pebbling and aching for his touch.

He pushed the robe off her shoulders so it slid away from her breasts to rumple at her waist. She was baring her breasts to Connor. And it felt so right.

'You're beautiful,' he said huskily, cupping her breasts in his strong, sure hands, caressing her nipples until pleasure shot through every pleasure pathway, heading straight to between her legs. 'Absolutely beautiful.'

'I… I'm glad you think so,' she murmured. 'You're pretty darn beautiful yourself.'

With hands that trembled with impatience, she pushed his robe away to plant her hands on his hard, warm chest. She was met with an impressive wall of muscle; he really had been working out. She kissed from the smooth hollow beneath his ears, along his chin, knowing her face would be red from the pleasing scrape of his stubble, but not caring as it felt so good, until she met his mouth to claim it again in a kiss.

He kissed her back, hungry and possessive. Then broke away to plant small warm, kisses down her neck until he reached her breasts. She gasped her pleasure and delight, moaned when he kissed and tongued one nipple while rolling the other between his fingers.

She realised she had pushed him up against the wall, too overcome by passion to really be aware of what she was doing. Until he broke away from the kiss.

'Shall we take this somewhere more comfortable?' he said, panting.

'Good idea,' she said, holding on to him for support.

'Your bed or mine?'

'Whichever is closest. The carpet will do at a pinch.'

He looked a little shocked 'You continue to surprise me.'

'I hope I never stop surprising you,' she said with a teasing smile.

'I look forward to lots of surprises.' He swung her up in his arms.

'Connor! This is so romantic. But you don't have to carry me.'

'But I want to. Besides, you're very light.'

'You're very strong.'

He made carrying her seem effortless. He took her to the nearest bed, which happened to be his, and laid her down on it. He undid the ties from her robe, she did the same for him and they were both completely naked. Her hungry gaze took in his perfect male body. Broad shoulders, powerful chest, six pack, long, strong limbs. She had to clear her throat before she spoke.

'It's a long time since I've seen you without clothes. You've changed.'

He laughed. 'I should hope so. That was a long time ago. I was most likely running around under the garden hose with my brother.'

'We were so innocent. There must have come a time when our parents decided we were too old for naked shenanigans and sharing a room but I don't remember.'

She walked her fingers down across his chest, admiring, wanting. 'I should be feeling awkward, being naked. I don't think you've even seen me in a bikini since I got my first training bra.'

'You've got absolutely nothing to feel awkward about,' he said. 'You've got a lovely body. The loveliest.'

The transition from just friends to something altogether more intimate seemed so relaxed, easy and incredibly exciting.

'This is different, isn't it?' she said breathlessly. 'Crossing boundaries into the unexplored. We're so familiar with each other and yet this is so very different.'

'Can you stop analysing this and just enjoy it?' His voice was hoarse.

'Yes, I— *Oh!*'

She couldn't have spoken more even if she'd wanted to. All she could think about was the intense pleasure of Connor caressing her in her most intimate places. He seemed to know intuitively what would please and arouse her. She bucked against his hand, aching for more. Wanting him inside her. But not completely oblivious.

'Protection?' she managed to choke out.

'Got it.' He reached to the nightstand beside the bed. Connor donning a condom was a sight she had never imagined she would see. She found it incredibly arousing. She offered to help. He offered no objection.

'Now,' she said. 'I need you. Please.'

When Connor pushed inside her, she felt utterly complete. They found each other's rhythms straight away, each stroke sheer ecstasy, building to the peak. She came with a cry of intense ecstasy, followed by Connor's shout of release.

For a moment she lay close to him, still shaken by the power of her orgasm, the intensity of her joy in having him so close.

'Yeah. I know,' he said.

'What do you mean, *you know*? I didn't say anything.'

'You were going to say, why did we wait so long, weren't you?'

'How did you know I was going to say that?'

'I know you so well.'

At the same time, she answered her own question. 'Because we know each other so well.' Making love with Connor was everything she'd fantasised it to be and more. There was a connection that was way more than physical. She laughed and Connor did too. Then they started to make love all over again, completely in tune with each other's needs.

Much later, she lay replete within the circle of her best friend's arms.

Best friend to best lover.

'Connor?' she murmured sleepily.

'Yes?'

'That was better than the very best Connor hug.'

'I should hope so,' he said, smiling. It was the indulgent smile he gave her when she said something he found particularly cute.

'Like a hug with benefits.'

'A hug on steroids.'

Now completely unselfconscious about her nudity, she lifted herself up on her elbow so she could see his face. 'You know this changes everything?'

'I know.'

'We won't be able to go back to being just friends.'

'Who would want to?' he said. 'Friends is good. Lovers is better.'

'Agreed,' she murmured. Best friends and lovers—what more could she want?

CHAPTER ELEVEN

FOUR DAYS LATER, Ana found herself in jeweller's heaven—her great-uncle Istvan's jewellery store in downtown Pest. She loved the traditional opulence of it all. Plush carpet. Chandeliers. Display cabinets of mellow timbers and spotless glass that showcased necklaces, bracelets, rings and earrings made from glittering diamonds and precious coloured gems such as sapphires, emeralds and rubies, as well as semi-precious gems. There were both classic and contemporary styles. Small breakout rooms were as much for security as the comfort and privacy of clients trying on fine jewellery with an attentive salesperson. She could have spent hours browsing and admiring the exquisite creations, all made here.

But what interested her most was the design studio and workshop on the floor above. When she'd been fifteen, it had been like stepping into another world, one where she'd immediately known she belonged.

Her uncle—so like his brother, her beloved grandfather Zoltan—took her upstairs. At the entrance to the studio, she stood in awe. There was an artisan seated at each work station, concentrating on the intricate task of hand-crafting fine jewellery. She breathed in the subtle scent of solder and melting wax.

'I'm seeing this room through different eyes,' she said.

'When I was fifteen, I knew nothing about jewellery making. Now I truly appreciate what I'm seeing here. Yet, in some ways it seems different. Not surprising, as it's ten years later.'

'Traditional techniques are at the very heart of our craft. However, we also keep up to date with new technology. Lasers, computer-driven programs and 3D wax printers are something I would never have dreamed of when I was your age. Yet they have earned their place here along with our more traditional tools.'

Ana looked around her with even more respect. 'I'm so looking forward to spending the morning here with you. There's so much I know I still need to learn.'

'It's a shame you can't spend more time with us. I know you've studied in Australia, but there's nothing like working in a studio like this to really hone your skills. Only one of my grandchildren has followed me into the business. I like that my Australian great-niece also shares the interest. Your online store is inspiring. I know this is your honeymoon, but maybe you could consider returning to Budapest to spend more time here. Perhaps for six months?'

'Seriously? You'd have me here? Working? Learning?'

'The door is always open for you and your charming new husband. You both could stay with your great-aunt and me.'

'That's a wonderful invitation. I would love it. Six months might be too much time away from home. But three months? Perhaps later in the year?'

'Whatever is convenient for you.'

Ana was dreading the time when she and Connor would end their marriage of convenience and file for divorce. No matter which way they explained it, their families would feel at best upset, at worst deceived. And she would be heartbroken. Because it would be the end of her friendship with him. How could she possibly return to just friends after all they'd shared on this honeymoon? How could she bear to hear him talk about his latest girlfriend? Or make plans for his life that didn't include her? Three months in Budapest away from him, away from everything at home, would be a good escape.

The next day, Connor sat holding hands with Ana on a sight-seeing cruise boat. It was taking them on an hour-long round trip to see some of the Budapest sights from the vantage point of the River Danube. She was bundled up in a quilted puffer coat, wearing boots, a hat and gloves. So was he. It was the fifth day of their honeymoon and they had managed to see up close and inside several of the fabulous neo-Gothic buildings they now viewed from the river from a different perspective. After they'd managed to drag themselves out of the bedroom, that was. But wasn't that what honeymooners did? Made love at any opportunity?

The boat passed the magnificent Houses of Parliament, so expansive they seemed to take up most of the river frontage on the Pest side. They had been one of the first of the beautiful Budapest buildings they'd visited. The next day, they'd walked over the Chain Bridge and taken the steep funicular up Castle Hill to explore the castle and the Fisherman's Bastion, with its multitude of turrets. They'd listened to a classical music concert in the ornately beautiful Matthias Church. Then walked around the well-preserved old town, marvelling at how lovely it was. On another day, they'd listened to a choir in the awe-inspiring St Stephen's Basilica back on the Pest side.

But what Connor had enjoyed most was wandering around downtown Pest with Ana, just taking in the Opera House, the galleries, shops, cafes, restaurants and the various landmarks. He was fascinated by a different city and a different way of life. When they'd veered off the main streets, they'd found themselves in a cobbled square around an ornate fountain, as if they'd stepped back in time. Or they'd come across a monument to a long-ago prince or general on horseback. There seemed to be a lot of equestrian monuments in Budapest, much to Ana's and his delight. They'd taken selfies in front of each one they'd encountered.

Ana had exclaimed at the number of posters promoting art galleries, concerts, the ballet and the opera—Budapest was a cultural city. The previous day, she'd spent a morning with her Great-Uncle Istvan in his jeweller's workshop, learning from him. Connor had roamed the city on his own. 'More of a case of learning how much I didn't know about designing and making jewellery,' she'd told him on her return.

The previous night Ana's second cousins—the children of her mother's cousins, who were around the same age as Ana—took them on a ruin bar crawl, which had been a lot of fun. The cousins had been amazed at Ana's fluent Hungarian.

Yesterday afternoon they'd braved one of the thermal mineral spas for which Budapest was famed. They'd chosen the elegant art nouveau Gellert private baths in Buda for their experience. Connor hadn't really cared much for sitting in his swimming trunks in a large bath of very hot mineralised water, full of strangers, then getting into another even hotter one. But Ana had loved the experience, telling him it was very good for the skin. She wanted to go back.

Another welcome discovery about Budapest was that the food was every bit as good as Ana had assured him it would be. They'd eaten in a traditional Hungarian restaurant, serenaded by violinists playing folk music, and had been offered Tokaji, the famous Hungarian sweet dessert wine. Another memorable meal had been in the downtown Market Hall, which they had discovered by chance as they'd walked around the area. Duck breast and red cabbage served in enamel bowls in a fashionable restaurant overlooking the river to Buda had been another highlight.

A disproportionate number of meals had been delivered to Ana and him via room service as they'd made up for lost time in bed. He was greedier for Ana than he was for food. And she seemed to feel the same way about him.

Ana's wise grandfather, Zoltan, had told him Ana needed to spend time in Budapest. To appreciate that her heritage was as much this cultured and sophisticated city as it was the Outback of South Australia. To appreciate that she didn't need to feel second best because of the way her father had deprived her of knowledge of her Australian family. What pleased Connor most of all about this trip was that it was having exactly the effect he'd hoped on Ana. He had never seen her happier or more confident in herself as a person.

He watched her now. They were each listening to a headphone commentary of the landmarks along the river. His was in English. Ana had chosen to have the Hungarian one, as she wanted to expose herself to as much of the language she could while they were in Budapest. The descriptions of the landmarks were interspersed with the music of Franz Liszt, Hungary's famous nineteenth-century composer.

The trouble with them being on holiday in such a different place, discovering a whole new relationship as lovers, was that talk of the future had been put on hold. During these honeymoon days—and nights—discovering each other in a very different way, he'd decided he wanted to secure a future with Ana. Forget this pretend marriage scenario. He wanted her as his wife for real. He just hoped she felt the same.

There were just a few plans to fall into place before he actually said anything to her. The most important of those plans was buying a house. Not just any house, but a house in St Kilda that Ana had always liked. It was a grand old house in the style Australians termed 'Federation'. They'd passed the house when walking home from primary school. Even then she'd liked it.

After they'd announced their 'engagement', he and Ana had discussed where they would live after the wedding. They'd decided on her house, which made sense. She had a guest bedroom and she didn't care for his ultra-modern apartment. Truth be told, neither did he. It was more an investment than a home. All his real estate purchases had been investments. Back in Melbourne, Ana had told him that, once her inheritance was settled, she intended to knock on the door of the house she admired and make an offer for it. Ana knew from chatting over the fence with the widowed owner that the large house and garden were getting too much for her.

The day after they'd first made love, Connor had instructed an estate agent to negotiate the purchase of the house on his behalf. It would be an excellent house for them to live and later raise a family in. That was how serious he was about making this mock marriage a real one. He loved her and he wanted her as his wife. But how did he talk marriage to a woman to whom he was already married, and who had repeatedly said didn't want to be tied down by marriage?

It was snowing in Budapest, big, white flakes drifting slowly down from the sky to frost with white everywhere it landed. But it was as if the sun was shining in Ana's heart. Exploring the city with Connor was like carrying her own sunshine with her. After the river tour ended, they strolled hand in hand from the dock back towards their hotel. She couldn't bear to let go of his hand. Had to keep glancing up to reassure herself he was there. When he caught her eye, his smile reassured her. Then he dropped a kiss on her mouth, their lips frosty cold.

So this was what it was like to be in love—truly in love. She loved Connor. She couldn't deny it for a second longer. She'd never felt anything for anyone else that came close to her feelings for him. Something about him called to her heart like no one else had.

She'd fallen in love with him back when she'd been fifteen, about the time of that first kiss. She hadn't been too young to fall in love—maybe too young to do anything about it, but not too young to feel that emotion as fiercely as she had. She'd never fallen out of love with him. Just repressed it and denied it. No wonder she'd never found love with anyone else. Her heart had put the shutters up against anyone who wasn't Connor.

Did he feel the same for her? Sometimes she thought so. Other times she couldn't be sure. They'd certainly crossed out of the friend zone. The sex was amazing—passionate, energetic, tender at times. But, emotionally, she wasn't sure if Connor felt the same way she did. There was the friendly banter, laughs and multiple orgasms. But was there love? And, even if there was love, was there a future?

As far as the mock marriage went, they were still in the same uncertain place. Connor hadn't changed his views on trust and commitment. Or, if he had, he certainly hadn't told her. Was this a friends-with-benefits scenario? She'd never been in such an arrangement to know. Was the plan to stay lovers once the honeymoon was over and they were back to faking a marriage in Melbourne? They had discussed, to keep up the pretence, he would move into her house for as long as it took for the inheritance to come through. Then they'd separate and divorce proceedings would commence once the statutory year of separation had passed. One way or the other, that wouldn't be later than the end of May. Rose would either marry or she wouldn't by that date.

The uncertainty was beginning to make Ana feel edgy again. She would have to say something to Connor. But that wouldn't be easy. She didn't know how or where to start. She thought about it with every step on the walk back to the hotel.

When they got back to their suite, they took off their warm coats and boots. But not for long. Almost straight away, Connor got a call which he took in the other room. 'I'm going to have to go out again,' he said, when he came back.

Darn. Further delay in that much-needed talk about their future.

'Money Club business?'

'No.'

'Shopping?'

'No.'

'Don't tell me—you're sneaking out for another thermal bath?'

'No.' He seemed distracted, as if he'd barely heard her. He hadn't even cracked a smile at the thought of him visiting the spa. 'I'll tell you when we catch up again. Can we meet at that coffee house in an hour? I know you love it and want to go there again.'

Ana's grandmother had taken her to the splendidly ornate coffee house on Vörösmarty Square on her first visit to Budapest when she'd been fifteen. It was a combined café, cake shop and chocolate shop. What wasn't there to love about it?

But her mouth went dry at Connor's evasiveness. Why would he want to go out in Budapest without her? Was he already tiring of her non-stop company? After all, it wasn't a real honeymoon.

Her old insecurities came rushing back. *Was it something she'd done wrong?* Suddenly she didn't feel at all like coffee and a slice of *dobos torte*.

'Sure. I'll see you there in an hour,' she said, forcing her voice to sound normal.

He'd been gone for half an hour when his phone rang. In his rush to go out, he'd left it on the table in the living area. She let it ring out, but it rang again. There was something about an insistently ringing phone that got to her. She picked it up.

'Connor O'Neill's phone,' she said.

'May I speak to Connor, please?' It was a man's voice.

'I'm afraid he's not here; can I take a message for you?'

'Is that Mrs O'Neill?' Again, her mind went momentarily blank at the name.

'Yes. Yes, it is.'

The man identified himself as a St Kilda estate agent.

'Could you please tell him, the sale completed half an hour ago. He's now the owner of a magnificent house in St Kilda.'

The agent told her the address. She knew the house only too well. A big, old, turn-of-the-twentieth-century house on one of the best streets in St Kilda. She used to walk past it on the way to the restaurant from school. All gabled roofs, ornate carved wood trims and stained glass. A beautiful house she had seen deteriorate in recent years as the upkeep had become too much for the elderly widow who lived there. Worth multiple millions. It was her dream house. She'd planned to buy it when her inheritance came through. Why would Connor buy it for himself when he knew how much she wanted it? Knowing him, it wouldn't even be to live in. It would be as an investment.

'Congratulations, Mrs O'Neill,' the agent said.

'Th...thank you,' she said, and disconnected the call.

Connor had bought a house? That house? And he hadn't told her. Why? There was no real reason he should tell her of his business dealings. But a house. A house was such a personal thing. That particular house was so beautiful. It should be *her* house, not an investment for the Money Club.

She slipped on her coat and gloves. She wasn't wearing the lavish engagement ring. She'd taken it off when she'd spent time with her great-uncle and hadn't put it back on. He would spot it as a lab-made diamond and might ask questions. Not that there was anything wrong with lab-made. Some found that kind of diamond more ethical and environmentally friendly. But a lab-made diamond lacked the tiny imperfections of one that had formed underground over millions of years. Fake. Like her marriage to Connor.

Her feet dragged as she made her way over the slippery,

cobbled streets to the coffee shop. For the first time, she felt reluctant to see her friend. She would have to challenge him about the house and she didn't like confrontations. She loved that house. He would probably maximise profit by turning it into apartments or, worse, pull it down and rebuild.

He was there at a table, waiting for her. She could tell by the tense set of his shoulders something had happened. She hung her coat on a rack and went towards him. He got up to greet her, unsmiling. Why? What had happened after he'd left the hotel? What had the call been about that had taken him away from her? And what had upset him? It couldn't be as bad as picking up the phone to find her fake husband had gazumped her on the house she'd told him she intended to buy. He was a fine person to talk about trust.

She certainly didn't feel like smiling. In fact, she could hardly bear to look at him. They exchanged terse greetings. She didn't meet his gaze. The waiter took her order for coffee. No cake; it would choke her. She took out his phone from her shoulder bag and slid it across the table to him.

'Thank you,' he said, taking it. 'I realised I'd left it behind when it was too late to turn back.'

'I answered a call for you,' she said.

He frowned. 'Who from?'

'An estate agent in Melbourne. It's very late in the day there. Congratulations. Apparently you're the owner of a beautiful Federation house in St Kilda. The sale just completed.'

'Good,' he said, still unsmiling. 'I was waiting for that news.'

'Why did you keep that secret from me, Connor—that you'd gazumped me on the house I told you I wanted to buy? I know we're not really husband and wife, but we are friends.' *Just friends.* 'You didn't need to exclude me.'

'I wanted to wait until the sale actually completed. And tell you when we had a talk about our future.'

'And when was that going to be?' she said.

He leaned across the table towards her. 'Perhaps after you told me you were planning to spend three months living in Budapest and working with your great-uncle.'

She gasped. 'How did you—?'

'Find out about that?'

'Yes.'

'That call I took back in the hotel was from your great-uncle.'

'Why would he call you?'

'He thinks I'm your husband, for one thing. Is it true? Are you planning to come and live here? I can't believe you didn't tell me.' Connor's mouth was set in a tight line, his eyes cold.

'It was something I discussed with him, yes. An idea— more his idea than mine, actually. I could learn so much from him. But, Connor, I wouldn't do that without talking it over with you.'

'Wouldn't you?' he said.

'Like I wouldn't buy a house without telling you. Especially if I knew it was your dream house. Especially after the last few days. I thought… I thought we'd… Never mind.'

'I wanted it to be a surprise for you.'

'For me? Really? Why would you make a purchase like that without involving me? I'm really over people making decisions on my behalf. My parents. My grandparents. Surely not you too?'

He frowned. 'It seemed the right thing to do. I knew

you'd always liked that house. I'd planned to buy in St Kilda for a while. I had estate agents keeping an eye out for the right house for me from back when I was living in Sydney. The agent told me only recently that particular house had just gone up for sale. There was immediate interest in it. I had to move quickly to secure it.'

'It actually went on the market? What happened to the old lady who lived there?'

'She's gone to live with her daughter. It got too much for her to upkeep.'

So she would have missed out on the house anyway. The owner had told her she would contact her if she was thinking of selling, but the lovely lady's memory probably wasn't the best. Still, it was a decision she should have made for herself.

'I'm glad. For her, I mean. She was a nice old lady. I'm glad she's being looked after.'

'Her family knew the value of the place right down to the last cent.'

'Lucky you got it, then,' she said. She still couldn't understand why he hadn't told her.

'Not luck. Hard negotiating skills,' he said. 'Seriously. I bought the house for you, Ana. Because I knew how much you loved it. Not to control you, but for us to make a home together. I really wanted to surprise you. A wedding present, if you will. But, if you feel so strongly about it, how about I put the house in your name? Then, when you inherit, you can buy me out.'

Make a home together? What did he mean by that? 'You'd do that? You'd seriously do that?' she said.

'Yes,' he said. 'If it makes you less cranky with me. I could see us living there.'

'As…as friends?'

'We'll always be friends.'

Her heart sank. *Just friends.*

His gaze was intent, searching. 'But also as more than friends. As…as a couple.'

'Seriously?' Ana paused to take in the import of what he'd said.

He nodded. 'But then I heard you're planning to live in Budapest. Without saying a word to me.'

'You know why I talked to my great-uncle about coming here to live?' She kept her voice low. The café was large and busy, but she didn't want such a private conversation to be overheard. 'It was because when we got divorced, as planned, I would have somewhere to run to. My escape. I would have to be far away. It would be too painful to have to see you. My ex-husband.'

Connor frowned. 'When Great-Uncle Istvan told me about the visit, I assumed you wanted to get out of the mock to come and live here. To put me behind you.'

'That's not what I want at all,' she said, her voice unsteady.

'Me neither,' he said.

'I love you, Connor.' The 'L' word slipped out without her planning it. 'There. I've said it.' *She felt it.* 'The thought of not being with you is unbearable. You talk about being a couple, yet we've said nothing about a future with each other. And…and we're in the situation where we're married but not really married.'

The Connor smile was back, easing the tense lines of his face. 'You love me? As more than a friend?'

'Yes,' she said. 'I think I've always loved you. There I go, throwing myself at you again.'

He reached over the table to take both her hands in his. His green eyes searched her face. 'I love you too, Ana.

With all my heart. I believe I've always loved you. I just didn't recognise it.'

'Can you say that again, please? The "I love you", I mean? I really, really like the sound of it.' She was smiling, at the same time trying to stave off tears of joy.

'I'll say it as many times as you want. These last few days have been the happiest of my life.'

'Oh, Connor.' She blinked to hold back the tears. 'I… I can't tell you how happy that makes me. I love you so much.'

'If that's what you want, I'll say I love you twenty times a day for a lifetime,' he said. 'I want us to stay married. To have a real marriage. A committed marriage.'

'But…but you said you didn't want to get married. For real, I mean. You didn't trust yourself to not act like your father.'

'And you said you wanted to fly free without being tied down by marriage.'

'Marriage to anyone but you, I meant,' she said. 'I know you won't clip my wings, Connor.'

'When it comes to loving you, I trust you. More importantly, I trust myself,' he said.

She kissed him across the table. 'I've always known I could trust you.'

'I know you have. You've always believed in me.'

'And you've always been on my side.'

'I want us to live in that house together, Ana. I bought it for us. It needs total renovation, but I think you would enjoy that. It's a family home. We could raise a family there.'

'A family? We're talking children?'

'Yes. A real marriage. With everything that comes with it: Children. A dog. A cat. When we're both ready, that is. I don't want to push you into anything.'

'I couldn't think of anything more wonderful,' she said, kissing him again. It was a sweet kiss of affirmation, love and a happiness that was bubbling through her.

Connor pulled back from the kiss. 'You haven't asked me why your great-uncle called me. It's unlike you not to be more curious.'

'I've been too busy being happy that you love me like I love you. But now I'm curious. Why did he call you?'

Connor pulled a small velvet box from his jacket pocket. It had her uncle's store logo engraved on it. 'He called me to tell me this was ready to pick up.'

'You bought me jewellery?'

Connor flipped open the box and took out a ring. A gorgeous blue sapphire, baguette-cut, flanked by two baguette diamonds on a fine platinum band.

Ana gasped. 'Connor, that's my dream ring.'

'I know. I remember you telling me that's what you'd make for yourself. I thought, if we're going to have a real marriage, we should have a real engagement ring.'

She kissed him again. 'It's perfect. Absolutely perfect. And made by my great-uncle, which makes it even more perfect. What did you tell him?'

'That you didn't much care for the diamond ring I'd chosen for you. That I wanted to get you a ring that you'd love, as you'd be wearing it for the rest of your life.'

'He'd understand that.'

'So how do I propose to a woman I'm already married to?' Connor paused for a breath. 'Ana, my love, will you be my wife—my wife for real?'

Ana thought her heart would burst with happiness. 'Oh, yes, Connor. Yes, yes and yes!'

He slid the ring over her wedding band on the third finger of her left hand and kissed her again. 'I love you.'

'I love you too.' She would never tire of saying it.

There was a smattering of polite applause. Ana looked around to see they had quite an audience of smiling people at the tables nearby. She held up her hand to show them her ring and smiled, her heart so full of joy she wanted to share it with the world.

She was Connor's wife. And she'd found the best of all possible husbands living next door.

EPILOGUE

Garrison Downs,
first week of February, summer

GARRISON DOWNS IN February was sweltering. The sun
beat down from a sky bluer than the bluest Waverly eyes
onto the red dirt and thirsty grey foliage. It was too hot
even for insects to hum. From the homestead gardens
wafted the light, fresh scent of lavender. Could there be
a greater contrast to the snow-frosted Budapest she and
Connor had left just ten days ago, Ana thought.

And this time Ana had a feeling of coming home. That
she belonged here on the sprawling Outback kingdom of
the Waverlys. Not a permanent home. Not that. Not now.
Maybe not ever. Her life with Connor was in Melbourne.
And Budapest too.

They had already started work on the restoration of
the St Kilda mansion which they planned to make their
permanent home. The major work would be done while
they spent three months in Budapest—she working with
her great-uncle, Connor working with an international
veterinary aid organisation. Their house would be ready
for them when they got back. Connor joked that he hoped
there would be nice neighbours, so that any children they
might be blessed with could make friends with the kids

next door. After all, that was how he'd met his wife when she had come hurtling through the hedge.

But that was for the future. The reason Ana felt at home here now was not so much the property, the cattle business, the beautiful homestead or even the horses. What would keep her coming back to Garrison Downs was her sisters. That was why she was here now, for the unveiling of the new portrait of all four of them.

Rose, Eve and Tilly had brought unimagined joy into her life—they were the greatest gifts her father had bequeathed to her. The Horvath family had also embraced the sisters as new family members brought into the fold. It turned out Lili had spent quite some time with Rose and Eve at the wedding. Past resentments and pain had been well and truly buried. Eve's baby, due in June, would be welcomed with excitement and love as the first grandchild in the extended family.

Ana's friendship circle had also been widened by the men her sisters had married. On their recent visit to Chaleur, she and Connor had immediately connected with the charming Prince Henri, who made Princess Matilda so happy. Nate had become a friend too, as well as their trusted lawyer.

There was just the one dim cloud on the horizon of her bright future at Garrison Downs. All four sisters had to be married by the end of May. Three of them were now married. Only Rose remained unwed. Her oldest sister had assured the others not to worry, there were plans afoot. But she would give no further detail. It wasn't in Rose's nature to tantalise, but tantalise she had with that hint that her husband hunt had commenced. It remained for them all to see how it ended. Ana felt confident that Rose would never allow Garrison Downs to fall out of Waverly hands.

Another reason that Ana now felt at home here, was that the ongoing speculation and gossip swirling around the family since her father's death had been addressed by a public acknowledgement of her. The Waverly family had just released a carefully worded statement to the press. It welcomed into the family Holt's youngest daughter to a woman other than his wife, their half-sister, Anastasia. The statement had finally lifted the oppressive shadow of secrecy she had lived under all her life. Already there was avid interest in such a juicy story. All media requests for interviews and background material were being professionally handled by Eve, the family's own PR maven. Eve would fiercely protect their privacy and dignity.

The unveiling of the new portrait of the four Waverly sisters had now become symbolic of their unity. Eve had suggested the painting might even become a focus for a carefully curated story about the newly united family to feature in one of the weekend newspaper magazines. The large painting was to be hung in the family dining room in the space vacated by the old one. The sisters had commissioned the same eminent artist who had painted the original portrait, as well as the portrait of Holt that hung in his study. He'd been a friend of Holt. It was in honour of Holt's memory that he had come out of retirement to do the new portrait. In return for a hefty fee, of course.

With Tilly in Chaleur, the four sisters weren't able to come together at the same time to pose for the portrait. On her previous visit, Ana had followed the artist's instructions to pose informally with Rose and Eve on the steps of the back veranda of the homestead, near the big, old dented metal bell that was a feature. Lindy, the housekeeper, had stood in for Tilly, even though she was a head shorter. The artist had then painted from photographs and his memories of Garrison Downs, which he had visited on many occasions.

The bell used to be attached to the original old settler's cottage to call back home for meals the workers of generations gone by. As children, the three older sisters had known it as a signal to cease whatever mischief they were up to outside and come in.

Now the sisters and the two husbands headed into the cool of the air-conditioned homestead to view the portrait. Ana couldn't help a gasp when she saw it, echoed by both of her nearby sisters and Tilly, watching via video. Connor held her hand in a firm grip. Her beloved husband knew this would be an emotional moment for her. He was there, as he always had been, caring for her and supporting her. They'd gone from friends to lovers. Lovers was infinitely better!

The portrait, done in oils and entitled *Sisters*, was outstanding, breath-taking in the way it portrayed its subjects. Not only did it capture the beauty of the four young women but somehow also their intelligence, kindness and the pleasure they took in each other's company. The significance of the bell was that it had called the four sisters home and would continue to call them home at different times of their lives.

Although their colourings were different, there was a facial resemblance in all four of the sisters that clearly showed they were related. But it was the Waverly eyes, masterfully painted to look so blue and alive, that were the ultimate proof of their shared DNA.

Eve had suggested they all wear blue. It had been a genius idea. Rose wore a tailored trouser suit in a deep powder-blue, brown hair pulled back in her signature ponytail. She, the boss, was closest to the bell.

Tilly was carefree in denim overalls, with her luxuriant blonde hair flowing loose below her shoulders and her wide, generous smile caught halfway to laughter. She sat on the top step, her knees hugged to her chest.

Eve looked elegant in a fitted pencil dress in a clear ice-blue that didn't show her baby bump at all. Her pale-blonde hair was pulled back in a bun, her expression relaxed and open to all the happiness that had found her.

Ana was pleased with the way she was portrayed—close, connected, very much a part of it, as if she had always been on that veranda with her sisters. She wore a pretty dress with big puffed sleeves in the softest shade of indigo. Her black hair was in a messy bun, soft tendrils framing her face and gentle, thoughtful smile.

Integral to the portrait were the sister bracelets Ana had crafted for each of them with intuition and affection. Also connecting all four sisters was River. The big old border collie, his head resting on his front paws, lay by Rose's feet, the other three sisters within patting distance. The artist had captured River's sweet doggy smile and caught his long, feathery tail mid-thump.

'I think we all scrub up well,' said Rose, pride in her family underscoring her voice.

'Yes, we do,' said Eve. 'I can't fault a thing.'

'I just wish I could be there to hug you all,' said Tilly, through the video phone, her voice shaky. Her royal duties still kept her in Chaleur and, as Garrison Downs was so far away from the principality, it was impossible for her to have made a quick trip to visit for the weekend as Ana and Connor had done. 'But I'm there in spirit,' she said.

'The Outback princesses of Garrison Downs in their full splendour,' said Connor.

'Without a doubt, the most beautiful sisters in Australia,' said Nate.

'My sisters, the sisters I always dreamed of being with,' said Ana, her voice choked with emotion.

Connor pulled her tight against his chest and dropped a kiss on her mouth.

What had her mother said, back in the dire days of the husband hunt? *Love comes to you when you don't expect it. You have to be open to love for it to find you.*

Love had found her, big-time. Not just the love of Connor, her once-in-a-lifetime love, her husband, the man she adored, her best friend. But also the different kind of love she had found with her sisters.

And she couldn't be happier.

* * * * *

CLAIMING HIS BILLION-DOLLAR BRIDE

MICHELLE DOUGLAS

MILLS & BOON

To Ally, Rachael and Kandy.

Ladies, you're absolute goddesses!

I'm missing the daily emails, the flurry of questions, the brainstorming and the laughter.

I heart you guys so hard.

Wanna do it again sometime? :)

PROLOGUE

Garrison Downs,
June

ROSE STARED AT George Harrington who sat behind her father's desk in her father's chair and it took all of her strength not to stand up and yell at him to get out from behind it. The aging family lawyer didn't deserve that. He'd checked with her first, had asked her permission. It made sense that he sat where the rest of the room could see him.

But it still felt like sacrilege.

Glancing out of the French windows at the ancient gums, golden grasses and red dirt in the middle distance, she searched for calm, aching to turn and clasp Tilly's hand, but afraid if she did she might actually burst into ugly sobs. She wouldn't freak Tilly out like that. Concentrating on her breathing, she sent Tilly all the *buck-up, you're-not-alone* sister vibes that she could.

For the past month, she and her sisters had survived the shock of their father's death, the national outpouring of grief that had followed, and all the pomp and ceremony of a state funeral. Only allowing themselves to grieve in tiny pockets of downtime. For Holt Waverly, their father, had been a national icon, a legend, and everyone had wanted to claim him as their own.

Everyone had had a story they'd wanted to tell. Everyone

had wanted their share of the… In her darker moments she called it drama, but she knew it was a combination of shock and grief—lesser than hers admittedly, but real nonetheless. She'd managed to say all that was right and appropriate when cameras had flashed in her face half blinding her, microphones shoved under her nose and questions barked at her.

'Your father's death must've come as a shock?'

'How much of an impact will this have on Garrison Downs?'

'You must be missing him?'

She'd had to steel herself over and over. Calling the media morons wouldn't help anyone, it wouldn't do Holt proud. And she'd do him proud now if it killed her.

As aware as she was of Tilly on the sofa behind her, she was equally aware of Eve on the big screen on the back wall, video-conferencing in from her office in London.

A bitter smile twisted through her. When she said she and her sisters had got through the shock and ordeal of the last month, she meant she and Tilly. Eve hadn't been here. Eve hadn't come home. Not even for the funeral.

Rose had reconciled herself to never knowing what had happened between Eve and their father, but to not come home…to not—

Don't think about that now.

Once this will-reading was done, she could stride out of here and make sure the section of fence at Devil's Bend had been fixed, get an update on Jasper's swollen fetlock, ensure that Aaron, her head stockman, had a handle on the bore-running rota she'd set up, and that Ricky and Blue, the new station hands, were keeping their late-night partying within limits. The boys were young, but complaints had been made and there were phone calls from fretting mothers to negotiate. After that she really needed to make a start on the backlog of correspondence, schedule an appointment with the accountant, and at some point next week she needed to check in with Franz Arteta about their contract.

There was *so* much to do. Her father had made it look easy, but it wasn't. At least, it wasn't for her. How on earth was she supposed to fill such big shoes? How—?

Don't think about that now.

She refocussed on the view outside again. There were too many people in the room—she could see their reflections in the window glass as they moved—and George Harrington's voice droned on and on.

Bequests were made to various agricultural organisations, and the academic and industry-based research projects Holt had sponsored, a generous donation made to the arts—no doubt in honour of Tilly, which briefly made her smile—and an ongoing commitment pledged to the fund set up in their mother's name for cancer research.

Eventually George paused, cleared his throat. 'To my daughters, I leave all my worldly possessions not listed hereupon, including, but not limited to, the entirety of Garrison Downs.'

The voice seemed to come from a long way away. And now that the reading of the will was drawing to a close, Rose contrarily wanted to slow time. These were the last words her father would ever speak to her. She wasn't ready. He should still be here laughing with them, offering advice in his quiet laconic way, riding out on his black stallion, Jasper, and living to a ripe old age here on the land he loved.

'Let it be known that it is my wish that my eldest daughter, Rose Lavigne Waverly, take over full control of management of Garrison Downs. If that is *her* wish. If not, I bow to her choice.'

She flinched. She'd always expected to take over one day.

Her father and grandfather had instilled in her a deep love of the land, had groomed her to one day take up the reins of Garrison Downs.

But not yet.

'At this point, could we please clear the room,' George said, 'of everyone bar family?'

She let out a careful breath, didn't turn to watch as people filed out. Perhaps Dad had left them some final word—a loving message meant for their ears only.

George took off his glasses and rubbed his hand across his forehead.

She leaned forward.

'There is a condition placed over the bequest. One that has been attached to the property since its transfer to your family years ago.'

George laid his glasses on top of the papers in front of him. 'As I'm sure you know, the history of Garrison Downs is…complicated, what with your great-great-grandmother having won the land from the Garrison family in a poker game in 1904.'

That poker match had become local legend—one of those tales of derring-do that was bandied about whenever the beer flowed too freely. But it had also been the cause of a lot of ill will between the Waverly and Garrison families.

'Any time the land has been passed down since, certain conditions had to be met.' He read from the will directly. 'Any male Waverly heir, currently living, naturally inherits the estate.'

'Naturally,' Rose murmured, rolling her eyes.

'But,' George continued, 'if the situation arises where there is no direct male heir, any and all daughters, of marrying age, must be wed within a year of the reading of the will, in order to inherit as a whole.'

She stared, tried to make sense of the words he'd uttered. On the screen behind her, Eve laughed.

She swung around. 'You think this is *funny*?'

'I think it's hilarious, Rose. I mean, come on, what century do you think we're in, Harrington?'

Eve sounded so sure. Rose shook her head. This had to be someone's idea of a sick joke. 'What am I missing?'

'The land,' Tilly said quietly, 'is entailed to sons. If there is no son, the Waverly women can inherit, but only if all of us are married.'

Rose gripped the arms of her chair so hard her fingers started to ache. Then she leapt up to pace. 'That can't possibly be legal, not in this day and age. Surely?'

'Too right, it can't be,' Eve said, sounding battle-ready.

'It is…arcane,' said George. 'But it has been a part of the lore of this land for several generations. So far as I see it, and so far as your father must have wanted, it stands.'

She slammed her hands to her hips. 'How has this never come up before?'

'Sons,' said Tilly. 'Dad was an only child. Pop only had brothers, though one died of measles and the other drowned, meaning the farm passed straight to him. Waverlys have always been most excellent at having at least one strapping farm-loving son. Until us.'

Rose swung to Tilly, lifted her hands as if to say, *What the actual…?*

Tilly nodded, silently saying, *I know, right?*

But there was no time for that. She planted her feet, turned back. 'And what happens if we refuse to…marry?'

'If the condition is not met, the land goes back to the current head of the Garrison family. Clay Garrison.'

'That double-dealing, underhand, two-faced old goat can't tell the back end of a bull from the front.'

George winced. 'The son seems a reasonable sort—'

'*Lincoln?* If he stopped partying long enough to even notice the level of responsibility coming his way...' She pressed her palms to her eyes and tried to stop treacherous toes from curling as pictures of Lincoln flooded her mind. 'If our land, our home, the business that we've built—' *that her father had built* '—fell into their hands, I—I can't even think it.'

This land was her destiny and had been ever since she'd understood what that word meant. She couldn't let her father down, Pop, all the Waverlys before her...or the generations of Waverlys to come. A wave of dizziness shook her and she braced her hands on her knees, forced herself to breathe slowly and deeply.

'Don't waste your time worrying about it, Rose, because it isn't going to happen,' Eve assured her from the screen. 'Not now. Not ever.'

George's gaze moved from her to Tilly...and Eve...and to the far wall. 'As it stands, unless all four of Holt Waverly's daughters are married within twelve months of the reading of this document—'

'Twelve months?' Rose straightened. 'But I can't... I'm not... I mean, none of us are even *seeing* anyone right now. Are we? Eve? Tilly?'

Tilly shook her head.

Rose went to glance at the screen but stopped herself at the last moment. What was the point? Eve shared so little of herself these days.

'Wait.' Tilly sat bolt upright. 'Back up a second. You said *four* daughters. There are only three of us.'

Rose followed Tilly's gaze to a slight dark-haired woman she hadn't noticed, sitting in their mother's chair. The young woman rose.

'Who are you?' Tilly asked, not unkindly. But then Tilly

was constitutionally incapable of unkindness. It was one of the things they all loved about her.

The unknown woman swallowed, looking as if she wished herself a million miles away. 'Ana.'

'Who are you talking to, Tilly?' Eve said. 'I can't see.'

Her father's chair squeaked as George raced out from behind the desk, moving towards this Ana, his hand outstretched. 'Come forward, girl.'

Ana moved forward with a hesitant step.

'Anastasia, this is Matilda Waverly.' George smiled at Tilly. 'That there is Rose. And up on the screen is Evelyn. Girls, this is Anastasia Horvath.'

All the hairs on Rose's arms lifted. *Four* daughters.

No, that couldn't—

'Ana, here, is your father's daughter. Your half-sister. And therefore, according to your father's will…'

The rest of George's words faded away. *Half-sister!*

Spots formed in front of her eyes. The room spun. She'd known her parents' marriage had experienced rocky moments, but her father had adored his wife. He'd adored *them*. He'd have never…

But Anastasia's eyes were the same piercing blue as hers, Tilly's and Eve's. As Holt's. And George would know. He'd *know* the truth. He'd never allow an imposter to claim part of Holt Waverly's legacy.

George collapsed to the arm of the velvet sofa saying something about them still having their trusts and being wealthy women in their own rights. 'But the land itself, the Garrison Downs station and all of its holdings, will belong to the Garrison family unless you, Rose, Evelyn, Matilda, *and* Anastasia, are all married within the next twelve months.'

Even Ana was expected to shoulder this ridiculous burden?

When she'd never been allowed to be a part of their lives?

Reaching out, Rose grabbed the back of her chair, pieces of a giant jigsaw puzzle assembling themselves in her mind, falling into place—making a picture she didn't want to see.

'Rose?' Tilly started.

'Hang on, Evie.' She lifted her head to meet Eve's eyes fully for the first time in too long. 'Did you *know*? Is this why—?'

'I have to go,' said Eve just before her face abruptly disappeared as she disconnected from the call. Rose stared at the blank screen, her chest burning. Evie had known about her father's affair.

Oh, Evie, you shouldn't have had to bear that on your own.

She clenched her hands so hard she started to shake. How dared he? How dared her father keep a sister from them?

She stared at the door, willing him to walk through it and explain, to make things right somehow. A harsh laugh scraped her throat raw. An impossibility. An impossibility even if he were still alive!

Clenching her hands, she started for the door. If she didn't get out of here, she'd explode, and nobody in the room deserved that. 'I can't—I don't have time for this. I have a station to run.'

But before she strode out of the door she pointed at Ana. 'Stay!' She barked it like an order, as she would at some cocky station hand who'd tested her authority. She didn't mean to sound so bossy, but her voice was beyond control.

Continuing through the door, she hollered, 'Lindy, can you see that the yellow suite is made up for Anastasia, please? She'll be staying with us for a bit.'

CHAPTER ONE

ROSE STRODE INTO Holt's office, seized the calendar from the wall and counted the days down to the big red X marked in June.

Ninety days.

Ninety days! What the freaking heck...?

Flipping back, she counted again. Why had she left it so long?

Tilly had married her Henri and was a *princess*—oozing ecstasy and joy as was her wont. Evie was blissfully married to Nate with a baby on the way. And now Anastasia, who she'd not have blamed for clutching her trust fund to her chest and running for the hills—

She spun to glare at Holt's chair, but she didn't rant and rail at him as she had the day of his will-reading. She didn't speak to him at all. 'Beat the crap out of him, Pop,' she murmured instead.

She didn't know if other people spoke to their dead, but she'd spoken to her grandfather ever since he'd died when she was nineteen. Her grandmother, not so much. Unless it was to point out the stupidity of all of Katherine's previous strident advice. Her mother she'd chat to in the garden—telling her how her roses were coming along, describing the scent of the jasmine as the heat of a spring day cooled...telling her how much she missed her.

Swinging away, she slapped the calendar against her leg before hanging it back on the wall. Ana hadn't turned her back on them. Instead she was now married to her childhood friend, Connor, and so in love it hurt.

Her sisters had *all* met the terms of that stupid conditional bequest. Which meant Rose was now last man—*woman*—standing. If she didn't want to let her sisters down, she had to marry. If she didn't want to lose her home, she had to marry.

And the thought of losing Garrison Downs...

Reaching up, she retied her ponytail with fingers that shook. She *couldn't* let that happen.

Glaring at the calendar, she tilted her chin. 'Ninety days.' Not impossible. She pushed her shoulders back and swallowed. 'Piece of cake.'

'Talking to yourself again, Rose?'

Eve sauntered into the office in all her maternal contentment and smug in-loveness, and it made Rose want to laugh and wrap her sister in a bearhug. 'I don't get as much sense from anyone else.' She nodded at Evie's glorious baby bump. 'But when you pop out my niece I might finally get some decent conversation around here.'

Eve grinned, but sobered when she glanced at the calendar. 'You don't have to marry. You know that, right?'

Just like Evie to cut straight to the chase. But...

Of course she had to marry. It was the only honourable thing to do. With Evie finally making Garrison Downs her home again, after it had taken so long to lure her back... Oh, no, Rose wasn't risking that.

Reaching out, she traced a finger across that big red X. 'But I believe I'm going to.' She'd do whatever necessary to keep Garrison Downs.

'You haven't been on a single date in the last nine months.

You spend all your time with cattle and stockmen—' Evie broke off, eyes narrowing. 'You can't marry Aaron.'

She turned, curious to hear her sister's objections to her marrying Garrison Downs' head stockman. 'Why not?'

'He's fifteen years older than you!'

'So?'

'And he's being a pig to you at the moment.'

'I have it in hand.' Though, in truth, it was taking longer and proving trickier than expected. Holt would've had it sorted already—

She cut the thought dead, but not before a bone-crushing weight slammed down on her shoulders.

'And I saw him and Lindy looking very cosy the other night.'

Ah, a romance was brewing between Aaron and their housekeeper...

'Aaron was Plan B.' And he could just as easily be replaced with Johnno or Nick or one of the other stockmen.

'Then who on earth is Plan A?'

Folding her arms, she leaned back against the desk, the plan that had been brewing in her mind for the last few months emerging in a starburst of decision. 'Lincoln Garrison.' Energy powered through her when she said his name, lifting the weight from her shoulders and tossing it to the four winds.

'Linc Garrison?' Evie's jaw dropped. 'Are you mad?'

'Okay, Rose, you're going to be cool, calm and collected.' Dragging in a breath, Rose did all that she could to turn herself into the epitome of unflappable self-possession.

Don't forget sassy.

The façade slipped. What the hell...? *'No!'* The word

echoed in the chopper's tiny cabin. *Jeez*, this was real life, not a soap opera.

Go on, Lincoln would like sassy. Channel your favourite soap-opera heroines.

A reluctant smile tugged at her lips. What she was about to do would make a great plot line in any of her beloved soaps—*The Bold and the Beautiful, Coronation Street, Home and Away*—but she needed to keep things sensible and businesslike.

And that was what this was—a business proposition. Marrying Lincoln would safeguard Garrison Downs' future. What was more, it would help her accomplish another objective. If she and Lincoln married, if they came to know one another better—and in an ideal world became friends— they could bring the ridiculous feud between their families to an end.

In the scrub below a mob of kangaroos were startled from their morning siesta and scattered, their red-grey coats gleaming in the sun. From her current position, she couldn't see a single dwelling, though one of their stock camps would soon come into view. The cattle stations in the South Australian outback were seriously isolated. Out here neighbours ought to pull together. It'd be in both Garrison Downs' and Kalku Hills' best interests, and the district's, if she and Lincoln could learn to work together.

And while she'd never say it out loud, not even under the threat of torture, she couldn't help wondering if the Waverlys owed the Garrisons some kind of reparation. The way Louisa May had acquired the station, the bad blood it had created… the rumours that Louisa May Waverly had cheated Cordelia Garrison of the land. None of it had sat well with her.

Forty minutes later she landed the chopper in the home paddock of Kalku Hills, as Lincoln had directed her to in his email. She noted his blue Cessna parked on the airstrip to her left and an army of butterflies gathered beneath her breastbone.

Don't be silly. She had nothing to be nervous about. She was simply presenting a business proposition. Nothing more. *Be cool. Be calm. Be businesslike.*

As if her thoughts had conjured him, Lincoln appeared on the homestead's veranda, ready to welcome her. A giant of a man at six feet four, and all of it broad hard muscle. Folding his arms, he leaned against a veranda post and she let out a long, slow breath.

Lincoln's movements were always unhurried, almost lazy, as if he had all the time in the world. As if it was too much of an effort to exert himself. Even when playing cricket he preferred to hit a boundary over pushing himself to run.

Today he wore suit trousers and a business shirt, and she thanked whatever God had prompted Evie to insist that she wear a little black skirt and a pale blue blouse. And black court shoes that were immediately covered in red dust when she leapt down to the ground.

She might not be at home in the fancy rags, but she was at home in the red dust. And while the business proposition she'd come to discuss might not be conventional, it was practical…and sound. And it was time.

Giving herself no further time to rehearse what she'd say, or consider what Lincoln's reaction might be once she'd said it, Rose moved in the direction of the homestead and the man waiting there, his hair glinting gold in the sunlight.

The homestead at Kalku Hills was sandstone, and it was big and beautiful in its own way. But it wasn't built on the same scale as the Garrison Downs homestead. There were no gardens, no pool, no frills. Though, as Clay's wife—Lincoln's

mother—had left him twenty years ago, Rose suspected crea-
ture comforts weren't a high priority for the Garrison men.

'It's nice to see you, Rose.'

Lincoln held out his hand when she reached him and she
shook it, her mouth going dry. It was always like this, the
immediate physical impact, whenever she drew too close to
him, as if time were simultaneously speeding up and slow-
ing down. 'Hello, Lincoln.'

He didn't let her go immediately. Dark eyes travelled la-
zily across her face and something inside her trembled. No
doubt he clocked the dark circles beneath her eyes and the
fact she wore no make-up. Lincoln had dated some of the nation's most beautiful women. Word on the street was that he
was a man with a discerning eye and a short attention span.

What the hell was she doing here? For a moment she was
tempted to wheel away and speed back to Garrison Downs.
A woman like her could never tempt a man like him.

Going to play the craven little virgin now?

That had her pushing her shoulders back. She had plenty
to tempt him—namely land. Lincoln Garrison might be a
freewheeling playboy, but he wasn't an idiot. He'd recognise
a good deal when he saw one. And while he might be as hot
as sin this was a *business* meeting.

'It's *really* nice to see you, Rose.'

She rolled her eyes. The man was also incapable of not
flirting. And while she mightn't be blonde and busty, whenever he saw her Lincoln never failed to give her one of those
lingering glances of appreciation that he seemed to save just
for her. As he was doing right now.

For a moment she was tempted to flirt back, let herself
imagine his expression if she allowed her gaze to make an
equally slow perusal of his body. Because one question had
always plagued her. What had seemed like a lifetime ago,

Lincoln had asked her on a date. She'd declined, but she'd always wondered…

What if she'd said yes?

Her gaze lowered to take in the big, broad lines of him, and the pulse in her throat pounded. Maybe…

With a start she pulled herself back into straight lines, cleared her throat. 'So you already said.'

Those tempting lips tugged into a wider smile and it was all she could do not to groan. This would be so much easier if he looked like…*an ordinary man*!

'It was worth saying twice.' With the smallest hitch of his head, he led her inside, glancing back over his shoulder. 'You look great.' His gaze drifted down to her legs. 'You dressed up.'

'So did you. Don't walk into the wall, Lincoln.'

He was in no danger of walking into the wall, but she needed him to stop looking at her like that or she might just dissolve into a puddle at his feet.

'This is a business meeting,' she added as he gestured for her to take a seat in the office. 'I wanted to look good.'

She waited, kind of fatalistically, for him to say something smooth like, *You always look good.*

'Why?'

She was glad when he didn't. 'Because I want you to say yes to the proposition I'm going to put to you.'

With a grin, he took the seat behind the desk. 'My reputation precedes me, huh? Show me a pair of pretty legs and I'm putty.'

He thought her legs were pretty?

Focus, Rose, focus.

When tea had been served, he lifted his mug to his mouth and surveyed her over the rim. 'I was intrigued when you requested a meeting. You said you had a proposal to put to me?'

'Yes, quite literally.'

Dark blond brows shot up. 'Literally?'

'As in precisely or exactly or accurately.' She sipped her tea before setting it on the desk. 'I've come to ask you to marry me, Lincoln.'

Lincoln Garrison was rarely lost for words. But he stared at Rose Waverly's composed and very beautiful face and couldn't think of a single thing to say.

He could think of plenty of things he'd like to do. Number one on that list was stride around the desk, pull her into his arms and kiss her until neither one of them could think straight. Nothing new in that, though. He had the same urge whenever he saw her.

One kiss. They'd shared one kiss. Seven years ago. It shouldn't have had such an impact.

But it had, and, determined to do something about the unfamiliar longings, the sleepless nights, the *need* that had burned through him, Lincoln had asked Rose out. He hadn't cared that she was a Waverly and he a Garrison. He hadn't thought she'd cared either.

He'd been wrong.

I'm sorry, Lincoln, I can't hurt my family like that. Please don't ask me again.

After that he'd given himself to a series of other women, always hoping he'd find someone who'd fire his blood the way Rose did. He'd partied hard, had played up to the playboy image with which the tabloids had labelled him. It had amused him at the time. *Stupid.* Now most people wrote him off as shallow, bent only on pleasure.

Rose would too. Yet now she was asking him to *marry her*?

He clenched his hands to the underside of his desk, out of

her sight, as he fought an unfamiliar dizziness. 'Did you just ask me to marry you?'

She nodded, as composed and in control as ever.

He refused to allow so much as a flickering eyelash to betray his disorientation. 'Why?' He eased back, stained his voice with amusement, but when she glanced down at her hands and went deathly still, he wished he hadn't. 'Why, Rose?' he repeated more gently.

Why would she ask him to marry her? Because, while he might've been hung up on her all these years, she sure as hell hadn't been hung up on him. He'd done his best not to take it personally. She hadn't appeared to be hung up on anyone.

Swallowing, she folded her hands in her lap and her pallor hit him. She'd lost weight since he'd last seen her—at Holt's funeral—nine months ago. Was she looking after herself? Did she have someone keeping an eye on her to make sure she wasn't working herself half to death?

He'd read the recent press release the family had issued, welcoming their half-sister Anastasia Horvath into the family. Holt's youngest daughter. To a woman not his wife. The news had rocked him. It had rocked the district. It had rocked *the nation*. Rose had been forced to deal with a lot these last few months. It hurt something inside him to see her looking so tired and drawn.

'Lincoln, I'm going to let you into a closely guarded secret.' He couldn't keep his brows from shooting up and she smiled weakly. 'I know relations between our two families haven't always been favourable.'

An understatement if there ever was one.

'But fences ought to be mended. And I figure we need to start somewhere.'

He leaned towards her. 'By you and me marrying?' Had he stepped into some alternate universe?

Just for a moment her gaze drifted to his shoulders and she moistened her lips as if suddenly parched.

Things inside him clenched.

Giving herself a shake, she dragged her gaze back to his. 'I ought to clarify that when I say marriage, I mean a mutually beneficial business arrangement. A temporary agreement. A paper marriage.'

He sat back, any desire to ease her nerves dissolving. 'Do go on,' he drawled.

To her credit, she kept her head high and her gaze steady. 'What I'm going to tell you now, Lincoln, is in the strictest of confidence.'

'Why would you trust me?'

She stared at him for a long moment. 'Sometimes you have to choose to believe the best in people. You and I *don't* have to carry on Holt and Clay's animosity. I'm very much hoping we won't.'

And there it was—her honesty…her decency—the reason he'd been unable to prevent his feelings from becoming tangled up in her in the first place. Why what he felt for her had always been more than physical. Rose was tough and capable and equipped in every way to run a huge operation like Garrison Downs, but what no one else seemed to see was how… It sounded biblical, which probably went to show how bad he had it for this woman, but how pure of heart Rose was.

'If you betray my trust… I guess that'll answer any question I have about the kind of man you are.'

'You can trust me, Rose. You have my word.'

Nodding, she moistened her lips again. 'There was a condition attached to my father's will, dating back to the time when Louisa May Waverly first acquired Garrison Downs.'

'When she won it in a poker game, you mean?'

'Yes.'

The poker game that had created so much ill will between the two families.

'The conditional bequest is old-fashioned. It states only a son can inherit the estate. If there are no sons then the daughters will inherit, but only if each daughter is married. They have twelve months from the reading of the will to fulfil the terms of the conditional bequest.'

The breath punched from his lungs. 'You *have to marry*?' She *had to marry* if she wanted to keep Garrison Downs? 'What kind of archaic…?' He tried to rein in his wild thoughts. 'Why are you asking *me*?'

For the briefest of moments her gaze fixed on his mouth and things inside him clenched and clashed. Her eyes darkened and he wondered if she was remembering that kiss they'd shared. It occurred to him now, with the space of the intervening years, that maybe it *had* rocked her world as much as it had his. Maybe it had shaken her so much it'd sent her running scared.

I can't hurt my family like that.

Both Rosamund and Holt were now dead. Rose's choices couldn't hurt them any more.

'Why am I asking you in particular?'

He crashed back to the here and now.

'Because if my sisters and I don't marry, the land will return to the current head of the Garrison family.'

He *couldn't* have heard her right.

'Which, obviously, is your father.'

Damn it all to hell!

He bit back something rude and succinct. His father couldn't get wind of this. If he did—

Rubbing a hand over his face, he banished the ugly images rising through him.

'Now, of course…' Rose's fingers formed a steeple '… I

could marry one of the Downs' stockmen. Any one of them would do it to oblige me and I'll have fulfilled the conditional bequest.'

The thought of any one of them with Rose had his hands curling into fists.

'But…'

His heart pounded against the walls of his ribs. It took a superhuman effort to remain in his seat. 'But?'

Those extraordinary blue eyes met his, extraordinarily candid. 'It only seems fair to give you first right of refusal. I'd like to mend fences, Lincoln. I'd like us to be friends.'

'No, Rose, you want us to be husband and wife.'

'A *paper* marriage, though, Lincoln.' She seized her tea, took a huge gulp. 'We'd be friends who temporarily marry for mutual benefit, and then remain friends afterwards. I'd like the future generations of Waverlys and Garrisons to get along, wouldn't you?'

Yes.

Her nose wrinkled. 'I don't like your father. Sorry. Hence the reason I'm asking *you* to marry me rather than him.'

He didn't like his father much sometimes either. And she couldn't marry Clay, couldn't give him even the smallest of opportunities to gain a foothold at Garrison Downs.

'And while I'm on the topic of people I don't like… My grandmother would've hated me to marry a Garrison. I know I should be above such things—' she gave a small grin, and he found an answering grin building inside him '—but apparently I'm not.'

'I didn't like your grandmother either.'

'She was a bitter woman.' She hesitated. 'Your father is becoming an awful lot like her.'

Her words burned a path through him, but only because they were true. Who else saw what Rose saw? If his father wasn't careful, he'd lose his standing in the district, and his reputation. Linc planned to do everything in his power to prevent that from happening.

In truth, Rose's proposal couldn't have come at a better time. If he wanted to prevent his father from making the biggest mistake of his miserable life, Rose had just handed him the means to do it. But he refused to appear too eager. Even he had his pride.

'Why should I say yes to this proposal of yours? I suspect as soon as the demands of the will are met and the estate passes to you and your sisters, you mean to divorce me.'

'As I said, this would be a business deal.' She clasped her hands lightly on the desk. 'You know that parcel of land my family has always refused to sell to Kalku Hills?'

Camels Bridge? That stretch of land linked two separate portions of Kalku Hills land. Owning it would allow easy movement between the two. It would save the station time, effort and money. What was more, that land came with water rights. It was, quite literally, worth its weight in gold. 'I know it well.'

'It would be your wedding present.'

He blew out a long breath. That was generous. *Really* generous. He couldn't resist the sport of seeing just how far he could push her, though. 'Would you consider throwing in your Angus bull?'

'Carnelian Boy?'

He nodded. The stud fees for him were phenomenal.

She hesitated. 'I wish I could say yes but I can't.'

Lifting the snow globe his mother had sent him for Christmas when he was eleven—the year she'd left him alone on the station with his father—he shook it. Watched all the pretty flakes swirl before slowly settling.

'I can't in good faith… The thing is, poor old Carnelian

had a run-in with a barbed-wire fence and his breeding days are over. Now, if you still want him, that can be arranged, but I suspect you're not looking for a pet.'

'Hell, Rose.' He set the globe down with a clatter. 'I'm sorry.'

'Yeah, it sucks.'

He doubted Holt would've been so honest. His father sure as hell wouldn't have been.

It's only fair you get first right of refusal. I can't in good faith...

'Honour is a big thing for you, huh?'

She scowled. 'Yes.'

It made him laugh.

Her scowl only deepened. 'Is it for you?'

He nodded, but said aloud what he knew they both were thinking. 'Except you're a Waverly and I'm a Garrison and we don't trust each other.'

Her sigh sounded loud on the air, but she shook herself upright. 'Which is why my sisters, their husbands, as well as my head stockman, all know where I am and what time I'm expected back. If I'm not back by that time, they'll send out a search party.'

He tried to hide his shock. 'You think I'd kidnap you?'

'I only have three months to fulfil the conditions of the will...and this is a big country.' Her eyes started to dance. 'It's also true that I might be a little bit addicted to soap operas.'

Soap operas? He choked back a laugh.

She leaned towards him, a frown pleating her brow. 'I know we've not spent a lot of time together, Lincoln, but I've known you all my life...'

He waited, his chest growing tighter with each passing second.

'What I do know of you, I like.'

It was as if someone had cut the strings of a puppet—his insides sagged, his heart though took flight.

She stared back, half defiantly. 'I've never seen you be mean to anyone.'

With every word she spoke he fell a little deeper for her. But was it real? Or had he built Rose up in his mind because she was the one that had got away?

His hands clenched and unclenched. He'd always wanted a chance with this woman.

'You're well liked in the district. That's a good character reference.'

'So are you.'

'I'm considered reserved and standoffish.'

Ah, the ice queen tag had reached her ears, then.

'You're well respected,' he said quietly. 'Your judgement is considered as sound as your father's.'

She flinched at the mention of her father. He wished he could hug her.

You could hug her if you were married.

Oh, he was going to marry her, all right, there was no doubt about that.

Glancing at her watch, she shot to her feet. 'Look, I understand this is a lot to take in and that you'll need time to consider your decision. I'm afraid I can only give you a week, though. I've left this far too late and for my family's sake I—'

'If we married...'

He gestured for her to sit. She sat.

'I'd want to maintain the appearance of an actual marriage. I'd want people to think it real.'

'Why?'

'My father is going to be a...challenge. Him thinking the marriage is real will help me manage that.' And that was all he was going to say on the subject.

She chewed that over for a moment. 'You'd have to move to Garrison Downs.'

He nodded.

She nodded too. Not in agreement, but digesting his words. 'It's a moot point until you come to a decision.' She stood again. 'It was good of you to see me at such short notice, and—'

'I'll marry you on one condition, Rose.' He stood too.

Her hands twisted together. 'What's your condition?'

'That for the duration of our marriage, you don't break our wedding vows.'

She blinked. 'You're talking about fidelity.'

'No man likes to be made a fool. I'd promise the same thing. It wouldn't be fair otherwise.'

She gaped at him. 'Lincoln, you're not exactly known for your…abstinence.'

It stung that she thought him incapable of it.

She straightened, her hands on her hips. 'I won't lie to my sisters, and they'll keep the secret if I ask it of them. Other than that, I agree to all of your terms.'

Moving around the desk, he stuck out his hand. 'Deal.'

She clasped it, her grip firm. 'Deal.'

Leaning down, he pressed his lips to her cheek, inhaled her surprisingly light floral scent. 'A pleasure doing business with you, Rose.'

Her breath hitched. 'Likewise.'

She tugged her hand from his with more haste than necessary, and he bit back a grin. Did she really think they'd be able to keep their hands off each other for the next three months? He suspected a paper marriage was the last thing either of them wanted.

CHAPTER TWO

EVE AND NATE were waiting for Rose on her return.

The strange pulse pounding in her throat made it hard to breathe. The touch of Lincoln's lips still burned against her cheek.

Eve searched her face. 'How did it go?'

'Mission accomplished.' Dusting off her hands, she turned to Nate. 'Could we get a wriggle on with this? Organise a special licence?' Because the sooner this was done, the sooner Garrison Downs would be safe. Maybe then she'd breathe easier.

'How soon are you hoping for?'

She knew the norm was a month, but... 'Two weeks?'

The air whistled between his teeth but he gave a slow nod. 'Given where we are, the distances involved, the fact muster will start soon and the responsibilities you and Linc both have... We can make a good case.'

'Excellent.'

Evie grabbed her arm. 'Boss, are you sure about this?'

'I am, I promise.' She squeezed her sister's hand. 'Now, as you know, it's nearly autumn—'

'Which is the busiest time of the year.'

Rose strode off to get changed, but called back over her shoulder, 'The skirt was a great idea, by the way. I think Lincoln is a leg man.'

'Get back here right now and tell me *everything*!'

'Gotta go, Bambi.'

With a grin, she kept walking. She'd do everything in her power to ensure her sisters didn't think she was worried about marrying Lincoln. She had no reason to be worried. She'd wanted him to say yes. He'd said yes. It was all going exactly to plan.

Lincoln's image rose in her mind, the way he'd looked at her, the expression in those dark eyes…the touch of his lips.

She waved a hand in front of her face. Lincoln might be an incredibly attractive man, but there was too much at stake for her to indulge in idle fantasies about him. She'd secure Garrison Downs' future, and do what she could to bring an end to the enmity between their two families. She wasn't letting hormones interfere with that.

Thankfully muster would start soon and she'd be way too busy to think about anything else. But for the first time in a long time, she considered the parts of her life that she'd ignored and neglected for the sake of Garrison Downs and her role here. A familiar burning itched through her. A fire Lincoln had lit seven years ago when, knee deep in mud, their clothes ruined, they'd kissed—

She cut the thought dead. She and Lincoln were different people now. For God's sake, his last girlfriend had been a model—the face of one of Australia's leading cosmetic companies! A man like him wouldn't look at a woman like her twice, and she had no intention of making a fool of herself pining for someone so far out of her league.

God, she was having enough trouble running the station without buying more trouble. Work. That was what she'd focus on. Nothing more.

While Rose was getting ready for bed that evening, her phone rang. She pressed the receiver to her ear. 'Hello?'

'Hello, Rose.'

Lincoln. His voice sounded like a promise and all of the fine hairs on her arms lifted. 'Hello, Lincoln.'

'I have questions.'

She curled up in the chair in her bedroom. 'Fire away.'

'What's your favourite snack?'

It startled a laugh from her. 'Snack?'

'I'm a big chip man myself. If you give me a bag of potato chips I'll hoover them back in record time.'

'Favourite flavour?'

'Salt and vinegar.'

She made a note to stock up. 'My weakness is ice cream. Any flavour. All the flavours. And if a new flavour comes onto the market, I have to try it.'

'When did you last eat a bowl of the good stuff?'

She blinked. She couldn't remember. 'Not for a while.'

'That's too bad. You should always take the time to eat a bowl of ice cream, Rose. It's the little things.'

She found herself suddenly and insanely hungry for ice cream.

'Next question: when are we actually getting married?'

She shook herself. 'In two weeks' time, hopefully. I'll keep you posted.'

'Registry office in Adelaide?'

'That's the plan.' She frowned. 'Unless—'

'Nope, that's fine with me.'

'Okay.' She eased out a breath. 'That brings me to a question of my own.' Shooting to her feet, she strode across to the French doors and pushed outside to the back veranda and the cool night air.

'Which is?'

She grimaced at the night sky—deep and dark and dusted with a thousand stars. 'How are you going to juggle your responsibilities at Kalku while you're living at Garrison

Downs?' Lincoln might spend half the year gallivanting around the countryside doing playboy things, but he always returned to help out during muster. When he was home, he worked as hard as the rest of them.

Kalku Hills was nearly as large as Garrison Downs. Under Holt, though, the Waverly holdings had prospered and flourished in a way Kalku Hills had never been able to match. Whatever else she thought of her father, Holt had known cattle and had a deep understanding of the land.

He'd also had an unrivalled business brain, had known how to broker deals and seize opportunities. Under Holt's stewardship, Garrison Downs had become one of the most successful stations in the country. And she had to find a way not only to maintain that legacy, but to carry it on—to continue the expansion, the innovation…the profits.

Weight slammed down on her shoulders. How on earth could she—?

'You've got this, Boss. You know what you're doing.'

She waved a hand in front of her face to dispel her father's voice—*I'm not talking to you!*—dragged her mind back to the matter in hand. 'We can find ways to negotiate it,' she offered. Both stations had planes. Commuting would be involved.

'There's nothing to negotiate. My father fired me this afternoon.'

She digested that in silence. 'Okay.' She kept her voice matter-of-fact. 'If we're going to marry we need to speak plainly, agreed?'

'We promise honesty, Rose, or we call it off here and now. Otherwise there's no point. You want to create a strong working relationship going forward, yes? The only way that's going to happen is if we can learn to trust one another.'

He was right. 'Honesty,' she agreed. 'So with that in mind… Rumour has it that when you're home your father fires you every other day. Now, I expect that's a wild exaggeration, but there's probably a grain of truth in there somewhere.'

'Ah, but the difference is that today I chose to believe him.'

He sounded remarkably cheerful about it. She grimaced. 'He fired you because you told him you're marrying me.'

'He fired me because he's making some truly stupid business decisions, and I challenged him about them.'

He spoke calmly, without anger or rancour. But a memory rose in her mind. She'd been eight years old and in the general store at Marni—the nearest town for a hundred and fifty kilometres. She'd been idly perusing the horse blankets, wondering if she could talk Dad into buying her a flash blue and orange one, when she'd rounded the top of the next aisle—work boots stretched on one side, swags and camping equipment on the other. There'd been bedrolls, camp kettles, enamel plates and mugs. At the other end of the aisle eleven-year-old Lincoln had stood with his father, Clay.

Clay's hand had been raised. It had come crashing down on his son's shoulder with a force that had made her flinch. 'Read it!' As he'd shoved a price tag under his son's nose, that big broad hand had lifted again. 'I said read it!'

Trembling, Rose had reached out a foot and knocked one of the shiny cook pots off the shelf. It had clattered to the floor with a crash, rocking back and forth with a tinny racket. Both father and son had swung around.

Planting her feet, she'd glared at the older man. Lincoln might not know his numbers, but he didn't deserve to be hit like that!

And then Dad had been standing behind her, one hand on her shoulder. With an oath, Clay had stormed off. 'Okay, Linc?' Dad had said.

Lincoln had nodded, then he'd turned and disappeared and the tightness in her chest had slowly eased.

Her father had squeezed her shoulder. 'I'm proud of you, Boss.'

She'd felt good then, until she'd wondered who'd been proud of Lincoln.

'You still there, Rose?'

With a start, she realised her cheeks were wet. She wiped her hands across them. Not long after that incident word had gone around that Lincoln had dyslexia and some kind of hearing issue that had required surgery.

'I'm here.' She recalled the open-handed blow delivered to a young boy's shoulder and her hand clenched around the phone so hard her fingers started to ache. 'I guess he was never going to take the news well.'

'Telling him I was marrying you was simply the icing on the cake.'

The grin in his voice had her biting back a grin of her own. It took an effort to keep her voice steady and level. 'Would you like to come and stay at Garrison Downs early?'

'He isn't kicking me out into the cold, cold snow. I'm not homeless.'

'Never said you were, but your father has a bad temper and I expect he's not that pleasant to be around at the moment.'

Silence greeted her words, and she winced. Had she gone too far?

'I can hold my own.' The words were uttered quietly enough, but steel threaded beneath them.

She nodded. 'I don't doubt that for a moment.' If it were anyone else giving him a hard time, she wouldn't worry, but it was different when it was family. 'That, however, wasn't the question I asked. I asked if you wanted to come and stay at Garrison Downs. It doesn't need to be here at the house.

There's a vacant stockman's cottage at the outstation at the moment.'

Walking back into her bedroom, she closed the French doors and leaned against them, stared at the bed. The thought of Lincoln here in her house...

He's going to be in your house, not your bed.

She pushed away from the doors, wrapped common-sense practicality around her like a cloak. 'Lincoln, you know what it's like at this time of year. We're ramping up for muster. You and your Cessna would come in real handy here.'

With the inheritance left to him by his grandfather, Lincoln had bought a racehorse. It had won a lot of races. The prize money had funded the plane and his playboy lifestyle.

'Are you trying to poach me?'

'You're the best in the business. I'd be a fool not to. Anyway, it's not poaching if you're between jobs. I can offer you a contract position for the autumn.' That way he'd be his own boss. 'You can set your own rates.'

Even if he charged twice the going rate, he'd be worth every penny.

'I'll admit I'd like a first-hand look at how you run your operation. Would that bother you?'

'Nope.' He might not hold the reins at Kalku Hills yet, but one day the station would be his. And even if he decided to fritter his time away on inane things—like parties on yachts and movie premieres—he'd hire someone who'd do a better job than his father.

'Is there anyone staying in the cottage out at Ned's Gorge?'

'Nope.'

'Then you have yourself a deal.'

She laughed. 'And here I was thinking the day couldn't get any better.'

'You should do that more. Laugh,' he added before she could ask. 'Are you in bed?'

She climbed beneath the covers. 'Yep. You know we keep early hours out here.'

'Then I'll wish you sweet dreams in just a moment. But first… Will you wear a dress to our wedding?'

An odd note had entered his voice and she blinked. He sounded almost…*vulnerable*. She shook the thought away. 'You want me to wear a dress?'

'More than life itself.'

The words were threaded with a sultry heat and a slow burn started up at the centre of her. Lincoln wanted to see her in a dress? He'd thought about her in a—

'As you so rarely wear dresses, it'll make things look more convincing.'

She crashed back.

'It'll give the ceremony…gravitas.'

He was right. She rarely wore dresses, preferring trouser suits for more formal occasions. She was careful to keep her voice even and crisp. This was business, nothing more. 'Long or short?'

'I don't mind. Just wear something that makes you feel pretty.'

She blinked again. Reminded herself *again* that he didn't mean anything by it.

'What would you like me to wear?'

And she found herself laughing again. He really was every bit the charming shallow playboy the tabloids made him out to be. 'Whatever you think will give the best impression.'

'Sweet dreams, Rose. I'll look forward to speaking to you again soon.'

She suspected her dreams were going to be anything but sweet. 'Goodnight, Lincoln.'

A dress she felt pretty in?

Leaping out of bed, she fired up her laptop to check out her favourite online shops. She wouldn't choose anything too fussy. But she was seized with a sudden desire to make him see her as a woman—just for a few short hours. An attractive and sensual woman, rather than some unsophisticated backwater cow hick.

The next day, when a delivery of rocky road ice cream was flown in from Marni, she laughed. That evening she ate a huge bowlful, enjoying every luscious mouthful.

Lincoln rang her every few days. Always at night as she was getting ready for bed. It became a thing. Sometimes he simply rang to say goodnight. Other nights, if she wasn't dead on her feet, they'd chat longer.

'Tell me something about yourself that I wouldn't know.'

'I'm addicted to *The Bold and the Beautiful*.'

His laugh, all rich warm caramel, made her crave something sweet. 'So that's the soap opera you meant when you mentioned being addicted?'

'One of them. Your turn.'

'I'm good at cricket...'

'That's not a secret.' He'd been the star at the district's annual cricket match for the last decade.

'Ah, but what you wouldn't know is that I'm just as good at chess.'

No way. He didn't seem *serious* enough to play chess.

'You still there, Rose?'

She shook herself, channelled mock outrage. 'Are you challenging me to a game of chess?'

'Rumour has it you're the best in the district. And I can't resist a challenge.'

Said with typical male arrogance. 'I'll look forward to it. I don't play for money, though. Unlike Louisa May and Cordelia, we won't be wagering the station.'

'I'm sure we can think up stakes that are more interesting than that.'

Her eyes narrowed. Had he meant that to sound suggestive?

'Now tell me something else.'

She thought for a moment. 'I call Evelyn Evie, and Matilda Tilly.' She hesitated. Not because she was ashamed or embarrassed, but because it was still so new. 'And I call Anastasia Ana. But nobody calls me Rosie because I hate it.'

'Lots of people call you Boss, as that's what your dad called you.'

She could've hugged him for not peppering her with questions about Ana.

'I'm not going to call you Boss and I won't call you Rosie either. Rose is a beautiful name and it suits you perfectly.'

A funny lump lodged in her throat. 'Do you prefer Linc or Lincoln?'

'Everyone calls me Linc, but you've always called me Lincoln. I like it.'

So did she.

'Next… Do you mind if I hire a photographer to take a few tasteful shots for the press release announcing our marriage?'

Closing her eyes, she grimaced.

'A shot of us exchanging vows, emerging from the registry office married. And then maybe a snap or two of us celebrating at some swish establishment that evening.'

Her eyes snapped open. 'We're spending *the night in Adelaide*?' Her voice rose. What the hell…?

'Rose,' he said gently, 'it's supposed to be our wedding night.'

Damn. She should've seen this coming. The only request

Lincoln had made of her was for her to maintain the pretence that this marriage was real. That meant toeing these kinds of lines, playing these kinds of games.

'These aren't going to be tabloid-style shots.'

She tried to unlock her mouth to say okay, but her jaw remained stubbornly clenched.

'And obviously we won't be sharing a room. I'll book two rooms.'

Her jaw promptly released. 'I should've thought of all this myself. But yes, the photographer…a night in Adelaide… fine.'

She heard him move. Was he in bed too? Or maybe out on the porch of the cottage staring up at the stars. She opened her mouth to ask, then closed it. It seemed too personal.

'Are you inviting anyone to the wedding?'

She snuggled down under the covers. 'Just Eve and Nate. You?'

'My father.'

She scowled at the ceiling.

'I haven't spoken to him since I left Kalku, but it only seems right to give him the chance to be there.'

She hoped for Lincoln's sake that Clay showed up to support his son. 'Do you ever see your mother?' Cynthia Garrison had left Clay and Kalku Hills when Lincoln was eleven.

'Once in a blue moon. She's remarried, has a new family. I'm part of a mistake she wishes she'd never made.'

'You're not a mistake, Lincoln.' Though he'd certainly drawn the short straw as far as family went. No wonder he sought approval and appreciation elsewhere, found it so hard to settle down. 'Don't let your parents make you feel bad for the mistakes they made.'

He was quiet for a moment. 'You'll probably miss your mum on the day.'

Her eyes burned. Her mother would be appalled at Rose marrying for such pragmatic reasons.

'I liked your mother. She was beautiful, classy, elegant. You're a lot like her.'

Her head rocked back. No, she wasn't! Eve and Matilda had Rosamund's beauty and elegance, not Rose. Beside her mother, she'd always felt rough and coarse.

'You must miss her.'

'Every single day.' Her mother had died of pancreatic cancer seven years ago. Even now the speed of it sickened her. Six weeks from diagnosis to death. Not that Rosamund had told them about her diagnosis. She'd kept that to herself. They'd only found it out after she'd collapsed. Everything had changed in the blink of an eye and none of them had been the same since.

'Your mother was always kind to me, always went out of her way to make me feel welcome. You do the same, Rose. It matters. It means a lot.'

A lump lodged in her throat, making it impossible to speak.

'You still there?'

With a superhuman effort, she dislodged it. 'I wish she could be at my wedding and I wish you'd had the chance to know her better. But I'll have one of my sisters there.' And that meant everything.

'Did you know there's supposed to be a diary of Cordelia's hidden somewhere at Garrison Downs?' he asked one night a few days later.

Rose sat upright in bed. 'A diary?'

'Yeah, my great-grandma told me about it.'

It probably contained a rant or ten about Louisa May and an itemised account of all Waverly offences and shortcomings. Though, one didn't lie in their own diary, did they? Perhaps it revealed how Cordelia had come to lose Garrison Downs in such a reckless fashion?

That poker game between the two women had gained legendary status. Cordelia Garrison wagering a cattle station in a game of cards against Louisa May at the beginning of the last century and losing it. The ensuing scandal and uproar reverberating down the generations.

If they found the diary and discovered the truth… It could help lay old ghosts to rest.

'Or it could make them worse.'

Her grandmother's strident outrage whipped through her, making her flinch.

Oh, right, like I'm going to listen to you, Grandma.

'It's probably long since been lost or destroyed,' Lincoln said.

'I can say with hand on my heart that nothing like that has ever been found.' Or if it had, she'd never been let in on the secret.

'It'd be something to find it though, wouldn't it?'

Something in his voice made her smile. 'A treasure hunt?' She tapped a finger against her chin. 'Old House is probably the best bet.' Old House was the original station homestead. 'Eve and Nate have set up house there. I'll mention it to them, tell them to keep an eye out.'

The night before the wedding, Rose and her sisters gathered for celebratory drinks in Holt's office. She avoided the room whenever she could, refused to work in it, but it was the room with the technology, so…

Tilly in Chaleur appeared on the giant screen soon followed by Ana in Melbourne. Her sisters exchanged surreptitious glances and, from her seat on a pile of cushions that she and Evie had thrown on the floor, Rose rolled her eyes. 'Okay, girls, gather round.'

Everyone leaned closer.

'You know why I'm marrying Lincoln. You know it's a marriage in name only. But I also want you to know that I don't regret doing this, not for a moment. I'd do a whole lot more to safeguard the Downs' future. I just want us clear on that.'

Tilly and Evie exchanged raised eyebrows.

'Now, before the two of you pile in I want to mention a couple of things.'

Tilly pursed her lips. Evie folded her arms. Ana watched, her gaze serious.

'First up, Lincoln signed the prenup without a murmur of complaint.' He wasn't entitled to any part of Garrison Downs beyond Camels Bridge, just as she wasn't entitled to any part of Kalku Hills.

'That's…heartening,' Ana offered.

Rose shot her a smile. 'He hasn't raised any red flags—it's a tick in his favour. The other thing I want to say is that I've always wanted the two stations to work together rather than pulling in separate directions. It's insane for us to be at constant loggerheads. It'd save both stations a lot of time and money if we could work cooperatively. Holt would never see sense on the subject.' She ground her teeth together. 'Frankly, the way he and Clay have acted over the years is disgraceful.'

Tilly's jaw dropped. 'Rose!'

She blinked. 'What? I didn't agree with him about everything.'

'I know, but when the two of you argued you never sounded like…*that*.'

'Like what?'

'Furious,' Eve supplied.

Tilly nodded. 'You worshipped the ground Dad walked on.'

Once maybe, but… She hadn't spoken to them about it. The last nine months had been hell, and the time had never felt right. 'I *am* furious.' She grew tense with that fury all over again. 'I'm *never* going to forgive him for keeping Ana from us.'

'Oh, Rose.' Ana's bottom lip wobbled.

She retied her ponytail. 'That's a discussion for another day. The fact is Holt was brilliant in a lot of ways, but he could be a jerk at times too. He enjoyed playing top dog in the district, and he loved rubbing Clay's face in it.'

'Clay isn't a very nice man, though,' Tilly murmured.

'Agreed. But going forward I think Lincoln and I can forge a stronger working relationship between the two stations. It's beyond time the bad blood between our families came to an end.'

'Hear, hear.' But Evie's brow pleated. 'Can you trust him, though?'

Rose's heart sounded loud in her ears in the sudden hush of the room.

Tilly stared at her. 'What do your instincts tell you?'

Both Tilly and Evie leaned towards her. Rose pressed her fingers together and swallowed. 'Lincoln might refuse to live his life seriously, he might bounce from woman to woman, but he's *not* his father. I believe he can be trusted.'

Both her sisters sagged in relief. Evie glanced up at Ana. 'Rose's judgement is practically infallible.'

Rose's stomach gave a sick kick. Dear God, if it let her down this time… Swallowing her doubts, she forced up her chin. 'Hey, here's something. Lincoln's great-grandma told him that Cordelia's diary is supposed to be hidden somewhere at the Downs.'

'Ooh!' Tilly clasped her hands beneath her chin. 'How

wonderful if we could find it.' As an historian and a graphologist who was called upon to give advice about the authenticity of old letters, this was totally Tilly's jam.

'I reckon Old House is our best bet,' Rose said.

'Oh, my God! Nate and I will tear the house apart. If it's there, we'll find it.'

The women talked for a little longer before signing off and promising to talk again soon. Both Tilly and Ana wished Rose well for the following day.

But as Rose readied herself for bed that night, thoughts of Cordelia's diary circled through her mind. The enmity between the Waverlys and the Garrisons had an origin, even if that origin was now shrouded in hearsay and speculation. She understood, even sympathised, with everyone's excitement and curiosity, but a part of her couldn't help wondering if finding that diary would open a whole other can of worms that would be better off remaining buried.

CHAPTER THREE

LINCOLN CHOSE TO believe that the unhindered sun that dawned on the day of his wedding was a good omen. Rose wore a dress in a shade of deep dusky pink that matched her name, the material caressing her curves with a loving attention that had his mouth going dry. He couldn't believe he was going to marry this woman.

His father didn't show. Rose glanced around, but didn't say anything, just reached up to trace a finger down his tie—pale blue silk, covered in a print of pink tea roses. He shrugged. 'Made me think of you.'

Curling her hand in the crock of his arm, she turned them in the direction of the reception desk. 'Let's go do this.'

The service was fast and efficient—'i's dotted and 't's crossed. Before they knew it, they were standing blinking in the sun again. Rose glanced up and her lips twitched. 'Here's to the beginning of a beautiful friendship.'

He sent her a lazy grin. 'Ah, Rose, we'll always have Adelaide.' That twitch blossomed into a full-blown smile, and hope burned a path through his chest. 'I made a lunch reservation at the Grand Hotel in Glenelg.'

Eve gave a delighted squeak.

'And booked two ocean-view suites for the night.' The views of the Southern Indian Ocean from the hotel were stunning.

Rose's smile faded. He maintained a deliberately cheerful manner, refusing to let thoughts of his playboy reputation mar the day. She might doubt his intentions, but he planned on being the perfect gentleman.

Seducing Rose would only reinforce her view of him. He needed to take things slow. Call him a sentimental fool, but he actually wanted her to like him before they embarked on a sexual relationship. *If* they embarked on a sexual relationship. He refused to take anything for granted.

'You deserve a night away from the station, Boss. It'll do you good.' Eve folded her arms. 'You ought to make it two.'

Rose shook her head. 'There's too much to do.'

'An extra night wouldn't make any difference…except giving you a bit of a break.'

Eve was worried that Rose was working too hard?

'Besides, you and Lincoln must have things you want to discuss away from prying eyes. You can give me the orders for the rest of the week and I'll make sure Aaron gets them.'

'Aaron knows what needs doing for the next few days.'

'Yeah, but will he do it?' Eve muttered. 'I heard you arguing with him again the other day.'

Rose was having trouble with her head stockman?

'Evie, one night away is more than enough.'

He thought of his father then and nodded. 'It is.' He clapped his hands. 'The plan. Tonight I thought dinner at a waterfront restaurant that does an amazing seafood platter. After that…' He shrugged. 'We were both up at the crack of dawn so I can't see us dancing into the wee small hours, but… Do you like whisky, Rose? There's supposed to be a speakeasy somewhere close by that does tastings. I thought it might be fun.'

She glanced up, moistened her lips. 'Dinner, followed by

the speakeasy and then a relatively early night sounds good to me.'

'And then home tomorrow?'

'Perfect.'

And he made sure it was. He kept her laughing, made sure the conversation flowed, and didn't make a single inappropriate move. As he fell into bed at midnight, he couldn't remember the last time he'd enjoyed himself more.

Eve met them on their return the next day. Linc swooped down, lifting Rose into his arms before they could step inside the homestead.

Startled blue eyes blinked into his. 'What are you doing?'

Was it his imagination or was her voice a fraction high? He might want to take things slow, but it didn't mean he didn't want her aware of him. 'I believe it's traditional for the groom to carry the bride across the threshold, Mrs Waverly.' He'd taken for granted that she'd keep her own name, but as to the title... 'Do you want to be a Mrs, or would you rather remain a Ms?'

'I think, perhaps, I'd rather you put me down before you dropped me.'

'I'm not going to drop you.' He grinned, loving the feel of her in his arms. 'I'll be happy to hold you all day until you decided the Ms or Mrs question.' He manoeuvred through the doorway with care. And then just stood there, patiently waiting.

At least, he hoped he looked patient. An armful of warm delicious woman had everything starting to throb. 'Don't you worry about me, Rose.' He widened his smile. 'Like I said, I could do this all day and not break out in a sweat.'

'Okay, okay. *Mrs* Waverly, all right? It'll keep the lawyers happy.'

'Perfect.' Reluctantly he set her on her feet.

When he straightened, he found Eve biting her lip as if try-ing not to laugh. 'Refreshment time!' She linked arms with Rose and led the way through to the kitchen.

The homestead was luxurious—a series of spacious elegant rooms with large creamy interiors and dark antiques—grace-ful and classic. It dazzled and charmed in equal measure.

'You should be taking it easy, Evie.'

'Morning tea with my sister and her new husband, espe-cially when neither Lindy nor Nate will let me lift a finger, doesn't count as hard labour. It *is* me taking it easy.'

Which made Rose laugh. And that made him smile. The sisters' closeness fascinated him. As a boy, he'd watched Rose and her family on race days and show days, hungry for what they had, wondering what it'd be like if he had a brother or sister.

'Lincoln, this is our housekeeper, Lindy.'

A dark-haired woman, probably a decade older than Rose and half a head shorter, glanced up from the jug she was filling with ice cubes. 'Welcome to Garrison Downs, Mr Garrison.'

'Linc,' he automatically corrected.

'Many congratulations to both of you on your marriage.'

'Thanks, Lindy, much appreciated.'

'Lindy's homemade lemonade is to die for,' Eve said.

Rose nodded. 'And her date scones.'

He filed all of it away.

That evening Linc strolled into the living room to find Rose curled up on the sofa with a pile of paperwork. River, Holt's retired border collie, dozed on the floor nearby. Rose glanced up as he set a neatly wrapped package on the coffee table in front of her. 'I bought you a wedding present.'

River stood to sniff it. Lincoln ruffled the border collie's ears. He'd ordered this present two weeks ago, after getting off the phone to Rose that first night.

She set the paperwork to one side. 'You didn't have to do that.'

'I wanted to.'

'I…uh…have something for you, too, but you'll have to wait until tomorrow. We ran out of time for me to show it to you today.'

They hadn't, but he didn't challenge her. After morning tea with Eve and Nate, Rose had given him a comprehensive tour of the house—which hadn't included a peek inside her bedroom, but she'd touched the door as they passed to indicate it was hers. She'd placed him in the room next door and had left him to *settle in*, then had disappeared for the rest of the day.

He sat beside her now, close, but not too close. He might not be the playboy she thought him, but nor was he a saint. He wanted her aware of him, unable to ignore him. He leaned in, breathed deeply. 'You smell great.'

'I…uh…it's probably my shampoo.' She edged away a fraction, her tongue snaking out to moisten her lips.

It was still there. The heat between them. It chafed at her in the same way it chafed at him. The knowledge hummed through him. 'Go on.' He nudged her. 'Open it.'

Leaning forward, she tore the paper from the gift. 'A chess set!'

'Ah, but not just any old chess set—a *themed* chess set. A *soap-opera*-themed chess set.'

Pulling it free from its box, she lifted out one of the pieces, her bark of laughter making him grin. 'Where are on earth did you find it?'

'You can find anything on the Internet these days.' Not quite true. He'd had this one specially made.

She turned the piece over in her fingers—a baron masquerading as a moustache-twirling villain. 'This is amazing, Lincoln. I love it!'

He'd known she would. 'Wanna play a game?'

She hesitated.

'You can tell a lot about a person by the way they accept defeat.' He seized a king—a smug tycoon wearing a Stetson and holding a fistful of dollars. 'And I'm looking forward to seeing your face when I trounce you.'

She placed a swooning maiden on the board. 'You know I'm going to wipe the floor with you?'

'In your dreams.' With a lazy finger, he touched the tiger eye set into the bracelet she wore. She'd worn it the day she'd proposed. She'd worn it yesterday, too. 'This is pretty.'

She stilled. 'Ana had one made for each of us. They're all set with a different stone. She calls them sister bracelets.'

The tiger eye suited her. 'What's Ana like?' He kept setting up, not wanting to make a big deal of his question.

'Incredibly talented. Smart. Strong.' The words were short and clipped. 'Why?'

He fought an urge to close his eyes. Despite everything, he was still a Garrison. And she a Waverly. Trust wasn't part of their DNA.

Pushing an ottoman across to the other side of the coffee table, he sat down on it and folded his arms too. 'I envied you all when I was growing up, did you know that? I wished my parents had given me a brother or sister before their marriage imploded.'

Something in her face softened. 'I'm sorry. I shouldn't have snapped. I'm just sick of the gossip.'

He nodded.

She kept setting up the board, not meeting his eye. 'Sisters are the best. And Ana is a sister. She's one of us.'

It was enough. For now. 'Okay, game on. You be white.'

Rose found it ridiculously difficult to concentrate on chess. Lincoln wasn't doing anything exceptional. He wasn't flirting. But she was minutely aware of him. When he'd leaned in earlier to sniff her, gooseflesh had broken out on her arms. It had taken a superhuman effort not to chafe them away.

She glanced at him, glanced back at the board. Of course he wasn't flirting. She'd made it clear she wanted a marriage in name only. And she was well aware that a woman like her had nothing to tempt a man like him. If only that worked in reverse.

Gritting her teeth, she told herself this was nothing but a mixture of nerves and relief. Tomorrow she could bury herself in work and everything would return to normal again.

Seizing one of her pieces, she moved it. 'Pawn to Queen Four.'

He responded with, 'Pawn to King Three.'

Her brows shot up.

He winked at her and it made her chest catch. 'Didn't think I'd know the lingo?'

'Sorry, I used it without thinking. It's not the way they call games any more, but it's the way Pop taught me.'

They played in silence, but every time she glanced up she found those dark eyes watching her. Once she swore she saw heat in their depths. It made her blood leap.

Don't be stupid!

But the long-ago memory of Lincoln ringing to invite her to dinner lifted through her. Things had leapt inside her then too, and she'd had to clench her eyes shut to dispel the image of the way his eyes had flared before their one and only kiss. She'd wanted to say yes so much it had hurt. She hadn't. She'd said, 'Lincoln, we can't go on a date. I can't hurt my family like that.'

'It's *just one date*, Rose,' had been his reply and she'd felt like an idiot then, because it had felt like so much more. But it wasn't. It was *just one date*.

His words had snapped her out of foolish daydreams, had

her pulling herself back into straight lines. 'Thank you for the invitation, but I don't have time for dating at the moment. Please don't ask me again.'

It hadn't been a lie. After her mother's recent death, her father had needed her in ways he never had before. She'd refused to add to his pain—his consuming grief.

She'd been proven right in not dating Lincoln, though. He'd gone on to date *so many* women. She'd have just been one in a long line. He'd have broken her inexperienced heart. And she'd have hurt her family for nothing. For heaven's sake, even now whenever she saw his picture in the newspaper, some beautiful woman on his arm, it sent a sting through her.

Glancing up, she found a frown in those bitter chocolate eyes. 'Where did you just go?' His face gentled. 'You looked so sad.'

Lincoln might have the attention span of a flea when it came to women but it didn't change the fact that he was kind. And her heart was still every bit as inexperienced now as it had been seven years ago. She couldn't misinterpret that kindness. She needed to be careful. Before she could come up with a reply, Lindy appeared in the doorway.

'Linc, a delivery just arrived for you.'

Lincoln stood with his familiar indolence. 'I sent some things on to Marni from Kalku. Was going to borrow a vehicle and collect them tomorrow. Someone must've sent them on.'

'That's uh, not what this is. It's a...special delivery from your father.'

Clay hadn't shown up at the registry office yesterday. This could be an olive branch. Or it could be mischief. Rose stood too, and prayed for Lincoln's sake that it was the former.

Reaching into the corridor outside, Lindy brought forth a small animal carrier. Inside was an ugly marmalade tabby. Rose had a sudden image of her mother sitting in Holt's office with an elegant chocolate and cream shorthair on her lap, stroking its fur and cooing softly.

She raised an eyebrow in Lincoln's direction, but he was already striding across to take possession of the crate. 'Thanks, Lindy.' Walking back, he set it on the ottoman. Kneeling down he said, 'Hey there, Colin. How you doing, buddy?'

A loud purring immediately filled the air.

Mischief. Definitely mischief. 'Why would your father send you a cat?' She did her best to keep her voice neutral.

'How do you feel about cats, Rose?'

Not enthusiastic. Not when they had working dogs. Not with dingoes around. Damn it, cats could do a lot of damage to the native wildlife, were a disaster if they went feral. All farmers knew that.

He grimaced at whatever he saw in her face.

'Tell me he's microchipped, registered and desexed.'

'He is.'

'He'll have to be an inside cat.'

'Absolutely.' He glanced across the room. 'How's River with cats?'

'Fine. My mother had a series of shorthair Burmese cats when we were growing up. River came to an understanding with the last one. But...' She gestured at the cat and raised her hands. 'Why?'

One broad shoulder lifted. 'He's a stray I picked up in Adelaide last year. Half starved, half dead. I took him to a vet—not registered or microchipped. The vet was going to put him down.' He rolled his shoulders. 'It seemed a bit harsh.'

Oh, God, why did he have to be such a gorgeous big... *marshmallow*?

'My father wasn't a member of the Colin fan club either.'

Hence the reason Colin was now here in her living room. Biting back a sigh, she moved across to crouch in front of the carrier. 'Hello, Colin, welcome to Garrison Downs. I'd appreciate it if you'd be on your best behaviour for the next couple of days while we get to know one another.'

Easing back, she nodded at Lincoln to let the poor cat out.

When the door opened, Colin's head emerged. He looked as if someone—or something—had chewed off half his ear. The rest of him followed with a regal air at odds with his appearance. Lincoln's lips twitched. She bit back a grin.

Lifting his head, he sniffed the air and then, with an unholy yowl, swung in the direction of River quietly dozing on the other side of the coffee table. River lifted his head, instantly alert. Upon seeing the cat, he stood and shook himself, gave a friendly bark.

A signal Colin clearly misinterpreted as a call to arms as he immediately charged the poor dog. River might be old but he was still nimble. He took off around the room with the cat in hot pursuit.

'Do something,' she yelled at Lincoln.

'Colin! *Stop that!*'

'Very effective.' At her signal River made straight across the room to her, jumping up on the coffee table and scattering the chess pieces in all directions before leaping onto the sofa. Rose moved to shield him and, with one hand held out, hollered, 'Stop!'

Amazingly, Colin did.

'You want back in your crate?' she threatened, pointing at the crate.

Colin sat amid the debris of the coffee table, curled his tail around himself and started cleaning one paw. Lincoln scooped him up, grinning. 'You've a way with him already.'

Rolling her eyes, she glanced behind to find Lindy holding onto the doorway convulsing with laughter. 'I'll get the trays and bowls and whatnot out of storage, shall I?'

'Thanks, Lindy.'

She turned and then tried not to melt at the sight of the big strong man holding the big ugly kitty who clearly adored him. Lincoln stood there looking impossibly wonderful. Impossibly gorgeous. Impossibly out of reach.

He glanced up and froze at whatever he saw in her face.

Oh, God. Had she been making big cow eyes at him?

Very slowly he eased Colin to the floor. Then he ambled across until they stood so close she could see the lighter amber flecks that glinted in his eyes. 'If you ever want to change the terms of our agreement, Rose…'

He was talking about sex. She took a step back, her heart pounding. 'I don't.'

He raised an eyebrow.

Damn it! She couldn't very well deny that she'd been checking him out. 'Look, you're an attractive man, but…no.'

He folded his arms, looking as strong and sturdy as a mountain. 'We're consenting adults. We find each other attractive.'

He found her attractive? Fat chance. She'd probably do as a stopgap. But she didn't want to be anyone's stopgap. Instinct warned her that this man would threaten her peace of mind…and even her heart, if she let him.

And that was out of the question.

'We're not going to dance this particular dance, Lincoln. There's too much at stake. We might both be footloose and fancy-free—'

'Neither of us is footloose and fancy-free.' His eyes flashed. 'For the next three months we're *married*.'

Her heart hammered in her throat. 'I'm not going to break the promises I made you. But you have a reputation. I expect you'll find three months of abstinence…challenging.'

'That's harsh.' One eyebrow cocked. 'Especially in light

of the fact that I've not been with a woman in over fourteen months.'

Her jaw dropped. 'But…' That was impossible. 'You've been photographed with eight or nine different women in the last year!'

He sent her a slow grin. 'Been counting, Rose?'

She had. But she wasn't admitting as much.

'I expect it's been a while for you too.'

If she told him she'd never had a lover, would he laugh out loud, run scared, or see it as a challenge? None of those scenarios filled her with enthusiasm.

She fixed him with what she hoped was a glare. 'All I want is for us to be friends. And if that's not possible, then for us to at least not be enemies.'

'I want that too.' The expression in his eyes flattened. 'And just for the record, our relationship won't ever become physical until you like me rather than loathe me.'

'I don't loathe you!'

But she found herself talking to thin air. Lincoln had already marched from the room.

CHAPTER FOUR

LINC LEANED BACK in his chair and sent Rose a slow grin when she strode into the kitchen the next morning. 'You're looking radiant this morning, Rose.' The unguarded hunger he'd surprised in her eyes last night still had him wondering if he ought to be fanning the flames rather than taking things slow.

She startled, glared, and then rolled her eyes at Lindy, and he knew she thought he was flirting for the housekeeper's benefit.

'Looks like we've a morning person in our midst.'

Lindy's chuckle could be heard over the spitting and crackling of bacon. Reaching for a mug with 'Boss' stamped on it, Lindy filled it to the brim with hot dark coffee and pushed it across to Rose, who promptly buried her face in it.

When she surfaced a few moments later, everything about her had sharpened. Coffee, it seemed, was a non-negotiable first thing in the morning. *This.* Hunger and possessiveness shot through him in equal measure. He wanted *this*—to learn everything about Rose; to know her in ways no one else did.

'Thanks, Lindy.' Rose plonked down on the seat across from him.

Lindy placed poached eggs in front of Rose, and bacon and eggs in front of Linc, and a towering plate of toast between them. 'It's nice to have another morning person around. Reminds me of the way it was when Holt was here.'

Rose's face instantly closed.

That expression… He eased back. From where he was sitting, it looked less like grief and more like anger.

Holt had always been larger than life—a walking, talking, living, breathing legend. A man who could do no wrong. The news of his affair must've rocked Rose to her very foundations.

Not a topic he meant to raise today, though. 'What's on for the day?'

'I need to get a report from the outstation, check in with the trucking companies to make sure we're coordinated for the muster. And we have a vet visit at the stud that I want in on. After that it's routine maintenance on the bikes and quads.'

'Where would I be most useful?'

'Tomorrow I'd say out on Judy, checking herd locations, but today there's something I want to show you.'

His ears pricked at something in her voice, at the bright flash of blue in her eyes.

'After that, the choice is yours. It's—'

She broke off, already on her feet when Aaron strode into the kitchen. 'What's wrong? Is anyone hurt?'

Her head stockman shook his head.

Linc didn't stand. He eased his chair back and stretched out his legs. He preferred to conserve his energy—only kicking into action when necessary. And he wanted to assess the dynamics here. Rose had mentioned that Aaron was overseeing the building of the new yard on the central western boundary. Why was he here?

'We have a problem.'

Rose put her hands on her hips. 'Which is?'

Aaron flicked a glance in Lincoln's direction. The dislike in his eyes had Linc's mind whirring, though he was careful to keep his posture deceptively lazy. This was one of the reasons people dismissed him as a lightweight—he gave nothing away. It made them think he wasn't paying attention, wasn't processing what was happening. It had given him an edge more times than he could count.

Aaron's face twisted. 'Cattle have gone missing on the south-eastern boundary.'

The boundary with Kalku Hills? Things inside him tensed. Had his father taken advantage of the fact that both he and Rose had been in Adelaide? Had he whisked the cattle away while attention was elsewhere? His gut clenched. It was clearly what Aaron thought.

'We're talking over a thousand head of prime—'

'Thank you, Aaron, I'm well aware of the numbers.'

Her face tightened and his chest hollowed.

Blue eyes flashed. 'Why am I hearing this news from you? Why hasn't Nick rung it in to me directly? Why aren't you overseeing the building of the new yard?'

The safety of those yards was a prime concern of every cattleman in the country. If the yards didn't hold, if just one element was overlooked, it could spell disaster.

'It's just as well I am here! I not only—'

'You mean to tell me you never *left*?'

'Johnno is more than capable of overseeing the yard and—'

He doesn't have the experience you do! You had no right—'

She broke off, breathing heavily, glancing at Linc. She moderated her tone, clearly not wanting to upbraid the man in front of him. Probably wise. 'You and I are going to have a serious conversation *very* soon, Aaron. I want you out at that yard now.'

'What about the missing cattle?'

'Lincoln and I will take care of it.'

'Him?'

Aaron's face twisted before he started around the table in Linc's direction. Linc stood in one unhurried motion. If the man threw a punch, he wasn't giving him a height advantage.

Aaron stabbed a finger at him. 'If you hurt her, me and the boys will take you out the back and beat you senseless and leave you for the dingoes.'

'Aaron!' Rose snapped. From the corner of his eyes he saw Lindy cover her mouth.

Linc moved in close to Aaron. Aaron was a big man, but Linc was bigger—taller and broader—and he used all of that now to deliberately loom over the other man, though he was careful to keep a pleasant expression on his face. 'And if you hurt Rose you'll have to answer to me. I won't need anyone else. I'll be enough.'

'All right, enough.' Rose moved between them and pushed them apart.

'You know what the Garrisons are!' Aaron flung out an arm. 'You know they can't be trusted!'

'Careful, Aaron.' Her voice had gone dangerously soft. 'Are you accusing my new husband and my father-in-law of stealing Garrison Downs' cattle?'

She moved in close, deliberately in Aaron's face. She might be half a head shorter, but she bristled all over and it reminded him of the way Colin had charged River last night, smaller but fiercer. 'You need to be very sure before you start throwing accusations like that around.'

She said the words as if by rote. He'd bet she'd learned them at her father's knee.

'You can ruin a good reputation with unfounded accusations, and out here one's reputation is their livelihood. You *know* that.' Reaching up, she grabbed his hat from his head and slapped it against his chest. 'No hats in the house! You know that too. Now go.'

She strode back to the table and seized a piece of toast, bit into it ferociously. Aaron didn't move. She turned back, her eyes narrowing. 'And?'

'Franz Arteta rang. He's put a hold on the contract.'

Her shoulders drew as tight as the strings on a freshly strung tennis racquet.

'And when the Graziers Association rang to ask if you'd give the annual address, I told them you'd be delighted to.' He smirked. 'If you're not up to it, though, I'll do it.'

Lincoln wasn't taking that sitting down. 'Everyone knows you've wanted the association gig for the last five years, mate, but that's not the way to go about getting it. If they'd wanted you, they'd have asked you.'

Aaron turned a dark shade of red.

Ambling around the table, Lincoln rested an arm across Rose's shoulders. 'I've wanted it for the last five years too. Rose, though, will do a brilliant job.'

A shiver swept through her, not visible, but he felt it. She didn't want to give the annual address? But it was considered an honour. Holt had given the address multiple times and—

Ah... Holt's were ridiculously large shoes to fill. It'd be enough to intimidate anyone.

He kept speaking to give her time to collect herself. 'You know she's the right person, I know it, and more importantly the association knows it.'

Silence stretched through the room. Seizing his orange juice, Lincoln downed it in one go. 'I am, however, the best pilot in the district. Guess I better go get ready. You two probably have other things to discuss.'

'Nope.' Aaron started for the door, clearly realising that if Lincoln left, Rose would give him *what for* in no uncertain terms. 'I'll get out to the new yard now.'

Rose glanced at Lincoln and he waited for her to tell him she didn't need anyone to fight her battles for her. Instead she gestured for him to sit and finish his breakfast. 'That was nicely done. You put him in his place, but placed yourself on his level too.'

'Wouldn't work for you, not when you're the boss.'

He wanted to ask how far Aaron was overstepping. He wanted to know why the association address intimidated her. And who the hell was Franz Arteta and what contract had he put on hold? If he could, he'd fix *all* the things.

'Finish your breakfast, Lincoln, we've a long day ahead of us.'

She spoke as if on automatic pilot, her mind racing behind the blue of her eyes.

'Yes, ma'am.'

She started, her lips hooking up in a reluctant smile. 'The girls always did call me bossy boots. Sorry.'

'Forgiven…on the proviso you sit down and finish your breakfast too.'

She did. When they'd finished up, she stacked their plates in the dishwasher, Lindy having long since moved on to some other chore. 'Lincoln, while you're here I don't want you putting up with any insults—veiled or otherwise. I want that nonsense knocked on its head as soon as it shows its face.'

'I can look after myself, Rose. I keep telling you that.' She opened her mouth, but he got in first. 'No hats in the house, huh?'

'No boots, no hats—my mother's rule.'

He loved the inbuilt continuity and unspoken respect of it. 'I won't forget. Now for this reconnaissance—plane or chopper?'

'The plane would get us there faster, but the chopper will give us more manoeuvrability.'

'Chopper,' they both agreed.

An hour later they were flying across Garrison Downs' southern boundary.

'Rose, I don't know what kind of trash talk Aaron's been indulging in, but the district thinks you're doing a brilliant job.'

He pretended his attention was on the land stretching away beneath them, but from the corner of his eye he saw the way she rocked back in her seat as if his words had shocked her. The way her hands half lifted as if to press against her eyes.

His jaw clenched. *Damn Aaron.* Rose had enough on her plate without him undermining her. 'We both know what Garrison Downs means to the local economy. It's not fair, I know, but people have been watching, waiting, trying to calculate the fallout from the change in circumstances.'

He met her gaze briefly. 'But there hasn't been any. The transition has been seamless. Everyone is impressed with the job you're doing. Seriously impressed.'

Moistening her lips, she nodded. 'Good. Not that they're impressed with me. That's neither here nor there. But that fears have eased. I know…' A breath shuddered out of her. 'I know how worried people have been. I'm glad confidence in Garrison Downs is building again.'

'Holt is a hard act to follow, but you've got what it takes to step into his shoes. You know your land, you know the business, you know the challenges facing the industry. Don't let anyone convince you otherwise. From where I'm sitting, you seem to be doing it with ease—with one arm tied behind your back while standing on your head.'

She huffed out a laugh and he let out a careful breath. Rose had the weight of the world on her shoulders. He'd do whatever he could to lighten her load.

Twenty minutes later they were flying over the area where last week Lincoln had called in his sighting of a large herd. Nothing. Not a steer or heifer in sight. Rose craned her neck to look at the control panel. 'The coordinates are right.'

This was exactly where he'd have expected to find them. 'Want me to check the fence line with Kalku?'

'Yes, please.'

He heard her sigh through the headphones. She had to suspect Clay was behind this. Acid burned his throat. And maybe him.

Not once had she asked him if he thought his father responsible, though. He still hadn't worked out how he'd answer if she did. Would he tell her the truth?

Or would he lie?

Damn it! Fact of the matter was he thought his father as guilty as hell. He should never have invited Clay to the wedding, should never have let him know he'd be away from the station for even a day. He'd been so careful during the last fortnight, making his father aware that he was patrolling the boundary with an eagle eye.

Clay had always believed that Garrison Downs should've been his—that it'd been stolen from him a hundred and twenty years ago—but Linc never had. What Clay refused to see was that he'd have never made a success of the place the way Holt had. That was what really stuck in his father's craw. It was why he hid behind that ancient poker match with its rumours of cheating and foul deeds, bleating about what could've been.

Seizing the binoculars, Rose focussed on something below.

Linc rubbed a hand over his face. How the hell was he going to convince Rose to trust him when—?

'Lincoln, can you take us down?'

He crashed back, stared at the land below. What the hell had she seen?

Rose stared at the tracks made by a quad bike—fresh tracks—and the familiar marks made by a mob of cattle on the move and bit back something rude and succinct.

She couldn't look at Lincoln, afraid her thoughts would show on her face.

'Rose.' Lincoln pointed to a brand-new section of fence—a recent repair. As if it had been cut to allow a herd of cattle to pass though. 'There was nothing wrong with this boundary when I flew over it a few days ago.'

He'd been keeping an eye on their boundary with Kalku? Had he been scouting for his father? Feeding Kalku the locations of Garrison Down cattle?

Her stomach churned. In marrying Lincoln, had she made the sorriest mistake of her life?

'Hold your horses, Boss. You know—'

Shut up. I'm not talking to you.

'I knew nothing about this, I swear.'

The low throb in his voice burned through her. Stalking over to the fence, she forced herself to assess the ground on the other side, searching for clues. Frowned.

'If my father is behind this—'

She whirled on him. 'We *don't* make unsubstantiated accusations.' She pointed a finger at him. *'Ever.'*

Corded forearms folded across a substantial chest. 'You sounded like Holt then.'

From beneath the wide brim of his hat, his mouthed kinked up and her heart did some dumb lamb-like cavort thing. She forced her gaze away. 'Yeah, well, it was one of the things we did agree on,' she bit out.

The anger she harboured against Holt was getting harder and harder to contain. She needed to get a grip. She didn't want anyone, and certainly not Lincoln, sensing what she refused to say out loud—that there were multiple issues she and Holt hadn't agreed on.

Like hiding a daughter away as if she was something to be ashamed of.

Like not letting her know her sisters.

The injustice of it—the moral bankruptcy—still burned

through her as fierce and hot today as it had when Harrington had read the will nine months ago.

Boss—

But that wasn't where her focus should currently be. She turned back to Lincoln. 'Do you remember Roddy Jackson?'

Squinting into the sun, he nodded.

Rumours had started getting around that Roddy, a local grazier, wasn't paying his suppliers. Somehow the rumours had gathered momentum and people began to cross the street so they didn't have to talk to Roddy whenever he went into town. One day he was refused service at the pub.

He'd gone home and had tried to take his own life. Luckily he hadn't succeeded, and it had eventually come to light that his accountant had been cooking the books. Roddy hadn't been responsible at all. It had made a huge impression on her.

It had made a huge impression on Holt, too. Out here a person's reputation was everything.

The hard light in Lincoln's eyes as he stared at the ridge in the distance, and the white line of his mouth, had her swallowing. Maybe he wasn't responsible for this. Maybe he and his father weren't working together to steal her cattle.

We don't make unsubstantiated accusations.

She straightened. She'd take her own advice. She'd keep her eyes and ears open, and judge based on the evidence she saw—*not* hearsay or inherited suspicion.

And what was the current evidence? She breathed out slowly. 'Look at the ground on the other side of the fence, Lincoln.'

He did as she ordered. She had to stop doing that—barking orders at him as if he were some green station hand. Air whistled between his teeth. 'No tracks.'

She folded her arms and rested back against a fence post. 'Not one. The cattle will still be on Garrison Down land somewhere. An experienced cattleman on a quad bike, with a good working dog—' and they all had good working dogs '—could easily cut a thousand head of cattle into five separate herds of two hundred. Or even ten herds of a hundred if he had the time and inclination.'

'My father?'

'Holt and Clay have been at this nonsense since they were teenagers.' A tit-for-tat back-and-forth that passed for sport out here.

Lincoln's jaw clenched. She shrugged. 'I wasn't supposed to know.'

'Why the hell didn't I know too? Where was my head at?'

'Rumour had it your head was always taken up with your latest busty blonde.'

That had him grinning. 'Is that an unsubstantiated rumour?'

'Not if the pictures in the papers are anything to go by.'

Those dark eyes surveyed her as the smile slowly dissolved. 'Just so you know, Rose, they weren't all blonde, nor were they necessarily busty.'

Fourteen months.

He'd not been with a woman for fourteen months. Why had he told her that?

She pushed away from the fence. It didn't matter. It was none of her business. And she *didn't* care. 'Come on, let's go find my missing cattle. Those hills to the north are our best bet.'

CHAPTER FIVE

IN MARCH THE days were long and warm, but the evenings held a welcome hint of coolness. Rose pulled clean air into her lungs and let it out slowly, her fingers idly ruffling Blossom's fur. Like River, her working dog, Blossom was a lilac border collie. She'd had her since she was a pup. Unlike River, though, as a working dog she was relegated to the back veranda.

They both enjoyed the early evening stillness, broken only by the 'chet-chet' chattering of a flock of galahs, their feathers flashing pink and grey as they flew in to nest for the night, the horizon softening from a deep orange to muted bands of lilac and blue.

The French doors to Lincoln's room opened to her left. He strode out—freshly showered and wearing a pair of low-slung denims and a white T-shirt. If she were the director of a soap opera, she'd have made that T-shirt ridiculously tight so viewers could appreciate every superb muscle.

Actually, as a director she'd probably have him ditch the shirt altogether.

Oh, for heaven's sake.

Swallowing hard, she forced herself into relaxed lines. 'Evening, Lincoln.'

He turned with that customary indolence. 'I wondered where you'd disappeared to.'

It'd been a fraught day, searching for the scattered cattle, but they could both relax now. The cattle had been found. She gestured at the view. 'I love it out here at this time of day.'

He nodded. 'The gardens here are a real treat. Up for an amble?'

She accepted the hand he held out, let him pull her to her feet. He didn't relinquish her hand, but wrapped his fingers firmly around hers. The bare skin of his arm brushed against the bare skin of her arm. Her throat went so tight it hurt. What did he think he was doing? Gritting her teeth, she tugged her hand from his. Did what she could to ignore the warmth and temptation of the man.

They walked in silence for a bit. 'Rose, are you worried about giving the annual address for the Graziers Association?'

The question took her off guard.

'I get the impression you are, but I don't see why you would be.'

She folded her arms tight across her chest. 'Ooh, let me see... Maybe because they only asked me hoping I'll dish up the inside story on the family scandal.'

'You're selling yourself short.'

He pointed up at the sky and she glanced up to see the first stars starting to emerge. Rolling her shoulders, she unfolded her arms, tried to relax. Reclaiming her hand, he squeezed it and everything inside her tensed again.

'Your insights on taking over the reins of a large enterprise like Garrison Downs—the challenges, the pitfalls...the joys—that's what people want to hear about.'

Nuh uh, he was wrong.

Except...

She frowned. What he described was exactly what she'd wished she'd had a chance to hear and learn from.

'Your experience, that's what's of real use to people on the land. It's gold, Rose. Rose gold.'

And then he grinned as if delighted with the pun and she had to choke back a laugh.

'You have an opportunity to help, to make a real difference. That's why you were invited to be the speaker.'

She had no idea what to say, her mind whirling with the new spin he'd put on the issue.

'Mind you—' he winked '—if you wanted to include some salacious gossip, the tabloids would love you.'

Huffing out a laugh, she tried to run him into a grevillea. 'Very helpful, Lincoln, thank you.'

He grinned, glancing around. 'Your father had the gardens built for your mother, didn't he?'

She welcomed the change of topic. 'Theirs was a whirlwind romance, but once my mother found herself out here so far from family and friends and all that she knew, it was tough for her. She became homesick.'

Her mother's lovely face rose in her mind, the faraway look in her eyes whenever she spoke of her home, and a familiar ache gripped her chest. She did what she could to breathe through it. 'So Holt created this garden for her. It was her pride and joy.' Her solace and her comfort. 'When Da—Holt had New House built, one of the things that excited her most was enlarging the garden. The garden connects both homesteads while providing both households with privacy.'

Rounding the corner of the house she gestured across the lawn to the lights twinkling behind a hedge of lilly pilly—Old House, the original homestead. It must've been a nightmare for Rosamund to move to Garrison Downs and then be forced to live with her mother-in law. Other than their love for Holt, the two women had had nothing in common.

'Did you tell Eve about Cordelia's diary?'

'I told all the girls. Eve's been scouring the place, but so far no luck.'

He squeezed her hand. 'I'd love it if we found it.'

She made herself smile, but things inside her tensed. What did Lincoln expect to find in that diary? Evidence that Garrison Downs still belonged to his family?

She shook herself. 'Tilly would go mad for it.'

He glanced down. In the gathering darkness it was hard to read his expression. 'What's your favourite part of the garden?'

'My mother's was the rose garden. Come and see. We're very proud of it.'

He pulled her to a halt. His thumb brushed the inside of her wrist, back and forth, making her pulse jump and pulling her skin tight.

'I didn't ask to see your mother's favourite part of the garden, I asked to see yours.'

Hers? 'It's not particularly picturesque.' Not in the same way the rose garden was.

'Show me anyway.'

And still that thumb brushed across the sensitive skin of her wrist. Gritting her teeth, she turned them to the right. She *could* ignore it. She *would* ignore it.

Except she couldn't. And the awareness built inside her until she wanted to scream. For heaven's sake, all he was doing was idly running his thumb back and forth. He probably didn't even realise he was doing it!

On the pretence of gesturing to a large gum, she tugged her hand from his again and moved across to sit on the swing that hung from one of its branches—a swing with a seat broad enough for three sisters. 'This is my favourite spot in the garden. Evie, Tilly and I turned this into our unofficial clubhouse.'

And Ana should've been here with them. She started to seethe. If Holt had—

'What did you do here?'

She pulled her mind back. 'Evie would spin tales of princes and princesses and fairy-tale castles while Tilly would regale us with stories of the Taj Mahal and the Colosseum and Stonehenge.'

He gestured. 'May I?'

She shuffled over and he took a seat beside her. Their shoulders touched and she inhaled his scent—clean and fresh, but laced with something darker that had an edge to it, like leather or fresh firewood. It complemented the night perfectly.

'And what about you?'

'It's where I plotted how to make sure I could join the muster when I was thirteen. How to talk my mother into letting me do my last few years of school via correspondence rather than at boarding school. It's where we plotted to sweet-talk our old housekeeper, Mrs Bishop, into making ANZAC biscuits, how to break the news of some misdemeanour to our parents, and how to wrangle someone to take us into Marni.'

His laugh, low and rich, had an added potency in the gathering dark and goosebumps raced across her skin. The moon had started to rise, a large golden disc. She pointed, turning to see if Lincoln had followed the line of her arm, to find him staring at her, his eyes deep and dark.

'Has the swing witnessed any stolen kisses?'

Flirting came as easily to him as breathing. 'I'm sure it's seen its fair share.'

'Any of them yours?'

Maybe it was the beauty of the night—the stars and the scent of roses drifting across the lawn—but she felt suddenly lighter and freer. Since she'd married Lincoln, a weight had lifted from her shoulders. And it made her feel...hopeful. Rather than close him down, she raised an eyebrow. 'Why? Tempted to steal a kiss?'

'More than life itself.'

His eyes blazed in the light of the moon and that dark hungry gaze drifted to her lips. A pulse started up deep inside. He stared at her with the same intensity that he had seven years ago, and she knew in that moment he was going to kiss her.

More to the point, she knew she was going to let him. She wanted to know if her memory of that long ago kiss was real. Or if she'd blown it out of proportion.

Lincoln's mouth lowered towards hers with unhurried deliberation, and they hovered there between breaths, savouring the moment. Down by the river a spotted nightjar called a series of rising notes.

And then Lincoln's lips were on hers and they were neither urgent nor fierce and yet everything inside her quickened and shifted. Her mouth opened—on a gasp or whether to draw more of him in, she had no idea. But he accepted the invitation without hesitation, one hand cupping the back of her head while he thoroughly plundered and explored. Her fingers curled into the material of his shirt to pull him even closer so she could plunder him back.

Need coursed through her like a grass fire—an instant and fierce conflagration that was mindless and demanding. They careened across the grass, and she couldn't even remember standing. At the last moment, Lincoln turned them, his back crashing into the huge gum behind, his hands gripping her hips as though he'd never let her go. Hell, he'd have bruises. He'd—

But then his mouth was on hers again and there was nothing lazy or slow about it and her mind splintered. Hands slid beneath her shirt—strong and warm against her fevered flesh. Excellent idea. She slid her hands beneath his shirt too, explored the hard contours of his stomach. Slid them upwards to explore that glorious chest, ran the flat of her palms over flat male nipples that beaded intriguingly and made her hungry to explore more.

'Rose.'

Her name sounded ragged, as if dragged from some deep place inside him.

'Rose.'

This time it was accompanied with the tiniest of shakes. She forced her gaze upwards. Eyes slumberous with desire stared down at her and she almost stood on tiptoe to kiss him again. But hands at her ribcage held her in place, and she belatedly realised the question he was asking—did she want this to continue?

Hell, yes.

She swallowed. But...

She swore.

He released her immediately.

She took a couple of steps back, sucking in a breath. She was a virgin. At twenty-nine. And, yes, she knew it was laughable, but there were reasons. If they were to continue, she'd have to tell him.

And she wasn't sure...

She lifted her chin. Why shouldn't she embrace what he had to offer? Surely she was finally due something just for herself? She'd put that side of her life on hold for so long...

His eyes glittered in the dark and a hard thirst gripped her. She wanted him with an intensity that took her off guard, but it didn't automatically follow that she should fight it.

'Do you think we can be lovers without damaging a potential friendship?' she asked, clenching and unclenching her hands.

He nodded and moved a step closer. 'Do you want to become lovers, Rose?'

'Yes.' She held up a hand when he took another step towards her. 'But there's something you ought to know first.'

'Okay.'

She hitched her head in the direction of the homestead. 'C'mon, we need a drink for this.'

They kicked off their shoes, washed their hands, and she led him through to the piano bar—the most grown-up room in the house with its ebony baby grand, glittering chandelier and indulgent white carpet. And Holt's best whisky. Lincoln whistled when she pulled the bottle from behind the bar. She poured them both a generous measure and pushed a glass towards him.

Too keyed up to move to one of the chairs, she paced across to the piano, her feet sinking into the white carpet that was so insanely difficult to keep clean. As kids, they'd never entered this room without permission.

She turned, leaned against the baby grand. 'What I'm about to tell you isn't particularly edifying, but…here goes.' She took a fortifying sip. 'Have you ever made a really bad promise?'

He rested back on a bar stool. 'I suppose we all have.'

'When I was fifteen, my grandmother made noises about putting Pop in a nursing home.' Her grandfather, Cec Waverly, had been gored and tossed by a mickey bull when he was thirty-eight. It had left him partially crippled.

'Was your granddad that…?'

'Incapacitated? Unwell?' She shook her head. 'My grandmother was simply a mean-spirited woman who wanted to manipulate everyone around her. I begged her not to put Pop in a home, told her he belonged at Garrison Downs.'

The memory could still make her stomach churn. She knew now Holt would never have allowed that to happen, but she'd only been fifteen and so easily manipulated. 'I loved Pop. We were close. He taught me to identify the tracks of wild animals, taught me survival skills necessary to the land, and he taught me how to play chess.'

'Rose, what did you promise?'

She slugged back the rest of her whisky in one hit, let it warm the cold places inside her. 'In return for not putting Pop in a nursing home, I promised my grandmother I'd remain a virgin until my wedding night.'

His head rocked back. She wanted to curl into a ball and hide from his shock.

Don't be a drama queen.

'Why would she demand such a thing?'

'She seemed to think I could use it as some kind of bargaining chip to snare myself *"an important husband".*' She rolled her eyes. 'Nobody could accuse my grandmother of progressive attitudes.'

Anger burned bright in his eyes. 'Did she demand the same of your sisters?'

'No, thank God. She said I'd be the one to take over the station, that Evelyn and Matilda would leave for what they thought were brighter pastures, which apparently made them fools.' Her hand clenched around her now empty glass. 'She said that as I would be the Waverly to take over Garrison Downs, we couldn't have me doing anything that would bring shame on the family. Quote, *"I won't have you marry someone unsuitable just because you have a bun in the oven."*'

He swore.

'My sentiments exactly.' She attempted a smile. 'In case you don't know, that's a line from the movie *Mamma Mia*.'

He didn't smile back. His hand clenched so hard he'd started to shake. 'Rose, are you telling me you're still a virgin?'

'Yes.' Her cheeks burned, but she refused to look away. 'Not because of that promise. I figured Grandma's lies and manipulations made it null and void. But I didn't figure that out until my first year of university.'

She stared into her glass, wished she hadn't guzzled her drink so fast. 'A few weeks after I started seeing someone though, and before things had progressed that far, my grandmother died. I came home—for the funeral and to help out where I could—and by the time I returned to university the guy I'd been seeing had moved on to someone else.'

He dragged a hand down his face. 'Rose...'

'Oh, he didn't break my heart, though he sure as hell hurt my pride. But the thing is, no one else has seriously tempted me since.' She swallowed. 'Other than the night of the Bachelor & Spinster ball when I was twenty-two...'

'When we kissed.'

He remembered it too. Something inside her shook, though in relief or fear she couldn't tell. She forced a shrug. 'It seemed stupid to sleep with someone just for the sake of it. It didn't help that I was working my butt off. I completed the face-to-face components of a four-year degree in two. That didn't leave much room for socialising.'

'And since university?'

She eased down to the piano stool. 'There has always been something more important that needed doing, that took precedence. Pop died when I was nineteen, Mum when I was twenty-two. Holt needed me.'

She rubbed a hand over her face. 'I had a rule not to sleep with anyone who worked here, figured that'd be asking for trouble. And it's not a simple hop, skip and jump into town.'

'Rose, it's only an hour to Marni from here.'

It sounded appalling, laid out so starkly. 'I thought that one day I'd see someone and *bam*—sparks would fly.' She stood and moved across to him. 'And now it has. With you.'

Lincoln stared down at her with eyes that throbbed. And then he stepped back. 'Excuse me, Rose. I need some air.'

Rose stared after him, started at the sound of the front door closing. Moving across to the bar on legs that felt like lead, she poured herself another whisky. But she couldn't drink it. Her stomach churned too much for that.

What did you think was going to happen?

Lincoln was a man of the world with sophisticated tastes, and she'd just proven she was as unsophisticated as they came. Her insides shrivelled to the size of a hard dry nut. He clearly didn't want to mess with a naïve little virgin.

Pressing her palms to her eyes didn't ease the way they burned. Was Lincoln worried the naïve little virgin would fall in love with him? She dragged her hands away. She might not be worldly, but she wasn't an idiot. They both knew this arrangement was temporary.

But Lincoln walking away confirmed what she'd suspected and had been stupid not to heed—that he simply wasn't that into her. She should've listened! If she had she wouldn't be feeling such a fool now.

Instinct continued to tell her that Lincoln wasn't like his father, and she still mostly believed that. But Clay *was* his father, and she'd be a fool to ignore that fact. And she was through being a fool.

Lincoln wanted Camels Bridge. And he might also be happy to turn a blind eye to any mischief his father caused. Her stomach churned. His kisses might even be a ruse to string her along, lull her into a false sense of security. Discovering she was a virgin, though, might've pricked his conscience. Maybe messing with a virgin was a step too far in whatever skewed code of conduct he operated under.

She abandoned her drink. She needed to get *relations* between her and Lincoln back on a strictly business footing. She refused to let him leave her feeling so exposed and foolish again.

CHAPTER SIX

LINCOLN PACED THE perimeter of the garden, Rose's words echoing in his head. She was a virgin. He'd been about to fall on her like a starving dog. But...

She was a virgin!

He'd had to walk away before he'd done something he'd regret. Like surrendering to his intoxicating greed and taking what she offered with an unholy intensity. Without giving her a chance to catch her breath or think better of her decision. Or before he could work out if he could keep the promise he'd made her—*Do you think we can be lovers without damaging a potential friendship?*

To be Rose's first lover... He'd be a fool to think it wouldn't be momentous. For both of them—him as much as her.

He braced his hands on his knees. She didn't need some impatient, uncontrolled brute pawing at her. She deserved a man who'd take things slow, who'd bring her passion to deliberate but unhurried life, who'd encourage her to explore it without restraint.

He *wanted* to be the man to do that.

In the piano room, all he'd been able to think about was dragging her into his arms and making her his. *Right then.* Kissing her until she was mindless and begging, joining their bodies with a savage joy. His body had shaken with the effort of holding back.

Hence the need for a breather.

Gulping air, he straightened. She needed someone who'd focus just on her and her needs, not themselves. And he *could* be that man.

A wild uninhibited joy flooded him, making him feel more alive than he had in all of his thirty-two years. As he glanced towards the house, the light in Rose's bedroom came on like a beacon—and he answered the call, immediately starting towards it.

Rose opened the French doors on his second tap. She hadn't started getting ready for bed yet, still wore the same jeans and T-shirt she'd had on earlier. It was all he could do not to sweep her up in his arms and kiss her.

'Lincoln, I've had a rethink. And the sex thing?' She shook her head, her voice cold. 'Not going to happen.'

The ground beneath his feet tilted and he battled a sudden wave of nausea. 'You want to tell me why?'

She folded her arms and sent him a wide fake smile— one that appeared deliberately designed to annoy, which incongruously had him battling a grin. She was magnificent.

'I'd be delighted to. I just told you something I've never shared with anyone, and your response was to walk away.'

Hold on. He'd done that so—

'It makes me think you're no more trustworthy than your father. Or my grandmother.'

His head rocked back. He hadn't considered how she might interpret his leaving as he had. His chest clenched tight. His hands opened and closed, feeling strangely bereft. The last thing he'd meant to do was hurt her. 'I'm sorry if my leaving like I did made you feel bad. It was the last thing I meant to do.'

Her only answer was a shrug.

He moistened his lips. 'You want to know why I left like I did?'

'It doesn't really matter now.' She started to close the door. 'It's been a long day. I'm going to bed. *Alone.*'

'I left before I could do something appalling like fall on you like some starving wild animal.'

She froze just for a millisecond, but it was long enough for a sudden gust of breeze to snatch the door from her fingers and send it crashing back into the room. He glanced behind her, his gaze landing on an object sitting on her dresser, and he froze. She followed his gaze and swallowed.

Striding into the room, he seized the piece of amber sitting there. This was the token he'd given her when he was eleven years old—after she'd witnessed Clay hit him in the general store. Back then, this piece of amber had been one of his most prized possessions.

He turned to her with it on his palm. 'You kept it.'

Reaching out, she took it from him, colour staining her cheeks. 'It always felt like a symbol of a friendship that should've been. But I think I've always been a sentimental idiot where you're concerned.' Her gaze clashed with his. 'I felt bad that you had to put up with Clay and his terrible temper, and over the years I've let that colour my judgement.'

'We promised each other honesty, so I'll give you honesty, Rose. I went on my dating spree seven years ago because you wouldn't go out with me.'

Her eyes widened and her jaw sagged. He felt like an idiot saying it out loud, but in leaving so abruptly, he'd made her feel small and diminished. He'd do anything he could to make up for that.

'Our kiss at the dam that night rocked my world. I wanted more of it. When you wouldn't go out with me, I figured there'd be other women who could make me feel the same way.' He planted his feet, his glare defiant. 'But I was wrong.'

She glanced away, retied her ponytail.

'So the fact of the matter, Rose, is that I can totally see why you were waiting for another moment like that before sleeping with someone.'

She folded her arms tight across her chest.

'I went looking and didn't find what I was looking for. You stayed put and didn't find what you were looking for. And here we are. Again. Feels like we've come full circle.'

Her eyes throbbed in the dim light of her bedroom lamp.

He advanced on her. 'A woman like you deserves more than to have some guy fall on her and paw at her like an animal. You deserve to be wooed, you should be spoiled, and made to feel beautiful…special.'

Her chin lifted. 'It's a pretty line, but my understanding is that you've had a lot of practice at spinning pretty fictions.'

He bent at the waist until they were eye to eye. 'You shouldn't believe everything you hear.'

She shook her head. 'We're not going to do this.'

His heart dropped to his feet.

'It's too risky. What about tomorrow…and the day after that?' She stabbed a finger at him. 'What I want is for us to develop a halfway decent working relationship and that doesn't include sleeping together. We both know that could complicate things. And complicated is the last thing I need right now.'

He'd missed his chance, had played this all wrong. And now he needed to back off and give her space.

'What's at stake here for you, Lincoln? A piece of land. For me it's my home and my sisters' home. My livelihood.' She slapped a hand against her chest. 'My *life*.'

She shouldn't define her life based on the station. No

matter how profitable that land might be, she was worth so much more than that. An ache spread through his chest. Somewhere nearby a tawny frogmouth's hoot vibrated on the night air.

Rose was carrying the weight of the world on those slim shoulders. He wanted to make her life easier, not harder. It took a supreme effort, but he forced his legs to carry him through the French doors until he stood on the veranda again. 'There's more at stake for me than you give me credit for.'

Her gaze travelled over his face, but she remained silent.

'What happened between Cordelia and Louisa May all those years ago has rippled down through the generations. What happens between us now, Rose, can have the same effect on the generations to come. I don't want to leave a legacy of bitterness and hate in my wake. And I don't believe you do either. I'll do whatever I can to make sure that doesn't happen. You have my word.'

Turning, he disappeared into the darkness before his resolution crumbled, but in that moment he made a resolution. He was going to make this woman fall in love with him or die trying. He was now playing for longer than three months. He was playing for keeps.

Lincoln stared at the contract he held. The kiss in the garden two day's ago had solidified exactly what he was doing here at Garrison Downs; why he'd married Rose; what he was hoping for.

While he wanted to be in a position to prevent his father from causing harm—to both Garrison Downs and himself— and while it was also true that he'd do what he could to mend fences between the two families, what he most wanted was to win Rose's heart.

He'd never found the same fire with any woman that he'd

experienced with Rose. He'd gone looking for it, but no woman had inflamed and captivated him the way she had.

And he suspected now they never would.

There'd been a connection between the two of them since that day in the general store. Cemented by their one stolen kiss. At the B & S ball where separately, and unbeknownst to one another, they'd slipped out to catch their breath, take a rest from the noise and revelry. He'd seen her ambling on the opposite side of the dam from him, and at the same time they'd both seen the distressed calf that had been caught in the mud.

Neither of them had hesitated—even though he'd been wearing a tuxedo and she a fancy ballgown. They'd waded in and had managed to wrestle the calf free. Her dress had been ruined, her arms and legs caked in mud, splatters on her face and hair, but her eyes had sparkled and she'd laughed.

Taking her hand, he'd helped her back to drier ground where they'd grinned at each other like idiots and then... It felt like a dream when he thought about it now. The grins had faded and something electric had arced between them and his head had dipped towards hers and hers had lifted towards his and their kiss had flared in the night like some bright promise—full of fire and vitality.

They'd eventually stumbled apart. She'd lifted a hand as if to touch her lips, and he'd had wit enough to reach out and stop her, her hands still as muddy as his. But she'd threaded her fingers through his and had squeezed tight. And he'd squeezed back. Then laughter from the nearby group approaching had had them springing apart. One of her sisters had appeared with a few other friends and laughed when she'd seen the state of Rose and her dress. 'Mum's going to pitch a fit when she sees you.'

'Calf in trouble. Dad'll get it.'

'Come on, let's go get you cleaned up.'

And then she'd been moving away from him, but before she'd disappeared she'd turned back—had sent him a single glance that had burned itself onto his soul.

But she'd refused to go out with him when he'd rung, and he'd never really understood why. After yesterday's kiss, though, he wished he'd stuck around and found out, fought harder to convince her they belonged together.

He stared down at the document he held. After the stunt his father had pulled, she had to be wondering if she'd made a major mistake in marrying him. But maybe this would help.

He had three months to win her trust, to make himself indispensable…to make her fall in love with him. He'd use whatever tools he had at his disposal.

Striding into the living room, he found her curled up on her lounge with some report or other. Rose, he'd discovered, was always working. If she wasn't careful, she'd burn out.

She wore shorts, and the sight of those long legs with their smooth tanned skin had him prickling and itching all over. He ran a finger around his collar only to realise he wasn't wearing one.

'I have something for you.'

With the tiniest of frowns, she took the document he held out to her. With hands in pockets, he watched the emotions play across her face as she read it. Slamming upright, though still reading, she crackled with an outraged energy that had him thinking of summer storms and the way they could light up the entire sky.

That was what Rose was—a natural phenomenon. She might act all cool and reserved and aloof, but underneath this woman was fire and flame, thunder and lightning.

She slapped a hand to the contract. 'You can't do this!'

He grinned, doing his best not to stare at those amazing legs. 'Yeah, I can.'

'You can't just *give* me your plane, your horse, and your cat.'

Holding her gaze, he nodded. 'They're the three things I love most in the world.' Then he aimed for levity. 'Despite appearances to the contrary, I love my father too, but you can't give people away. There are laws against it. I checked.'

She huffed out a laugh. 'Lincoln, be serious. This—'

'I've never been more serious. I want you to trust me. I want you to know that I plan on keeping every promise I've made to you. I want you to believe me when I tell you I'm not working with my father to harm Garrison Downs or your position here in any way.'

She stared at him, her eyes wide and uncertain, but she wanted to believe him, he could see that too.

'If I don't, you get to keep Judy, that's what I call the Cessna, along with Thunder my horse and Colin. And I know *you* know how much those things mean to me.' Out here, a man's horse was everything. The Cessna was a symbol of freedom, of autonomy. And while Colin wasn't worth anything materially, he'd stolen Linc's heart. Losing any of them would gut him.

She pressed a hand to her brow as if trying to understand why he was doing this—why he'd risk these things.

'Once I've kept all of my promises, I ask that you return that contract to me so I can destroy it.'

She shook the paper at him. 'You've not stipulated that here.'

'I know. I also know if you promise to do it, you will. I don't need that in black and white.'

'You should protect—'

He pressed a finger to her lips. 'I know you're a person of honour. When you make a promise, you keep it. I trust you.'

Straightening, she held his gaze. 'In three months' time, once you've fulfilled all the terms of our agreement, I promise to return this contract to you.'

'Thank you.' Job done. He'd made a start.

And now to induce her to a bit of downtime. He gestured at the television. 'Now, come on, you have me intrigued. Put on an episode of *The Bold and the Beautiful*.' He knew she recorded them. 'I did some research while I was out at Ned's Gorge and there's a villainess who intrigues me.'

'Oh, she's deliciously awful. I love her.'

Curling up on the sofa, she tossed the report to the coffee table. River leapt up beside her, his head on her lap. Lincoln sat on her other side, not too close, feet on the ottoman. Colin leapt up and started to clean himself on Lincoln's lap. She glanced at Lincoln, a quizzical light in her eyes. 'You sure about this?'

'Positive.'

Huffing out a laugh, she reached for the remote.

'All I'm saying is that I don't understand why she had to throw such a big temper tantrum.'

At his side, Rose laughed and the morning air grew brighter as they moved towards a complex of well-maintained outbuildings. Even the red dust seemed tinged with gold. 'It's because she's the ultimate drama queen—*drama* being the operative word.'

'The guy was such a patsy. He let her walk all over him and then he needled her—*deliberately*.'

'It's because he thinks she's in love with his dead brother.'

He halted. 'Isn't she?'

'Nope.' She halted too. 'She was only pretending because he was blackmailing her.'

'You *cannot* be serious.'

'A soap's joy is in all of its crazy sauce over-the-topness, its melodrama.' Her eyes danced. 'But underneath all of that there are some universal truths.'

'Like?'

She swung away, still grinning. 'Perhaps we can explore that more fully with another episode tonight.'

That had him laughing. Maybe soaps would never become his thing, but he'd sure as hell enjoyed sitting beside Rose as they'd watched not one but two episodes last night. 'Nice try, but tonight I'm challenging you to another game of chess.'

'Fine. Now do you want to see the stud or not?'

She'd offered him a tour after breakfast and he'd leapt at the chance. She knew from their pre-wedding phone conversations that he'd eventually like to establish his own stud. 'Yes, please, ma'am.'

With a snort, she pushed into a huge, well-ventilated shed. Inside a central cement corridor was lined on both sides with stalls, many of them with access to yards outside. The Downs' stud stock.

Garrison Downs had one of the most successful breeding programmes in the country. She walked him through their operation, showed him the bulls she hoped would eventually prove as successful as Carnelian Boy, and he couldn't help but be impressed. 'You're doing great things here.'

'Holt had the initial vision. And he made sure to hire the best people.'

'Maybe, but you've the knowledge and the passion to take it to new heights.'

'We'll see.' Her lips twisted. 'The Arteta contract Aaron mentioned yesterday is an exchange programme I've been wanting to set up between us and a Spanish stud who are doing interesting things.'

His ears pricked. 'You brokered the deal yourself?'

She nodded. 'Holt saw the potential when I told him about it, but he wasn't convinced.'

But he could see that she was.

She dragged both hands through her hair, retied her pony-tail. 'It's been years in the making...so much red tape, going back and forth so many times... I thought it was all finally in the bag.'

A cold finger raked his spine. 'Any idea what's up?'

'Nope, but as I have a call with Mr Arteta in an hour, I guess I'll find out soon enough.'

He opened his mouth, but she shook her head. 'I now want to introduce you to our pride and joy. Junior here is the latest and will be one of the last of Carnelian Boy's offspring. He's only two weeks old. What do you think?'

He cast an expert eye over the calf and the air whistled between his teeth. 'I think I can honestly say I've never seen a better proportioned bull calf in my life, Rose. He's extraordinary.'

Her swift smile was his reward. 'I'm glad you like him as he's your wedding present.'

CHAPTER SEVEN

SURPRISE AND DELIGHT raced across Lincoln's face. He stared from Rose to the calf and back again. 'I wasn't serious when I asked for Carnelian Boy. I was…'

'Seeing what else you could negotiate? It was business. I don't blame you for that.'

'Want the truth?'

The low chuckle that emerged from the depths of him brushed across the bare skin of her arms, making her want. She hadn't stopped wanting since their kiss in the garden two days ago. She dragged her gaze from that far-too-tempting body. 'Regardless of how unpalatable it might be, I will always choose the truth, Lincoln.' Even if she didn't like it, the truth was something she could work with.

'Your proposal had knocked me for six. I was playing for time while I tried to find my feet again.'

She couldn't think of a single thing to say. She could think of a lot of things she'd like to do.

For pity's sake, stop thinking about kissing him!

He gestured at the stall. 'This is a tremendous gift. You might want to rethink—'

'Or I might not.'

'You—' He broke off, then, 'Your father would strongly advise you against it.'

'Oops.' She hoped her shrug carried every bit of nonchalance she wished she could feel.

His eyes narrowed.

She narrowed hers too. 'And your father is doing cart-wheels and singing show tunes at the fact you've given me your cat, your horse, and your plane?'

Those hypnotic lips did that slow-grin thing and she had to look away, pull in a breath. 'You want us to trust each other. You want us to like each other.'

'Rose, I already like and trust you. But, yes, I want that.'

'And I'm choosing to believe you're sincere.'

Please God, don't let her be wrong about this man.

She recalled the haunted expression in his eyes when they'd stood on the south-eastern boundary with evidence of Clay's troublemaking surrounding them. Instinct told her Lincoln wasn't involved, and after his gesture last night…

She'd chosen to believe he wasn't. 'We have a business deal, and I intend to keep my side of the bargain.'

'As do I.'

Please God, let him mean that.

'But this gift…' she nodded at the calf '…isn't about business.'

Dark eyes turned almost black. He took a step closer, and she could hardly breathe. 'What is it about?'

'It's a thank you.'

'For agreeing to your proposal?'

Her mouth went dry. She shook her head. 'For making it as easy as you could. For being kind about everything rather than cocky and arrogant.'

'Cocky isn't my style.' He frowned. 'Rose, I want us to be true partners.'

The way he said *'true partners'* made her chest lurch. The expression in his eyes when his gaze had landed on the piece of amber in her room…the tone of his voice when he'd said he didn't want to leave behind a legacy of hate. The passion in his eyes seven years ago after they'd kissed. The joy and excitement that had raged in her heart...

Blossom nudged Rose's knee, whined. Reaching down, she scratched her ears, tried to get her racing pulse back under control.

If Lincoln broke his promises to her...

Ice crawled across her scalp. It'd break something inside her. Somewhere along the line, she'd become invested in...

What? This marriage?

Not the marriage. *That* was business. But in becoming friends with Lincoln, in forging a connection with him. In working with Kalku Hills rather than against them. If he was toying with her—

Sidestepping him, she leaned her arms against the stall door, stared at the calf. She'd decided to believe him sincere. Worrying and doubting now would only undermine that. If her judgement let her down, if he didn't keep his word, it would hurt her in ways she couldn't begin to imagine. But some things were worth taking a risk for, worth making a fool of yourself over.

She gestured to the calf. 'I know you'd like to start your own stud. This is a gesture of goodwill—a token of my hopes for the brighter future I'm hoping we can forge. But it comes with no strings.'

Reaching down, Lincoln took her hand and lifted it to his lips, brushed a kiss across her knuckles that had her skin tingling. 'I've never been given a finer gift in my life. I will cherish him. And I promise to look after him to the very best of my ability.'

The sheen in his eyes had a lump lodging in her throat. Swallowing hard, she reclaimed her hand. 'I know you will.' After clearing her throat a couple of times, she glanced at her watch. 'I need to get back for my phone call. In the meantime, you need to come up with a name for this guy.'

'I'm going to call him Waverly Rose.'

He said it without hesitation and another lump stretched her throat into a painful ache.

'If that's okay with you?'

She nodded. It was very okay.

'He's going to be the finest stud bull in the country.'

The lump dissolved and she gave a slow grin that ended in a laugh. Lincoln stared, his gaze fixing on her mouth. It had butterflies gathering in her belly. 'He'll be in the top three. Garrison Downs will have the other two.'

He really needed to stop looking at her like that! 'Did you want to chat to Lori, who's in charge of the breeding programme?' She called Lori over and introduced them.

He shook the other woman's hand. 'I'd love to talk to you about what you're doing here, but I'm expecting a delivery that I need to be on hand for.'

Rose nodded when Lori glanced at her. 'When he has the time, it would be great if you could talk him through whatever he'd like to know.'

'Sure thing, Boss. Whenever you're free, Linc, you know where to find me.'

He nodded his thanks and then kept easy pace beside Rose as they made their way back to the homestead.

'You know Jackson?'

She glanced up. 'One of your stockmen, right?'

'One of Kalku's stockmen,' he corrected. 'He's bringing Thunder over for me this morning, driving my car.'

With a horse float, he'd have had to go the long way around, which would take at least six hours. 'I'd have organised a car and horse for you while you were here.' She kicked herself for not mentioning that earlier.

'I wanted my own. And, anyway, Rose, he's yours now.'

'Only if you break your word.' And she couldn't believe

he'd risk his horse, his cat and the Cessna. She'd never put Opal and Blossom up as collateral, not in a million years.

'Anyway, people would talk if Thunder remained at Kalku.'

Frowning, she halted beneath a huge red gum that stood at the edge of the garden. The shadows of the leaves moving in the breeze made intriguing patterns on his face. 'Is there anything else we should do to make this marriage appear real to the wider world?'

One broad shoulder lifted. 'At some stage we should probably go into Marni and shout a round at the Royal to celebrate.'

They should.

'But not today.' He urged her forward again. 'Once Jackson gets here, the two of us will unload and then I'm flying him back to Kalku.'

'We'll give him lunch first. And tell him to jump in the pool if he wants to cool off. It's a dusty drive.'

'Thanks, Rose.' They vaulted up the steps at the rear of the house and toed off their boots in the mudroom. He held the interior door open with his hip before plucking off her hat and placing it on its usual peg and setting his beside it. 'Want to go for a ride later?'

'Sure.' Jasper, her father's horse, needed exercising. Jasper had been grieving since Holt had died. She tried to spare the stallion whatever time she could.

'Coffee?'

She swung to stare. *Really?* 'That sounds great.' She could get used to this.

Twenty minutes later, she had the phone clasped to her ear. Mr Arteta had proven a tough negotiator over the last two years and she respected that, but she'd thought they'd ironed out every kink and crease in their arrangement.

After greetings had been exchanged, she cut straight to

the chase. 'Señor Arteta, I thought we had an agreement. You gave me your word.'

'But you did not inform me of all the information.'

Her brows shot up. 'What information are you referring to?'

'It has come to my ears that the ownership of Garrison Downs is now in question.'

Hot blood turned to ice in a heartbeat. 'I beg your pardon?'

'And that due to a condition in your father's will, your cattle station will pass once more into the hands of the Garrison family.'

How had he heard that? Her hand clenched so hard she started to shake.

'Do you deny it?'

To lie would be the death of the deal. And she didn't want to lie, though she cursed the fact that this news had reached his ears.

'Miss Waverly?'

She pulled herself together. 'There was an ancient stipulation in the will that said the station would only pass to the daughters if they were married.'

'My understanding is that *all* daughters must be married, *sí*?'

Her lips twisted. He was not only reliably informed, but well informed. Though he was missing one key piece of information. 'Then you'll be pleased to know that I'm now *Mrs* Waverly. All four Waverly daughters *are* married. You can rest assured that Garrison Downs will remain in Waverly hands.'

'I very much hope you are not mistaken, but I refuse to risk so much in a venture that could so easily turn to dust and ashes. If and when Garrison Downs is once again securely in your hands, Mrs Waverly, we will talk again.'

The line went dead and she stared at the handset before slamming it down. 'What the freaking heck?'

Someone cleared their throat in the doorway and she spun around. *Lincoln.* Holding a tray with two mugs of coffee and a plate of date scones. 'How much of that did you hear?'

'Enough.'

He set the tray down and pushed a mug into her hands. 'I suspect you'd prefer something stronger, but it's still a bit early.'

Far too early, and she didn't want her brain fuzzed by alcohol. 'How did he find out about Holt's will?'

Her words shot out like an accusation and Lincoln's head rocked back. 'I didn't tell my father about Holt's will, Rose. I told him nothing about you and me except that we were getting married.'

She reined in her frustration, ground back her suspicions, forced herself to recall her earlier resolution. 'You told me the day I proposed that you'd keep all I said in confidence. I believe you.'

But did she?

Or was she being a fool?

He raked a hand back through his hair, making him look deliciously rumpled like a hero in a sitcom.

'I don't like to ask this…'

She slammed back.

'But can you trust your staff?'

He meant Aaron. 'My sisters and I haven't told anyone about the will except the men we've married.'

He raised an eyebrow. She grimaced. These things had a way of getting about, but they'd been so careful. 'Aaron shouldered a lot in the months after Holt died. I—we were all in shock…' There'd been so much to do.

'Understandable.'

'And he's finding it hard to relinquish control now. Not because I'm a woman.' Aaron wasn't sexist. 'But I'm younger, less experienced, and I have some views that are different from Holt's.' He missed her father almost as much as she did.

He nodded, but those eyes remained watchful.

'So yeah, he's pushing my buttons and we're clashing a bit, but… I trust him.' And she did.

Beyond Lincoln, framed in the glass of the French doors, red dust billowed along the driveway. She nodded towards it. 'Looks like Jackson's here.'

'I better get out there. But, Rose—' dark eyes met hers '—ring Nate. Find out if anyone has requested to see the will.'

Could they do that? 'Okay.'

Rubbing a hand across her chest, she watched him stride away. If she was wrong about him…

If she was wrong, she could bring all of this crashing down around their ears. Her sisters would be without their home—a place they could turn to if they ever needed refuge. *She'd* be without her home. She couldn't imagine a life for herself apart from the one she had here at Garrison Downs. Didn't want to imagine it.

Lincoln *could* be stringing her along; he could be working with his father. If he'd told Clay about that ancient conditional bequest…

Reaching out, she gripped the back of Holt's chair. Had she handed Garrison Downs to them on a platter?

He gave you Judy, Thunder and Colin.

He might consider them a small price to pay to win the larger prize of Garrison Downs.

Deep inside she didn't want to believe that. Deep inside some instinct urged her to believe he was a man of honour.

'Your judgement has always been sound, Boss.'

She batted her father's words away. She'd been wrong about *him*. But if her judgement let her down now…

She couldn't bear to think about it. She recalled Pop's words from long ago.

'This land is our legacy for all the generation to come, for all the children that are yet to be born.'

If she lost it, she'd never forgive herself.

Pressing her palms to her eyes, she forced herself to think. *Right.* She pulled them away. She'd act as cool and calm as she knew how. But from now on she'd watch and assess Lincoln's every move, weigh everything he said and did. Then she'd decide what to do.

When he dropped Jackson back at Kalku, Lincoln searched for his father, but Clay had gone to ground.

He left a note on Clay's desk, as well as instructions, with both Jackson and the station cook, requesting his father call him. Instinct told him Clay was behind the current mischief Rose was dealing with, but how the hell had he found out about that conditional bequest?

Rose trusted Aaron, but… Aaron had a chip on his shoulder the size of the ridge country to the north.

Once back at the Downs, he toed off his boots in the mudroom, the racket of a vacuum cleaner sounding from inside. Even given the lushness of the lawns surrounding New House and the nightly watering that damped it down, the red dirt still found its way inside.

Silence sounded and Lindy walked through from the formal living room, wiping her hands on a cloth. She smiled when she saw him. 'I have a message for you from Rose.'

He maintained a lazy posture, but things inside him pulled tight. 'Yeah?'

'Drink, Lincoln?'

'I'll help myself to something, Lindy, you don't need to wait on me.' Ambling through to the kitchen, he opened the fridge and pulled out a jug of homemade lemonade, poured himself a glass. 'What did Rose have to say?'

Did his voice soften whenever he said his new wife's name or was that just his imagination?

'That something's come up and she can't go riding with you this afternoon. She was needed elsewhere.'

Needed? Or was that a convenient excuse to avoid him?

Hooking out a chair, he sat, silently cursing his father. He and Rose had made progress in the last couple of days—he still couldn't believe the generosity of her gift this morning. Everything he'd learned about her since they'd married had consolidated what he already knew—Rose was the epitome of generosity and integrity. And beneath that hard-working, cool, calm and collected façade lived a passionate heart.

But a part of her had to now suspect him in league with his father.

Glancing up, he found Lindy watching him. Downing his lemonade in one go, he sent her an easy smile. 'Guess that means I get first shower.'

Lindy twisted a tea towel in her hands. 'Linc, you need to know that for Rose the station comes first.'

Damn it. How glum had he looked?

'She's—'

'It's a big responsibility,' he cut in. 'And it's been hard since her father died.' He didn't want anyone thinking he felt neglected. Jeez, pathetic much? 'Anyway, it wasn't Rose I was thinking of just then, but my father.'

She grimaced. 'Have a run-in with him when you were over at Kalku?'

He didn't answer, just rolled his eyes and said, 'Family,' in his drollest voice, making her chuckle.

But when he stood under the shower a short time later, hot water beating down on him, Lindy's words came back to him.

'For Rose the station comes first.'

A month ago he'd have agreed with her, but now…

Lifting his face to the spray, he rinsed the shampoo from his hair. As much as she loved the place, it wasn't Garrison Downs that came first for Rose. It was her sisters.

He envied the bond she shared with them.

Rose, though, had a big heart. He hoped she'd find room for him in there too—once he'd proven himself to her. Closing his eyes, he let the water beat at him. Any other scenario didn't bear thinking about. Any other scenario would tear the heart from his chest.

Linc glanced up when Rose returned with yet another folder. That was the third time in an hour. He folded his arms and raised an eyebrow.

'What?'

'Why aren't you working in the office? It'd be more efficient than all of this toing and froing.'

She plonked back down on the sofa. She wore shorts again. He tried not to notice. 'It still feels like Holt's office, not mine.'

It had to be hard surrounded by all of those memories. 'Then do something to make it yours.'

'Like what?'

'Change the paintings, go for a new colour scheme, fill it with your own knick-knacks.'

'That'd feel like sacrilege. And anyway—' she waved a hand at the room '—when I'm out here with the TV and chess set I can pretend I'm not really working.'

He raised his eyebrow higher.

'Anyway, you can't talk. You don't seem to be making much progress on whatever it is you're working on.'

'That's true enough.'

She frowned. 'What are you working on?'

'Edits for the latest edition of my book.'

She blinked, leaned towards him. 'Did you just say… you've *written*—'

'*Co*-written.'

'A *book*?'

He rifled through the pile, located the earlier edition and handed it to her.

She stared at the cover, turned to the title page. 'You have a PhD in Economics? You're *Dr* Lincoln Garrison?'

He shrugged.

She stared at him, stared back at the book. 'You've written a book on *economic theory*?'

'*Co*-written with my thesis supervisor.'

'Who just happens to be a professor with thirty years' experience who's considered a leading light in the field.'

She gaped at him. He shrugged again.

'Why don't we know about this? Does your father know?'

'Why should you? And yes.'

'Because you're a local boy! Everyone would be so pleased for you. So proud. And rather than teasing you for—' She broke off with a gulp.

'Being a hard-partying playboy?'

She eased back, folded her arms. 'You haven't been partying hard, though, have you? You've been working on your PhD and writing a book and…?'

She gestured for him to fill in the other gaps. 'Doing the odd guest lecture and some private consulting.'

She stared at him for a long moment. 'Why have you been hiding your light under a bushel?'

'The people who need to know know, Rose. And, besides, I did party hard there for a couple of years.'

Blue eyes sharpened. Slowly she nodded. 'You don't want

to make your father look like a complete and utter clown, that's why.'

Her perception shouldn't surprise him.

'You can't win with that man, can you? You go away and do something amazing like this…'

She thought it amazing? His chest expanded.

'Yet rather than brag about your accomplishments, he complains to all and sundry that you've abandoned him and left him to run the place on his own, and…*dismisses* you as shallow and irresponsible. Even though you come back every muster to lend a hand.'

That just about summed it up.

'And, when you are home, he won't listen to your ideas for improvements to the place.' She held up his book. 'When you clearly have the expertise to advise him. Why not?'

Her eyes flashed and he had to fight the urge to reach for her. 'Because he wants to be the one to singlehandedly turn Kalku's fortunes around. He wants the kudos for turning it into as thriving an enterprise as Garrison Downs.' His father refused to relinquish control. He was driven to try and achieve the same level of success that Holt had—to enjoy the same respect and esteem. Lincoln's arguments always fell on deaf ears.

'And that right there is why he's going to fail. Nobody can do it all. A good manager understands their individual team members' strengths and utilises them.' She tossed her reports to the floor. 'I've had enough for one day. Game of chess?'

'Absolutely.'

'You be white this time and we'll see if we get any further through this game than we did the last one.'

'I'll be your white knight whenever you want, Rose.'

'You think these up on the spur of the moment or store them for the right occasion?'

But her lips twitched, and he found himself grinning.

They sat in their usual spots—Rose on the sofa, Linc on the ottoman. River rested his head on Linc's foot, while Colin butted his head against Rose's left arm.

'Give over, you crazy cat.' Pushing him to his back, she scratched under his chin without looking at him. Colin wrapped his front legs around her arm, his purr as loud as a tractor.

Lincoln made his opening move. 'Can I ask you something?'

'Sure.'

'Why wouldn't you date me seven years ago?'

She froze. Easing back, she swallowed. 'I wanted to.'

'But?'

'Do you remember running into me and Mum in Marni the week after the B & S ball?'

He did. He'd done his level best to get Rose alone, but it had proven impossible with Rosamund there.

She moistened her lips. 'Then the following weekend the Marni Cup was on.'

It had been winter. The season of outback social activities. He'd tried to get Rose alone that time too, but hadn't managed it. There'd been too many people, too many distractions. Their eyes had caught and held more than once, though. When he'd smiled at her, she'd smiled back.

'My mother took me aside a few days later, said she'd noticed the way you looked at me.'

He'd wanted to kiss her. He still did.

'And the way I looked back.' She stared at her hands and things inside him clenched. 'She told me there was something I needed to know.'

A vice squeezed his chest. What had Rosamund told her?

'Lincoln, Clay once did his very best to cause trouble in

my parents' marriage—insinuating to each of them that the other was being unfaithful.'

His stomach plummeted.

'I was shocked. I said it would never have worked, that their marriage was too strong. She said, *"It is now, but there was a time when it had the potential to cause real mischief. Did cause real mischief."*'

Colin batted his head against her arm. She curled her fingers into his fur as if seeking comfort. Lincoln ached to reach across and draw her onto his lap.

'I now know Mum knew about Holt's affair. I suspect your dad was just flinging mud in the wild hope it would cause trouble. Which it almost did.'

Acid churned in his gut. 'My father has been an unhappy man most of his life.' The words emerged from numb lips, a fire banking under old hurts.

'My mother said it would hurt them to have Clay in their inner circle.' Her throat bobbed as if she'd swallowed a tennis ball. 'She also said that if it was true love she'd never stand in my way, that love was too precious.' Her gaze lifted. 'But, Lincoln, we barely knew each other.'

He nodded. He didn't blame her, not for a moment.

'And then she died so unexpectedly. And while I knew you weren't like your father, Holt needed me in ways he never had before. I couldn't add to his burdens.'

'I'm sorry, Rose. I'm sorry my father has been the cause of so much pain for your family.'

She reached out and squeezed his hand. 'You're not responsible for your father's actions. None of us ever considered that you were.'

But it didn't change the fact that his surname was Garrison.

She bit her lip. 'Maybe I shouldn't have told you. It paints your father in an ugly light.'

'I'm glad you did.' But things inside him pulled tight.

The phone rang. Reaching across, Rose lifted the receiver. 'Hello?'

Shaking Colin free, she picked up a bishop to move it— Linc blinked when she placed it back on its original square.

'One moment, please.' Covering the receiver, she grimaced. 'Speak of the devil…it's your father.'

His mouth tightened. 'I left a message for him to call. Thought he'd ignore it.'

They both stood and she handed him the receiver, ducking beneath the cord, clearly intent on giving him some privacy, but he hooked an arm around her waist and pulled her back against him.

'Dad.' With Rose so close, he started to throb.

'What was so darn important I had to ring you asap?'

Linc cut to the chase. 'I want to know who your contact at Garrison Downs is. I want to know who's feeding you information.'

'Don't know what you're talking about.'

He'd always been able to tell when his father was lying. 'I know you're behind the trouble Rose is having with her contracts.'

Clay gave an ugly laugh. 'And what if I am?'

Rose glanced up, her eyes wide.

'Serves both her and Holt right for counting their chickens. Arteta had the right to know the truth.'

Gently detaching his arm, Rose plonked down on the ottoman, fondled River's ears when he padded over to her. Linc missed her warmth, the feel of having her so close.

'And what *is* the truth, Dad?'

'That you're a *traitor*!'

Clay shouted the words so loud Rose winced.

'I've seen the will—'

Linc sat beside her and held the phone between them so she could listen in.

'How?'

'I have my sources.'

Who here was feeding him information?

'You great big lumbering lug!'

Rose's mouth dropped open. Snapping it shut, she retied her ponytail.

'You've played right into that hussy's hands.'

Linc's hands clenched so hard he started to shake, but Rose nudged him. Mirth brightened her eyes, turning them an intriguing shade of opal. *Hussy?* she mouthed silently, and he found himself grinning then too.

'I'm going to tell you how you're going to fix this. First thing in the morning you're coming home and we're going into Adelaide to have this marriage annulled. And then we're going to start court proceedings and take back what's ours.'

Linc shook his head. His father's bitterness had become an obsession. 'Garrison Downs was never ours, Dad. And despite the name on the front gate—Garrison Downs is Waverly land through and through. It's time you came to terms with that.'

'You listen here—'

'I'm not annulling my marriage to Rose, I'm not divorcing her, or giving you any extra rope with which to hang yourself.'

'For heaven's sake, Linc, you idiot! Think with your head for once rather than a different part of your anatomy. You always had the attention span of a flea, but—'

The phone was snatched from Linc's hand.

'Nobody speaks to my husband like that.' Rose's eyes flashed. 'What a dreadful man you are, Clay. And a terrible father. What gives you the right to speak to anyone like that, let alone your own son?'

'Well, we all know what a sterling father Holt turned out to be, don't we?'

She paled and Linc feared that if his father had been in the room, he'd have punched him.

Her chin lifted. 'Holt had his faults, as we're all well aware, but he never put his daughters down. He never called them awful names or complained about them all over town. He respected us and made sure we knew we were loved. *That's* what a good parent does.'

She blinked as if her words had surprised her.

The line went dead. She stared at it. 'And he never hit us,' she added in a harsh whisper. Slamming the receiver down, she paced around the room, River at her heels as if to give her comfort.

'Doesn't it bug you, the way he talks to you?' Her eyes spat fire.

'I don't let it bother me any more.'

She stabbed a finger at him. 'You shouldn't let anyone speak to you like that.'

She looked magnificent fired up in outrage, and his hunger burned hot and fierce. He pointed at the phone. 'You stuck up for me.'

'I know, I know, you can fight your own battles.'

She started pacing again. River moved to sit in front of Lincoln, stared up at him expectantly. She swung back. 'Except you weren't.'

In two strides he stood in front of her, capturing her hands. 'There's more than one way to win a war, Rose. And I'm winning this one by refusing to allow his bitterness to infect me, by living my life the best way I see fit.'

Hauling in a breath, she nodded. 'You're doing a fine job of it too, Lincoln. You should be proud of yourself...proud of all you've achieved...proud of the man you are.'

Her words punched through him.

Her gaze lowered to his mouth, her pupils dilating.

He had no idea who moved first, but their mouths moved together, hot and hungry, and wildly out of control. Falling down to the ottoman, he took her with him. She kissed him like a starving woman, like a drowning woman, like a woman who wanted everything.

Pulling her flush again him, he let his hands rove across her back, down her hips…lifting her until she half straddled his thighs, both of them balancing precariously on the ottoman. He had to brace one hand behind him to prevent them from toppling over.

She gripped his shoulders, that sweet mouth continued to ravage his and he kissed her back with the same hunger. He slid his hand up the bare skin of her thigh and she dragged her mouth from his to pull air into her lungs. When he pressed the hard ridge in his trousers against the juncture of her thighs, a moan left her lips.

Spots danced across his eyes, but he gathered together the shreds of his control. She'd said she didn't want this, and he wasn't losing her trust now. Claiming one more drugging kiss, he stood and lowered her feet back to the floor, but he didn't release her. 'You said you didn't want this.'

She stared at him, breathing hard, her fingers clinging to his arms as if needing to hold onto something solid.

'Just for the record, I do, but…'

Reaching up, she pressed her fingers to his lips, the pulse in her throat fluttering like a wild thing. 'I do too. And I'm tired of fighting it.'

A surge of heat and need nearly unmanned him. 'Can I tell you what I want?'

She nodded.

'Two nights—you and me alone with no one else around.

I know muster is starting, but you'll have me to help when we get back.'

He didn't want Lindy in the house with her vacuum cleaner and dusting cloth. He didn't want Aaron coming in with some disaster. He didn't want Eve coming over for afternoon tea and a gossip. He wanted Rose to be all his for two days. He wanted to show her how good it could be between them.

'I want to do things to you that will make you scream.' He wanted to bliss her out so much she'd never want to let him go.

Her eyes widened. The pulse at her throat pounded like a wild thing. 'In the morning we'll take some supplies and head out to my favourite place on the station.' Her voice was nothing more than a husky whisper.

'Swag rolls and tents?'

'There's a cottage.'

'Sounds perfect.'

She took a step away from him, as if needing air. 'Pack your swimming trunks.'

'We're not going to need clothes, Rose—any clothes.'

'Then pack sunscreen.'

He laughed, but then imagined rubbing sunscreen across her naked flesh. His breath sawed in and out of his lungs. Backing up, he turned and left before the curve of Rose's lips and the way her eyes glittered could unman him.

CHAPTER EIGHT

ROSE PULLED HER four-wheel drive to a halt beside a rustic two-room cabin, her stomach coiled tight, heat throbbing in places she shouldn't be thinking about just yet.

Lincoln raised an eyebrow. 'This is your favourite place on Garrison Downs?'

'I'll show you why in a bit.' She couldn't believe her voice sounded normal. 'C'mon, let's set up.' She'd focus on the practicalities rather than the burning need building inside her, rather than the memory of Lincoln's lips on hers, his hands on her overheated skin and—

Stop it!

Lincoln did a reconnaissance of the cabin while she collected the blow-up air mattress. He grinned when he saw it. 'Nothing but the best for the Lady of the Manor.'

'Just call me Princess Rose.'

'You're not a princess, Rose, you're a queen.'

The tone of his voice—low and husky—and the light in his eyes made her go shivery and weak-kneed.

He'd swept the floor with the old broom and pointed it now at the air mattress. 'I suppose it's my job to pump that up?'

'As much as I'd love to see your muscles gleaming with the effort…'

He nearly dropped the broom. *Ha!* Look at her being sassy.

'This is one of those self-inflating numbers.'

Setting it to the floor, she pulled the appropriate cord and the queen-sized air bed promptly inflated. Lincoln eyes dark-ened. When they lifted to hers, he moistened his lips as if parched, and an answering thirst raked through her.

Silently they returned to the car for the next load. She was aware of his every step, could imagine the heat from his body and the shape—

Gritting her teeth, she grabbed an armful of bedding and stalked back to the cabin. Rather than her usual swag roll, she'd brought quilts and pillows, and she arranged them over the mattress now.

Standing back, she admired her handiwork.

'A bed fit for a queen,' Lincoln said directly behind her when he eventually brought their bags in and set them on the floor.

Was it too much? 'I wanted to make it look nice.'

She rolled her shoulders. Maybe—

Lincoln turned her, cupped her face in those big strong hands, and her pulse went crazy and so did her breath. Naked need had to be plastered across her face.

'It's perfect. I love it. I want to fix it in my mind so I'll never forget.'

She'd never forget the way he looked at her this very mo-ment. Not if she lived to be a hundred and twenty.

His gaze lowered to her lips and things inside her leapt. He was going to kiss her and—

Releasing her, he took two steps back, and she remembered his words from earlier in the week—'I won't fall on you like some starving beast.' Maybe they were both trying to be on their best behaviour. The thought gave her heart.

'I didn't think to bring a camera.' She kept her voice light, shooed him back into the front room, forced herself away from the temptation of that bed. Mobile reception was non-existent out here. She'd left her phone at home. They had the satellite phone in case of an emergency.

'I did.'

She pulled to a halt in the front room. He'd been busy. While she'd been making the bed, he'd unpacked the rest of the car. The Esky keeping their food and drinks cold rested in the corner beside the airtight container of dry food as well as the crockery and cutlery. It weighed a tonne and she'd planned to leave it in the back of the four-wheel drive and yet Lincoln hadn't broken a sweat bringing it inside.

'Say cheese!'

A flash went off, making her blink.

'I thought a few holiday snaps could be fun.'

He sauntered across, bent down until they were eye to eye. 'But no naked photos, okay?'

All she could do was nod. But, of course, all she now wanted was to see him naked. Which was probably his plan, and the thought made her laugh.

'Okay, now is the time to don your swimmers if you want to wear them.' Grabbing the towels she'd slung over a chair, she sauntered outside.

'Are you planning on skinny-dipping, Rose Waverly?'

His voice was filled with laughter and she grinned at the sky. 'I'm wearing my swimmers under my clothes.'

He appeared a few moments later, wearing swimming trunks and a T-shirt. He winked at her and took the towels. 'Thought I'd better be a gentleman.'

She wanted to say, *What a shame*.

He gestured around. 'This seems an odd spot for a stockman's cottage. Especially one of this size.'

A flock of budgerigars lifted from the golden grasses nearby and flew off in a bright flash of green. 'That's because it's not. It's a holiday cottage Holt built for us.' She set off up the track. 'We'd come out here a couple of times a year for some R & R. We loved it.'

They walked steadily upwards for five minutes. Topping

the rise, they eased around a sharp bend, and Rose gestured in front of them. 'And now you can see why.'

Red sandstone cliffs rose up all around—grand, ancient, timeless. Beneath them stretched a large rock pool. Still and deep, the water reflected the sky above.

Lincoln let out a low whistle.

'It's something, isn't it?' she murmured.

'I've not heard a whisper about this place before. It's amazing.'

'It's called Cordelia's Leap.'

Named for one of his ancestors.

He turned, and their gazes caught and clung. 'Thank you for bringing me here.'

For no reason at all—or maybe for *all* the reasons—her mouth went dry. She swallowed again, cleared her throat, dragged her gaze away from midnight eyes—eyes that belonged in a bedroom—and shucked off her shorts and T-shirt in double-quick time before remembering she'd meant to make a seductive show of it. Except she needed a cold dousing *now*.

Lincoln's lips parted and his chest rose and fell, his eyes devouring her.

'The water is cold. And deep,' she shot over her shoulder, before vaulting lightly across the rock platform and diving in.

Gah! The water was *freezing*. She welcomed the shock of it, though—the way it cleared the fog around her brain, the way it chased away the thudding heat that had her in its grip.

Surfacing in the middle of the pool, she turned back to face him. The heat immediately built through her again as he hauled his shirt over his head in one smooth motion, and she was finally free to admire those powerful shoulders and broad chest. He looked as rugged, grand and timeless as the sandstone surrounding them.

And he was hers. It might only be in this moment, or for

a few days…or for a few months at most. But the knowledge that this man was married to her and that they were going to become intimate had a thrill humming deep inside—not some temporary frisson either, but a bone-deep vibration. She had no idea what it meant, but she didn't care.

He dropped his shirt beside her clothes. Pausing, he bent down, and when he stood again he held a box in his hand. Turning it over in his fingers, he kinked an eyebrow in her direction.

The box of condoms must've fallen out of her shorts' pocket. 'I'm a safety girl.' It was a line from the movie *Pretty Woman* and she'd always wanted to use it. 'One unexpected pregnancy in the family is quite enough.'

Dropping the box on their pile of clothes, he sauntered down to the water's edge—unhurried, in control, and she'd never wanted a man more. He didn't hesitate when his feet touched the water, but strode in and was in front of her in four powerful strides of those beautiful arms.

'You are beautiful.' She didn't mean to say the words out loud, but couldn't hold them back.

'So are you.'

No man had ever called her beautiful before, but the expression in his eyes had her believing him—*he* found her beautiful.

One strong arm went around her waist and he pulled her flush against him. Their legs brushed against one another and she flattened her palms against his chest to steady herself.

'I'm not going to ravish you out here in this extraordinary place, Rose.'

'No?'

She couldn't keep the disappointment from her voice and a sudden gleam lit his eyes. 'Those rocks look hard and unforgiving, and when we make love I want you focussed on nothing but me and pleasure. But we can play, if you'd like.'

Both of his hands slid down her sides, his thumbs brushing the sides of her breasts making her gasp. They made a slow sensual journey all the way to her hips. Hooking his hands beneath her thighs, he locked them around his waist, and one fingertip slid beneath the elastic of her swimsuit to travel from her hip, and slowly-oh-so-slowly around.

It stopped. 'I could provide you with some…temporary relief.' If possible, those eyes darkened further. 'I'd love to make you come apart right now.' That fingertip moved again.

She wanted that too—desperately. But for their first time she wanted him with her. 'Fair's fair, then.' She could barely make her voice work. 'As long as the play is two-sided, and I get to do the same to you.'

Her hands made a bold exploration along his shoulders and across his chest, her fingers tiptoeing down his abdomen—the muscles, that gloriously defined six-pack, all clenching in the most flattering manner—to dip below his waistband. Before they could reach their destination, she found her hands empty and she was treading water again.

'I'm trying to play the gentleman here and not rush you, but I want you too much.'

He'd moved several feet away, and he breathed heavily, labouring over his words. His face looked ravaged and she finally glimpsed the control he'd imposed on himself.

She gestured between them. 'Mutual,' she whispered.

He moved closer but didn't touch her. 'This water is freezing, but I burn for you. I want you *now*.' The words were raw and filled with need, and something aching and primitive soared free inside her.

Without another word, she swam for shore. He kept pace beside her. When they reached the rocks, he lifted her out, but released her as soon as her feet hit solid ground. They towelled off, put their shoes on, but didn't bother with the rest of their clothes. Taking his hand, she led him back to the cabin.

He closed the door behind them. Holding his gaze, she lowered the straps of her simple one-piece and peeled the suit from her body to stand before him naked. She didn't want to be coy, and she wanted all barriers between them gone. He drank her in like a starving man. He started towards her, but she held up a hand and gestured. 'Your turn.'

He sent her one of those maddeningly slow grins. 'You'd like to see me naked, Rose?'

The blood pounded in her ears. 'More than life itself.'

He obliged. Flipping open the snap on his trunks, he let them fall to his feet before stepping out of them.

Lincoln was built on the most perfect lines she could imagine for a man. He was big. But perfectly proportioned. And she wanted what was about to happen with every atom of her being.

The appreciation burning in Rose's eyes almost undid him.

Lincoln gathered together the ragged shreds of his control and pulled them tight. He wanted her with a primitive need he'd not experienced before. He wanted her in ways he hadn't known a man could want.

But more than that he wanted to make this special—he would *not* rush. Sauntering across, he snaked a hand beneath her hair and tilted her head, claimed her mouth in an unhurried kiss. Her lips, soft and pliant, opened beneath his, and he tasted her slowly and thoroughly, memorising the shape of her mouth, the texture of her lips, the taste of her. She kissed him back with a hunger she didn't try to hide, with nothing held back. Her arms slid around his neck and her body pressed against his and stars burst behind his eyelids. He had to drag his mouth away to gulp air into starved lungs. 'You're sure about this, Rose?'

'Positive.' She swallowed. 'You?'

Her flash of vulnerability caught at him. 'Never been surer about anything in my life.' Before he'd finished speaking he was pressing kisses against her neck, grazing her earlobe with his teeth. A gasp, a tiny moan, and her body arching into his. Her hands reached out to touch and explore and while he hungered to feel her hands on his burning flesh, he couldn't risk it just yet.

Capturing her wrists lightly in one of his hands, he held them behind her back. 'What are you—?'

Her shocked cry when he closed his mouth around one nipple, the way it beaded as he lathed it with his tongue, dragged a moan from him too.

'Lincoln.' She almost sobbed his name.

'I want to learn your body, Rose.' He kissed his way across to her other breast, his fingers brushing against the side of it, while his lips and tongue applied themselves to pebbling it into urgent hardness.

The way her breath sawed in and out, the way she moved restlessly against him, the gratifying sounds she made—

With a wrench, she pulled her hands free. 'I want to learn your body too. I want to discover what makes you weak at the knees, what makes you tremble. I want—'

Capturing her hands, he pressed a kissed to both palms. 'Sweetheart, my control is thin.' Nearly non-existent. 'If you touch me now, I can't guarantee I'll be able to contain myself. You can explore my body to your heart's content later this afternoon or tonight or tomorrow. I promise.'

Eyes the colour of sapphires glittered in the light pouring in at the window. That colour would stay with him till his dying day.

'For now, please let me focus on you. Please?'

Her eyes grew suspiciously bright. Wordlessly, she nodded. Then she captured his face in her hands. 'I want you with me this first time, Lincoln.'

He'd planned to make her come first with his lips and tongue.

'Please let me have that.'

Nodding, he lifted her into his arms and strode into the bedroom, laid her down on the mattress among the nest of quilts. And then all talking stopped as he applied himself to her pleasure. Kissing her until she panted, working his way down her body until she arched and moaned. Her cry when he touched his mouth to the sensitive heart of her made him feel invincible. He kissed and licked and touched until his name was dragged from her throat. Only then did he sheath himself in a condom and kiss his way back up her body.

Desire-slicked eyes gazed into his. 'I want you, Lincoln. *Now.*'

But he felt the unconscious stiffening of her body, and he had every intention of dispelling it before joining their bodies and making them one. His fingers moved down to damp curls, trailing through them, tugging gently, a finger sliding over her most sensitive nub. Her hips lifted, her legs parted and moved restlessly.

'You taste like the finest wine.' He slid a finger inside her, the silken feel of her almost undoing him. 'I love touching you and feeling you.'

'Lincoln.'

His name was a long, low moan and he saw that she was lost again, a slave to the pleasure he was providing, and only then did he nudge himself against her entrance and, meeting no resistance, slide inside.

Her pulsing heat had him clenching his jaw. Her eyes flew open and stared into his. He brushed her hair from her face. 'Did I hurt you?'

She shook her head. 'I thought—'

Her breath caught when he moved and her head fell back. 'Oh, God, Lincoln, you feel so good.'

'That was the plan, sweetheart.'

Short fingernails dug into the muscles of his back. 'I'm sorry,' she panted. 'I have to touch you. I need to hold onto something solid before I...'

He clenched his jaw harder, kept moving rhythmically, steadily. Her body moving with his—urgent, seeking. He'd have to start reciting his times tables soon. 'Before you...?'

Her breath came in short sharp gasps. 'You said you wanted to make me scream.'

'More than life itself,' he gritted out.

'And... I am going to scream!'

With an exultant cry that rang through him like a bell, her muscles clenched all around him as she found her release. The pull and pulse that enclosed him startled a shout from him too—of surprise, pleasure, joy. His body took on a rhythm of its own then, demanding, seeking, wanting everything—all of this woman—as he hurtled into a kaleidoscope of sensation and release.

He came back to himself, to find he'd collapsed on top of her. Probably crushing her. He started to move away, but her hands on his back flattened—a silent plea for him to remain where he was. Taking some of the weight on his forearms, he stared down at her flushed face—her eyes still closed, damp tendrils of hair curling around her temples—and something in his chest lurched. He forced himself to roll away. They lay side by side, staring up at the ceiling. Reaching out, he took her hand, threading his fingers through hers. 'You okay?'

'I'm more than okay, Lincoln. That was...'

'Yeah.' He couldn't find words for it either. 'It really was.'

'You were worth waiting for.'

He turned his head to meet her gaze. 'So were you.' And

he meant it. He'd waited seven long years. And he'd wait another seven if he had to.

There was no going back now and the realisation had an icy hand squeezing his heart. He'd always considered himself half in love with her—she fascinated him, he found her attractive—but he hadn't known her, not really. But he did now in a very real and elemental way. He knew her sense of honour, had witnessed her love for her sisters, saw how hard she worked, and now he'd experienced her passion. He'd made love to this extraordinary woman and it slammed into him now that he never wanted to let her go.

'You're looking awfully serious all of a sudden.'

He crashed back, made himself grin, pointed at his face. 'This is the look of a man who is suddenly ravenous. Is it lunchtime yet?'

'I think we can make our own rules up while we're here. If we want it to be lunchtime, then it's lunchtime.'

Leaping up, she grabbed his T-shirt. 'May I?' At his nod, she hauled it on over her head. It came to mid-thigh, and, while he much preferred naked Rose, it looked cute on her.

She shot him a sassy look over her shoulder. 'I've always wanted to do this. In all the best soaps, after a couple have made love, nine times out of ten she ends up wearing his shirt.'

He couldn't help but laugh.

Planting her hands on her hips, she nodded. 'That's better. Now let's get you fed, and then maybe a bit later...'

That hot gaze roved down his body with naked appreciation and he found himself going hard again.

She stared as if fascinated. Resting his hands behind his head, he did his best to look hot and sexy. 'And a bit later?'

The pulse at the base of her throat fluttered. 'Maybe we can do that again.'

'You know what, Rose? I don't think it is lunchtime just yet.' Reaching out, he tugged her down on top of him.

'So I can have my wicked way with you now?'

'Absolutely.'

With a delighted grin, she set about doing exactly that.

They ate a late lunch of salad, bread and cheese—cleaning up afterwards and stowing the food safely away, not wanting to encourage the wildlife to explore their sanctuary. Yawning and lazy, they napped. When they woke, he made tea and they sat outside to watch the sky flame with late afternoon colour as the sun descended in the west and the day lost its heat.

'I don't know if this is the right time or not, Lincoln, but can I ask you a personal question or two?'

'I wouldn't mind asking you a couple myself.'

He wouldn't ask her how she felt about spending a lifetime with him. Not yet. It was too soon.

Folding her arms, she stood, her eyes wary. 'You want to ask about Holt and his affair, and how we all really feel about Anastasia.'

He stood too. 'I'd like to know about all of that, sure, but they weren't the questions I had in mind.'

She blinked. 'Oh?'

He refused to be drawn. 'Ladies first.'

'Would you like to come for a walk?' She pointed. 'I'm hoping to find some pretty rocks beneath the ridge along there. Ana, who makes gorgeous things—' she held up her wrist to display her bracelet '—might like them.'

'Sure.'

They walked and fossicked. Tenderness and an unfamiliar dread warred inside him. He'd always sensed making love with Rose would rock his world, but he hadn't realised how deeply. Hadn't realised it would bind him to her in a way he would never be able to change.

Don't think about that now.

For now, he'd focus on being what she needed him to be. And pray to God that he could win her heart.

'Ask your questions, Rose.'

Eyes bluer than the sky above turned to him. 'You're under no obligation to answer or—'

'Ask your questions, and I'll answer if I can.'

Bending down to pick up a pebble, she turned it over in her fingers. 'Your father treats you terribly, and yet you tell me you love him. What kind of relationship do you have with him?'

He took the pebble from her—a shard of granite—and replaced it with a piece of quartz, a ribbon of agate inside it. 'It's complicated.'

She searched his face.

'I love my father, Rose. He's not unremittingly awful. When he forgets to nurse his grudges, he can be good company.' He let out a breath slowly. 'I understand why he does what he does. I understand his vulnerabilities, and it makes me ache for him.'

She glanced away.

'All of which is compounded by the fact that I hate so much of what he says and does. I agree with so few of his opinions and attitudes.'

She glanced back.

'What you're really asking me, though, is if I'd lie to protect him.'

Her mouth fell open—that soft, kissable and surprisingly mischievous mouth.

'The answer is I don't know. Probably… To an extent. There's a line, though, which I won't go beyond.'

'Which is?'

'I won't let him hurt you.'

CHAPTER NINE

LINCOLN'S WORDS ECHOED through Rose. *'I won't let him hurt you.'* She stared at him, moistened her lips.

His face could be carved from granite. 'You have my word.'

The flash in those dark eyes, the way his lips firmed, had things inside her clenching, heating...melting.

Making love with Lincoln had been a revelation. She'd expected pleasure, but she hadn't expected such joy; hadn't known she'd want to throw her arms wide and embrace the world. Or that a lump would lodge in her throat at the sheer beauty of it. She'd never felt closer, more attuned, to another living soul.

Swallowing, she pulled herself up short. That was her in-experience talking. She needed to be careful. In three months this marriage would end and Lincoln would return to Kalku Hills, with the deed to Camels Bridge in his hand.

She couldn't read too much into this, couldn't let herself fall for him. The horizon turned a soft pink. She *wouldn't* be the silly naïve ingenue.

'You don't believe me?'

Slamming back, she silently cursed herself. Her thoughts should be focussed on securing Garrison Downs' future, nothing more. This thing with Lincoln was temporary, but Garrison Downs was her home, her sisters' home, and she needed to safeguard it for the generations to come.

Lifting her chin, she met his gaze. 'I believe that you don't want your father to hurt me.'

'But?' He placed another rock in her hand—a beautiful deep red. 'Jasper.' He added another. 'Rock crystal.'

She stared at them. 'How do you know the names of them all?'

'When I did my undergraduate degree we were encouraged to study a strand unrelated to our main course. Some people did creative writing, others studied philosophy. I did geology. But back to the subject at hand.'

His father.

'You can't control what your father does. You can probably influence it, but…' She lifted a shoulder, let it drop. 'Which means you can't protect me from the results of his actions, not fully.'

Those large capable hands clenched and unclenched, as if he'd like to take on the world. To protect her?

The thought turned her insides to jelly.

'And the other thing—' Dark eyes met hers and just for a moment she wanted to weep. He looked as solid and steadfast as the ridge of red rock behind them. 'I don't believe you'd choose me over him. You've known and loved him all your life. You've known me for no time at all.'

He nodded, not in agreement but as if he should've realised that this was what she'd think. 'Then that just goes to show how wrong you can be.' He smiled, the creases around his eyes crinkling. 'It's good to know you're not infallible, Rose Waverly.'

Infallible, *her*? Give her a break.

'You said you wanted to bring an end to the bad blood between our families. I want that too. I don't want my children riddled with the same bitterness that my father has fallen victim to. I want my children to be happy and to thrive.'

Children featured in his future?

Her mouth went strangely dry.

'If my father does something to damage Garrison Downs and I support him in that, I will rightfully earn your undying resentment.' Bracing his hands on his knees, he stared at the ground. 'And then this mistrust and the bitterness and the attempts to undermine each other will continue into the future.'

Straightening, he shook his head, placing another pebble in her hand. 'I don't want that.'

That she did believe. Reaching out, she touched a hand to his cheek. 'Let's do our best to make sure that doesn't happen.'

Everything about him sharpened—determination settling across his features—and then he pulled her into his arms and kissed her with a dizzying intensity that had her dropping all of Ana's pebbles as she wrapped her arms around his neck and tried to climb inside his body.

Before she knew it, they were back at the cabin and falling down onto the mattress, making love with a fierce intensity totally at odds with their earlier slow tenderness. She loved the primal ferocity, loved that he knew exactly what she wanted and how to give it to her. She loved that when he started to slow, to remember her relative inexperience, she could touch him in a certain way, move and clench in a certain way, and his groan would ring in her ears as he flung headlong back into heat and passion.

It made her feel strong and bold.

And then she was undone—begging and crying out his name—more naked than she'd ever been in her life.

Afterwards she lay pressed against his side, her head on his shoulder, his hand trailing lazy circles on her back, her fingers drifting across his stomach.

His hand stilled. 'I have no control where you're concerned. I shouldn't have—'

'Oh, yes, you should.' She glanced up and met those dark eyes. 'I loved every moment of that.'

He grimaced. 'Maybe so, but tomorrow you're going to be sore in places you never even knew you had.'

'Yet I've never felt more physically sated in my life. So if I'm sore tomorrow it'll have been totally worth it.'

He grinned. 'Hungry?'

'Starving.'

They built a fire and when it had died down they cooked potatoes in the embers. Sitting on large flat stones while they waited for them to cook, they opened a bottle of wine, ate cheese, crackers and olives, and then big slices of chocolate cake. They'd meant to save that for afterwards, but they were both too ravenous, and they decided if they wanted to eat dessert before their mains then they could.

Turning the potatoes in the embers, Lincoln glanced across. 'Did you want to continue our earlier conversation? I kind of cut you off.'

In the best possible way, though.

'You still have questions about my father.'

She didn't know if it was a statement or a question. 'Yeah, but...' He raised an eyebrow when she hesitated, and she shrugged. 'I don't want to spoil the mood.' She gestured back behind them. 'What just happened in there... It felt...'

Very slowly he set the barbecue fork down and moved across to crouch down in front of her. 'What did it feel like?'

She'd promised to be honest. Even when it was hard. *Especially* when it was hard. Pleating the material of the shirt she wore—his shirt—in nerveless fingers, she forced her gaze to his. 'It felt like it meant something.' And then she made herself laugh. 'Listen to me—the naïve little virgin.

Throughout the ages women have mistaken physical pleasure to mean something more…a meeting of the souls or—'

'It felt momentous to me, too.'

The very quietness of his words had her heart picking up pace. It startled her how much she wanted to believe him.

You can choose to believe him.

Behind him, crystal stars glittered in a navy sky. She *could* choose to trust him.

Swallowing, she lifted her chin. 'What happened this afternoon felt like a promise.' A promise of what she couldn't really say—a promise of a brighter future, perhaps.

'Yes.' He said the word slowly, as if he felt the truth of that in the depths of himself.

'I don't want to spoil that with talk of your father.' It felt too new, too vulnerable for such realities.

Leaning forward, he pressed a kiss to her brow. 'You and I, we're good, Rose.' He moved back to the fire. 'And talk about our fathers need have no effect on that. So ask your questions.'

Their relationship had shifted today. She hadn't realised making love would have such a momentous impact on *them*. But clearing the air was probably a good idea.

'Does your father really hate us Waverlys?'

He served the potatoes onto two plates and came back to sit on the stone beside her. Balancing their plates on their knees, they broke the potatoes open, slathered them in salt and butter, and waited for them to cool enough to eat.

'You don't understand how much he envied your father or how Holt's success ate away at him. It all escalated after my mother left.' One broad shoulder lifted. 'She was a city woman, like yours. But your mum stayed.'

The legend that was her parents' marriage rose up around them. People might mock it now, discredit it, but there was a solid truth to the love Holt and Rosamund had had for one another. Their marriage hadn't been perfect. But it didn't change the fact that they *had* loved each other.

'It wasn't easy for Mum in the early days. I remember her crying. I remember some dreadful fights.'

She hadn't told anyone other than her sisters about that, but she didn't want him thinking her parents' marriage had been picture perfect. There was the myth and then there was the reality. He'd been so alone, and it mattered. Her heart ached for the young boy he'd been. She'd been so lucky to have her sisters.

'Mum never stopped missing her home. But she stayed, and it made all the difference.' And it had. 'Even though we now know she had a strong reason to leave, she made the decision to stay and fight for her marriage.'

Lincoln's mouth turned grim. 'Mum leaving broke something inside my father. He turned inward and blamed all of his misfortune on Garrison Downs having been lost in that poker game all those years ago. As if there'd been a blight on the family ever since. He believed that if Garrison Downs was his, he'd have all that Holt had—the success, the plaudits of the nation, the family.' He rubbed a hand over his face. 'And just so you know. That day in Marni when you saw him hit me in the general store...'

Her fork of potato halted halfway to her mouth.

'Mum had only been gone a month and what you saw was the culmination of all his fear and frustration. He apologised later. He never hit me again.'

'Good.'

'I dreamed of finding Cordelia's diary when I was a kid because I'd hoped it'd frame the poker game in a way that would...' He shook his head. 'I don't know. Help him come to terms with it all.'

What if it did the opposite, though? What if—?

'My great-grandmother said that the goings-on back then were vastly exaggerated. If she'd lived longer, I'd have eventually known the right questions to ask, but…'

Rose abandoned her food as a growing foreboding grew inside her. 'What are you afraid your father is going to do, Lincoln?' Because it had finally occurred to her that one of the reasons Lincoln was here, one of the reasons he'd agreed to marry her, was to prevent his father from doing something…awful.

Lincoln made a decision in that moment to trust Rose with the truth. What had happened between the two of them this afternoon had changed things. He knew now that he loved this woman. With *all* of himself. He was hers, body and soul. To admit as much, though, would send her scurrying for the hills in a panic. Too much, too soon.

He wouldn't spook her. He'd win her trust, then he'd win her heart. He was smart and resourceful, and she loved making love with him. He *could* make this happen.

Sharing his concerns about his father would help cement the trust growing between them. Lifting a portion of potato to his mouth, he bit into it, letting the warmth and steam rise into his face. He nodded at her plate. 'Eat up, Rose. This is one of the joys of camping out.'

She did as he bid.

He waited until she'd taken a couple of bites before speaking again. 'You ask what I'm worried my father will do. I'm afraid he's going to try and steal some of your cattle.'

Her potato dropped to the ground with a splat. Picking it up, he threw it into the fire, placing the rest of his cooled potato on her plate and reaching for a new one to break open and slather in butter.

'Before you ask, I don't have any solid proof.' He held up a hand. 'And before you say anything, it's not rumour-mongering if it's kept just between ourselves.'

After the briefest of hesitations, she nodded.

'All I have is half a telephone conversation I overheard. All I caught was a truck being arranged to go north on your western boundary.'

'That's the furthest boundary from Kalku Hills.'

It was.

'To divert suspicion that Kalku could be responsible?'

'Possibly.' He ate more potato. 'Or because it's the last area you generally muster. It'd give Clay a chance to get out there undetected.'

'This is why you've been going out in Judy so much. You've been patrolling the boundaries.'

Bingo.

She ate her potato, staring reflectively into the fire. It occurred to him then that one of the reasons he loved her was that she didn't fly into a panic or throw a tantrum or make a drama out of a what-might-happen situation. She really was every bit as cool, calm and measured as she appeared.

Except in bed.

Then she was every inch the passionate, fiery siren.

Maybe she wouldn't panic if you told her you loved her?

His lips cracked into a smile. No, she'd be freaked.

'What are you smiling at?'

He shook himself. 'Your lack of drama. The fact you're not jumping about and waving your arms in a rage.'

'I save that for when things actually happen, not on the off chance that they might. Lincoln, if your dad does this and gets caught, he'll be ruined.'

If he was caught, the fool could go to jail.

'Do you think talking to him would help?'

'I want to say yes, but...' His father had lost all perspective. He wanted to prevent Clay from going too far, from taking a step he'd not be able to come back from. 'If he thought we were onto him, I'm worried he'd just change the plan.'

'And Garrison Downs is big. It's a lot of country to keep an eye on at a time when we're about to be all hands on deck.'

'Yep.'

She stared into the fire. 'Would it help if I gave Kalku Hills access to Camels Bridge now? Early?'

He straightened. 'You'd do that?'

'In an instant if it would help soften things between him and the Waverlys.'

'It'd give him another access point onto your land.'

'We'll be mustering there later in the week. Once we're done, he can drive the cattle through from the north if he wants. I'll let Aaron know as soon as we're back.'

'He might reward your kindness with—'

'Or he might not. But at least I've extended an olive branch. In the meantime, we remain vigilant.' Her gaze returned to the fire. 'Holt was one of the country's leading graziers,' she started slowly.

'He was a legend.'

'And he enjoyed that position, but sometimes, Lincoln, he could've wielded that power with more grace. He enjoyed rubbing his success in your father's face. I know your father needled him every chance he got, but Holt could've ignored it, been the bigger man.'

Rose had worshipped Holt. It was unsettling to hear her criticise him. 'There's a lot of history between our fathers. There'll be things that happened we've no knowledge of.' He glanced down, noted the stubborn jut of her jaw. 'Why are you so angry with him, Rose? Why do you call him Holt now instead of Dad?'

Startled eyes met his. The light from the fire danced across her face, and in that moment her beauty sent a shiver through his heart. If he couldn't make her love him... A weight pressed down on his chest. If he couldn't win her love, life would go on—an endless grey lonely life, a mockery of a life. If this risk didn't pay off, he'd be half a man.

'Is that the personal question you wanted to ask?'

He eased back. 'It's a spur-of-the-moment question. One you don't have to answer.'

Her nose wrinkled, and she refilled their glasses from the bottle of Shiraz.

'If he were here, he'd hate hearing me calling him Holt rather than Dad.' She sipped her wine. 'It's childish, imma-ture, but oddly satisfying.'

He winced. She didn't look particularly satisfied. 'Be-cause of the affair?'

'No.' Those lovely lips turned down. 'Not that I condone what he did. But I remember a period when there were awful fights. Truly awful, Lincoln. I'd have been no more than four or five. Mum wasn't there for a time. But then she returned and things went back to normal.'

Rosamund had left?

'I asked Da— Holt about it a few years ago.'

She might be angry with her father, but he sensed her love for him threading below her words.

'After Tilly was born, Mum had severe postnatal depres-sion.'

The air whistled between his teeth. 'Hell.'

'She'd been uprooted from all that she knew and trans-planted into a totally alien—and isolated—world. She had three children in quick succession. On top of that she had to deal with my grandmother—who wasn't sympathetic to her plight—while Holt spent long hours on the land…sometimes days.'

'That's a lot for anyone to handle.'

'He said it was like she'd changed overnight. She alternated between being withdrawn and then raging at him. He thought she'd gone from loving him to hating him in the space of a few of years. She accused him of ruining her life and—' She broke off, stared at her hands. 'She was hospitalised with depression for a short time. He thought their marriage was over.'

Linc could barely get his head around what she was telling him. 'I had no idea…' Holt and Rosamund had always presented such a united front, had always seemed so deeply in love.

'That they were less than perfect?' She gave a low laugh. 'It's why my view of marriage has never been as rosy as Tilly's. I knew they'd had a rocky patch. I knew Holt had thought the marriage was over. I didn't know about the affair. While I can't condone it, I can understand him seeking solace.'

'Why are you so angry with him, then?'

Her eyes flashed. 'For keeping a sister from us! Ana should never have been hidden away like some dirty little secret. We should've had the chance to know her. She grew up thinking we'd resent and loathe her if we'd known about her. He should've publicly acknowledged her, and she should've had all the same advantages we had growing up.'

Reaching out, he pulled her into his lap, wanting to soothe her agitation. 'But Ana is in your life now and she knows you love her.'

'Yes, but—'

'Rose, your father loved all of you—the fact all four daughters inherit Garrison Downs proves that.'

She folded her arms and glared at him, but she also rested

back against him as if she belonged there. 'So you're saying I should just forgive him?'

He traced a finger down her cheek. 'You will forgive him.' Her lips trembled. 'You love him and you'll eventually forgive him just like you'd forgive one of your sisters if they hurt you.'

He stared down at her, aching for her. She'd lost her father, had all she'd known about him turned on its head. It was enough to rattle anyone. 'Did your mother know about Ana?'

Her hair brushed his cheek as she shook her head. 'She knew about the affair, but, according to Ana, Holt and Lili had ended things before they discovered Lili was pregnant.'

'If she'd known he'd had a child to Lili, how would Rosamund have reacted? Would it have been one obstacle too many?'

She glanced up, swallowed.

'It would've devastated you all if Rosamund had given up on Holt and demanded a divorce. It would've torn your family apart.'

Her eyes swirled with confusion, agitation.

'It's only natural Holt would want to save Rosamund from further pain. He would've done just about anything to keep your family together. That's understandable.'

She frowned. 'But—'

'And Ana had Lili. There would never have been any question of Ana coming to live at Garrison Downs. She'd have remained with her mum. Holt was financially responsible for her. He didn't abandon her.'

'No, but—'

'You had a wonderful childhood with your parents and sisters. Clearly your parents' marriage emerged even stronger.'

'Well, yes, but—'

'And Ana has had a good life with her mum.'

'Of course! Lili is wonderful.'

'Holt had to know that the news would hurt you. But maybe the hurt you're suffering now is the lesser hurt than if your family had been broken apart.'

'But what about the hurt Ana has suffered?'

It was a wail in the night and he tucked her hair behind her ear. 'It's easy to rewrite the past into the shape we want for it, but if your parents had divorced and you'd been forced to spend half your time in England with your mum and half here at Garrison Downs—your lives completely upended—isn't it possible you'd have felt some resentment towards Ana?'

He pressed a finger to her lips when she opened her mouth.

'The scenario in your mind is one in which everyone is acting as their ideal best selves. All I'm saying is that the reality might have been different. And the fact is, you can't change the past. All you can do is make the best of your present.'

'Hmph. Why do you have to sound so reasonable?'

'I don't like seeing you tied up in knots. You deserve to be happy.'

She glanced down at her hands. 'I've been lucky, I know. I've an embarrassment of riches when it comes to family. I've no right to complain.'

'Your dad betrayed your trust, and, while I don't doubt he regretted it, you've every right to feel hurt and let down. But, Rose, don't forget that a mistake—even a big one—doesn't mean he wasn't a good man. It doesn't mean all of your memories of him are a lie. It doesn't mean everything you thought of him is a lie.'

The inherent truth of Lincoln's words seeped into Rose in a slow trickle. She moistened her lips. Some of the things she knew about her father were still true. 'He was a good cattleman.' Her heart thudded. 'And a good businessman.'

'One of the best.'

In her mind's eye she saw Holt on Jasper, the black stallion cutting behind a mob of cattle, man and horse moving as one. Momentarily removing his hat to swipe an arm across his brow, he caught her eye, winked and grinned, looking every inch the legend he was.

Her throat thickened. 'He was a good dad to Evie, Tilly and me.' He'd taught them to ride, to swim, to navigate home by the stars. He'd encouraged them to follow their dreams, had wrapped them in his love.

She gave a sudden sob. He'd hurt her. He should never have kept Ana a secret from them. But he hadn't kept Ana a secret forever—he'd sent Ana to them, had made sure Garrison Downs was hers too. It hadn't all been a lie.

Lincoln pulled her against his chest and let her cry. One large hand stroking her hair.

The storm was brief, but cleansing. 'Thank you,' she whispered. 'I feel as if I have my dad back.'

'I only told you what you already know in your own heart.'

She lifted her head to meet his gaze, glancing beyond him to the star-jewelled sky. Pushing off his lap, she disappeared inside the cabin, returning a moment later with a couple of blankets. 'Have you ever made love beneath a starry sky beside a campfire?'

'Is that what you'd like to do?'

'More than life itself.'

He took the blankets from her and kissed her deeply. 'Your wish is my command.'

CHAPTER TEN

TWO DAYS AT the waterhole with Lincoln weren't anywhere near enough, but the muster couldn't be delayed any longer. They packed up camp, and Lincoln dangled the car keys from his fingers. 'May I?'

At her nod, he held the passenger door open for her as if she were a queen, saw her seated, and then he negotiated the rustic track with an unhurried ease that had her shifting in her seat and wishing...

What? That they could've stayed at the waterhole forever?

She focussed on the scenery instead. Thanks to the past year's record rainfall, native grasses stretched away in all directions, waves of gold bending in a soft breeze. She loved it—all of it. The dry dusty plains to the west, the pockets of Eucalypt forests beside the river, the lushness surrounding the lakes, the flinty red hills. She even loved the red dust that settled on one's hair and eyelashes.

Yet none of it could distract her from the man beside her. He was beautiful. He made love beautifully. He *had* made her scream. He'd also made her beg, sigh, laugh...and a couple of times he'd damn near made her cry.

She was sore in places she'd never known she had. But it was a good sore—the same as after a hard day in the saddle, wrangling cattle. And it didn't dampen the desire rushing through her now. She wondered if she'd ever get enough of him.

It's called a honeymoon phase for a reason.

And yet she couldn't imagine the intensity fading.

Naïve little virgin.

'Do you know I haven't asked my personal question yet?'

Lincoln's words had her crashing back. He hadn't?

'Guess I had other things on my mind.'

His lazy grin heated her blood.

'Wanna ask it now?'

He nodded. 'You mentioned that one unexpected pregnancy in the family was enough—referring, I suppose, to Eve and Nate. How would you feel if we did become unexpectedly pregnant?'

The *we* surprised her, but she appreciated it too.

'Not sure I expect an answer. It's probably not something you've considered. But if the idea horrifies you…'

Her stomach performed a slow forward roll—not of horror, but of longing. Her mouth dried at the pictures that played through her mind.

Dear God. She couldn't have those kinds of longings with this man. While she couldn't imagine ever tiring of making love with him, she wasn't foolish enough to believe the feeling was mutual. He might no longer be the playboy the district considered him, but it didn't mean he was ready to settle down.

'I like kids,' he continued, 'and I very much want some of my own eventually. You?'

She had to swallow before she could speak. 'I always figured they'd feature in my future.'

'If we had a child, Rose, it would change things.'

'Understatement much, Lincoln?' She laughed, but absurdly she wanted to cry.

'I don't want to be a part-time father. And from what you just said, I'm guessing you wouldn't want to be a part-time mother.'

No! She wanted her child—children—growing up with her. She stared at that hard, lean profile and suddenly blinked. 'Are you saying that if we became pregnant, you'd want to remain married?'

He looked at her then, those dark eyes briefly blazing. He didn't say anything, just gave a hard nod.

Her stomach clenched. Her chest clenched. And somewhere lower down clenched too. *Don't be absurd.* The idea was too ridiculous for words.

'I don't want you thinking I'm going to be lax with contraception. I mean to be careful. But no method is a hundred per cent effective. So if the idea of an unplanned pregnancy appals you, you might want to consider an additional form of contraception besides condoms.' He shrugged. 'You might want to anyway. In an ideal world, a planned pregnancy is best.'

And yet his tone almost implied the opposite—that an unplanned pregnancy wouldn't appal him.

He flicked a glance at her when she remained silent. 'Didn't mean to freak you out.'

'Not freaked out.' *Liar.*

'Just figured it was something we should consider.'

'Absolutely.' He deserved more from her, though. He'd raised a difficult topic and had been startlingly honest. 'The situation you just described doesn't appal me, Lincoln. But you're right, it's not ideal.' No matter how much it might tempt her.

He raised an eyebrow as if aware there was something she wasn't saying.

'I'd hate to trap you in a marriage that wasn't your idea, and not what you wanted.'

He grinned. 'It might not have been my idea, but it was a good one, Rose. I'm enjoying it so far.'

She couldn't help but laugh. 'I'll make a tele health appointment this week.'

Reaching across, he took her hand and squeezed it, rested it against his thigh. Ahead of them, three emus raced off to the right on long, gangly legs. Emus were considered a symbol of survival and adaptability. And maybe that was what she and Lincoln would do—adapt and survive. The thought had her lips lifting.

For the next three weeks, it was all hands on deck as they mustered in the station's south-eastern corner—the boundary closest to Clay Garrison and Kalku Hills. Rose kept her eyes peeled for signs of unusual activity, but nothing raised alarm bells. Nevertheless, she heaved a sigh of relief when they had the cattle vaccinated, ear-tagged, and those going to market on trucks and rumbling off to the sale yards.

Every evening, Lincoln checked in with Jackson, the Kalku Hills stockman, to find out how things were going next door. Clay had gone quiet. She didn't know if she ought to be worried or not.

But each night, regardless of how hard they'd worked during the day, she and Lincoln made love. Apparently they were never too tired for that.

Mustering eighteen thousand head of cattle across fifteen thousand square kilometres would take a full three months, and yet Rose was careful to ensure her staff had rest days. She didn't want fatigue causing accidents or mishaps.

'You mind if I head over to Kalku?' Lincoln asked during one set of rest days.

'Of course not.' And yet something inside her sank.

'They're mustering a tricky bit of terrain and the helicopter pilot has come down with appendicitis.'

'Ouch.' Kalku Hills was Lincoln's home. Of course he

wanted to help. 'You're free to spend your time however you want, Lincoln. You don't have to help here with the muster if you'd prefer to be at Kalku.'

'I *want* to be here.'

For now. But in three months' time—*two* months' time, she amended. When their agreement had been fulfilled, Lincoln *would* return to Kalku. She'd be a fool to forget it.

'It's the first time Dad has asked anything of me since…'

Since they'd married? She nodded.

'And I want to check that everything is as it should be over there.'

She and Lincoln were consolidating a new working relationship they could take forward into the future. She had absolutely no reason not to trust him.

'You be careful out there,' was all she said.

'Always. But tomorrow night I'll be challenging you to another game of chess. Hopefully this time we can finish it.'

That had her grinning. 'I'll look forward to it.'

The following afternoon, the sound of Lincoln's plane landing shook Rose from the torpor of having sat too long with the accounts. Today she'd faced her demons. After their conversation about Holt at the waterhole, it had felt like time— time to stop avoiding the office, to claim it as her own and start working in it rather than grabbing her laptop and the accounts and settling elsewhere in the house.

Lincoln believed in her. The district's fears had eased. She hadn't messed up. And while it still felt too soon to take over the running of such a massive operation, this was her home, her legacy…and she had a vision for Garrison Downs' future. She *could* do it.

Seating herself behind the desk, she'd thought she might feel awed or a fraud…burdened by all she'd found herself responsible for. But she placed the piece of amber that Lincoln had given her all of those years ago on the desk, alongside the glass horse—named Peridot—that Tilly had sent her from Chaleur, and the silver pen that had been her twenty-first birthday gift from Evie. Touching her tiger's eye bracelet for luck, she set to work. And once she started, she became lost to the work and was ridiculously productive.

She'd felt as if her mother had been sitting in her chair by the window, her love and pride reaching out to her daughter, her quiet strength bolstering Rose's own resilience. At her back she'd felt a presence too—Holt—not intimidating or intrusive, just *encouraging*. She felt, for the briefest of moments, as if she had the very best of both her parents.

In that moment she'd realised she carried that inside her— that she would always have it. A weight had lifted and she'd cried, but the tears had been a release. They'd allowed happy memories to surface—her mother's smile, her father's laugh. Christmas as a child with her sisters, bouncing and excited. Family dinners. Picnics. Bedtime stories.

She wanted to tell Lincoln about it all.

Maybe he'd like a cold beer by the pool?

Or she could join him in the shower, perhaps...

Standing and stretching, she lost herself in that scenario until she glimpsed his tall broad form sauntering through the gums at the edge of the garden. When he halted and glanced to his right, she craned her neck to see what he was looking at.

After the briefest of hesitations, he set his footsteps in that direction. Stepping out onto the veranda, she started after him, wanting to know what had caught his attention. Blossom followed at her heels, her nails clicking on the veranda's tessellated tiles.

Lincoln had passed through the garden and now started

up the low rise in the direction of the old settler's cottage. She opened her mouth to call out to him, but closed it again. What had he seen?

You mean, what is he up to?

'Grandma,' she murmured, 'if I want your opinion I'll ask for it.'

Her eyes narrowed. There was something almost furtive about his movements that had a chill settling across her scalp. Topping the rise, she watched in silence as he ducked straight inside the cottage. Her heart pounded. Probably due to the stories Pop had told her about the giant brown snake that used to live there.

Lincoln was up to something. Acid burned her stomach. And she knew exactly what it was—he was hoping to find Cordelia's diary. Why would he do that behind her back?

With a single gesture she sent Blossom behind the cottage out of sight, before creeping up to one of the two windows. Inside, Lincoln checked the walls and rafters. Ducking down when his gaze turned in her direction, she crept across to the other window. When she peeked in again, she found him crouching down and running his fingers along a row of stones as if... Was he counting?

His fingers halted, and even from where she stood she heard his quick intake of breath. Prising a stone loose, he lowered it to the ground. Nestled in the gap behind lay something wrapped in calf leather, tied with a piece of knotted cord. Reaching in, he took it out and blew the dust from it, staring at it reverently before placing it carefully beneath his shirt.

Tiptoeing around the corner, she flattened herself against the wall. His footsteps faded as he strode back towards the homestead, the afternoon shadows lengthening. She didn't emerge until he was out of sight.

Why hadn't he told her he'd worked out where the diary

was? And what the hell did he think was in it? Spots danced at the edges of her vision. Had she been a fool to trust him?

Bracing her hands on her knees against a wave of nausea, she pulled air into cramped lungs. He'd said he'd wanted to find the diary to help Clay come to terms with the past. She had no reason not to believe him.

'Stop being obtuse, Rose. That diary could damn Louisa May. And if it does—'

She tried to block out her grandmother's voice. Even if it did, the land had been in Waverly hands for the last hundred and twenty years. It was the Waverly family who had made Garrison Downs what it was.

If Lincoln wasn't trying to make mischief, though, why hadn't he shared the treasure hunt adventure with her? She covered her face with her hands. Had he slept with her simply to throw her off the scent? Had he been searching all this time while her back had been turned?

Blossom whined and nosed her leg. Crouching down, Rose buried her face in her fur. Eventually she straightened, faced what needed to be faced. Lincoln had been playing her for a fool. *She* had been a sentimental fool.

She took the shortest route home. She'd been naïve and now she needed to work out what the hell to do. She headed straight into the office.

'Afternoon, Rose.'

She slammed to a halt. Lincoln sat in the chair on the other side of the desk, grinning that grin she should never have allowed herself to believe in, but even now it had things inside her softening.

Nausea churned.

Don't throw up.

She couldn't let him see how badly his betrayal affected her. She couldn't…

Stumbling around the desk, she sat. She'd ask him to leave. Tonight. *Right now.* And she wouldn't ask—*she'd order.*

She opened her mouth, refusing to look at him, staring instead at her hands as she flattened them on the desk. 'Lincoln…'

She blinked. Directly in front of her sat a leather roll tied with cord, the cord still knotted and intact. She stared at it and then at him. He *hadn't* taken it. He *hadn't* hidden it. He *wasn't* a wretched, black-hearted traitor.

'Tut-tut. Boots in the house? I'm shocked, Rose Waverly.'

Her mind had blanked. She tried to find her way back to the surface. 'Holt's office, his rules.'

'Your office now. Your rules. Which are?'

'Boots allowed. In here. Not the rest of the house.'

His grin widened at her choppy sentences.

She pointed at the leather pouch. 'Is that…?'

'Cordelia's diary? I'm hoping so.'

He hadn't stolen it, hadn't hidden it away. Her vision blurred. He wasn't hoping it contained something that would take her home from her.

She couldn't move. She could only stare from the leather pouch to him and back again. 'But…*how*?'

'My father is still being pig-headed. Which irritated me more than usual today. Got me thinking about the diary again. And when I was flying in, I saw the old settler's cottage and wondered—what if those old tales weren't referring to the original homestead but to the original *dwelling*?'

A deliciously broad shoulder lifted. 'While we've been on muster, I've been trying to remember everything Gran told me. She said I shouldn't believe what everyone said about Louisa May…and something about *three up and six across*. Like it was some private joke. Today, when I flew over the cottage, I realised it was a direction.'

He *had* been counting!

'Three stones up—'

'And six across.' And here the treasure was, right in front of her. She'd been right to trust him.

The relief hit her like a punch, pulling her from her daze. Rather than reaching for the calfskin parcel, though, she shot around the desk to fling herself into his arms.

'Whoa! I—'

But her mouth had claimed his, fierce and possessive. He kissed her back with the same intensity, breaking off to gasp when her hands tugged the hem of his shirt from his jeans to flatten against the hard flat planes of his stomach. 'Rose, I—'

Dragging him to his feet, she led him to the sofa and pushed him down. 'Want me to stop?'

He shook his head.

She closed the French doors. She locked the office door. His eyes blazed when she turned back to face him. Standing in front of him, she undressed—slowly and seductively, like some soap-opera starlet—but it worked because his breathing grew more and more ragged.

'Rose, you're killing me.'

And then she proceeded to make love to him with her hands, her mouth, her body—telling him in a language that needed no words how much she admired him, how much she desired him…how much she *liked* him.

But then there were no more thoughts—just sensation. Glorious sensation.

Afterwards, when they could move again, she lifted her head from where it was pressed against his neck. She'd straddled him and she should probably move and give the poor guy a chance to breathe again. His hand on her waist stilled her. With his other hand, he lifted her chin until liquid dark eyes bored into hers. 'Did something happen today? Anything I should know?'

She cupped his face, let her hands drift down to enjoy the

strength of his neck, before sending him a straight-from-the-heart smile—one she couldn't have contained if she'd wanted to. 'Only that I missed you.'

Something flared in his eyes, and she thought it might be hope. Maybe both of them were becoming more invested in this temporary marriage than they'd meant to. The thought should terrify her.

Instead she recalled his earlier words about his father being difficult and a hard determination settled in her chest. This man had never had a proper family of his own, not one who loved him unconditionally—not a warm, loving, sharing family. But she could give him a taste of that now. She could share what she had with him.

Something in Rose's face made Lincoln's heart beat harder. The way she'd made love to him just now...

She'd made him feel *cherished*. He searched her face. The light in her eyes...the smile on her lips... Was she starting to care? Something fierce and fiery rushed through him.

He ground back the declaration pressing against his throat. It was too soon to tell her he loved her. They had time. He wouldn't spook her.

'What?' he asked instead as she continued to survey him.

Easing off his lap, she started hauling on her clothes, grinning at him over her shoulder. She pointed at the leather pouch on the desk. 'Family conference in thirty minutes.'

He stilled. Except his heart, which thudded like a wild thing.

'Ever since we Waverly sisters have heard about it, we've been dying to know what's in that diary.'

She was including him in that inner circle? He'd finally get a peek behind the curtain and be a part of the family that had enthralled him his whole life? He opened his mouth but not a single sound emerged.

'Chop-chop.' She clapped her hands. 'You need to make yourself respectable. I messed up your pretty hair.'

That had him grinning. Speaking of messed hair…

She turned on her phone and sang the first line of Sister Sledge's 'We Are Family'.

'Girls,' she dictated into the phone, 'Lincoln is the man of the hour. He's found the diary. I'm opening it in thirty minutes. You know what to do if you don't want to miss it.'

He heard the pings as her sisters all immediately answered. They sounded like excitement and love and belonging.

Thirty minutes later he was seated behind the desk next to Rose. Eve and Nate sat on the sofa at right angles to them. At Rose's insistence that Eve have the most comfortable seat in the house, he and Nate had moved it. Up on the giant screen on the back wall, Matilda and Prince Henri appeared in one window, and Ana and Connor in another.

Matilda squealed when she saw everyone and immediately blew kisses. Ana waved, her shy smile broad.

'Show me my future niece,' Matilda demanded.

Eve rose and smoothed a hand over her stomach with a big grin and soft eyes. 'Isn't she beautiful?'

'Gorgeous!'

Coos and excited murmurings filled the air. Matilda danced in her seat, clapping her hands, Ana shot so far forward that Connor slipped an arm around her waist to stop her from falling off her chair, while Rose just grinned. The broadness of her smile and the way her eyes shone made his breath catch. *This.* This was what he wanted.

Nate caught his eye and winked.

Matilda sobered and pointed. 'Rose, I hope you're making sure she's not overdoing it, that she's taking it easy.'

'Nate is taking perfect care of her.'

'Cross my heart.' Nate lifted a hand and crossed his heart, the tattoos on his forearm endearingly at odds with the quaint gesture.

'Pfft, Eve won't listen to you. But Rose, now…she's the Boss.'

Lincoln glanced at Rose, but her father's old nickname only made her grin.

'We're all terrified of her when she's on the warpath.'

'And we all know that's a load of old cobblers, but I *am* going to call this meeting to order.' And with that Rose held up the leather roll. It was the first time she'd touched it and it was as if the very air stilled as all eyes turned to stare at it.

'Tilly, you're the expert. How should we do this?' She lifted the pouch closer to the camera.

Matilda bent down, gestured for Rose to turn it over. 'The leather is in good condition, but that cord…' She shook her head. 'The historian in me is urging you to pack it up and send it to me. If I can't get hold of the right equipment to protect and date it, I know people who can.'

'You always were a comedian, Tilly,' Eve trilled. 'You know that's not going to happen. Those in favour of opening the roll here and now, raise your hands.'

Rose and Eve both raised their hands.

'Ana?' Rose kept her voice gentle.

Ana squirmed. 'Sorry, Tilly, but I'm dying to know.' She raised her hand as well.

'No need to apologise, Ana Banana.' Matilda raised her hand too. 'Me four. Just, Rose…try and be gentle.'

Rose glanced at Lincoln. 'As Lincoln is the one who found it, and as it probably belongs to his great-great-grandmother, perhaps he should do the honours.'

'What, with these big lugs?' He held his hands up, shaking his head. 'No, you have at it, Rose.'

Settling the pouch in front of her, she took a deep breath and did her best to gently unknot the cord, but it promptly disintegrated.

'Don't throw it!' Matilda wrung her hands. 'It can be used to help date the package.'

Rifling through the desk drawers, Rose emerged triumphant with a Ziploc bag, which made her sister laugh. 'Dad always had a collection of those on hand for my discoveries.'

After the cord had been carefully stowed inside the bag, Rose gently unrolled the pouch. Inside was a package of…

'Letters,' Rose said, pulling them out. 'Not a diary. Letters addressed to Cordelia Garrison…'

His ancestor.

She turned the top one over. 'From Lissy May.'

'Louisa May,' Eve and Matilda breathed at the same time.

'And some addressed to Louisa May from Cordelia too.'

'Read them, Rose!'

That burst from Ana, but both Eve and Matilda nodded.

CHAPTER ELEVEN

ROSE CAREFULLY SHUFFLED through the letters. Lincoln's gaze caught on those fingers, recalled the feel of them on his overheated flesh in this very room earlier, and had to swallow.

'This one is dated first and it's from Louisa May. *"Dear Cordelia, A poker match? A poker match! I nearly fainted when Elinor Conklin informed me that the town was agog with the news that I'd won Garrison Downs from you in a poker match. She said she'd had the words direct from the horse's mouth—you—so that there was no use me trying to deny it. You'd have been proud of how I rose to the occasion. I shrugged and asked her if she'd like to be invited to our next game. You've never seen anyone make their excuses quicker. She hightailed away as if I was the most wicked of women. I had a hearty laugh afterwards, but seriously you should've warned me. To my surprise, rather than making me persona non gratis, it appears that my standing in the community has risen in some circles. Miss Delia Gray, who's so high in the instep, deigned to stop and ask after my brother when I was in town yesterday. And, yes, Michael's health is improving, thanks to your kindness. And reports of our wild deeds do not appear to have scared Ned Waverly away as the dear man continues to pay me court. Is it wrong of me to hope that soon I shall be Mrs Edward Waverly? I'm sure it's most unladylike, but you know what they say—as soon as a woman turns to gambling she loses all decorum. But seriously, I implore you, dearest Cordelia, to accept the deeds back to Garrison Downs as soon as you're sure we've scared off Geoffrey Bannister, as that is, I believe, your design in starting such a rumour. I can imagine the difficulties Arthur is now making for you too. Much love, your faithful friend, Lissy May.'"*

Rose set the letter down. 'They weren't enemies. They were *friends.*'

'Not just friends,' Eve said, 'but besties.'

'Sisters of the heart,' Ana breathed.

Matilda stared at the letters as if she ached to hold them for herself. 'There *wasn't* a poker match.'

Apparently that was a rumour started by his great-great-grandmother.

'Oh, hurry.' Matilda groaned. 'Read the next one.'

Rose picked up a second letter. 'This one's from Cordelia. *"Dearest Lissy, How I wish I could've seen your face when Elinor told you of our iniquitous deeds. Don't be too cross with me. I was in the process of writing to you when your letter came. I did not think you would be going to town for another six weeks at least and believed that I, thus, would have time to tell you what was afoot. However, let's get to the heart of the matter. Garrison Downs is yours, my dear friend, and there's nothing my dreadful brother Arthur can do about it—regardless of how he might bellyache and complain around the district that I've ruined him. He squandered his own inheritance from Grandfather, and I won't allow him to squander mine. As you well know, Papa not only owns Kalku Hills, but vast swathes of land to the north-east. I am far from destitute. I repeat: Garrison Downs is yours, my dear. Not only have you saved my life three times, but Arthur has done you and Michael a grave disservice. My con-*

science won't rest easy until amends are made. I know that
if I should ever need a place of refuge in the future, I will
always find one with you at Garrison Downs. Now, let me
tell you the colour Geoffrey Bannister's face turned when he
heard the news and came knocking on my door to demand
I refute such dastardly rumours. First it turned puce, and
then the most interesting shade of purple, and then a sickly
shade of yellow. It really was most fascinating to witness. He
informed me that I am a wicked wanton with no regard for
my future, my children's future or any respect for God Al-
mighty himself. What woman would want to lumber herself
with such a proselytising prig of a husband? I ask you. But
he will never again darken my door—his words, not mine—
and I cannot tell you the weight that has lifted from me. While
he wears the face of a Christian, underneath he is a sadistic
brute and I'm heartily relieved to be rid of him. Now I plan
to woo my Thomas properly and convince him to make an
honest woman of me."'

Rose set the letter down carefully, stared at her sisters.

'I want to know how Louisa May saved Cordelia's life
three times.' Matilda rested her chin in her palm. 'I bet there
was a brown snake involved at least once.'

There were a lot of ways to die out here. Even more back
then.

'Nursed her through a fever?' Ana offered. 'Jumped into
a swollen river and saved her from drowning?'

Eve snorted. 'Went to stay with her to save her from bore-
dom?'

A laugh burst from Rose. 'You're right, this pair are a riot.'

'I wonder what disservice Arthur did to Lissy and Michael, though?'

'The brother sounds like a piece of work, and Geoffrey

Bannister sounds even worse.' Rose picked up the next letter. 'Shall I continue?'

Rose read letters that detailed Cordelia's marriage to Thomas Sinclair, a lowly station hand, and how her father gifted Kalku Hills to the couple when Thomas agreed to take Garrison as his surname.

'No way.' Linc leaned forward, and she showed him the line in the letter. He eased back, grinning. 'Wait till my father hears about that.'

Her eyes danced before returning to the letters. They revealed that Louisa May married Edward Waverly and that they settled at Garrison Downs. It became clear that in the early days of their marriages, the two women relied on each other enormously.

When Cordelia gave birth to *'a bonny son'*, Louisa May and Ned were named godparents. As a gift to her new godson, Louisa May had a codicil attached to her will stating that if there were no Waverly sons to inherit Garrison Downs, and if the Waverly daughters were all unmarried, then the station would pass back to the Garrison family.

Rose sat back as if the air had been punched from her body.

'She didn't do it to punish us!' Eve burst out. 'She did it out of respect for her dearest friend and for the godson she loved. And because Cordelia had gifted it to her in the first place.'

'She adds here that the two of them know how hard it is for women on the land alone, and that she hopes all of their daughters find husbands as fine as their fathers, and that their sons should find wives with the love for the land that she and Cordelia have.' Rose shrugged. 'And that's it.'

They were all silent for a moment.

'They weren't enemies.' Rose swung to him, her eyes shining. 'They were besties.'

He couldn't stop from reaching out and touching her cheek. His heart swelled. 'Friends,' he murmured.

'Ooh, you two are making bedroom eyes at each other,' Matilda cooed.

Rose dragged her gaze from his. 'Shut up, Button.'

It made everyone laugh, and then she rose and scanned each of the letters, and sent copies to her sisters…and to him. She and Matilda discussed how best to get the letters to Chaleur for Matilda to verify them. None of them doubted that the letters were real, but official authentication would provide authority for this new version of the station's history.

He suspected Rose wanted that for him. He'd be able to take that back to his father, and maybe then Clay would finally look to the future instead of remaining mired in the past.

A new history. Friends. Not enemies. No poker match. No lying or cheating. Cordelia had gifted land that was legitimately hers to her dearest friend, and the two women had been each other's chief support. Sisters of the heart, as Ana had said. They'd been family.

And to be here now like this, in the middle of the Waverly clan, accepted as part of the family, he realised what a treasure that was. His father had wasted his life in bitterness. Lincoln wasn't making the same mistake. After today's revelations he was only more determined to make Rose his own.

They made love again that night, and Rose gazed into his eyes the entire time, let him see her most secret self, unedited—the awe, the ecstasy—as if she wanted there to be no secrets between them, as if she was trusting him with her very essence. It left him wanting to kiss her feet.

Afterwards they lay side by side as they waited for their hearts to stop racing and their breathing to slow.

'That was…'

She nodded. 'It was.'

He turned his head on the pillow to find her watching him. 'Okay?' he asked gently.

Was she rocked by the intensity of their lovemaking, worried that it was one-sided? He could put her mind at rest on that—

'I have a confession to make.' She rolled to fully face him.

He turned to face her too, his senses sharpening.

'I owe you an apology. I saw you heading for the old settler's cottage this afternoon and I followed you.'

He frowned. 'Why didn't you call out? We could've searched together.'

She glanced down, moistened her lips. 'Your manner seemed…odd. Almost furtive.'

He pushed up into a sitting position, resting back against the headboard. His temples pounded. Would she never trust him?

She sat up too. 'Why didn't you come and get me so we could make the discovery together?'

'It felt like a long shot. I didn't want to get my hopes up.'

She pleated the sheet between her fingers. 'When you found those letters…'

He covered her hand with his own. 'You thought I meant to keep them from you?'

'I went into instant melodramatic soap-opera mode, thinking they must contain something that painted Louisa May in a bad light, and that the only reason you married me was to get your hands on them.'

Her words shouldn't rake his soul so raw. She knew now she'd been mistaken, but a sick realisation had bile rising in his throat. 'If I hadn't placed them on your desk when I did…'

She nodded, her face pale. 'I'm sorry.'

He'd wanted to play the hero for her, to bring home the prize so she'd think him wonderful. Instead, he'd nearly wrecked everything.

'When I thought you meant to betray me, I was gutted.'

He stilled, a pulse ticcing to life. 'You were upset?'

She lifted her eyes to his and he saw the shadows stretching through them. 'I thought we'd become friends.' One slim shoulder lifted. 'More than friends, actually.'

Her openness, her vulnerability, stole his breath. 'Rose... sweetheart.'

'And the thought of losing that left me bereft.'

'You haven't lost it.'

'When I realised my mistake, I was so relieved and so elated.'

She cared.

The knowledge hit him sure and swift.

She cared.

It might not be love. But, like trust, given time it could grow.

'You didn't have to tell me any of that. Why did you?'

'We promised to be honest with each other.'

And she was a woman of her word.

'I figure that's especially important when it's hard.' Her fingers fluttered about her throat. 'If I could be that mistaken about your actions, it made me realise you could be mistaken about mine. It made me realise how careful we need to be. The trust is growing, but it's still in its infancy.'

From now on, he needed to make sure that all of his actions were transparent, that she wasn't in danger of misreading him. But...

His chest grew lighter, bigger.

She cared.

'Rose, I've been thinking. We could extend the length of our marriage beyond three months if we wanted.'

Blue eyes searched his. 'You don't think you'll be sick of me by then?'

She said it as a joke, but he didn't laugh. 'You want to know why I really married you?'

Her eyes widened.

'Because I've always *liked* you, always been drawn to you. I wanted a chance to get to know you. I've never felt for any woman what I feel for you. I wanted to know where, if anywhere, that might lead.'

Her mouth fell open.

'And maybe the relationship between us has an end date, but, as far as I'm concerned, it's not looming on my horizon any time soon. I, for one, would like to see where it could take us.'

He could've groaned out loud when she moistened her lips. 'Maybe...' Her voice was a croak. She cleared her throat and started again. 'Maybe when the mustering is done, you and I could go away somewhere for a week or two.'

Then she smiled and adrenaline pumped through him, his heart soaring light and free. She was open to exploring what was developing between them.

She *cared*.

CHAPTER TWELVE

ROSE PAUSED TO admire the sight of Lincoln and Thunder pivoting, wheeling to the right and then galloping to cut off a breakaway mob, directing them back to the main herd. Strong thighs flexing, spine and shoulders fluid, horse and rider moving as one.

Lincoln looked good on a horse. Seriously good. There weren't many who could boast horsemanship to rival Holt's, but Lincoln was one of them.

He's a good lad.

She smiled.

Yeah, but I bet Grandma's having conniptions.

Her father's laughter sounded through her, and she found herself grinning. Then someone shouted, 'Left flank!' and she and Opal spun into action.

The past month had been insanely busy—muster always was—but it had been heaven too. She loved this time of year. Mustering might be back-breaking work, but few things could beat being out under a peerless sky on Opal, bringing the cattle into the yards. *This* was where she belonged.

The other place she belonged, apparently, was in Lincoln's arms—when the sun had gone down and the stars had come out and the world had hushed and shrunk to just the two of them.

He turned to grin at her now and she grinned back, knowing he loved all of this as much as she did. From the corner of her eye she saw Aaron scowl, but ignored him. Aaron had stopped openly challenging her every decision, but she sensed rebellion lurking still beneath the surface.

They ushered the cattle into the giant yard, dust swirling all around. Then began the back-breaking work of drafting the cattle—calves for ear-tagging into one of the smaller yards, others for health checks and vaccinations into another, and those for the sale yards in yet another.

When the calves were done, she leaned down from Opal's back, to unlatch the gate and let them back into the main yard to find their mothers, backing Opal up first so the two of them would be out of the way of the stamping rush of hooves. She was dying for a cup of tea, and as soon as this was done they could stop for half an hour.

All around dust swirled, the air filled with the lowing of cattle. As she pulled her arm back, her bracelet—the one Ana had made—caught on the sleeve of her shirt, and the sudden wrench sent it flying through the air to land in the red dirt.

Her sister bracelet!

For two tenths of a second she considered leaping off Opal and trying to retrieve it, but the cattle were starting to move and she'd never be able to hold back the panicked press of bodies. With eyes burning—*her precious bracelet*—she eased Opal away.

And then Lincoln was there, dashing across the yard, flinging himself through the space with a speed that had her jaw dropping before fear kicked in. A tiny corner of her brain marvelled that a man as large as Lincoln could move with such speed, but mostly her heart lodged in her throat pounding so hard it hurt.

He'd be trampled!

Injured!

Her stomach gave a sick kick. Or worse.

One long arm swooped down to sweep up her bracelet. A fraction of a moment later a heifer barrelled through where he'd been, but then he took the hand she held out to him and vaulted onto the back of Opal behind her. She cantered them away, Johnno opening the main gate to let them through, slamming it behind them.

Her heart rate would never return to normal. *Never!*

The moment she brought Opal to a halt they both leapt from her back.

With a lazy, laconic grin that sent fury surging through her veins, Lincoln dangled the bracelet from his fingers. Red mist burst behind her eyeballs and she thumped his chest, and then she did it again because it seemed a better idea than bursting into tears. Though she doubted he even felt her blows—he remained unmovable. But while he might think himself indestructible, he wasn't!

'Whoa, Rose.' He held his hands up. 'Rose, I—'

'What the hell were you thinking?' she shouted, gesturing at the yards. 'You could've been injured. Or worse!' He could've died and it made her break into a cold sweat, had her fury redoubling. 'That was the stupidest, most idiotic—'

She broke off to wheel away and press her palms to her eyes.

'But I wasn't hurt.' His voice was low and steady, as if he were talking to a spooked horse. 'I know what that bracelet means to you.'

She spun back, stabbed a finger at him. 'It's not worth your life. It's not worth *anyone's* life.'

'I know what I'm capable of. I took a calculated risk. I knew I could scoop it up and get to safety before too many had come through the gate.'

She wanted to scream. Dragging her hands through her hair, she retied her ponytail, scraping it back hard and tight. 'One miscalculation and you'd have been a pile of broken bones, and the rest of us would've had to risk our necks to save you.'

His head rocked back.

She loved the sense of having Ana near—of having all her sisters near—but she'd been an idiot to wear the bracelet during muster. 'I don't need a hero, Lincoln. I need someone with a cool head who makes sensible decisions.'

He could have lost his life.

Clicking her tongue to Opal, who immediately trotted over, Rose was back in the saddle in one smooth motion. The rest of the crew had studiously turned their backs to them, and she winced. She shouldn't have raked Lincoln down in front of everyone like that. So much for the cool head she was known for. But if Lincoln had been hurt…

She glanced at him. He'd paled and his face had shuttered. He stared at her with a coldness she didn't recognise. Her hands shook. She'd yelled at him the same way Clay had done. She shouldn't have—

He could've been killed!

Opal danced sideways as Rose's hands tightened on the reins. She took advantage of the moment to soothe her horse, to grab at the threads of her shattered composure. 'I can't have anything else go wrong this year,' she said to him now.

She couldn't smile to soften her harsh words. Fire and ice alternately burned through her as she tried to blink away images of Lincoln's broken body lying on the ground beneath pounding hooves. 'Let's get back to work.'

She turned back to the yard and the work she wished would consume her. But no matter how frenetic, messy and physically demanding it proved to be, it didn't stop the sudden knowledge that had burst into her consciousness from pounding at her.

The fear that had gripped her when she'd thought Lincoln would be hurt…

The darkness that had engulfed her at the thought of him dying…

She'd gone and done the unthinkable. She'd fallen in love with her husband.

* * *

When they returned to the homestead that evening, Rose and Lincoln both went in separate directions.

Rose headed straight for her room to shower, pulled on her baggiest, most comfortable track pants and a fleece jumper, and collapsed to the side of her bed to try and make sense of the day's events. She'd fallen in love with Lincoln Garrison—the bad boy next door.

Only, he wasn't bad. He was… She rubbed her hands over her face. He was wonderful. Other than that daft risking-his-neck thing.

What are you going to do about it?

She had no idea.

She waited for one of the many voices she carried inside her to offer an opinion or advice—Pop, Grandma, Mum… Dad—but they all remained infuriatingly silent. She could talk to Eve…

She dismissed that thought as soon as she'd had it. Her sister should be focussed on the arrival of her new baby, on married bliss with Nate. Evie deserved all her current happiness. Rose wasn't casting a shadow on it.

Besides, she had a feeling that this was something she needed to work out for herself.

On impulse, she made her way through the house, across the pristine white carpet of the piano bar, to open the door to the master suite. Her parents' marriage hadn't been perfect, but their love had survived all that life, and their own mistakes, had thrown at them. Could she and Lincoln do that too?

'I've never felt for any woman what I feel for you.'

He'd practically told her he was ready to settle down. Maybe…

She dragged both hands back through her hair. Once they'd had a chance to cool off and a decent night's sleep…and she apologised for shouting at him in front of everyone, and he promised never to be so reckless again… Well, maybe the two of them could make a go of their marriage as her parents had.

She turned on the spot. It was time to look to the future. It was time for her to take her rightful place here at Garrison Downs. No matter how much she missed her father, she was now station manager. It was time she embraced the role fully.

Rose woke to someone knocking on the French doors of her bedroom. 'Rose, wake up.'

Aaron.

She was up in an instant. Grabbing her robe, she flew across the room to fling the door open. 'What's happened?'

He grimaced.

'Come on, Aaron, out with it.' Had the stock in the yards broken free? Been stolen? Did someone need medical attention?

'Something fishy is going on.'

She breathed a little easier. Not an immediate emergency then, but something that worried him enough to wake her in the middle of the night. A glance at the clock told her it was only eleven p.m.—not that late, then. A glance at the bed confirmed what she already knew. For the first time in a month, she'd slept alone. She forced her gaze back to Aaron. 'Go on.'

'You're not going to like it, but I've been keeping my eye on Linc.'

She resisted the urge to roll her eyes. Of course he had.

'He just took off in his car. Headlights turned off.'

He'd left? Without telling her? Her throat tightened into a painful ache. He'd thrown in the towel because she'd yelled at him?

You didn't just yell at him. You called him awful names and were totally unreasonable.

'And headed west.'

Her head came up. Kalku Hills was south-east.

'I'm going to follow. Thought you might like to come along.'

Oh, she was coming along all right, if for no other reason than to prevent this pair from coming to blows. 'I'll get dressed.'

They drove for forty minutes before they saw Lincoln's car parked by the fence that ran parallel to the road to Marni. On the other side of the fence was a car with a horse float. Aaron flashed their car's headlights to high beam, and Lincoln and his father were caught in its glare. Lincoln's hand rested on the gate of the horse float. A pair of wire cutters hung from his other hand.

They hadn't spoken on their return to the homestead. She should've searched him out and cleared the air. But she'd still been trying to wrap her head around the fact that she'd fallen in love with him. And the thought of him walking away when she told him… She hadn't been able to face it.

The mental toing and froing coupled with the labour of the day had left her exhausted. She'd thought it might do them both good to gain some perspective first. Instead, had Lincoln been concocting some elaborate form of revenge?

Her chest cramped. Had he rung Clay and told him he'd had enough, and it was time to move on whatever their plan happened to be—to steal her cattle? The thought left her feeling broken.

Show no weakness.

All of the voices she held in her heart united to impart that single piece of advice.

Show no weakness.

Hauling in a breath, she straightened. Very slowly, she pushed out of the car. 'Evening, gentlemen.' She ambled over, but everything inside her trembled. The fence remained between them. 'Would someone like to tell me what's going on?'

Lincoln stared at her, his eyes burning. 'Rose, this isn't what it looks like.'

Beside her, Aaron folded his arms. 'What does it look like?'

Nobody spoke. Her heart thudded so hard she thought they must hear it.

Clay snarled. 'No one can accuse me of anything.'

Aaron jumped the fence, pushing past both men to stare into the back of the horse trailer. 'Two steers.' He came back to stand beside Rose. 'Diseased, by the look of it.'

Clay had been planning to place diseased cattle on her property? But… Why on earth would he risk that disease then spreading to his own herd? Because it would. Eventually.

Leaning against a fencepost as if she hadn't a care in the world, she surveyed the older man. Fatigue threatened to swallow her whole. The act was senseless. He might hate the Waverlys, but he wouldn't do something so against his own interests. He shifted and she noted the cold calculation in his eyes. The…triumph?

She stilled. His hatred hadn't become mindless. Not yet. Her mind raced. He'd already achieved what he wanted to achieve.

Which was…*what*, exactly?

Clay clapped his son on the shoulder. 'C'mon, Linc, time to go home. I told you this would all end in tears. We'll get you a quickie divorce. And then we'll let the courts decide what to do about Holt's will.'

And then she saw it—Clay's plan. Lincoln had been set up. She and Aaron had been meant to find Lincoln and Clay like this.

For a moment she trembled. If she was wrong…

CHAPTER THIRTEEN

A BONE-DEEP WEARINESS descended over Lincoln, and he had to fight an urge to brace his hands on his knees. He'd ruined *everything*.

Rose had told him how fragile their trust was. He'd sworn he wouldn't break it. But he'd come out here on his own when Jackson had told him that something was going down. He should've brought her with him. He should've told her what he was doing.

She'd never believe him. Not now.

And he couldn't blame her. He knew exactly what it looked like. Diseased cattle. Wire cutters in his hand.

An invisible vice squeezed his ribs tight until he couldn't breathe, until he thought they might crack.

Hell, talk about *pathetic*. He hadn't brought her with him because he'd still been smarting from the dressing-down she'd given him this afternoon. And she'd been right to. Dashing amid flying hooves to save her bracelet had been fool-hardy. But he knew what that bracelet meant to her. And he'd do it again in a heartbeat. He'd been playing the hero for her.

Again.

She'd told him she didn't need a hero, but that was exactly what he wanted to be—her hero. But in coming out alone tonight he'd acted like one of those stupid, insecure men on the soaps she so loved.

She didn't need one of those.

She didn't need a hero either. What she needed was an equal partner who'd be honest with her.

And he'd blown it.

He'd played directly into his father's hands, and he couldn't blame her for having no faith in him now. He'd come out here to prevent his father from doing something he'd regret, help him save face without anyone else present. But Clay didn't deserve that kind of consideration. Another serious lack of judgement on Lincoln's part.

A grey and featureless future stretched out in front of him. The chance of winning Rose's heart might now be lost to him, but his father had another thing coming if he thought Linc was just going to fall in with his plans. Rose might no longer want him, but he wasn't divorcing her, not before she was ready.

Too soon or not, he wished with every atom that he'd told her he loved her.

He opened his mouth, but Rose spoke first. 'I'm afraid that will cost your son dearly, Clay. You see, he signed a contract giving me the Cessna, Thunder and Colin if he didn't keep his side of our bargain. And just so we're clear, his side of the bargain is to remain married to me.'

She leaned her elbows on the fence post and oh-so-casually rested her chin in her hand. She'd never looked more beautiful.

'And you know what? I'm not sure that's a price he's willing to pay.'

Clay's face twisted as he swung to Linc. 'You stupid idiot! What the hell were you—?'

Clay raised a hand. In a flash, Rose was over the fence and between them, her hand in the centre of Clay's chest pushing him back. 'Lay one finger on my husband, Clay, and I will deck you.'

Clay blinked. So did Linc.

'If you don't think Holt taught me how to fight then you'd be the idiot. And while you are a truly reprehensible human being, I don't think even you would hit a woman.'

Clay lowered his arm. 'Of course I wouldn't hit a woman.'

'Which means you'd just have to stand there and take it while I whipped your butt.'

He glanced at Linc. 'You going to let her speak to me like that?'

Linc shrugged and tried to keep the grin from his face. He didn't need a hero either, but he sure as hell liked watching Rose play one. 'I reckon you deserve it.'

'Why do you continue being such a pig-headed idiot? Why aren't you boasting about Lincoln's accomplishments near and far rather than putting him down all the time? Why won't you acknowledge his true worth?'

Her hands clenched into fists and Lincoln readied to grab her around the waist in case she did take a swing at Clay.

Those fists unclenched and she turned to Aaron. 'Did you know Lincoln topped his year at university, has a doctorate and has co-authored a textbook on economic theory?'

Aaron's jaw dropped.

'He advises government officials on how to best invest the nation's capital to benefit the economy, and yet his father ignores his advice, freely given, something that I'd happily pay for.'

Clay glared at them all. 'You know nothing!'

'What I know is that you love playing the poor put-upon victim—*"Oh, my wife left me!" "Oh, my son is off partying and neglecting his duties at home." "Oh, if only Cordelia hadn't gambled away Garrison Downs."*'

Clay took a step towards her, but Lincoln and Aaron stepped together to provide a defensive wall. Clay's face twisted and he stabbed a finger at them. 'Garrison Downs should be mine.'

'There was no poker match, Dad.'

He'd spent too much of his life feeling bad for his father, pitying him, trying to make up life's disappointments to him. It hadn't done an ounce of good. Clay refused to acknowledge what was good in his life, preferring to focus on his sense of injury. 'Cordelia *didn't* gamble it away.'

Clay took an unsteady step back. 'You found the diary?'

'Letters, not a diary. Letters Cordelia and Louisa May wrote to each other. They were friends, not enemies. And the land was Cordelia's in her own right. It didn't belong to her brother, Arthur—it never had. He'd already gambled his grandfather's inheritance away.'

'Lies,' Clay croaked.

'Cordelia gave the land to Lissy May for saving her life three times and to cover a debt of her brother's. She spread the rumour of the poker match to get rid of an unwanted suitor. There was no cheating, no lying. The two women were the best of friends.'

Rose pushed between him and Aaron to stand beside them. 'The reason Kalku Hills isn't as big a success as Garrison Downs is because *you* don't know how to put in a proper day's work. It's easier to whine than it is to work.'

Clay's jaw dropped.

'You don't make the best use of Kalku Hills' resources.'

'Now, look here—'

'And your biggest mistake was in not listening to Lincoln's ideas for improvements, because you couldn't bear to think he might know better than you. You can bet your bottom dollar I won't be making that same mistake.'

Linc stilled.

'I might lack my father's freakish business brain. Genius like that rarely comes along. But I mean to play to my strengths and I know what they are. For one, I'm an excellent judge of character.'

Her hand slid about Linc's upper arm and she held on as though she never meant to let go. His heart thundered like a galloping horse.

'And I know my land—every inch of it.'

'I—'

'And I might lack my father's wheeling-and-dealing charisma and know-how, but Lincoln doesn't.'

Clay stiffened, and in those few words Linc realised Rose had brought home to his father all that his folly and bitterness had cost him.

'Now this is what's going to happen.'

She sounded every inch the boss and he bit back a grin.

She pointed to Clay. 'If you come onto my land again to scatter my cattle to the four winds, I will report you to the police.'

Before his father could respond she swung to Aaron. 'And if I find out you've gone onto Kalku Hills land to do the same, I will fire you.'

Aaron's head rocked back. 'Whoa, steady on, I—'

'I mean it!'

She glared at both men. God, she was magnificent. How could she have ever doubted her ability to step into Holt's shoes?

'I don't care what the provocation, this stupid feud ends with this generation. Do you hear me?'

Aaron shuffled his feet and finally nodded. 'Aye, Boss.'

His words reflected the new-found respect in his eyes. Linc silently applauded her.

'And the other thing that's going to happen, Clay, is that you're taking those steers to the vet in Marni tonight and having them treated.'

'That'll cost me a packet—'

'You should've thought about that before you started this charade. Those animals don't deserve to suffer more than they already have.'

Aaron nodded. 'Agreed, and I think I might just go along with Clay to make sure that happens.'

'Before you head off…' Linc's gaze collided with his father's '… I want to know who your informant at Garrison Downs is.'

Rose tightened her grip on his arm. 'I've worked that out.'

She had?

Both their gazes moved to Aaron.

Aaron's eyes widened. 'It's not me!'

Rose nodded. 'I know.'

Linc stared. It wasn't? Then who…?

'Think about it, Aaron.'

She blew out a breath, looking suddenly tired, and he had to fight an urge to pull her into his arms.

He watched the other man turn options over in his mind.

'Who has had access to Holt's study to copy documents we wouldn't want shared?'

He saw the moment the realisation hit.

'Lindy,' Aaron croaked.

Damn.

'I'm sorry. I know the two of you have become close. I don't know why she'd jeopardise her position like that. It's a shame. I liked her.'

Aaron dragged a hand down his face. 'Money. Her mother is in a nursing home. It's costing her a fortune.' He pulled in a breath. 'Rose, look…she doesn't have a bad heart, I swear.'

Rose stared, eventually nodded. 'Decent people can do bad things when they're under a lot of stress.'

A lesson she'd learned from her own family.

'We'll see if we can sort something out.'

Aaron let out a breath. 'Thanks, Rose.' He turned back to Clay. 'Come on, let's go.'

Lincoln didn't watch them leave. He only had eyes for Rose.

Rose watched the tail lights of Clay's horse float disappear into the night. Only then did she turn to face Lincoln. How much of herself had she given away in her defence of him? And would he use it against her?

He's a better man than that.

'Rose, I—'

He halted when she held up a hand. 'I'm sorry I hauled you over the coals like I did out at the yards this afternoon. I shouldn't have said what I did. And I shouldn't have said it in front of everyone. I was no better than your father.'

'You're *nothing* like my father, Rose. In your shoes I'd have done exactly the same. And,' he added when she opened her mouth, 'you're forgiven.'

His eyes glittered in the starlight and she wanted him with a fierceness that took her off guard.

'I thought you were going to kick me to the kerb just then.' His chest heaved as if dragging in a much-needed breath. 'I thought you were going to send me packing.'

The ragged lines of his face and the slope of his shoulders told her that thought had gutted him. He *did* care for her. Her heart picked up speed. Given time, could she earn his love and make this temporary marriage permanent? 'Nuh uh. I bought you. I own you. That's a line from *Groundhog Day*, by the way. And I know I don't really—'

The rest of her words were cut off when large hands cupped her face and tilted it up to meet the demands of firm, lean lips. It was a kiss that turned her world upside down.

She swayed.

She moaned.

She opened her mouth and let him have all of her.

'I don't care if it's too soon or not.' He lifted his head, his breathing ragged, his voice raspy. 'I don't mean to spook you or freak you out, but I love you, Rose. I've always loved you.'

He... Wait, *what*?

'I've spent my whole life watching you, admiring you. And, as soon as puberty hit, lusting after you.'

Her jaw dropped, but her heart lifted, took flight like a majestic wedge-tailed eagle. 'No way,' she breathed.

'Yes way.'

He released her, leaving her strangely untethered.

'But things between our families were...'

'Complicated.' She nodded.

'And I was a couple of years older than you and I...'

'You what?' He'd only ever asked her out on one date. He'd never told her he was crazy about her.

That he loved her.

'I wanted to wait until you'd finished university and had seen a bit of the world—experienced a bit of the world.'

He bent down until they were eye to eye. She ached to touch him.

'I never expected to be your first lover, Rose, but I sure as hell wanted to be your last one.'

Her pulse...her heart...everything raced and danced and swooned. It took a force of will to drag air into lungs that didn't want to work; to make sense of all he was saying.

'If you felt that way, why didn't you ask me out on another date?' The words burst from her like an accusation.

'A date you turned down, let me remind you.'

More fool her. But…would she have been ready for all of this seven years ago?

'And you asked me—begged me—to never ask you again.'

Oh, God, she had.

'I hate men like Cordelia's Geoffrey Bannister. I never wanted to become someone like that. I had no intention of badgering you. You'd said no, and I had to respect that.'

She couldn't move, couldn't speak…could only stare.

'But I knew it was inevitable that we'd see each other throughout the year. And every single time I'd make a point of seeking you out, to say hello, to flirt a little.'

'I remember.'

'You never gave me any encouragement, but I refused to give up hope that one day you might.'

She'd been too afraid to, had never in a million years thought he could be serious about her.

'But when you asked me to marry you, I finally had an opportunity to prove we belonged together. You'd given me three months and I meant to make the most of them and win your heart.'

Her eyes burned. She pressed her hand to his cheek. How had she ever managed to deserve this wonderful man?

'I nearly destroyed it all when you told me you were a virgin.'

She grimaced. 'I thought my revelation had turned you off.'

'I was so angry with your grandmother for extracting such a promise. But more than that I was appalled at my own re-action—a kind of primitive possessiveness.'

He raked a hand through his hair and paced in front of her. 'I wanted to leave some kind of mark on you that de-clared you mine. As if I was some alpha wolf or something. I wanted you so badly I was afraid I'd hurt you. And I wanted our first time to be special. Something you could always look back on with fondness.'

Shaking his head, he halted in front of her. 'I needed to get my head back on straight. I didn't stop to think what message I might be sending you. I was such an idiot.'

'*Not* an idiot.' She gave a low laugh. 'I feel as if our relationship has been one step forward and three steps back, but it's been worth it. All we've been through has forced me to acknowledge the kind of man you are. And I like that man.'

His eyes blazed in his face. 'Are you saying I have a chance at winning your heart?'

He hadn't realised…?

She raised both hands heavenward. 'Why do you think I lost my temper so completely this afternoon? I was so afraid of you being hurt…or worse. I knew I was beginning to care, but that… *That* was the moment I realised I was in love with you. And it scared me witless.'

He stared as if her words made no sense and then his hands curved around her shoulders and he was lifting her onto her tiptoes. 'Say that again.'

'I love you, Lincoln. You're the best man I've ever known. You do your best to look after everyone—and you do it in kind, subtle, and unconfrontational ways. You don't ask for fanfare or acknowledgement. You just see what needs doing and you do it. You're honest and honourable, and you know what those things mean to me. If I was given the tools and the power, I couldn't create a man who would suit me better. You're perfect for me. And I want to be perfect for you.'

He stared at her as if he couldn't get enough of her and the words she was whispering to him. This beautiful man had never had anyone truly appreciate him. But she would if he let her. A tear spilled from her eye and then another. She'd appreciate and love him until her dying day.

He thumbed away her tears. 'Don't cry, Rose.'

The words were a whisper on the night air. 'Happy tears,' she whispered back. He deserved so much more than he'd ever been given. He deserved everything. 'When I get too serious, Lincoln, you make me laugh. When I get too caught up in work, you distract me and make me see all the wonders around me. You make my life so much better. And this may be shallow, but I love what you look like, I love your body. And making love with you is my very favourite thing.'

She found herself suddenly released.

She swayed. He was supposed to kiss her now, not release her!

In the red dirt in front of her, he went down on one knee. She pressed trembling fingers to her mouth. Reaching up, he took her hands in his. 'Back at the homestead, hidden in the depths of a drawer, is the engagement ring I bought for you and swore I'd give to you before our temporary three-month marriage was up. I had it especially designed so you could wear it while you work—flat so it won't catch on anything—a yellow diamond set in platinum. I see it and I think of you—strong, enduring and beautiful.' His grip on her hands tightened. 'Rose, will you do me the very great honour of agreeing to being my *forever* wife?'

'Yes!'

The word rang out in the silence of the night and his grin was *everything*. Bending down, she kissed him, and then she was in his arms and he was whooping and spinning her around and she'd never known it was possible to be so happy.

Later, much later, stretched out beside him in her bed, she lifted her hand to admire the way the diamond caught the moonlight. 'It's the most beautiful ring I've ever seen.'

Catching her hand, Lincoln kissed it, before folding it

against his chest. 'If I'd known Ana designed jewellery, I'd have commissioned her to make it.'

'Except she'd have told me and let the cat out of the bag.' Propping her head on her hand, she stared down at him. 'How would you feel if I commissioned her to make us new wedding rings? These ones were just a prop.' She gestured to the ones that they wore.

'Prop or not, this one means a lot to me.' He twisted it around on his finger. 'Could she melt some of this gold into the new rings?'

'Of course she can. She's a marvel.' She stared at her wedding ring then too. 'That's a nice idea.' A symbol of how their relationship had evolved.

He reached up and kissed her. 'Now tell me what else is going through that beautiful head of yours?'

He read her so well. 'How would you feel if we had a ceremony renewing our vows? I want everyone to know that I love you. I want them to know you're my family—that I've chosen you because there's not a better man alive for me, that I want you as the father of my children, and that I want you at my side for the rest of my life.'

Reaching up, he kissed her again—slowly and oh-so-thoroughly—and then she was on her back and he was moving above her and they were moving as one and it was a long time before either of them spoke again.

'That was a yes, by the way,' he said when their breathing had returned to normal. 'I love you, Rose. Forever.'

She met his gaze and smiled with all of herself. 'Forever.'

EPILOGUE

Garrison Downs,
mid-September

ROSE STARED AT her three sisters—all here together *in person* at Garrison Downs for the first time in what felt like forever—and her heart expanded until it felt too big for her chest.

Evie, Tilly and Ana sat side by side on the swing chattering like bright and bubbly rainbow lorikeets in their wedding blessing finery. A lump lodged in Rose's throat. Tilly, glancing up, caught her expression and nudged the others. They all quietened like schoolgirls in a classroom and it made her smile because their demure exteriors didn't fool her for a moment.

'Right, I'm now calling this meeting to order.' She pressed her hands together. 'I love you guys.' Despite her best efforts, her eyes filled. 'I know you know that, but I love you bigger than my own heart.'

'Oh, God, Rose, stop!' Evie pressed hands to her cheeks. 'You'll have me ruining my make-up.'

'Make-up, schmake-up,' Tilly scorned. 'It's our party and we can cry if we want to.'

Ana held up a small make-up bag. 'We can touch up.' Her grin grew shy. 'I brought it along just in case.'

Tilly wrapped Ana in a hug. Evie winked at Rose. 'Guess you have free rein, then, Boss.'

Rose met her sisters' gazes one by one. 'I love each of you more than I love Garrison Downs. I know you're all aware what this station means to me—Garrison Downs is my life. But each of you, as well as Lincoln and the families we're all creating, are my heart.'

Their eyes welled then too and Rose's vision blurred, and though she blinked hard, it refused to clear. 'I never expected any of you to marry so that we could keep the station.' She gave a shaky laugh. 'So that *I* could keep the station. Only now that we have, I can't tell you how happy I am that we did, because the men we've married are not only hard-working, honourable and decent—'

'Don't forget hot,' Evie piped in.

'*So* hot,' Tilly crooned.

'Dreamy,' Ana murmured.

Lincoln's powerful form rose in her mind and she found herself grinning. 'I could *never* forget that, but… They love us in the way we deserve to be loved—with all of themselves. And I couldn't want more for us in life partners. Not in a million years could I have imagined such a happy outcome.' She pressed her hands to her heart. 'Thank you. From the bottom of my heart, thank you.'

And then her sisters swooped on her as one, and they were group-hugging and crying and murmuring loving nonsense, and it made Rose's heart sing.

When they'd dried their eyes and had retouched each other's make-up, Rose said, 'Don't forget that Garrison Downs is your home. You're building other homes too—homes where you're loved and where you belong, and that's as it should be. But don't forget the Downs will always be here for you. And I'm very much hoping we can manage at least one in four Christmases here.'

Linking pinkies, they made a pact.

'I have one final announcement to make.' She pulled in a deep breath. Her three sisters promptly sat on the swing again. 'Lincoln has had his father sign a statutory declaration relinquishing any claim the Garrison family have to this land.'

Tilly clapped her hands. 'He is such a good guy!'

'How?' Evie gaped. 'Clay is a—'

'I know!' Rose cut in before Evie could call him something horrible. The man *was* her father-in-law. 'Lincoln told him that if he wanted to mend their relationship, that's what he had to do.' To her utter amazement, Clay had acquiesced without a murmur.

Ana's eyes shone. 'Good for him!'

'If you're all in agreement, I'll have the will changed so that no future generation of Waverly women find themselves in the same predicament we did. We've been ridiculously fortunate, and I wouldn't change a thing about these past fifteen months, but I don't want my daughters or their daughters facing that same dilemma we did. All in agreement of having that conditional bequest removed, please raise your hand.'

Four hands shot in the air.

Perfect.

'Okay, is there any other order of business?'

'Me! Me!' Tilly leapt up.

Rose took her vacated spot on the swing, linking arms with Evie and Ana.

'Louisa May's and Cordelia's letters have been officially verified. They're definitely legitimate, dating back to the early nineteen hundreds—and all is true and correct. Louisa May and Cordelia were besties, sisters of the heart, and I think we should sing that out loud and proud to the rest of the world.'

They all cheered.

'Anyone else have anything to say?' Tilly moved to lean against the swing, a hand circling its chain.

'I don't need to stand to say it,' Evie said. 'I just want you all to know I'm so glad to be home. I never knew I could find so much *happiness* here.'

Rose squeezed her sister's arm. 'You're back where you belong, Bambi.'

'I get jealous sometimes when I think of the two of you here.' Tilly let out a gusty sigh. 'And then I remember I'm a princess living in a castle with my prince charming...' She trailed off, making them all laugh.

Ana shot to her feet. 'I want to say something.'

Tilly promptly took her seat, her arm twining through Rose's.

'I just... I want to say... Well, just that I'm so glad you found out about me, so glad you're my sisters.'

'And we are too!'

And then there was more hugging, followed perhaps by a little more necessary touching-up of their make-up.

'So,' Rose finally said, 'are we ready to do this?'

'Yes,' her sisters chorused.

Arm in arm they walked around to Rosamund's glorious rose garden. One by one they walked down the aisle towards their respective husbands—Prince Henri, Nathan, Connor, and Lincoln—who watched them with steady, intent eyes. The late afternoon air was filled with the sounds of birdcalls, the scent of spring and the happy sighs of all who were present.

In front of the people who mattered to them most—family and friends, and the entire township of Marni—they renewed their wedding vows, their voices clear, strong and sure. After the wedding blessing a cheer went up from the assembled crowd. Photos were taken and congratulations flowed and then people began to move in the direction of the ballroom for the celebration banquet.

Before they could follow, Granny Lavigne came up with the latest addition to the family, Evie and Nate's daughter, Hope—the most adorable bundle of blonde hair, chubby legs, and the trademark Waverly blue eyes. Granny Lavigne kissed them all and told them how proud and happy she was for them.

Rose glanced at the nearby roses.

We miss you, she silently told her parents. *We love you.*

Tilly gave an excited wriggle. 'I can't wait until my little bundle of joy meets you all.' She and Henri had announced that they were expecting a baby in March. There'd been much celebration at the news.

'Ana?' Tilly nudged their youngest sister.

'Clucky,' she admitted. 'Working on it.'

Ana's family—her mum, Lili, and her grandparents—immediately started talking at once. Rose grinned. They were quickly becoming some of her favourite people. She was beyond glad that they'd come to Garrison Downs...that old hurts were being healed.

'Rose?'

Evie's voice hauled her back and she found all eyes had turned to her. She touched a gentle finger to her new niece's cheek. 'Well, as I don't like long being outdone by you lot...' Across their heads she met Lincoln's gaze. His grin made her heart swell. 'I guess I'll probably start working on it too.'

'Our babies will be the best of friends.' That was Tilly.

Evie's eyes danced. 'They'll be trouble. Into all the mischief.'

'But in the best way.' Ana grinned.

'And we'll love every moment,' Rose agreed. 'But they're not allowed in the piano bar until they're at least sixteen.'

Laughing, they made their way towards the ballroom to dance and celebrate the night away.

* * *

Later, as Rose danced a sedate number with Aaron, they passed the table where Lincoln's father Clay held court and overheard him brag that it'd be his grandchildren who would one day run Garrison Downs. 'Surprised he has the gall to show his face,' Aaron said with a growl.

'Lincoln told him he'd not be welcome today until he apologised to me. Which he did—comprehensively, too. I think he was genuinely ashamed of himself.' A truce had been called and she was grateful for it. 'I think Dad's death sent him off the rails for a bit.'

Aaron grimaced. 'Holt's death sent us all into a spin. I know I've apologised—'

'No more apologies!'

He cleared his throat, nodded. 'I don't know how to say this without sounding patronising, but… I'm proud of you, Rose. You've single-handedly dragged everything back from the brink and we're now as productive as we've ever been. You've filled shoes I never thought could be filled.'

'I didn't do it single-handedly. I've had all of you working with me, just like Holt did.'

Aaron held her gaze. 'Holt's very best legacy is his daughters. He'd be so proud of you.'

She blinked hard, swallowed. 'Thanks, Aaron. Now, I think it's time for you to go and find Lindy. I told her she wasn't to work tonight, but she keeps ducking into the kitchens.'

'She wants the night to be perfect. She's just doing what she can to make amends. She's so grateful you've let her stay. I am too.'

That one act had won her Aaron's and Lindy's undying loyalty and she didn't regret it for a moment. She pushed him in the direction of the kitchen. 'Go dance with your girl.'

When she turned, she found Lincoln standing behind her.

Without a word he pulled her into his arms and they swayed together in perfect harmony. Had she ever known a moment of such perfect contentment?

'I have something I want to show you.' Lincoln led her through to the primary suite, which they'd finally made their own.

She waggled her eyebrows. 'Oh?'

A low chuckle left his throat. 'Behave, woman. I have a wedding present for you.'

She pulled him to a halt. 'You already gave me a wedding present.'

'This is another one.'

She loved her chess set—her *well-used* chess set. 'Can I say something first?'

He immediately stopped trying to shift her forward. 'Always.'

From where they stood, she could see a corner of the bed and its quilt of muted greens, pinks and golds. In the daytime those colours were reflected in the view from the picture window—lush green lawns, towering gums with olive leaves and pink blossoms, and, further beyond, the golden grasses and red dirt.

Home. Their home.

'I'm grateful every single day that you said yes when I asked you to marry me.'

His face gentled. He opened his mouth but she touched fingers to his lips. 'Marrying you is the single best thing I've ever done. The best,' she added firmly, when he frowned. 'Knowing you, loving you, being loved by you, has filled all of the spaces inside me that I never knew were empty. Thank you, Lincoln. Thank you for being patient with me, for not giving up on me, and for loving me.' Reaching up on tiptoe, she kissed him, and he kissed her back with an intensity that had her clinging to him.

Pulling back, his breathing ragged, he shook his head. 'You have the ability to undo me every single time.'

'Not true.' Her breathing was just as ragged. 'You're currently ahead in our chess tournament.' Because of course they were keeping count.

'Only by the skin of my teeth.'

As he spoke he ushered her forward, gestured at a simple frame hanging on the wall. She moved across to read it. 'This is the contract you had drawn up giving me Judy, Thunder and Colin. I gave it back to you. We—'

'It's a symbol of the fact that I'm all in, Rose.'

She turned back to him. 'I know you are.'

'You're sharing so much with me—your home, for a start.'

She cocked her head to one side. 'Well, my portion of it at least.' She placed her hand over his heart. 'We're family now. We share everything.'

He gestured at the frame before gathering her close. 'I never want you to forget that it's *you* that is most important in my life. I love the home we're creating, I already love the children we're going to make, and I love being a part of your already existing family, but it's *you*, Rose. None of it means anything without you.'

Some days she had to pinch herself to believe this amazing man was hers. 'I feel the same way.'

A lazy grin stretched across his face. 'I also thought, in a similar vein to Louisa May's and Cordelia's letters, it could go in the family archive to amuse the generations to come.'

She started to laugh, imagining the tall tales they'd spin for their children.

Glancing at the bed and then at him, she raised an eyebrow that had him chuckling. 'Later. You can't leave the party early when you're the belle of the ball. And make no mistake, Rose, you are queen of Garrison Downs.'

'And you're my king.'

His eyes danced and he gave one of those slow lazy smiles. 'Prince consort will do fine for me, as long as I'm king of your heart.'

'Always,' she promised. Before pointing to the contract on the wall. 'You're mine.'

'You bought me,' he agreed, dark eyes filled with laughter.

'And then you won my heart.'

He sobered. 'I'm never giving it back.'

'And I'm never letting you go.'

'Checkmate,' they said at the same time.

His head lowered to hers. 'Forever,' he whispered against her lips.

'And ever and ever,' she agreed, before his lips claimed hers in another toe-tingling kiss.

* * * * *

MILLS & BOON MODERN IS
HAVING A MAKEOVER!

The same great stories you love,
a stylish new look!

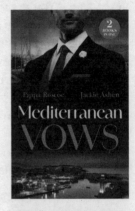

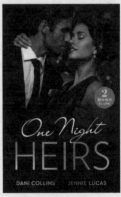

Look out for our brand new look
COMING JUNE 2024

MILLS & BOON

COMING SOON!

We really hope you enjoyed reading this book.
If you're looking for more romance
be sure to head to the shops when
new books are available on

Thursday 6th
June

To see which titles are coming soon, please visit
millsandboon.co.uk/nextmonth

MILLS & BOON

MILLS & BOON®

Coming next month

THE PRINCE SHE KISSED IN PARIS
Scarlett Clarke

Awareness prickled over her skin. A sharp inhale brought about a scent of pine mixed with a masculine scent that painted a vivid image of a handsome smile and brown eyes crinkled at the corners.

'Hello.'

Squaring her shoulders, Madeline turned and laced her fingers together as she faced Prince Nicholai.

'Your Highness.'

He looked incredible. Dressed in a navy suit with a silver tie, his hair combed back from his face, he looked every inch the austere royal. His face was smoothed into an expressionless mask that made his sharp features look more like a statue than those of a living person.

Something inside her chest twisted. She missed the carefree smile he'd given her on the rooftops of Paris, the naked emotion in his eyes when they'd met in the alcove. On those occasions, she'd seen the man behind the crown.

Now, though…now he looked distant. Unreachable. Untouchable.

Continue reading
THE PRINCE SHE KISSED IN PARIS
Scarlett Clarke

Available next month
millsandboon.co.uk

afterglow BOOKS

Afterglow Books are trend-led, trope-filled books with diverse, authentic and relatable characters and a wide array of voices and representations.

Experience real world trials and tribulations, all the tropes you could possibly want (think small-town settings, fake relationships, grumpy vs sunshine, enemies to lovers).

All with a generous dose of spice in every story!

OUT NOW

Two stories published every month.

To discover more visit:

Afterglowbooks.co.uk

LET'S TALK

Romance

For exclusive extracts, competitions and special offers, find us online:

f MillsandBoon

X @MillsandBoon

⊙ @MillsandBoonUK

♪ @MillsandBoonUK

Get in touch on 01413 063 232

MILLS & BOON

THE HEART OF ROMANCE

A ROMANCE FOR EVERY READER

MODERN
Prepare to be swept off your feet by sophisticated, sexy and seductive heroes, in some of the world's most glamourous and romantic locations, where power and passion collide.

HISTORICAL
Escape with historical heroes from time gone by. Whether your passion is for wicked Regency Rakes, muscled Vikings or rugged Highlanders, awaken the romance of the past.

MEDICAL
Set your pulse racing with dedicated, delectable doctors in the high-pressure world of medicine, where emotions run high and passion, comfort and love are the best medicine.

True Love
Celebrate true love with tender stories of heartfelt romance, from the rush of falling in love to the joy a new baby can bring, and a focus on the emotional heart of a relationship.

HEROES
The excitement of a gripping thriller, with intense romance at its heart. Resourceful, true-to-life women and strong, fearless men face danger and desire - a killer combination!

From showing up to glowing up, these characters are on the path to leading their best lives and finding romance along the way – with plenty of sizzling spice!

To see which titles are coming soon, please visit

millsandboon.co.uk/nextmonth

GET YOUR ROMANCE FIX!

Get the latest romance news, exclusive author interviews, story extracts and much more!

blog.millsandboon.co.uk